PRAISE FOR *THE FLOWER BOAT GIRL*

"A breathtaking saga of a real life heroine, so richly alive that the pages seem to breathe."
—CAROLINE LEAVITT, *New York Times* bestselling author of *Pictures of You* and *Cruel Beautiful World*

"Fast-paced plotting ... evocative prose and attention to detail. Will satisfy lovers of thoughtful historical fiction."
—*BookLife* from *Publisher's Weekly*

"A vivid and often compelling adventure with a sweeping, cinematic feel."
—*Kirkus*

"A thoughtful and penetrating novel that brings to life the world of Cheng Yat Sou, one of the most important yet least understood women in Chinese history."
—ROBERT ANTONY, author of *Like Froth Floating on the Sea*

"Convincingly renders Cheng's stranger-than-fiction trajectory to pirate royalty, punctuated by ripe Cantonese profanity."
—*South China Morning Post*

"Feign's work bears comparison (to James Clavell's *Tai-Pan*) both in its historical and geographical sweep, as well as in its readability and attention to regional historical detail."
—*Asian Review of Books*

"*The Flower Boat Girl* is historical fiction at its best."
—DIAN MURRAY, author of *Pirates of the South China Coast*

"A simply riveting read from first page to last."
—*Midwest Book Review*

Publisher's Cataloging-in-Publication data
Names: Feign, Larry, author.
Title: The flower boat girl : a novel based on a true story / Larry Feign.
Description: Silvermine Bay, Hong Kong: Top Floor Books, 2021.
Identifiers: ISBN: 9789627866541 (Hardcover) | 9789627866558 (pbk.) | 9789627866565 (ebook)
Subjects: LCSH Zheng, Shi, 1775-1844--Fiction. | Cheng I, Sao, 1775-1844--Fiction. |
Women pirates--China--Fiction. | Pirates--China--Fiction. | China--History--Jiaqing,
1796-1820--Fiction. | China--History, Naval--1644-1912--Fiction. | BISAC FICTION / Historical |
FICTION / Action & Adventure | FICTION / Biographical | FICTION / Women.
Classification: LCC PS3606.E54 F46 2021 | DDC 813.6--dc23

Grateful acknowledgment to David Hinton for permission to reprint his translation of
"Li the mountain recluse stays the night on our boat" by Po Chü-I, from *Mountain Home,*
copyright 2002 by David Hinton. Reprinted by permission of New Directions Publishing Corp.

"Fall Fragrance" excerpted from E.N. Anderson, "The Folksongs of the Hong Kong Boat People," in
The Journal of American Folklore 80 (1967)

"Fascination" by Ssu-K'ung T'u, translated by L. Cranmer-Byng, from *A Lute of Jade* (Dutton, 1909)

Cover and book design by Coverkitchen.
書法家黃沛旋先生. Chinese calligraphy by Wong Pui Suen.
Maps by Peter de Jong.

ISBN 978 962 7866 55 8

Top Floor Books
PO Box 29
Silvermine Bay, Hong Kong
topfloorbooks.com

the Flower Boat Girl

A Novel Based on a True Story

LARRY FEIGN

TOP FLOOR
BOOKS

for Cathy

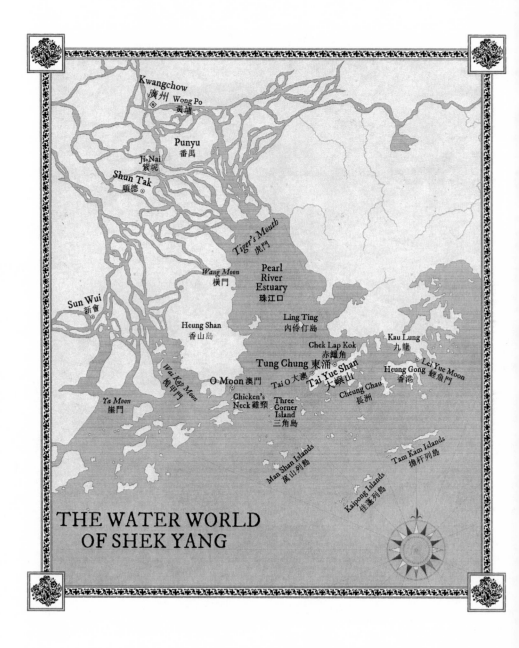

Kwangchow
廣州 Wong Po
黃埔

Punyu
番禺

Ji-Nai
紫坭

Shun Tak
順德

Tiger's Mouth
虎門

Wang Moon
橫門

Pearl
River
Estuary
珠江口

Sun Wui
新會

Heung Shan
香山島

Ling Ting
內伶仃島

Chek Lap Kok
赤鱲角

Kau Lung
九龍

Tung Chung 東涌

Wai Kap Moon
氹甲門

Lei Yue Moon
鯉魚門

O Moon 澳門

Tai O 大澳

Tai Yue Shan
大嶼山

Heung Gong
香港

Ya Moon
崖門

Chicken's
Neck 雞頸

Three
Corner
Island
三角島

Cheung Chau
長洲

Man Shan Islands
萬山列島

Tam Kam Islands
擔杆列島

Kaipong Islands
佳蓬列島

THE WATER WORLD
OF SHEK YANG

CONTENTS

PART I

I	Magpies	3
II	Red Slippers	13
III	Shame	19
IV	Wife	27
V	Lotus	31
VI	Sugar	39
VII	Lagoon	49
VIII	Moon Festival	63
IX	Pirate	79
X	Cheng Yat Sou	85
XI	Black Sails	99
XII	Borders	111
XIII	Chiang Ping	117
XIV	Deluge	125
XV	Poetry	133
XVI	Ink	145
XVII	Cavalry	149
XVIII	Spirit River	155
XIX	Sons	169
XX	Cove	175
XXI	Pillars	181

PART II

XXII	Hold	193
XXIII	Blockade	205
XXIV	Release	223
XXV	Partners	231
XXVI	Tai O	249
XXVII	Gathering	257
XXVIII	Haven Hollow	269
	The Pirate Pact	275

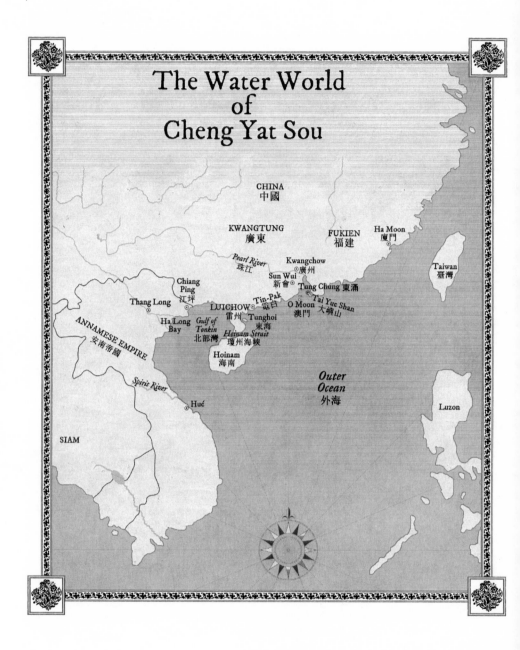

The Water World
of
Cheng Yat Sou

CHINA
中國

KWANGTUNG
廣東

FUKIEN
福建

Ha Moon
廈門

Taiwan
臺灣

Pearl River
珠江

Kwangchow
廣州

Sun Wui
新會

Tung Chung 東涌

Chiang
Ping
江坪

Tin-Pak
電白

Tai Yue Shan
大嶼山

Thang Long

LUICHOW
雷州

O Moon
澳門

Ha Long
Bay

Tunghoi
東海

*Gulf of
Tonkin*
北部灣

Hoinam Strait
瓊州海峽

Hoinam
海南

ANNAMESE EMPIRE
安南帝國

Spirit River

*Outer
Ocean*
外海

Luzon

Hué

SIAM

PART III

XXIX	Confederation	281
XXX	Shadow	293
XXXI	Proclamation	301
XXXII	Barbarian	311
XXXIII	Invincible	325
XXXIV	Following Ghost	339

PART IV

XXXV	Ceremonies	353
XXXVI	Po	373
XXXVII	Three Visits	377
XXXVIII	Conference	385
XXXIX	Night	395
XL	Drum	403
XLI	The Pirate Queen	409

Acknowledgements	413
Characters & Glossary	415
About the Author	421

AUTHOR'S NOTE

Names follow the Chinese format of surname followed by given name(s). Shek Yang's family name, therefore, is Shek.

Astute readers will recognize many of these characters by names such as Cheng I Sao (or Zheng Yi Sao), Zhang Baozi, and so on. The trouble is, in real life no one called them that. These spellings are transliterations from the Mandarin (Putonghua) readings of their names, used by western scholars and propagated into popular histories and thousands of online articles. The actual people did not speak Mandarin in everyday life—if they even spoke it at all—and would certainly not address themselves or each other in what was essentially a foreign language.

The dominant language of the south China coast was, and remains, Cantonese, which differs from Mandarin as extensively as Portuguese diverges from French. For this simple reason, names of people and places in this book are transliterated as they would have been spoken: using Cantonese. Since there is no standard romanization for Cantonese, I primarily use a variation of Yale transcription, which I consider easiest on the eyes and tongue for English speakers.

A character list and glossary are found at the end of the book.

嘉慶六年辛酉

PART I

—

Sixth Year

of the

Reign of Emperor

Ka-hing

—

1801

I

Magpies

I'll never believe in birds.

Especially magpies. Listen to them, squawking and clattering on the deck overhead, like armies battling on scratchy twig feet. The same thing every day before sunset—but today, they were more grating than usual.

I rose from the sleeping mat and pounded the ceiling. The customer in my bed snorted and rolled onto his side, offering a view of his scar-crossed coolie's back. I dared not hit the ceiling again, for fear of disturbing him and the anticipated tip. Let the birds wake him.

How did magpies become harbingers of good fortune? Was it because of that story, the one my mother loved to cry over? Every year at the height of summer, the magpies linked wings, forming a footbridge across heaven to unite a lonely weaving girl with her shepherd boy lover, just for one day.

"Why didn't she stay with him?" I always asked. "Why didn't she make the birds weave a bridge down to earth and let them both escape?"

Every year, my mother smiled at such questions. "Oh, Yang, my big-eyed girl, it's because a single day of pleasure so pure can last an entire year. Besides, we want to tell the story again next summer."

It was that time of year right now, the twenty-sixth summer of my life. Where was my bridge away from this place? Where was my shepherd? The magpies cackled back: *Ha! Not for boat girls! Not for whores! Certainly not for you, Shek Yang!*

Faraway drumbeats scattered my thoughts. They sounded like fishermen beating pig skins to herd fish into nets, but this was neither the right time of day for it nor their usual slow, steady pulse. This tempo was hurried and uneven, a palpitating heart.

I draped a shawl over my shoulders and stepped to the porthole, rested my chin on folded arms, and stared out at my world.

Eight wooden huts hovered on stilts over the hard mud, same as they always had. The beached junk at the end hadn't been there when I was sold away as a child. Now it looked as parched and worm-ridden as this old boat, the one my young body paid for, now my hollow haven. Beyond, the mudflats stretched out forever, empty except for an old woman on a skid gathering mudskippers and the girl with her clam bucket who I'd found squatting in the cabin when I returned after thirteen years away.

A fluttering sea breeze chilled my sweat. The air tasted of iron and salt: a storm was coming. The fish would be swimming deep. Then why had the fishermen's drumming grown louder, more erratic?

In a paddy field somewhere, buffaloes moaned. Pigs whined. Dogs barked back. The magpies chattered. I'd forgotten how noisy this place could be.

I'd forgotten many things about Sun-wui. As a little girl, this narrow inlet had seemed like a wide-open gulf, big enough to swallow the world. I'd forgotten the stench of fish on everything, every plank, every stone, the salt-sour taste in the air from shrimp drying on racks.

And the mud, the mud, always the mud. Black and squishy at water's edge but scouring young fingers when they dug down for clams. Spreading inland, the mud turned coarse, pockmarked with stones and crab holes, but never dry enough to earn the name dirt, never letting go of whatever it sucked in: boulders, driftwood, my father's stranded fishing junk.

Nobody knew where he was, where he'd gone or whether he was still alive. Nothing was left of him, my mother, or the family we'd once been, in this rotting carcass of a vessel: not a strand of rope, not even a familiar stain on the deck. This hollow hulk that he'd traded my young life for had been abandoned by its spirits.

The clam girl splashed through a pool in the mud, swinging her bucket, stooping to examine something that caught her eye. I turned my head away, but too late; the memory flooded in.

Years and years ago, another little girl had set down a clam bucket in nearly the same spot and picked up a dazzling red scallop. *I'll give this to my new baby brother or sister, due any day now,* I'd thought. I remembered shrieking with laughter when a hermit crab popped out a claw and tickled my hand before I set it down and it scurried away. I'd clung to this memory through the years on the flower boats, always recalling that

4

last perfect moment of my life, before...but I always stopped there, humming, shouting, anything to block out what came next, the blood across this very cabin's floor—no, I couldn't bear the thought, not even now.

Everything suddenly went quiet, like the world holding its breath. No drumming, no birds, no breeze. The air weighed on my head.

The shawl whipped off my shoulders; a rough hand seized my breast.

His breath filled my ear. "Again."

My revulsion was tempered by the thought of his purse. Another copper cash toward the cost of a proper boat, something for once that was mine.

"Need to pay two times," I said.

"First one too quick."

"Not my fault, dear." Composing my best working smile, I half turned to him as something caught my eye.

A ship crept past the headland, a stout three-masted creature of nearly black wood, sails tinted red by the setting sun. I would have taken it for an eat-water coastal trader if it hadn't been for an unusually tall deckhouse at the rear. It swung into the inlet. I was stricken by its bulging painted eyes.

It didn't belong here. Local Kwangchow vessels rarely had eyes carved onto the bow, and Fukienese ones were round. But these were high and elongated, squinting like a tiger preparing to pounce.

The coolie tugged my arm. "You hear me, you bitch? Said fine. Pay twice."

Two ships, now three, all with tiger eyes. Other than that, they really were nothing more than tattered old junks. Whatever they'd come for didn't concern me, unless they sought the kind of refreshment I offered for cash. Meanwhile, I had an impatient customer to appease.

This time he took more pleasure in making me earn my money than in the act itself. Skillful hand work was required to prime him into shape. Then he climbed on from behind and grunted and growled like a bull, in rhythm with the fishermen's drumming, his queue swinging past his shoulder into my face with every thrust. I made the necessary noises while picturing a treat for afterward—slices of fresh roast pork, or a bowl of sweet bean curd, or maybe his tip would cover both.

A sharp knock at the cabin door so startled me that I nearly bucked him off. He squealed in pain.

"Ah-Yang!" It was the little clam girl. She pounded louder.

What did she think she was doing? The stupid girl knew she was never, ever to disturb me when I was working. Hadn't I been kind to her? Given her the forward hold? Always sharing rice in exchange for a handful of clams? How dare she interrupt?

The latch jumped from the slot and the door creaked open.

I screamed, "Get out!"

The coolie threw himself off, smacked his head on a low beam, and danced into his trousers.

"Not you." I lunged for his leg, but he slipped away.

"Wait—you pay money!"

He nearly trampled the girl on his way out.

"My money, you turtle egg! Pay me!"

I almost crushed the girl myself as I stumbled through the doorway, pulling on my crumpled clothes. By the time my tunic was half buttoned, he was already bounding behind the fishing huts toward the paddy fields.

"See what you did?" I grabbed the clam girl's muddy shirt and dragged her out to the deck. Tears and sweat mixed on her face.

"Ah-Yang, I—"

The unmistakable crack of a musket shot singed the air. Magpies surged from the poop deck, forming a shrieking black cyclone overhead. With a high-pitched burst, they scattered toward the darkening hills.

The girl grabbed my arm and pointed across the seaward rail.

"I said pirates!"

I counted five junks. Men clambered over the rails into sampans; others jumped straight into the water. With the sun low behind them, they looked like cutout figures in a shadow play. No one had ever told me what to do in the event of a raid. Were they here to plunder? To murder? What would they do to women and girls?

"Run!" I yelled.

Back in the cabin, I flung open my storage chest, pulled out my best silk tunic, and grabbed a padded vest. What else to keep out of their hands? I sifted through a small pile of trinkets—hairpins, copper bracelets, a dented mirror—the pathetic vestiges of my former life. Let the bandits have them. All except an ivory comb which I tucked snugly into my hair.

I dragged the sleeping mat aside, reached under a loose floorboard, and removed my money purse with its reassuring metallic rattle.

The girl screamed from the doorway, "Ah-Yang! They're coming!"

"Don't wait for me. Go! Run!"

I stretched my hand deeper into the gap until it found the slippers. The embroidery caught on a splinter until I freed them with a gentle tug. Only a few threads damaged. I pressed the soft silk to my cheeks, as if they might still hold some residual warmth from my mother's feet.

I threw on the tunic and vest, stuffed everything else into pockets, ran onto the deck, and, without stopping, made a flying leap onto the hard mud below.

The first wave of pirates was just knee-deep in water. More surged from sampans and junks. Dodging mounds of fish bones and discarded nets behind the fishing huts, I met the clam girl crouched at the paddy's edge. Stupid girl! Why hadn't she run ahead?

Clouds of mosquitoes chased us along the muddy causeway and through a taro field before finally giving up on us as we ran through a fan palm grove. What lay up ahead was worse than stinging bugs. At the village gate, landsmen holding bamboo poles blocked fishing families from seeking shelter inside. One villager spotted us and waved a menacing pike. I tugged the girl's hand to move faster.

"Ah-Yang, I can't run that fast."

"You have to if we're going to get around those ox prick Puntis!"

Fishermen from neighboring huts tried to wrestle past the barricade, but they were no match for swinging pikes. Among the mob of defenders, I recognized men who'd visited my bed, though that would earn me no advantage. Those peasants and petty traders who called themselves Punti, so-called *natives of the land*—to them I, the girl, my neighbors, were all nothing but lowly Tankas—boat people, creatures of the water—little different than the pirates now swarming up the flats.

"How many of those bastards cheated you for your clams?" I said.

The girl struggled to run and speak at the same time. "I don't... know. A lot."

"Time to cheat them back."

I pulled her off the footpath into a patch of tall weeds. Men shouted at us, but we had the advantage of a relatively clear field. To intercept us, they'd have to wade through a swamp of broadleaves that would leave them itching for the rest of the day.

A gap between a house and a walled pigsty gave us a place to catch our breaths. It opened into an alley which hooked around a corner, leading us straight into a crowd surging up the market lane. Men carried elderly parents on their backs, older children dragged younger ones, while too many wives hobbled behind on tiny lotus feet. They might be daintier than us Tanka women, who never adhered to that tradition, but at least we could run to save ourselves. That was, if we could reach the Kwun Yam temple that everyone else was rushing to before its gates slammed shut.

I steered the two of us along the edge of the throng, past the bean curd shop, past the ironsmith, wedging ourselves through the herbalist's family who were carrying armfuls of precious roots and fungus somewhere out of reach of the pirates.

At last the temple structure appeared at the bend in the lane, surrounded by a sea of people.

"Our only chance is to squeeze through," I said.

A wild-eyed woman stepped between us and yanked the girl's head back by the hair, maybe searching for a missing child. Before I could reach her, I was struck in the face by a duck cage on a shoulder pole. The crazed woman vanished into the crowd. I spat out a feather and we plunged onward.

The temple's worship hall and lofts overflowed with squirming bodies, and the small courtyard teemed with people. Monks tried to lever the heavy timber gates closed as whole families pushed through, ignoring shouts of, "Women and children only!"

That was us: a child and a twenty-six-year-old woman. I picked up the girl and dashed for the narrowing entrance at the same time as ten or twelve others. I had my fingers on the gate's edge when something hard knocked the wind from me.

"No Tanka! No whores!"

A neckless pear of a man herded us back with a pike. He was no monk, rather some local vigilante. I put down the girl and attempted to step around him. In return, he mirrored my movements. We continued our crab-like dance while people bayed at us like dogs.

"Tanka whore! Tanka whore!"

The clam girl kicked the fat man's legs. "Get in the temple," I ordered. Instead, she dug her fingernails into his flesh.

The taunts grew louder. "Tanka whore! Water chicken whore!"

The fat man posed to skewer the girl with his pike. I grabbed the pole, attempting to twist him off balance, but he had the size and temperament of an enraged buffalo.

"Tanka whore! Filthy—"

The temple gate was closing. Just three or four steps to the left and I could slip inside. I would be safe; I would be free. But what about the girl? By the time I pried her from his leg, the gate would have shut, leaving both of us at the mercy of the Puntis and the approaching pirates. It wasn't my fault that the girl had made such a stupid move. Yet she had done it to save me.

Screams pierced my ears, shooting strength into my bones. I ducked under the swinging pike, peeled the girl from his leg and threw her through the narrowing gap between gate and wall. I lunged for safety, but too late. The gate slammed shut behind the girl, catching my sleeve in its great wooden jaws. I hammered and kicked, barely hearing my own voice.

"Open up! I'll pay you!"

My answer was the thump of the bolt sliding into its socket.

I was a pinned target for whatever punishment the fat Punti wanted to wreak. I turned my head to face my tormentor, but he was lost in the fleeing crowd.

At the far end of the lane, in the last evening light, pirates poured into the village.

I struggled to free my sleeve, but the silk was stubborn. With one foot against the gate, I finally yanked my sleeve free, tearing a gash in the material.

The first black turban appeared just steps away. An old man swung his walking cane at the pirate. A swish of a blade, then the cane and the fist holding it disappeared in a spray of blood. A woman was dragged past by the hair. Which way to flee? The lane was a simmering mass of bodies colliding on all sides, offering no sense of direction.

Spying a boy squeezing into a narrow gap between houses, I took my chances and bolted through the crowd. The alley was coal black and smelled like the cesspit of hell, but it might make a passable hideout until the raid was over. I slipped on something greasy, breaking my fall on what felt like a mound of garbage, as torchlight bloomed on the walls.

I crouched into a low curl, narrowed my eyes, and tried not to breathe. A scraggly-bearded figure raised his torch and peered into the passageway, baring his teeth as though he'd spotted me. I considered my defense: fingernails in the eyes or a sharp blow with my money purse? A balled-up wad of rubbish in the face was likely best.

A second pirate clapped the bearded one's shoulder. In a blink they were gone.

I stumbled out the other end of the passage into a smoke-filled lane drenched in red glow. Two female figures ran from a burning house pursued by bandits. A paper window steps away burst into flame. Somewhere inside, a woman pleaded.

It all became clear. The pirates were uninterested in men. Half the girls on the flower boats had been taken in village raids and sold into whoredom. I was never going back there. Death first.

Voices filled the alley behind me; there was no chance of retreat. I hugged the walls, creeping through shadows away from the fires. I nearly fell through an open doorway into a dark room, deserted except for a lingering odor of cooked chicken. A rear exit led to a private courtyard.

I tried a door on the other side but found it firmly bolted.

"I'm a villager! Let me in!" My pounding was answered by a lone dog's hysterical bark.

A dilapidated stone border wall functioned as a crude stairway to within reach of the roof. A misty light rain slickened the tiles. After hooking my fingers through a broken gap, I managed to hoist myself, crawl over the peak, and lay flat. The tiles thumped against my chest; no, it was my heartbeat. *Slow down, heart. You're safe here.*

From here I could see the entire market street and the hellish opera unfolding below. Pirates hurried from shops with sacks over their heads; others herded women through the muddy lane. Dogs, alarmed by popping flames, ran every which way.

My hands gripped the tiles so hard that one came loose. I was afraid—not about the fires or the people I recognized down there. Even as a child this village felt foreign to me. The taunts I'd endured—*Dirty Tanka! Motherless one! Drunkard's daughter! Leave your fish. No, I won't pay more!*—those had changed to *Tanka whore!* But the meaning was the same: forever contemptible, forever the outsider. Watching the place burn moved nothing in my heart. The fear in me was for myself.

A woman screamed somewhere below. I knew I shouldn't, but I crept toward the roof's edge to peek.

A heavyset man pinned a teenage girl to the mud while two other bandits tugged at her trousers. I felt more disgust toward the men than pity for the girl. She was Punti who, in normal circumstances, would fling a cutting look my way. Regardless, I had no power to change things.

The roof tile snapped free in my hand. How tempting to slide it to the edge in just the right spot and watch it drop straight onto a bandit's skull. If I pulled my head back in time...if the stocky one shifted just a bit closer—

A fist folded around my ankle and nearly twisted it off.

"Get off!" said a hog-gravelly voice. "You'll bring them here!"

I tried to jerk away, but he wrenched my foot until I thought it would break. Tiny piggish eyes peered through the weak light. Did he mean to push or pull?

"Let me inside then," I whispered.

"If it isn't the Tanka whore!" He sounded like I'd interrupted some hard drinking. He twisted harder.

"Let me in. I'll do you free."

"Not your choice. You do me anyway."

He tugged my leg, nearly losing his grip. I slipped down the rain-slick roof. "Let go, so I can climb up," I said.

"Lying slut. Try to cheat me." He leaned over the crest, his other arm reaching for my free leg. Then a surprised, swinish grunt.

A mound of dark flesh skidded downward, one arm flailing, the other firmly attached to my ankle. I grasped for a nail, a crack, a hole to cling, to break my slide, to pull myself out of the way. I realized too late—I still held the broken tile.

His full mass barreled over me into the dark, dragging my foot with him. "Let go!"

Then I had nothing left to cling to. My legs kicked free, striking air. Flames, blurred and spinning. I knew I was falling; I knew it would never stop. If I stretched out both arms, could I fly away like a bird?

My head struck something neither hard nor soft. Life drained into darkness and silence.

So, this was death.

Death was black. Death was numb.

Something poked my back. Laughter dribbled into my ears. My cheeks burned. Vision returned, my eyes filled with fire, which focused into a single flame. It was only a torch held to my face.

"A goddess fallen from heaven." Someone yanked me up by the armpits. Another pirate leaned close and leered.

Men surrounded me, all clad in black, except for a boy who stood out in his violet turban. He picked up something from the ground and

11

waved it in front of me: my ivory comb! I tried to grab it, but my arms were held fast from behind. The boy laughed and stuck the comb in a fold of his turban.

"Lucky you landed on him, not him on you," a pirate said.

I didn't understand until whoever held my arms turned me to look. My rooftop assailant lay twisted on the ground, a broken roof tile lodged firmly behind his ear.

"Lucky us," the tree-trunk shaped pirate said. He nodded to another, who bound my wrists behind my back and nudged me forward. The village burned around me, undeterred by the rain.

Death was fire.

My captor pressed me toward a line of shuffling women. *No! Not a slave again. Give me real death instead!*

I kicked backward, wishing for a groin, but met only air, answered with a knee in my spine and stinging slaps across my face. Every shred of strength ebbed out of me like icy rivers.

Death was ice.

Death was stones and debris stabbing my feet. Death was fists and pikes prodding me forward behind marching bodies. It was throbbing shoulders, dripping matted hair in my face that I couldn't flip away. It was sprawled figures illuminated by an oily golden glow—some moving, others stiff as logs. It was the hiss of snakes, or laughing ghosts, or rain-drops striking hot embers.

Death mocked me as I passed the last houses, where, overhead, the magpies, fooled by fires into a second sunset, squawked merrily in the trees.

II
Red Slippers

The storm snuffed out the moon and stars. Screams pierced the darkness at every heave and buck of the ship. There must have been fifty women and girls crammed onto the poop deck, exposed to the wind and heavy rain. Judging by the violent arch of each sway, I guessed that they'd anchored us outside the shoal past the northern headland in waters too rough and too far from shore to swim.

Some women huddled together, sobbing, while others like me hunched against the parapet for what little shelter it offered.

I braced myself for another big swell, though there was nothing I could do but dig my fingernails into gaps in the deck boards. A wave smashed the transom, spewing frigid spray over the rail and pitching the ship crosswise to a chorus of shrieks and whining wind. Brine on my cheeks tasted like tears.

No place, no person would miss me. No family to pry ransom from, I was as worthless as trash fish, as good as dead. At best, fodder for another brothel. I had to get away, even if I risked drowning.

Faraway lightning provided a glimpse of shore, too brief to seek landmarks, to judge distances. Did I have the strength to swim it? Unlikely in this weather, even if I could find my way in the dark. If the currents didn't take me.

Piss-yellow light pooled on the main deck below. A figure sprinted across and disappeared down a forward hatch. A thump somewhere and the light vanished. The pirates were all bunkered inside; I might steal a sampan, though not without assistance.

I raised my aching body and leaned on a rail, all thoughts of escape dissolving in the rain and spray pecking my face. White-capped water reached like fingers to lure me in.

I'd known more than a few flower boat girls who had made that terrible choice. I never knew whether it was cowardice or courage which stopped me from committing the same act. For now, I had to stay alert. When the right moment came, I could decide between cowardice or courage and free myself either way.

The wind and showers passed, and the ship settled into a gentle sway.

Lights appeared below again. For once I wished for darkness.

Men with torches swarmed the poop deck from both sides, shouting ugly words. Women collided into each other, rushing for the opposite rails. Sitting ones clung to each other and screamed to the heavens.

Should I jump? I still wasn't sure I could make it. I hid my face and folded into the shadows.

A ruffian with a long feathery beard leaned over with a torch in one hand, the other extended like a claw.

"A pretty one," he said, but he wasn't speaking of me. A young woman beside me squeaked like a mouse as he grabbed her jaw.

"Who's your husband, pretty girl?"

She clenched her mouth shut and whimpered. Feather-beard lifted her head, forcing her to rise. "What's his name?"

She gagged on the name. "Chan."

"Well then, Chan-tai, and what's his trade?"

While pirates gathered around the girl, I took a tentative step sideways on my knees.

Another man slapped the squirming woman. "Answer! What be his trade?"

"Wood—" She gulped. "Woodcutter."

Feather-beard wrenched her head back and grimaced. "How much is she worth, the delicate young wife of honorable Woodcutter Chan? Let's see the goods." He tore open her tunic and lowered his torch to her bared breasts. "What do you think, brothers? A hundred silver taels to return such ripe fruits to their master?"

I sneaked another few side steps. A pair of wooden crates in the corner presented a tempting hiding space.

I last glimpsed the girl hanging over a man's shoulder on his way down the ladder. Other men followed, hauling women who kicked and scratched while their abductors laughed. I had to move faster. I crept on my knees until the crates' deep shadow was just two or three steps away.

A girl, no older than thirteen, dashed in front of me and launched herself in a big, springing leap toward a gap in the rear rail. As a Punti, surely she couldn't swim. A man threw himself at her, grabbing her collar which tore off in his hand. She disappeared over the side with a yell.

Lucky you. The same man turned his attention to me. I was beyond his reach, but it was too late to hide. Faint outlines of hills formed in the distance. Soon the sun would be up. I had to take my chances and swim it.

I tensed my legs—now or not at all.

My scalp, neck, and shoulders ignited with pain. Someone lifted me clear off the deck.

"Who's this delicate little butterfly, all poised to wing away?"

I aimed a knee at my captor's groin, but he hopped back just in time. Pulling my hair skyward until I thought it would rip from my skull, he pressed his face close to mine.

"Where were you going, little butterfly?"

A pair of slug-like lips formed a hideous grin, his eyes little more than fissures.

My fingernails raked his face.

I expected a knife in the gut as a consequence. Instead, he laughed and twisted my head aside.

"More like an angry snake. What do you think, brothers? Should we—"

My fist smashed into his throat. The pirate lost his grip and staggered backward. I dashed toward the gap where the girl had jumped.

Two more steps...

Someone tackled me to my knees. A dagger appeared at my neck.

"You want to slice her, Captain? Or allow me the pleasure?"

The blade nudged my jaw up until I met the eyes of the man I'd struck. So, he was the captain of this pathetic junk who'd lost face in front of his wretched crew because of me.

The pirate captain gagged into his hand, studied his fingers and then, in a slow movement, extended his arm to the side, leaned back, and spun his body as if swinging an axe. The ball of his hand cracked my cheekbone. Deck and sky traded places. My skull struck wood.

The captain stood over me and spat.

"Send the snake bitch to my cabin."

The captain's quarters smelled of must and rancid oil. Dawn light seeped through a gap in the porthole shutter, barely illuminating a cramped cabin whose only ornament was a shrine at the back. A large porcelain seafarers' goddess Tin Hau squinted at me through the gloom. Fat beams hung so low across the ceiling that I would have to stoop to walk. That is, had I been at liberty to stand up at all.

I lay curled up with my arms and legs bound behind like a crab for market, trying to relieve the itch under my wet clothes, though every scrape of a rib against the bare floor shot pain up my side. My throat was so parched and swollen that I had to work to breathe.

I needed water. I needed escape, whether by jumping ship or through the refuge of sleep. I needed to shut out the thumping and cries which continued unabated on the poop deck directly overhead.

A latch rattled. The door slid aside. The captain stepped in without a glance my way. Head hunched under the low ceiling, he walked to the shrine, kindled fresh offerings, bowed, and mumbled prayers to Tin Hau. Incense smoke scoured my throat.

"You're a tough one," he said over his shoulder. "Pretty, too. Who's your master?"

Interpreting my cough as a flippant reply, he rushed at me. A sheathed dagger bounced on his hip.

"Your husband's name." He yanked me into sitting position and leaned closer. He smelled like the aftermath of a night of drinking.

I considered inventing a spouse. But what would happen when his scouts returned with the truth? He would kill me, or worse, keep me.

"Talk, little sister!"

His hand cupped my chin. I tried to squirm away, but his grip tightened.

"Untie me," I said.

"So, you do speak. Answer my question."

"Untie me!"

I snapped my head sideways and would have sunk my teeth into his wrist if his reflex had been a little slower.

The slap struck without my seeing it, then again, and once more. I fell, bucking and straining against my binds, screaming, "Untie me! Untie me! Untie me!" until my voice shattered into uncontrollable coughs.

A voice through the door: "Captain? The purser—"

"Not now. Fetch the water jar."

My eyes were swollen and too painful to keep open, nor did I wish to see the gloating look I heard in his voice. The sound of an earthenware lid scraping open, liquid pouring. My head was wrenched upright, a bowl tipped against my lips, like someone feeding a sick farm creature. Eyes closed, I clamped my mouth tight. Water dribbled past my chin.

"Untie—"

His wheeze said the rest. I girded myself for another slap.

"Remove her bindings," he said.

"Captain?"

"You heard what I said."

"But—"

"Now!"

Behind me, the sailor loosened the cords. I clenched and unclenched my hands, feeling them tingle back into life.

I heard the captain dip the bowl in the water pot. With one hand he pried open my jaw. Stale liquid filled my mouth.

I cracked my eyes open to take aim and spat the water in his face. "Dog! Let me go!"

The crewman waved a cutlass at me. The captain motioned him away, wiped his eyes, and, to my surprise, bared his teeth in a grin.

"Your husband must be a bull to handle a wild snake like you."

"No husband. No family. No money for you."

"Such stunning beauty without a husband?" He examined a fingernail and chewed it off. I looked back and forth at the door and the porthole. The crewman crouched at the entrance, eyes burning into me.

"Those cows up there..." The captain's eyes pointed to the ceiling. "All belong to me now. If no ransom, I sell to my crew. Forty taels for the prettiest ones." His palm grazed my breasts. "For you, I think eighty."

"I'll pay," I said, leaning forward, as much to hold his gaze as to distract from the bulges in my vest pockets. "Pay you one hundred to let me go."

"No family, you said. No money."

"She's lying," the crewman said. "Just fuck the useless bitch and feed her to the fish."

"Silver is in my house," I said. If I could convince them to take me ashore, I might be able to...what? One step at a time. "I'll give you two hundred, all I own."

The captain cocked his head at the crewman. "What do you think?"

"That she's lying trash."

The captain nodded and placed a hand on his dagger sheath. He ordered the crewman out.

He pulled out the dagger and slid it across the floor, far beyond my reach. He stroked my thigh.

I'd seen this look ten thousand times before: playing at seduction, wrapped in threat, inviting me to make the next move, to incite desire. Both of us pretending I had a choice. If I played his game to his ultimate triumph, would he take a chance on my lie? Something dangerous simmered behind those fat lips, that stony chin, and those cheekbones halfway to the sky.

His fingers traced down my nose and caressed my lips, while his breath dampened my cheeks. I tilted my head back ever so slowly, my mouth rounded and tongue curled like an orchid beckoning a bee. Two rough fingers slid into my mouth.

I bit down hard.

His skin was bitter. Ragged fingernails scraped my tongue. I willed my teeth into animal fangs, impaling his knuckles between iron jaws. I *was* an animal, not thinking of death or consequences, only of release.

His fist drew back for a punch, but with the advantage of two free hands I caught his forearm and twisted it down and back. My throat foamed over with blood-salted saliva, but even as I choked, my jaws clenched harder. He kneed me in the belly, knocking us both off balance. His head loudly struck the floor, mine smacked into his chest. He took that moment to yank firmly on my jaw with his trapped hand. Every muscle in my neck was on fire, crying to let go.

I punched myself in the chin.

Teeth struck bone and sinew. His cry was a python's hollow hiss.

A hidden pair of hands wrenched my arms behind me until my shoulders threatened to snap, my mouth sprung open, another man's knees sunk into my belly.

"I told you to kill her," he said.

The captain knelt in close, examined his hand, and wiped his bloodied knuckles on my cheek. His face was a shadow, eyes black slits over a wolfish grin.

"Beautiful as a butterfly, fierce as a tiger."

He pressed his lips onto mine and smothered me with a dry, leathery kiss.

"Tell the crew I'm taking a wife."

III
Shame

I was alone with the flies.

Light seeping around the porthole frame suggested it was midday. Someone had inserted a wedge behind the shutter with the obvious intention of discouraging escape. They needn't have bothered; any attempt to sit up sent swords of pain up my back. My head felt puffed up and empty as a fish bladder. I drifted back into darkness.

The aroma of fresh rice filled my nostrils. My eyes opened to a bowl cradled in a bony hand and followed the faded gray sleeve up to an old woman's creased face. My stomach yowled. Had it been days since I'd eaten?

The old lady propped me up against a rattan pillow and set the bowl in my hands. I shoveled in red rice and fish jerky with hardly a pause to chew or breathe until bones caught in my throat and I coughed a mouthful onto the mat.

"So, you're the wife."

What was she talking about?

Then I remembered. I shook my head. This wasn't the first time a man had declared his intention to marry me, usually in a voice heavy with drink, always forgotten before his next visit. I mopped stray rice grains from the bowl's rim with my finger and sucked them in.

The old lady unrolled a pouch filled with thread and needles, then flicked open a red kerchief and spread it across her lap. An embroidered flower was in progress. She threaded a needle with yellow silk.

"Do you talk?" she said.

I spat fish bones into my hand. "I'm nobody's wife."

"Ha! Thank your luck it's Cheng Yat and not one of those other monkeys."

"Is that the reptile's name?"

The woman laughed without taking her eye off her sewing. "You've not heard of him?"

"Heard of who? Why would I care about a sea scum bandit?"

"Careful, missy. Among us 'sea scum', he's a big man. You know Cheng Sing-kung?"

I shoveled in more food, plucking rice from my trousers.

"The Ming patriot," the old lady said. "Threw the red-haired devils out of Taiwan. But people called him a pirate. Cheng Yat's paternal great-great-grandfather."

I shrugged. I didn't need a history lesson; I needed a sampan back to shore.

The woman cackled like a duck. "Never met someone more ignorant than me before."

My next swallow of rice came right back up into the bowl. I set it down and picked my teeth with a fingernail.

"Dull company, you. Won't talk, only vomits," the old lady said. She snatched a slipper from my pocket. "What's this?"

"Give it back!"

She examined a frayed thread at the toe and reached for her sewing pouch. "Let me fix that for you."

"No!" How dare this stranger touch a single fiber of my mother's remains? I stuffed it back into my pocket, then hid my face behind my sleeve. Curse the old goblin for making me cry.

"Sleeve's torn. Maybe you'll let me fix that before the rip spreads."

"Help me get out of here," I whispered, trying to keep the pleading out of my voice.

"Ah..."

"I mean it." I patted the pocket holding my pouch. "I can pay."

"Don't be stupid. Life's not so bad for a woman on a ship like this. Better than where you come from."

"What do you mean, where I come from?"

The old lady chuckled. "You're water folk like us. Anyone can see that. But these..." She felt my fingers the way a shopper fondles fabric. "So long and smooth. Never seen a rope callus nor nicked by fish scales. And a full purse! I can guess what kind of boat you're used to. Sailing on your back, am I right?"

I hurled the rice bowl across the cabin, an explosion of grains and ceramic. "Stupid *baat po!* Get out!"

She chuckled and went on with her stitching.

"Girl, there's no shame in what you've been." She tied off a thread, rolled up her pouch, then collected porcelain shards on her way to the door.

The woman shot me a parting look. "And there's no shame in being a sea captain's wife."

I clenched my eyes and squeezed out the tears. What could that old hag possibly know about shame?

Shame began at seven years old.

The beach held just me and the shorebirds and, being low tide, the mudskippers. Ah-Ma called them kindred spirits, those land-walking fish who lived their whole lives in the mud. She wanted me out of the house that day. By the time I came home, she said, I might have a baby brother or sister.

I should have been able to quickly fill my bucket with clams, but I was in no hurry. There were too many prettier things to collect: a pebble so blue it might have been a jewel, a brilliant red scallop.

Ah-Ma would love these. She could put them on the side beam that stuck out like a shelf, a little sun and moon to brighten our home. Or maybe I'd give them to my new brother. I hoped it would be a brother.

I picked up the shell and squealed with laughter when a hermit crab stuck out a claw and tickled my palm.

Then I heard my name on the breeze.

A woman from the neighboring stilt house waved me over. I carried the heavy bucket, but the woman urged me faster. Something wasn't right. I dropped the clams and ran.

Before entering the cabin, I smelled blood. I heard my mother's weak cry.

My father yelled and stamped his feet. Ah-Ma's face was white against the bed mat, shiny with a big dark stain. Something lay beside her, wrapped in a bloody rag.

My father yelled at me, "It's your brother! See what she did!"

Ah-Ma tried to speak, but he drowned her words.

"She didn't have to push so hard! Couldn't wait! Those women— Choi-tai, damn her!—*Push! Push!*—all they can say! So much hurry! A boy needs to be ready to come out! Why'd you listen to those demons?"

He grabbed her shoulders and shook her like a sack as though if he shook hard enough another son, living this time, would come flying out. I rammed him off her and pummeled his chest. "It isn't her fault!"

Ah-Ba pried me off, then crouched in the corner and beat his head with his fists. "I want my son!" It was the closest I'd ever seen him come to crying.

I spent the day cleaning up, while Ah-Ba slumped on deck drowning himself in wine. The blood spilled from between Ah-Ma's legs until finally, in the morning it trickled to a stop.

I sat with her all day, dribbling broth into her mouth. I lay with her, not daring to move while her fingers faintly stroked my hair.

Late that evening, she whispered something about a package under a floorboard. In a shaft of moonlight, I unwound the dusty paper and found a pair of embroidered red slippers.

Ah-Ma strained to fill her lungs, then her voice crackled like wind sweeping empty shells, "For your wedding."

What a waste those final words were, I decided right then, at age seven. A wedding meant marriage, meant a man like him, a short life like hers.

I stepped outside to tell him. Ah-Ba smashed a wine jar against the deckhouse.

"How am I supposed to pay for two caskets?"

That, old lady, was just the beginning of shame.

He called me *Daai-dai,* a nickname many water folk gave their daughters. Its literal meaning: *bring a younger brother.* He spoke it with amusement almost verging on affection, but the intention was clear to a little girl; I was an obstacle on his path to having a son. My name was a conjure. I wasn't me.

He called me by that name long after it had lost its purpose, when I was the only one he had left. He called me *Daai-dai* while he trained me in the skills he would teach a son.

He taught me to fish. How to read water. How to properly dry nets, coating them with egg whites when there was money to spare—if he hadn't exchanged it yet for wine, if he hadn't gambled it into the air.

He taught me to read the weather: a crow's cawing meant fierce wind and rain, a goose feather on the water meant an approaching storm.

Always bad omens, always prohibitions, always something to fear.

My pride was in working the yuloh. Sometimes, I'd have to stand on my toes to swivel the oar into the thickest currents. But in calm and shallows I sculled as fast as boys twice my age.

Still, I hated the sea. The work was rough and busy and boring, all at the same time. The sun burned you. A squall could drown you. Sharks were enemies, dolphins and turtles taboo. And the rituals: prayers and offerings to the sea and sky, for every contrary wind, every promontory and river head. At least on the water, Ah-Ba could blame his troubles on the cursed gods. Always so sad, cocooned in his dark world.

By my thirteenth year, the thought of marriage loomed like an approaching gale that would sweep me away, but we never mentioned it out loud. Ah-Ba said we were fated to each other, though such talk grated on me. Any time he mentioned fate, it was like the weather portents: a choice between bad and worse.

Fate had nothing to do with gods on that night he came stumbling home drunk, screaming about being cheated by Puntis. This was nothing unusual; every four or five days he raged at the injustice he'd suffered at the fish traders or the fan-tan table. But that evening, he refused food and bolted himself inside the cabin. All night long, I heard things breaking.

For two days he didn't come out. He didn't speak. I left food by the door. Sometimes he took it; other times, birds got there first.

Then two men showed up and kicked in the cabin door. My father pleaded and promised, though I didn't know about what. Something cracked and he let out a throat-burning scream.

I found him lying on the floor. His face was swollen, blood dribbled from his nose. One finger dangled like a broken twig.

"Daai-dai, ask the neighbors for fish gall," he said. A remedy for pain.

"What did you do?" I said.

I dipped a rag in water and wiped his bloody lip. Something in his hurt and angry face made me think of a trapped animal who would just as soon devour its rescuer.

"You've been gambling," I said.

His eyes squeezed shut.

"How much did you lose? How much do you owe?"

A tear pushed between his lids.

"Tell me!" I said.

I made him repeat whatever he'd mumbled. "The ship. I lost the ship. It's all I have."

Days later he disappeared, and I didn't see him for another three days. The two men returned, but finding him gone, left without a word.

He came back before dawn, took in the ropes, and sculled past the headlands before raising sail. He pointed us upstream into the delta, not toward any familiar fishing ground. Were we running away? Where were we supposed to live? Where would we fish?

"They'll find us," I said.

He told me to change into my best Spring Festival clothes, which were small on me now. He thrust a sack at me and said to keep it close.

Midmorning, he pulled up to a boat anchored inside a small tributary. This was no fishing vessel. It looked like one of the square-sailed pig boats which ferried animals up the inland waterways. A woman emerged from the arched canopy at the back and waved.

What happened next is a jumble in my memory. People chased me across the deck, tackling me like a pig. I swung my sack at them; they laughed. Strong arms lifted me. The woman pried my jaws apart and commented merrily about my teeth while baring her yellow gap-toothed grin.

My father stood with his back turned while he counted silver from a purse.

The woman tore the sack from my hands and dug inside. Her hand came out holding my mother's slippers.

"Mine!" I lunged for them, but she lifted them out of my reach.

"Inside!" she ordered.

Someone shoved me. I tumbled into the gloom under the canopy where at least five other girls hunched over, hugging their knees and watching me with soulless eyes.

"My shoes," I pleaded.

The dark figure above me placed a foot on my chest and pressed me between two girls. The slippers dropped near my knees.

I screamed for my Ah-Ba. He leaned down and locked eyes with me. I couldn't hear what he said but read by his lips: *"Daai-dai."*

At least call me by my name before you turn away forever.

I caught a last glimpse of him back on his deck hugging the purse, a deep, sad frown scoring his face.

Is that shame enough for you, old lady? Because there's more.
Shame was not the first time a man pierced me, drawing blood.
Shame was not the next thousand who shoved their smelly pricks in
me before I turned fifteen.
Shame was not allowed amidst the showy merriment of the flower
boats.

It took thirteen years—half my life—before they informed me I'd paid off my debt. My father's debt.

They invited me to stay. They implored me. I was one of the best, they said: beautiful, artful, voluptuous, and poised. I knew how to arouse a man and keep him at his peak for just long enough and no longer. And they always returned. I had many good years left, they said. I could keep all the money, minus rent, minus perfumes and makeup and contraceptive herbs, minus drinks and food and servant boys' tips. I would be able to save, one day buy my own girls and manage a flower boat, live an easy life. That was the way the world went 'round.

Instead I returned to Sun-wui, intent to find him and punish him. But all I found was the old junk, empty and mired in mud, showing no trace of the man who sold my life away, not even a rumor, as if a man who could do such a thing wasn't worth a puff of air to the rest of the water folk.

Moving inside that boat felt like living inside my own bare womb.

Yet, there I owned my life for the first time. I had no debts, no obligations, no father, madam, or overseer. No man could buy me without my consent. No man could sell me. No man could lose me to a table covered with tokens.

Until Cheng Yat came and snatched me away.

That, old lady, is what shame is.
Don't ever speak to me about shame.

IV
Wife

The goddess Tin Hau's eyes appeared to follow me wherever I moved within the cabin. Legend had it that she was a real fisherman's daughter, like me. She saved her father and his crew from drowning in a typhoon, and was worshiped by seamen ever since. Eventually, she had been elevated to the rank of goddess, undisputed protector of all who live on the sea.

If this were true, which prayers to Tin Hau had I missed that might have saved my mother? Had my father's daily offerings and entreaties rescued him? Would this in turn have redeemed me?

I would not pray to the hollow porcelain goddess posing on her lacquered throne under a chipped headdress, offering only empty hope.

I had to rescue myself.

The porthole was open barely enough to slide a hand through. No amount of tugging made the shutter budge. My fingers protested each attempt to pry loose the wedge that held it. I needed a tool: an iron bar, even a musket rod might do if the wood was hard enough.

Maybe I'd find something in the captain's chest, a weighty crate of dense carved mahogany, pressed against the back wall. The key had been left in the brass bolt. I quietly slid open the clasp and raised the lid.

Purses bulging with what was certainly silver or gold ingots weighed down stacks of paper- and silk-wrapped packets. He wouldn't miss a purse or two, but first, I needed a way to escape.

My eye caught on an official-looking scroll. I slid it out of its embroidered sheath, but the wooden pin was too fat to act as a lever. The scroll unrolled onto the floor. Of course, I couldn't read—it didn't even look like Chinese—but I recognized the blocky red chops that indicated a person of authority. As I returned it to its place, my eye caught something more promising at the bottom of the chest: a bright yellow box adorned with a painted elephant encircled by more strange writing. Its heft suggested something of solid metal, maybe a dagger. I snapped open the clip to discover a large bronze name seal laid out on a satin cushion. It was cold to the touch, like something from the bottom of the sea. The flat engraved end was flecked with dried red ink—it had been used, but not in a long time.

What kind of pirate held onto such authoritative objects? Had they belonged to his famous ancestor? Or, more likely, were they stolen from some hapless official long digested by sharks? If they were plunder, why hadn't he sold them? The scroll and chop obviously had some meaning.

Neither was of use to me. Like the scroll pin, the chop was too wide and rounded to get a grip on the porthole shutter.

The cabin door rattled.

I rushed back to the chest. My scalp grazed a beam. As I hurried to put everything back in place, my head throbbed, my bladder protested.

I surprised myself by smiling. There might be another way out.

I knocked on the door.

"I need to relieve myself!"

No reply. Whoever had tested the latch had no intention to enter. I banged again, harder, repeating my words.

Somebody outside cleared his throat and spat.

I kicked the door again and again. I really did have to go.

"All right," I said. "Do you want to tell the captain you made me shit on his sleeping mat? Or shall I tell him?"

The latch rattled once more, this time with purpose.

It was the same squat crewman who'd pried me off the captain earlier. He pulled me out the door.

"Hands off," I said.

"Cheng Yat ordered—"

"I don't care. Touch me again, I'll bite!"

The day was later than I'd thought, the air beginning to cool, but even then, the light pinched my eyes. I leaned on the companionway rail, taking in the scene. The ship was at anchor, the shore a distant blur through a blanket of haze. The main deck stretched out below like a busy marketplace with human livestock. Female captives huddled inside a makeshift pen toward the front while men in black turbans bullied teams of bareheaded men—more Punti prisoners, I guessed—into hoisting incoming spoils over the gunwales. A chorus of men counted, "One, two, three", and a squealing pig tumbled onto the deck.

In the middle of it all, pirate women, wearing black trousers and tunics like their men, sat in a circle splicing ropes and darning sails. How extraordinary to chatter and laugh as if the commotion around them was routine daily business, though of course, it was.

My guard prodded me toward the stairs. "You said you have to—"

"I'm going. Hands off!"

At the bottom step, I nearly stumbled into a Punti woman lugging a water bucket.

"This way," the guard said. He pointed me up a ladder to a platform extending from the deckhouse like a narrow wing. Below me a sampan rode low in the water, crammed full of frightened villagers. I guessed them to be those whose ransoms had been paid, waiting to return to Sun-wui. A name was called, and one more blubbering woman clambered over the gunwale into the boat.

With a well-aimed leap, I could land between them and hide beneath their legs. If they would let me. If fifty pirates weren't all watching. If I didn't break my neck in the fall.

The guard, who required no intelligence to read my thoughts, grabbed my arm and pushed me toward the latrine, which consisted of a hole in the platform. A waist-high vertical plank served as a privacy barrier.

"You going to hold me while I shit?"

The guard let me step over the plank unaided. "No tricks."

I squatted over the hole and considered the hopelessness of my plan. That, in fact, I had no plan.

Someone whistled a signal. The sampan pulled away, the sculler turning it toward land. It teetered through a swell, carrying men who'd had me for a few copper cash and women who'd spat at my feet, who had just bought their freedom with silver or pigs. I wished the little boat would overturn and sink.

Inside the cabin, a steaming bowl awaited me. Beside it stood a needle and thread stuck into a patch of cloth which nearly matched my sleeve.

I couldn't see the departing sampan through the slit in the porthole, only wide-open water, an expanse of nothingness.

I pulled my mother's slippers from my pocket and stroked the toes, taming the broken thread, smoothing tiny ripples in the silk, trying to make at least one precious thing perfect again. I searched for a place to keep them safe: too visible under the sleeping mat; too thick with soot behind the shrine. I worked the heavy mahogany chest away from the wall, dropped the slippers into the gap, and pushed it back into place.

I settled in front of the congee bowl and watched its steam wisp and fade, while my heartbeats filled every corner of the room.

A hand slid under my tunic.

Jagged fingernails scraped my nipples.

Too dark to see, but not to smell: alcohol, fish, and smoke fumes smothered me. My trousers rolled past my knees. Coat buttons stabbed my ribs.

I wasn't ready, never would be ready for him. He pried my thighs open and stabbed like an angry wasp, before he spat on his hand and moistened me. He pierced, withdrew, and pierced again.

Thirteen years of habit brought a moan to my throat, but I made no effort to coat it with pleasure. His panting was a tempest in my ear.

He finished quickly.

His throat whistled in his sleep.

The porthole was wide open. I rose to my knees and leaned on the frame. Constellations crowded a brilliant sky, blending with the few wisps of clouds.

Almost as if I had called it forth, a star fell in a white burning streak: one brief and futile moment of beauty, silent and alone, before it died.

V

Lotus

M y eyes opened to gray dawn light. Chanting and scratchy incense smoke wafted across the cabin.

I had a view of Cheng Yat's back bent over toward the goddess. Leading the prayers was the chubby man in a black shiny robe I'd seen tallying prisoners the day before; the ship's purser, I presumed. Between them, a third man, whom Cheng Yat addressed as Taumuk—the ship's second-in-command—whose face looked stitched from leather.

Chants finished, the purser read from a book in his lap: "Favorable day for travel. Most auspiciously, you'll be delighted to know, toward south-southwest."

The Taumuk shot me a cold glance and mumbled to the others. Cheng Yat followed the man's gaze.

"Awake finally," he said, as though I was late for some business. The others looked impatient for me to leave. I was delighted to accommodate them.

No sentry guarded the door. No one tried to stop me. A fresh breeze blew, the clouds were thinning, and the air was clear. We were anchored in the same spot, perhaps two *li* from shore. I padded down the companionway stairs, weaved between men and women at morning chores, and squeezed into a crowd by a corner deck shrine. Someone muttered "Captain's wife", a statement of fact as unremarkable as the weather, which made it all the more grating. But men stepped aside at the words.

Behind the latrine barrier, I had a view of the now-empty sampan drifting at the end of a tether, though its yuloh was missing, which made it useless to me. Two local fishing boats kept their distance from the pirate junks.

Soreness between my legs reminded me of a more immediate problem. The bastard's seed was inside me.

I searched every corner of the deck for the old lady. I didn't know her name, who to ask for. The ship seemed enormous now, though it couldn't have been more than forty paces from transom to bow.

A younger woman climbed from a nearby hold with an armful of rolled mats. Old enough to be some sailor's wife, but too youthful to be a widow. I stepped in front of her and whispered, "Missy, please. I need contraceptive herbs."

Her contempt was clear; I was one of the new batch of captives. I was chattel.

"I'll pay." I pulled the purse from my pocket, which alarmed her more. Maybe she thought I'd stolen it from on board.

"I'm the captain's wife," I said, hating the taste of the words. But they worked. She had obviously heard the news.

She looked side to side and mouthed the words, "He'd kill me."

I slipped a wedge of Spanish silver into her hand, far more than a dose of herbs was worth. She passed me the mats and climbed down into her hold, returning with a small paper packet.

I unfolded one end: a handful of black ash.

"Lotus leaf?"

The woman nodded. Not the most reliable remedy, but better than nothing. She retrieved her mats and hurried away.

I slipped the sachet into my pocket and found the galley hold, where a cook labored in clouds of steam. The aroma of fresh boiled rice made my stomach sit up and talk.

"Bowl?" The cook held up his palm.

"No, but—"

"No bowl, no congee."

I considered whether he too required a bribe when a familiar feather-bearded face emerged from beside the stove and pointed. "Captain's wife."

The cook rummaged under the cutting ledge, blew dust and insect wings from a bowl, and spooned in rice gruel. He made a performance of dropping in an extra sliver of dried fish for his esteemed customer.

I hurried up the poop ladder, hoping for familiar company, even Punti ones, but the top deck was vacant. The other female captives, I noted bitterly, had likely been ransomed.

32

Sitting on a crate, blowing on the hot congee, I gazed across the water at the familiar shore which, as miserable and poor as it might be, I considered home. Yet here on this cursed ship, three times this morning, the words "Captain's wife" had earned me special treatment. In one direction, life as a mud-splattered whore, and in the other, perhaps a kind of privileged imprisonment. It was too much to consider.

I stirred half the lotus leaf ash into the gruel with my fingers, sucked them clean, and took a big swallow. The bitterness burned my empty stomach. Chewing a shred of salty dried fish somewhat reduced the urge to vomit.

A man said from behind me, "You're not going to bite my hand off again?"

Cheng Yat stepped from the poop ladder, arms raised in mock self-defense.

I gulped a large, acrid mouthful and covered the incriminating gray-streaked bowl with my hands. He settled beside me.

"What's your family name?"

I pressed the bowl to my face, licking clean the evidence. Before he could take it from me, I hurled it across the deck.

"Why don't you talk? You like to fight only!" He held my jaw, firm but not punishing, and turned my head to face him. "Speak to me like a wife," he said.

"Which one?"

"Which what?"

"Which wife? Number Three? Five?" I tried to pry his hand off, but his grip tightened.

"You speak in questions instead of answers. So can I: Do I have to beat you to make you tell me your fucking surname?"

"Maybe you do." I patted my left ribcage. "Here's a place you haven't kicked yet."

He let go, leaned back, and laughed.

"Shek," I said.

"Shek," he repeated, nodding. "I don't have the strength to ask your other name. Save that for later."

"How many wives?"

He stood and walked to the taffrail.

I repeated, "How many wives?"

"Not your concern."

"Finally, some truth. You're right, I'm not concerned with you or your damned devil ship."

He sprang at me, pressing my back onto the crate.

"Let me go, turtle's egg!" I spat at him and missed.

He leaned over me until his nose brushed mine, his breath heaving in my face. I avoided his look, but each time I turned my head, he moved his until our eyes met. He was toying with me.

His eyes sizzled.

"I like your spirit. You'll bear me powerful sons."

He let go, stepped to the forward rail, and waved a signal to someone below. A whistle came in reply. Someone shouted orders. Loud ratcheting filled the air, then a splash. The ship reared on its heel; the rudder had been lowered. We were about to sail.

Men swarmed the poop deck and hoisted the mizzen while the main sail rose skyward, engulfing me in its shadow. Firecrackers rattled at the bow, expelling bad spirits for the journey.

The ship leaned, battens creaking and whistling in the breeze. Hair blew in my face. I searched at my feet for a stray bamboo filament to tie it back.

When I stood, the landscape was already moving. Spirited away from this shore for the second time in my life to some new, unforeseeable horror.

But these thoughts didn't stick. I hardly paid attention as the inlet faded in the distance. My ears tasted the words they'd received, the way a tongue stirs a delicious morsel held in one's mouth. As brutish and despicable as this pirate chief was, as criminal and ugly and mean, no man—none of the tens of thousands who had entered my body and moaned in my face—not a single one had ever uttered such words. I'd heard my beauty lauded, bed skills praised, my breasts and hair and teeth extolled. But no man had ever before praised my spirit.

I finally found the old woman in a patch of shade by the small raised platform at the bow, where she mended a black linen blouse. She shifted aside to invite me out of the already scorching sun. The corner was still damp and cool from when they'd splashed down the decks, a good place to sit and pluck tiny white deck worms from my heels, another of the forgotten curses of shipboard life.

"Pretty-pretty miss, still keeping those lovely fingers nice and soft?"

I examined my other foot. "What's a woman supposed to do on this ship?"

"Same as a man except pee off the side, I suppose. Hee!"

"What's your name?"

"Never mind names. Sometimes even I forget. Ah-Yi will do." She dipped into her sack and removed a snarled mass of black thread. "Aiya! Help untangle this."

I guided the frayed end through one loop after another, but each maneuver seemed to lead to a new knot. Ah-Yi sucked in her breath at my incompetence.

"You sew?" she said.

"Not if I can help it."

"Good to sew. Gives us girls a chance to talk-three-talk-four. Here."

She pulled from her bag a black canvas slipper adorned with an intricately embroidered rose and an unfinished leaf. My lap received a needle and a comb spun with three shades of green thread.

I protested, "I don't know how to—"

"Foo. What kind of mother raised you?"

She got the message from the hang of my head, the pinch of my lips. After an awkward moment, she patted my knee.

"Don't want to sew, we'll find you something else. Know how to boil water? Hee! Even if you're the captain's wife—"

"Am I? Everyone accuses me of that. I've noticed no wedding."

"And I've noticed no virgin bride." The old woman's mouth stretched into a grid of yellow, black, and missing teeth. "We'll just have to imagine both."

My hand was too late to cover a small laugh, so I picked up the slipper. "What do I do?"

"The leaf. One side's finished. Copy it for the other side. See? Easy. Start with the dark thread, here."

I was in the middle of my first unruly line of stitches when a song rang out from overhead in a high voice:

> *Fall tangerines—*
> *Branches fill the jar;*
> *Fall night rain is perfect time*
> *For lovers near and far.*

A boy in a loincloth straddled the main masthead like a monkey, doing something with the sail bindings. I recognized him by his violet turban—the one who'd stolen my comb that night.

Fall colors each year
Just one time come around;
Fall wind whispers gently,
Stirring a fragrant gown.

Ah-Yi called into the air: "Cheung Po Tsai, don't you know any other songs?"

The boy slid down the mast, leaping halfway to land directly in front of me. He held up a foot. "Will you make me some fine slippers?"

Ah-Yi said, "I've told you more than once—"

"Not you, old auntie. Someone with prettier fingers can make my pretty shoes. Match this color." He patted his turban, then reached around my head and ruffled my hair, a move that angered me nearly as much as his next statement. "The ship's new mother. Ha!"

He ran off, leaving me so flustered that my next attempted stitch drew blood. I threw down the hapless shoe. "Curse him! And this too!"

There was something about the boy that disturbed me more than his impudent behavior. His singing, his teasing, his childish laugh—how could anyone exhibit such innocent joy in this miserable setting? A little trickster like the Monkey King, someone not to trust.

Ah-Yi dropped the slipper back into her bag. "Maybe best you stick to captain's wife's job." She slipped a thread through the hole of a large needle—in and out, in and out, while cackling like a chicken.

Her stupid joke upset me more. "Which man's wife are you then, old woman?"

She didn't answer right away. Fumbling in her bag a moment, she took out a tiny blue-and-white porcelain cup. "Dead man's wife," she said, finally.

Ah-Yi pressed the cup onto a fingertip and pointed it at me.

"It's a thimble. He took this from one of those foreign devil ships out of O Moon. Pretty, don't you think?"

I shrugged; I'd never seen such a device.

"Not for me, though. For his first wife." She tapped her chest with the thimble. "I was Number Two Wife. No children, me. So, Number

36

One treated me like a dog, her brats did too. Then soldiers caught him and—"

Her hand chopped the back of her neck. "That cut the tie binding me to that stinking cow."

"And she gave you this?"

"Let *me* tell the story. Both of us widows, she made me her slave. I took the thimble one night, showed the Taumuk, said she'd stolen it from the ship's bounty. So then..." Ah-Yi drew a finger across her neck while her eyes traced a trajectory over the ship's side.

Trying to hide my horror, I asked, "The children?"

"Worth a few ingots to a salt merchant. At least, the boy was."

"There was a girl?"

Ah-Yi's bitter laugh went straight to my gut. "You know better than anyone what happens to pretty little girls."

I raced to the latrine, pushed past a waiting sailor, and crouched behind the panel where I voided my lunch.

Something clattered onto the plank beside me.

My ivory comb. He'd stuck it in my hair.

I grabbed it before it teetered through the hole into the restless surf.

VI
Sugar

Days flowed, one into another, like swells in the sea.

On the third—or was it fourth?—morning since we'd sailed from Sun-wui, I leaned on a side rail with my bowl of congee and stared into the distance. All at once, a pod of pink and white dolphins surfaced alongside. Seamen called them *bak gei;* rhymes with "bad luck," my father used to say. Men hung over the gunwales, beating the hull with fists and poles to scare the creatures away.

Yet no man dared catch one to feed the crew. *Bak gei* were sacred fish, forbidden to eat. I'd almost forgotten what a web of contradictory superstitions sailors lived by.

Meanwhile I recognized another fear on board. As people went about their daily tasks, every so often they glanced toward the coastline to make sure it was still there. I caught myself doing the same. As much as I'd lived my whole life on boats, I had never been so far from shore for so long, confined to an infinity of chop and salt spray.

It was the seamen's age-old fear of losing sight of land, that we would cross an invisible line in the water beyond which we came untethered from the known world and dropped into the Outer Ocean, realm of wild and mythic danger.

My eyes shot grappling hooks to the hazy shoreline. From out here, the land wasn't split into farms and villages and towns and counties; it all blended together into a long, solid mass that shared one precious character: it wasn't this miserable pirate junk.

"I want to go home," I said, though I couldn't have named where "home" was anymore. A crewman oiling the rail nearby looked over and nodded.

Once more I filled my day by pacing the deck, counting the details: thirty-four steps from deckhouse to bow, twelve steps across the beam. Cannons: five on each side, no two alike. Winches: five, including the rudder. Companionway steps: eight. Same as yesterday, or had it been thirty-five steps then?

Crew—forty? Fifty? How to count them? The crewmen's holds were tight mazes of curtained partitions and narrow bunks where I might discover, like bugs under a rock, their wives and children, who I didn't yet know by name. Today a young mother called me Captain's wife and offered me a candied plum. When I sat and asked her name and how long she'd lived on board, she apologized and said that she had to clean her baby.

I was getting used to the crew calling me by that title. I almost welcomed it: it gave me reason to inhabit the same deck as these people; it granted me little favors. It also wrapped me in a kind of opaque screen. They made it clear in their exaggerated smiles that I was a usurper, an outsider, though born of the water world, yet too different to be one of them.

I joined the small crowd around the perpetual fan-tan game at a makeshift table over the fresh water tank, a commotion of shouted numbers and rattling brass. Lacking copper coins to play with, no one paid me attention, no one made room for me.

I squatted alone in a corner beside the deckhouse and watched a squall cross to the southwest.

Over my head, the boy, Cheung Po Tsai, sang the same song he'd sung day after day, morning and evening, something sad about the seasons. While the sun slowly broke free, for once I paid attention to the words.

> *Fall Fragrance bought and sold himself, the poem explains.*
> *Fall moon rays are bright, but likely come the rains.*
> *Though you scorn the traveler's way in fall,*
> *You can still meet old friends, after all.*

Buying and selling oneself I knew all too well; the same for dismal rains. But what was this thing that he held in the high notes, this miraculous notion called friends?

By the sun, we were headed southwest, and that was all I knew. I asked about our destination. A crewman laughed and told me, "We're fishing." Cheng Yat's five junks were a school of sharks, foraging for prey.

One blinding bright morning, ten, maybe twelve days since setting out to sea, a cry from the mast:

"Sail off the god side!"

Squinting into the sun, I found a dark spot on the horizon, at least as far from us as we were from the land. The men went deathly quiet.

The Taumuk ordered men to their stations, before he and Cheng Yat climbed the poop ladder.

Cheng Yat had pleasured himself with me only one time since that first night, and otherwise had nothing to say to me. So it was no surprise that he ignored me when I followed them aloft and listened from across the small deck.

The Taumuk held a spyglass to his leathery face, muttered, "Useless!" then employed it as a pointer. "He's no Kwangtung craft."

Cheng Yat tried the spyglass. "Are you an eagle? This thing is filled with mist."

The Taumuk raised his voice to the mainmast. "Wai! What sails? What course?"

"Three square! Fukienese," Cheung Po Tsai answered back, clinging to the masthead like a monkey. "Course to eastward, I'd reckon."

With a smug grin, the Taumuk tapped his brow. "These eyes don't need a spyglass, old man."

"Sailing singly, could just be fishing," Cheng Yat said.

Both men studied the distant vessel. "He's surely long spied the sun on our sails," the Taumuk said. "Headed east in this breeze, he's close-hauled, not set for speed, nor for fishing."

"Keeping far from land—he's something to hide."

The Taumuk scratched his lip and nodded. "Pepper, maybe bird nests. If he's bound for home, I'd wager a hold full of silver."

"This time of year, could be nothing but beans," Cheng Yat said.

"No, if all he had was beans, we'd smell their farts, even from here."

They laughed at the stupid joke, though I couldn't believe they'd left out the obvious guess as to its contents. How many ship's officers had I entertained over the years, listening to them boast about a successful run from Hoinam or Ningpo? They always came ready to reward my affections with a little sample of their wares. Spring and summer, if they'd come from the south, it was sweet snacks like red dates. From the north, they left sachets of fine tea. From time to time I received blocks of salt, which at least were good for barter in the market. But I always looked forward to this time of year, in the month before Mid-Autumn Festival, when I'd receive pretty little jars filled with crystals of pleasure.

"Sugar," I said.

I repeated louder: "I'll bet money they're carrying sugar."

They finally looked my way. Cheng Yat merely frowned, but the Taumuk stung me with dagger eyes.

What a fool I was. A rebuff would at least have been a show of respect. What had he said about admiring my spirit? Empty words from a hollow man.

I remained on the poop deck after they left, riding the swells and focusing on the distant trading junk. My mind soared with images of sneaking on board during the commotion of capture and buying passage to the nearest port. I patted my purse, as always tucked in my pocket. The longer I stared at the trader, the clearer the outline of its sails, the more my wild, unlikely thoughts turned into a plan.

The ship reared onto a steep ridge of water. I stumbled to the taffrail and held on tight, facing back toward the coast.

Except there was no coast.

We leveled over the peak. I wiped my eyes and looked again: where land should have been, a straight line between gray water and sky like a curtain had been sewn shut over the world.

The junk crested and tipped downward. I gripped the rail all the way to the bottom of the trough, then rushed down to the main deck where a rope snagged my foot and sent me stumbling toward an open hatch. I might have fallen onto a man cradling a large rusty ball if another hadn't pulled me aside.

"First time ever seen a body dodge a shot before it's even loaded." The accent was difficult to understand, harder to place; from a border town somewhere if I had to guess. Short and broad-chested, the man who'd saved me reminded me of a hawk, with stubby bowed legs and a neck as wide as his jaw. He carried the ball to the closest cannon and dropped it into an adjacent frame.

The hawk man waddled back, sat on a large wooden crate, and removed a smoldering pipe from his pocket. The man in the hold meanwhile came back up with another corroded black ball in his hands.

"Aren't you going to help him?" I asked the hawk man.

"Good question," he said. "Though I believe this old hunk of drift-wood first deserves a smoke."

We were being tossed by waves, about to attack another ship, yet this man sat pressing leaves into the smoldering bowl as though it were his only care in the world. "Someone needs to take it," I said.

The hawk man sucked his pipe, his nose pointing aside. "Goes beside the first." Did he mean me? Well, why not? I could use something to do.

It was heavier than I'd imagined. I staggered across the rolling deck, cradling the iron ball against my belly, and finally dropped it into the frame to laughing approval.

"Handles nine-catty shot better than some men!" The hawk man tapped his nose. "Including me."

My hands were smudged with rust. Metal flakes stuck to my skin. "Shouldn't these be polished before they're loaded?"

"Wah, hear that, girls? We've a munitions expert among us."

"Don't make fun. It doesn't take a scholar to figure that out."

"So, she's a scholar as well. Let me tell you something, little miss. Sit." He made room for me on the crate and took a deep drag on his pipe. "Polish those big bullets as much as you fancy, you're not likely to stuff it halfway down that barrel, much less get it to fire. Not unless you like hot metal blowing up in your face."

"What are you talking about?"

The hawk man stirred the pipe bowl with his little finger, casting red embers into the wind. He nodded to a third man, climbing out of the hold. "When's the last time that one's been fired?"

The new man counted on his fingers. "Don't know. Could be Thi Nai."

"Two years and some," the hawk man concurred. "We clean the bore then?"

"Don't recall myself."

Not that I was eager for a battle, but their behavior made no sense. "You're about to attack a trading ship, but instead of cleaning those barrels you're sitting around smoking?"

"Little miss—"

"Don't call me that! If you won't do it, then show me how!"

The hawk man tapped his ashes out and blew his pipe clear. "Melon Seed, you heard the lady. Show her how to clear a fouled bore."

The third man, Melon Seed, blushed, darkening the large freckles scattered across one side of his face that clearly earned him his nickname. The hawk man gave him a commanding wave. Melon Seed climbed into the gap in the gunwale, facing the end of the cannon and, bracing himself with one arm, dropped his trousers and pissed into the barrel.

"No better caustic to scour powder gunk," the hawk man said. The remaining man in the magazine hold passed up a ramrod with a rag wrapped around the end, with which Melon Seed mopped inside the barrel.

The hawk man pointed across the deck. "That old gun in the center? Narrower bore, more befitting a lady. Offer you a fresh rag, but we've only the one. Melon, you finished yet?"

"Does the captain know what shape these cannons are in?" I said. The cannon men chuckled.

"Little miss—" the hawk man began. "Sorry, don't know what to call you. Be assured, we won't fire a shot. Not from a big gun anyway." He nodded at the rack of cannonballs. "But we want them to think we might."

The other ship was clearly recognizable now as a three-masted trader, painted green with forward-facing round eyes in the Fukienese style. Would they survive a battle against us?

"How many cannons might they have?" I said.

A laugh rose from the magazine hold. "Hear that? How many cannons? How many you think, girls?"

"Go die!" I'd had enough of them. I stalked away.

"Cheng-tai!" the Hawk Man said. He'd called me Mrs. Cheng, not a welcome honorific at this moment. "Let me teach you," he said.

"Then call me Yang. What do I call you?"

The other cannon men laughed. "Won't say what name the girls use for me. Call me what you like."

"What about Hawk Man?"

He seemed to consider. "Suits me. Brains of a bird. Ha!"

I settled beside him again on the crate. He took another puff and raised a thumb at the trading junk. We were closing in faster.

"Take a look. He's no battle junk," he said. "And if he's a bandit, he's pretty far outside his territory to be working alone. What do you say, miss—er, Ah-Yang?"

"I suppose—" The ship heeled back with a force that stretched my stomach. The sea felt deeper here, the air thick and cold.

Hawk Man seemed not to notice. "He's a trader, no doubt. And no trader is going to carry weight that could be set aside for goods." He aimed his pipe at the newly cleaned cannon, unleashing a fresh spout of sparks. "Know how many catties of salt this beauty would displace? Three thousand? If he's any big guns at all, he'll have just one. All about money, sister. All about money."

Then the whole deck hushed.

The ship dipped into a massive trough and entered a new realm. This was the Outer Ocean I'd heard men speak of, usually with false bravado. The water was a deeper, rocky blue than I'd ever seen. The swells were white-capped mountains separated by wind-whipped canyons. Only gods and fish could survive here for long.

"Suppose it's time to prepare muskets," Hawk Man said as though he'd just thought of the idea. "Those we'll be rightly needing. We can use the lady's help."

He shut the lid of his pipe and stowed it in his pocket, then motioned me off the crate, raised the cover, and reached into a sack. His hand came out rubbing black powder between his fingers. He clicked his tongue. "Saltpeter's the problem. The bird shit in this batch holds too much damp."

The fear I'd felt moments ago was nothing compared to the fury that coursed through me now. He'd been smoking and spewing sparks atop the ship's powder store.

The Fukienese trader teetered through long, even swells, sails reefed and sagging, exposing its deck and bound crewmen and women to the ruthless force of the sun. Pirate sampans ringed the captured junk, along with tens of drowning chickens kicked overboard by Cheng Yat's men.

I steadied myself at the gunwale, witnessing the hapless vessel's ravishment by men from all five of Cheng Yat's ships. At first, the pirates appeared organized like a theatrical group, shouting and drumming while boarding the junk from all sides. Even the trader's crew seemed to be playing a role, as though they'd been through this a thousand times.

Then the strange plunder began. Pirates tossed sacks of rice and other dried goods overboard, half of them missing the sampans and dropping into the sea. Chicken cages flew from a hold and burst apart on deck, our men kicking the surprised hens over the wales like some crude sport.

"I don't understand," I said.

Hawk Man stood beside me, resting a long-barreled musket on the rail. "Looking for costlier loot."

We started when a large ball shot through an open hatch. It struck the water, then bobbed to the surface and floated.

"Coconuts?" Cheng Yat yelled from somewhere above. "Taumuk promised rare bird nests!"

A sampan set out toward our junk with two captives tied up in the middle. On the way a crewman plucked some still-living chickens from the water.

No sooner had it bumped alongside than a chubby, hairless man wearing nothing but short trousers tumbled over the gunwale, followed by a terrified younger companion. Our crew closed in so tightly around them that Cheng Yat had to squeeze through sideways.

The two men knelt in front of him, the younger unable to hide his trembling while the bald one looked up, strangely calm, as though he'd been through this too many times. It was quite apparent that he was their captain.

"What's your cargo?" Cheng Yat said.

"Have you no eyes?" the man said. "Coconuts. Bug-ridden unwoven hemp. Chickens. Rice." People snickered at his jumble of Hoklo and Cantonese.

Cheng Yat touched a cutlass to the man's bare belly. "You expect me to believe that? Coming from where?—Hoinam? Annam?—with a half load barely enough to cook a dinner? Where's the silver hidden?"

The bald man attempted to kowtow until the cutlass broke his bow. "I'm a poor sailor. Surname Ding. Any relations named Ding? Maybe we—aiya!"

The blade twitched in Cheng Yat's hand. A bead of blood dribbled down Ding's belly.

I averted my eyes. Why torment the man? More and more this episode took on the appearance of a show. When I turned back, Cheng Yat cast me the briefest of glances, enough to indicate the show was partly for me.

A purse thudded on the deck. "Here, all I have left," Ding said. "Please be kind and leave us an ingot or two."

The purser pressed through the onlookers and spilled out the contents. He bounced a bright yellow coin in his hand. "Twenty-two silver taels, a Spanish dollar, and this. Hardly a profit for such a long haul."

A gargled scream across the water turned everyone's heads. Two women were led at knifepoint into the trader's cabin, while a third, no older than sixteen, kicked and shrieked as her trousers were torn from her legs.

Ding's young companion lunged at Cheng Yat, then fell on his side, clutching a gash in his arm.

"Take what's left. Just let us go," Ding said, hands pleading.

"What do you mean, what's left?"

"Only a few catty-weight." The next word came out as a low grunt which he had to repeat:

"Sugar."

Cheng Yat's eyes spun in his skull until they found me. His brows moved as though they were lips speaking a message which needed no voice.

Still facing me, he lowered the cutlass from the man's belly and, using the blade to steady himself, crouched until his head was level with Ding's. Only then did he release me from his stare.

"Who are you fooling?" he asked the man. "You say you had sugar, yet you offer me floor sweepings?" He slapped Ding's fleshy face. "Dog! You sold it. Where's the rest of the money?"

"We—"

The younger man half rose and spat on the deck. "Fuck your old mother! One of you already stole everything!"

I watched Cheng Yat's hand whiten on the cutlass hilt and lift, slowly, like a cobra rising to strike. Yet his movement seemed false: the cultivated moves, the staged voice, his eyes—just now, another glance my way.

My eyes spoke back: *Your performance doesn't impress me. But I acknowledge that you're trying.*

A sudden big swell made him check his balance. Ding used the moment to throw himself over the young man and strike his forehead on the floor.

"I'm meat for your chopping board! I beg you, only spare my son and my women!"

The crew appeared disappointed when Cheng Yat lowered the cutlass. They preferred blood. A few grunted approval when he tapped the blade on Ding's chin. "Who did you say took your sugar?"

"A fat pig who spoke as if his testicles were bitten off."

Expecting murder, I was more than surprised by the grin unfolding across Cheng Yat's face.

"Did he call himself Vice Admiral Who Pacifies the Sea?"

Ding nodded. "The same."

Hawk Man chortled in my ear. "Talking about Wu-shek Yi."

Cheng Yat stood and leaned on the cutlass, affecting a mock-friendly tone. "When did you encounter my, ah, fat friend?"

"Two, three days. I don't know, south or southeast of the six-island lagoon. Please, every word's the truth. My son will fetch the rest of our silver, though I swear it isn't much. Don't kill us. Please don't take my girl."

Cheng Yat rubbed his chin, pretending to consider.

"I want only the sugar."

Fat Ding's sweaty body rose and fell on the deck like some slithering worm. "Thank you! Thank you, master!"

"I'm no master to a slug like you," Cheng Yat said.

Again he looked my way. Why this show for me? At that moment I despised him more than at any time since that first night. If his torment and humiliation toward this pitiful man and his family was meant to impress me, was I not then responsible for their suffering and pain? I wanted no part of this. All I wanted was release from this ugly pirate world.

Two men each lifted Ding and his son by the armpits and led them back to the gunwale. I ducked through the crowd of onlookers, keeping my head down, making sure all eyes were on the Fukienese. If I could slip into the sampan before the two men, wrap myself in a net, curl beneath a thwart, buy the sculler's silence with silver—

A hand blocked me. The man who thought himself an actor grinned in my face.

"The world will hear of the mercy of Captain Cheng Yat."

VII
Lagoon

Back on the flower boats, girls used to dream out loud about the luscious lives they might lead by marrying one of the ship's officers who frequented their beds: days of ease and adventure and colorful characters, all wrapped in promises, proving what great tale-spinners were men of the sea.

If only I could show them. Maybe only prison was more colorless, boring, and worm-ridden than spending day after day on a moving ship, but at least prison offered shelter from late summer sun and squalls.

Again, all I knew was that we were moving west in line with the coast. I could hardly tell. The sea, the sky, the land, always looked the same.

Cheng Yat's self-proclaimed magnanimity had nothing to do with me. He spent his days with the Taumuk or the purser and his ledgers, both of whom made it clear I wasn't welcome to hear ship's business.

Sometimes I sat with Ah-Yi, whose talk inevitably turned to women's prattle: babies, hair, and whose bloodline on board was mixed with whose, which thankfully—no matter how hard she tried to stretch it—never included my own. Although I finally managed to complete a full row of embroidery with a more or less even stitch, my second line always set out like a bird in flight and ended in a different land entirely.

What did I care about creating beautiful objects? I was far more interested in learning about guns. Beauty was fragile, something to exploit and abuse. Guns had power and purpose that beauty lacked.

Hawk Man was hesitant when I asked him to teach me, but I soon convinced him by actually getting things right. He and his two gun masters taught me about barrel gauges, trajectories, breeches, fuses, hammers, and frizzens. I discovered how to judge a cannonball's weight by sight and how and why to admire the smooth, tapered foreign cannon stolen in a port raid over rough-cast Chinese barrels. We took apart muskets and gingals and blunderbusses and the ship's one pistol.

I pushed their trust by prodding them to clean the cannons, which took two days and countless buckets of donated piss. The gun work kept my hands busy while a spirit deep inside me needed to prove to Cheng Yat and his smug officers that I was tough and smart and nobody's whore.

My aching arms were ready to quit for the day when Hawk Man said, "Bit more work to do," and dropped a sack at my feet, spilling a pile of tarnished and unfamiliar coins. "Best shot there is."

"You shoot money?"

"If you can call Annamese cash money. Wouldn't buy you a handful of pig shit. Plenty more down there." He demonstrated how to string them through their center holes before tying them into loops and bunches. "A big gun full of these'll turn a deck load of men into porridge."

At least the task could be done seated in the shade—until Cheng Yat appeared in front of me, tore a completed loop from my hand, and flung it into the water.

"Not proper work for captain's wife."

"Proper? What's proper, then, for the wife of a man of your standing? Maybe I should be plucking a zither?"

He laughed, at my admirable spirit I supposed, and swept the coins aside with a foot. "We won't need these anytime soon."

I followed his look past the opposite rail to a group of rocky islands jutting from the horizon.

The islets formed a rough circular lagoon in an expanse of surrounding sea. We entered from the northeast, passing between twin towering crags.

I took in this oddly quiet and separate world, a landscape of flat blue water and naked rock. Even the few sea birds kept to the outlying cliffs. By midday sunlight bounced from the surface, burning into one's eyes no matter which way one turned and heating the lifeless breeze. Men cooled the decks with seawater, women wove bamboo shavings into fans, and arguments raged over ownership of the few intact palm frond hats.

The largest island, formed of two scrubby round hills, vaguely resembled a turtle commanding the south of the lagoon.

Hawk Man said he'd been there years before, and that it was as barren as it looked, except for a small fresh water spring, which may have been our reason for stopping. Such news was consolation for the heat. It indicated a shore journey, a chance to get off this ship and feel solid ground, if just for half a day.

Cheng Yat directed Hawk Man to load two ready muskets in the sampan.

"Take me," I said.

Men loaded the boat with water gourds. Cheung Po Tsai stepped past, holding the yuloh over his head. I repeated my request.

"Room for eight, no more," Cheng Yat said.

His face made clear what a lie that was, as though I'd never ridden an identical sampan in my twenty-six years. Fourteen could squeeze in without danger. What game was he playing with me? Did he truly admire my spirit, as he'd claimed, or was I supposed to be his passive little whore? I wondered if even he knew.

"I can handle a gun," I said, though perhaps an overstatement at this point.

"Woman, this doesn't concern you."

I didn't know why I persisted. Maybe the heat had cooked my brain. Cheung Po Tsai fixed the yuloh to its pivot.

"Little brother," I called to him. "I can work a yuloh as well as a man. You're smiling. Yes, I can. How about a deal? Trade places for the day. I take yours at the helm, you take mine there." I pointed to the cabin.

Po Tsai blushed deep red. He and everyone else within hearing broke into horselaughs, including Cheng Yat. My face burned without my knowing why.

"Find the little chicken a dagger," Cheng Yat said. "She'll need more than a big mouth if we meet trouble."

I rode in the middle with my feet propped on one of many water gourds, more than were needed for a day's outing. A cross-current nearly swept us onto some rocks, but Cheung Po Tsai proved himself a powerful sculler.

I helped drag the sampan onto the sand next to a rotten, sun-bleached boat. Cheng Yat appointed a man to guard the beach. The rest of us followed him inland. The island had looked uninhabited from a distance, but the trail was well-trodden, walled in by tough, stunted shrubbery. We stopped in a shaded hollow to scoop water from the spring trickling beside an ancient tree. Cheng Yat and some of the men offered prayers to a collection of carved Buddhas inside a lightning scar on the trunk.

Our goal was a little temple at the top of the path. I was at the rear, halfway up the slope and drenched in sweat, when Cheng Yat halted and motioned for silence. He signaled the musket bearer to stand at his side and called, "I seek the fat wretch pretending to be Vice Admiral Who Pacifies the Sea!"

From above, the click of matchlocks. I felt for my dagger.

A high-pitched reply came from ahead. "I know that voice. Are you the great sea dragon who beds with dogs?"

"Don't be jealous. Dogs are prettier than you!"

A rotund bearded man in a blue suit met us on the landing. The trader captain had described Wu-shek Yi speaking like a eunuch, but he sounded more like a girl. "Old Cheng, ugly as ever. Looking for me, or a lucky accident?"

"Maybe something of both."

"Wah, and who's the willow-waisted beauty?" Wu said.

"My wife," Cheng Yat said. "But why are you making us stand in the sun?"

"Ha. You stay out here. Leave the woman to me."

The temple was musty and dark, but the stone floor was refreshingly cool. An unfamiliar deity reigned from a vestibule behind an altar table littered with empty bowls, as though no one had worshiped here in a long time.

Cheng Yat and Wu-shek Yi took the only two stools. I settled in a corner on the floor.

As men seem obliged to do whenever two or more are in a room, they drank. Cheng Yat removed the seal from one of his gourds, clearly never intended to hold water.

"How long has it been? Nine months? A year?" Wu took a deep swallow. "Cannons still ringing in my ears. And my prick's still ringing from those Annamese strumpets. Wah, sorry."

Wu granted me a smile. "Sorry. Old Cheng brings out my worst. What terrible stroke of fortune brought you to him?"

He thought he was teasing, but would he laugh if I told the truth? *I beat him in a fight and proved I was smarter than him. Now the devil won't let me go.*

Cheng Yat answered instead. "Found her waiting in my cabin."

The fat man's laugh sounded like he'd swallowed a flute. "Same old story! You and I are alike," he said. "Last man standing—or should I say last *boy*—after his band of thieves burned my master's ship. My good looks earned me the privilege of being dragged into his cabin. Ha! Anyway, one ship's the same as another, and no captain a greater or lesser scoundrel than the last, am I right, darling? Hope he isn't working you like a slave, as he did me."

I tried to conceal my reaction. Did his remark mean what I thought it meant? Wu offered me the gourd, but I waved it away. Cheng Yat was already flushed red from the wine.

"You handled yourself like a fool," he said.

"Thank the gods for making me a fool," Wu said. "Didn't take long to discover that anyone with half a brain can do this job. And possessing nearly half a brain myself, I seized the first opportunity to—"

"Steal one of my ships."

"Now, now, Admiral Cheng." Wu turned to me again. "It was never his. Taken in fair combat from Annamese rebels while he was farting in Haiphong. But we're still best of friends, as anyone can see."

"Friends, when convenient," Cheng Yat said.

Wu's smile dropped. "All jesting aside, my friend. I'm as loyal to you as a dog," he said, then turned to me: "And to anyone who shares his... should I say, close association?"

I had a creeping feeling of something lurking behind his words. Despite his bragging and the oddity of his voice, the man had a certain charm. But I was hot and thirsty, and the floor was hard. "May I have some water?"

"Ah, she talks! And here I'd thought I'd met the ideal woman— beautiful and mute. Not like my three."

"Three now?" Cheng Yat said.

"My second couldn't bear to be separated from her sister, so..."

I accepted a flask from one of Wu's men, slouched against the wall, and sipped water while the two old friends reminisced about people, ships, and naval actions in strange-sounding places. I gathered that they had served as paid mercenaries in Annam, a land I'd heard of only as a source of exotic fruits. I recalled the yellow elephant box and brass chop in Cheng Yat's trunk.

Their voices, the heat, and the exertion of the walk all conspired to make me drowsy. I got up, stretched, and set off to explore the little temple.

Crates and barrels packed a side chamber, which might have once been a monk's quarters. A single long chest looked like the twin to the musket store on Cheng Yat's ship. A doorway in the back opened into a small annex where two men dozed among dusty crockery, a cooking pit, and a smell like dead rats.

Back in the main hall, an ancient bell hung from a wooden frame so worn with age, I feared the slightest touch would send it crashing. The shrine was in better condition, its frame and deity repainted within the past few years. Some benefactor looked after this remote temple on the outer edge of the world—possibly the fat, drunken pirate in the center of the room.

In the loft overhead, behind a lineup of immortals along the ledge, was a cache of bound sacks, all too clean to have been there long. There were enough of them to make the platform sag.

I knew the moment I opened my mouth that I should have shut my lips and tied them with twine. I didn't know why I meant to ingratiate myself with these crude, bristly bandits, but if they expected me to accept being an accomplice to their deeds, then I wanted to be accepted right back.

"Is that the sugar?" I said, before I could gulp back the words. "If you're interested, I know the prices—" Wu-shek Yi's grin twisted into something sinister before I was halfway through my remark: "—it goes for in Kwangchow."

Or, more to the point, I'd heard them a year ago around this time, secondhand, from a warehouse clerk who liked me to stroke his oiled penis while he babbled about his job.

"Is that right?" Wu said. "I'm sure your pretty little face gets you a good price in the local market."

"Actually—"

Cheng Yat stomped the floor. "Enough, woman!"

"Where did you pick up this one?" Wu said. "Confide your business in bed, hah? And apparently mine as well. Makes her buck like a horse, I suppose?"

"Just a nosy old *baat gwa*."

"Enough talk." Wu put his grin back on and wobbled onto his feet. "Join me for a bite on my humble ship? Pork dumplings are good for the soul."

Cheng Yat teetered in the glare of the doorway. I waited for him to say something or to look my way, anything to confirm I was invited. Instead he clapped a crewman on the shoulder. "Back to the ship with her. And return with more wine."

The sailor refused to release my arm until we were well below the temple. A fluty voice drifted from overhead:

"...big trouble, my friend. A clever wife robs a man of his will."

And what about everything he had robbed me of?

Boredom devoured my spirit. Hawk Man's musket lessons didn't hold my attention. Sewing with Ah-Yi reminded me of my incompetence, not just with using a needle but in living my life. Most of the time I dozed in the cabin.

It was no secret that the fat, girl-voiced Wu-shek Yi had the sugar. I'd only offered some lighthearted help. I'd done nothing to challenge either man, nothing that might cost them face, nothing except show that I wasn't a stupid little whore.

But the larger question was this: why was I trying to prove myself to a couple of scum-of-the-sea thieves?

Whatever feeble breeze that had earlier rippled the lagoon now passed away altogether. I stripped off my clothes and cooled my body with a damp rag. Across the cabin, Tin Hau's eyes dared me to pray for relief. I wasn't desperate enough to put my faith in ceramic goddesses.

Once more I stuck my head outside. Still mid-morning. The sun seemed to have paused in its tired trek across the sky. How to get through the day? I pulled on trousers and a rough cotton blouse, plunked on a wide-brimmed hat, and pushed open the door.

People napped in the shadows, barely moving a leg to let me pass. I tiptoed across charcoal-hot deck boards to a section of rail in the mainmast's shadow and leaned over the side, staring into the clear green water. A few fish flitted past, deep where the water must have been cool. Tiny flecks of sea dust twinkled under the surface. I reached way down to scoop up a constellation of stars.

"Get back from there." It was the Taumuk, approaching from behind.

"I know how to swim."

"I said step back."

"Worried I'll fall in and drown? Captain will thank you for it."

"He wouldn't be the only one." He wiped his brow and reached for me.

"Fuck your old mother," I said. I stretched my arms forward and slipped easily over the side.

My chest and hips trembled at the sudden chill. I let my back, arms, and legs go limp, not knowing which way was up or down. How long had it been? Surrounded by water, nothing to cling to, unable to breathe, I was a child again, silent and free, cut off from the cares of the world.

Coming up for breath was like breaking off a kiss, gulping down clean, cool air, in a hurry for the next descent. Though I'd never once kissed for pleasure, I guessed that this was what it felt like, the intoxication of passion in the form of a swim.

A rope end splashed in front of me. I rubbed my eyes but all I saw was a tangle of outstretched arms.

"You must have fainted," a man called.

A woman said, "Grab the rope!"

My hat floated an arm's reach away. I flung it over the anxious faces at the gunwale.

I took three deep breaths and plunged back under, arms slicing the water, pulling me in, deeper and deeper. I bathed in brilliant green light, out of the ship's shadow. Below me, bottomless space. Above, crystalline light. Silver fish glistened. I attempted a loop, but dragged by heavy fabric, I lost half my breath righting myself.

I surfaced, lungs burning for air. The junk leaned under the weight of the entire crew crowding one side and waving me in. Hawk Man cupped his hands around his mouth, but I couldn't distinguish a word.

"Can you swim?" I said. "Come in! I'll teach you."

The Taumuk pushed to the rail, gripping a rope as though it were a whip. Him I could hear.

"Get back on deck! If the captain finds out..."

I didn't doubt that he would find out either way. I raised a hand to my ear, pretending not to hear.

He yelled above the frenzy, over the splash and gurgle in my ears, "No swimming allowed!"

Was it a trick of the light or water in my eyes? For an instant, his face was my father's. I remembered the day Ah-Ba informed me that

56

my swimming days were over: for modesty's sake, for hygiene, but most importantly, by tradition. Girls were forbidden to enter the water from the first day of the year we turned ten.

I took in a mouthful of water and spat a fountain. Tradition be damned and to hell with fathers and Taumuks. I still remembered my strokes.

"I'm the captain's wife, and I say swimming is allowed!"

I dove again, playing a child's game, slithering through the water like a dolphin. An explosion of air bubbles off to my side—a man's form curled into the water nearby. Our heads broke the surface at the same time. He spat out water and laughed. Another man dove expertly, like a spear fisherman. On another junk nearby, people leaned on the rails watching. Someone else leapt from the side. Soon the lagoon filled with men treading water, splashing and teasing each other like their souls had burst open.

"Women too!" I yelled.

A scream from near the bow. A young sailor's wife tumbled into the water. She came up thrashing and choking. "Can't swim! Can't swim!"

I swam to her, but by then a rope had been thrown. Once in her hands, she refused to be hauled back in, clasping the line, giggling and splashing her feet.

I dove farther next time, pulling into the shadowy depths until my arms burned and my lungs protested. I came up for air feeling hot in the face, almost drunk. I dove again, weaved among kicking feet, surfaced and dove again, passing under the ship to the other side. After surfacing for a quick gulp of air, I went deeper, beyond all strength in my shoulders and legs, ignoring my lungs' cry for breath—down and down until my body wanted to let go.

When I finally came up, clouds blotted the sun. A chilling breeze combed the surface into white-topped ripples. Ropes yawned as if the ship was waking from a nap.

I was the last out of the water, shivering and skidding across the deck, made slippery with rain.

As the sky cleared, the heat returned with renewed fury. I sat in the cabin doorway combing my hair, long-dormant muscles in my chest and shoulders aching with a kind of gratitude. People sat in the shadows, chattering happily. A woman looked up at me and smiled. A sense of peace permeated the air, along with the smell of chicken broth from the galley.

I went inside to borrow oil for my hair from Tin Hau's shrine—as a woman she would understand. When I came out again the sampan was docking. The Taumuk waved his arms and yelled to Cheng Yat before he even climbed on deck. I could guess the topic.

The companionway rattled under stomping feet, then Cheng Yat was in front of me, stinking of sweat and wine breath. He kicked the oil bowl away. "Inside!"

He tried to grab my hair, but the slippery oil foiled his grip. He blocked my escape and pressed me against the rail.

"What in nine motherfucking pricks did you do?"

There was no use arguing with him. I turned aside and furiously combed my hair.

"Throwing women overboard! Inciting mutiny among the crew!"

"I never—"

"Taumuk says you refused his orders to—"

"It was hot! Everyone was bored into convulsions! Ask them!"

People had gathered on the deck below to witness the drama.

"Tell him," I said to them. "The sun was baking us alive. You all swam of your own choice. Tell him!"

Each face I met turned away. The Taumuk leaned against the mainmast with folded arms and a sneer straddling triumph and contempt.

A voice rose from the crowd. "Captain!"

Hawk Man stepped forward, scratching the back of his head. My one defender, who deserved to be called friend. "I-I didn't, ah... Can't swim...but—"

"Then your opinion isn't wanted," Cheng Yat said.

He herded me into the cabin and slammed the door.

"What makes you think you command this crew in my absence? Answer me!"

"And where were you to command them? Oh, I can smell. Drinking with your fat eunuch!"

His slap knocked me onto my back.

"You bring bad luck to this ship. Make my Taumuk—make *me*—lose face in front of my crew!"

I backed away from him into the corner, shielding myself with the only thing within reach, a plaited rattan pillow.

"After you shamed me in front of my sworn brother."

"Who? Fatty Admiral? The sugar was right over your head. It was no secret. Were you going to say any—"

"Shut your lips! You wouldn't know driftwood from a casket. One more word—"

"And what? The strong man will beat me again?"

"Witch!" He lunged at me. I threw the pillow, but he knocked it aside. Immediately his hand gripped my throat. I pummeled his chest, tried to spit.

"Get rid of me!" I said. "You said it yourself—I don't belong here! Put me ashore, anywhere, I don't care!"

To my surprise, he released his grip and supported me by my arm until I caught my breath. He spoke in an almost apologetic tone, "It would be more merciful if I slit your throat now."

"If that's my only way off this ship, do it!" I said, raising my chin. But the fight had left him. He dropped me.

"Go. Run away. Leave if you insist," he said. "Or listen for once. You know what they'll do to you, right?"

Who were "they"? What story was he about to make up? I glanced at the door.

Cheng Yat settled on his haunches. "You think the locals won't know where you came from? A Tanka, but not from there, no family. Open your mouth, you don't speak like them. Sure, they'll welcome you—embrace you! Then drag you to the nearest garrison to collect their reward for capturing a bandit."

I didn't want to believe such ravings, yet the cold bluntness of his words gave me reason not to doubt them. "You can beg and plead— *Wah, the big bad pirate took me away and I ate his food and fucked him and opened my big mouth about stolen sugar and took command of his crew...but no, I'm not one of them, no, no, no*—Puntis are stupid, but not *that* stupid. Know what they'll do to you?"

He sprung up and pinched my eyebrow, just enough to hurt. I understood: death by a thousand cuts, starting with slicing off the eyebrows. I'd witnessed such executions in a Kwangchow public square. But those had been murderers and military traitors, every one of them men. I swatted his hand away and braided my hair, something to calm my trembling fingers.

"If you're a man, they mount your head on a pole. But a woman..."

He loomed over me now, as if he was enjoying himself. "Do you know what happens? Do you wonder? I thought you'd seen it all from your whorehouse window. I said, do you wonder what they do with bandit women?"

I worked furiously on my hair, saying nothing. He grabbed my half-tied braid and yanked my head back.

"The soldiers tie you down and take turns. For days sometimes. And when they finish, if you're still alive? I don't lie. You're auctioned to some fat Mohammedan trader to join his herd of slave girls in the western deserts—to fuck when he tires of fucking his goats."

Forgotten memories regurgitated like bile in my throat. The madam frightening us girls about running away. They'd been red-haired barbarians instead of Mohammedan traders, but the stories were remarkably alike.

What lurked behind his words? I'd cost him face; my desertion would cost him more. He could simply throw me out. Did he really care whether I stayed? Was he offering me a genuine choice? This strange man with the demeanor of a cobra could beat me or kill me without justifying it to a soul. But at this moment, more than anything, he confused me.

"Well?" he asked. "You prefer such a fate to lying around like an empress on my ship? Do you think any man will treat a wildcat like you better than I? The way I indulge you even when you go dipping your eyelashes to lure men into teaching you about guns? Ha! You think I'm too blind to see? What comes next? I turn my back and you pick up your old profession? You think I don't know you carry a purse in your pocket?"

"Bastard!" I let out a sob and tried to shake my head free, but he tugged my braid back as though strangling a goose.

"Answer me, wife!"

"Why do you want me? I don't understand! Why? Why?"

He abruptly let go. I fell forward, my chin struck the floor. He didn't try to stop me as I crawled to the door, shouldered it aside, and collapsed onto the companionway.

Something grazed my cheek, then another object soared past. My mother's red slipper skidded onto the planks beside me.

I lay on the poop deck gazing up at the half moon. As a child I'd strained for a view of Princess Sheung O, wishing I were her, who had that whole silvery planet to herself and spent her days playing in the heavens with her pet rabbit. Only now did I understand that Sheung O and I were the same, trapped inside worlds where we didn't belong, doomed to eternal loneliness.

I heard every sound in the cabin below me. The drone of Cheng Yat's evening worship, voices murmuring until late. Now, in the deep night hours, other noises seeped through the deck boards: giggles and laughter and groan after groan. The sounds of sex.

Which little slut was she? Or maybe he'd taken one of the crewmen's young wives as punishment for the crime of swimming. If so, they all deserved it. I'd given the crew an excuse to have fun, and they'd turned on me like fleeing rats.

I didn't understand why I was here. The more I resisted his determination to keep me, the more he insisted on calling me wife. Yet listen to him now, rutting like a pig for everyone to hear.

Clouds blanketed Sheung O's lunar realm. I smelled rain coming but didn't care.

Death or living death. Mohammedan's slave or sea bandit's courtesan. Even if his stories were untrue, what life awaited me off this deck? Resume whoring in the mud? Back to the flower boats, maybe become a sing-song girl? What sort of freedom was that?

Maybe I had freedom all wrong. Maybe freedom without limits was a trap. Even the magpies, free to take themselves anywhere, return to the same tree every sunset. Maybe freedom required a border, a fence, a canopy to operate within. Within the confines of a ship. Within the society of bandits.

I'd felt freedom swimming in the water, but then what? I pictured again the Taumuk's ferocious anger, then his gloating face, as if he'd vanquished a challenger.

I sat up and grabbed my chest; my heart pulsed all the way into my throat.

If the Taumuk saw me as a threat, as some kind of rival, didn't that imply I had the potential to be just that? Hadn't he and Fatty Wu, and Cheng Yat himself, showed me in a roundabout, hurtful way that I was *too* observant, *too* clever, that I was someone worthy of respect?

Yes, that was it! I could become that threat, be that rival, if only I were smart about it. Instead of taking punishment for every move I make, I would grab something for myself in this short, brutal life.

Drops pelted my face and turned into soft, steady rain. I was more concerned for my mother's shoes than for myself. Hurrying down the ladder, I felt giddy at my new-found role. I would play the wife he expected me to be while inserting myself into the cracks of this herd of scavengers until they couldn't get rid of me if they tried.

First, I had to claim my place by throwing out his little strumpet.

I yanked the cabin handle, but it was bolted from inside. I knocked and waited, knocked and waited, but the thumps and moans carried on. I kicked and pounded.

"Let your wife in!"

At last, movement inside, someone shuffling across the floor. The bolt scraped; the door creaked open.

Somewhere in the darkness Cheng Yat cleared his throat while the boy, Cheung Po Tsai, naked and sweaty, peered at me with shining eyes like a cat with a belly full of birds.

VIII
Moon Festival

"Down rudders!"
 At last, after eight or nine sweltering days—without further swimming—Cheng Yat gave orders to set sail. We were joining Wu-shek Yi's eight ships on a southwestward run to Wu's home base in Luichow in time for the Mid-Autumn Festival.

The morning we left the lagoon, it was as though a veil had lifted. Fresh wind in the face, the roll of the open sea, land moving again in the distance, all stirred the blood like a hearty gulp of wine. The crew, from whom I'd kept my distance, now treated me with cautious deference. I was still here, I was still alive, even after my alleged mutiny and fight with Cheng Yat. Before, they'd never known what to make of me and had been almost afraid to address me by name. Now I was Miss Shek when someone wanted to ingratiate themselves and, when they needed a favor, Captain's wife, though I still recoiled at the title. Only a few earned the right to call me Yang: those who'd stood by me, half of whom were the gun crew.

Hawk Man filled the long cruising days by immersing me in muskets, breeches, pins, pans, and powder. I threw my whole body into the work, despite grease-stained fingers and a permanent ache in my arms. The first time I repaired and mounted a flintlock by myself, I blinked away tears, not only at the gun crew's praise, but at the recognition of my first genuine skill that didn't require lying on my back. I felt useful and busy.

The one person I had no interest in seeing was Cheung Po Tsai, who seemed to appear in three places at once like some puppet play trickster. Moments ago, he'd stepped from the latrine right before I entered. Now he balanced one-legged on a gunwale, tossing fish guts to the birds.

I had heard the story of Cheung Po Tsai's abduction so many times—from Ah-Yi, other women, the cook—that it had taken the form of legend. He and his father were fishing far from shore in a small boat when pirates captured them. Cheng Yat took an instant liking to the handsome fifteen-year-old with the violet turban, who offered no resistance on his way into the captain's quarters—hardly the makings of an epic tale. No one said what happened to the father.

The fish offal exhausted, he danced on the rail singing songs to the sea and sky deities. How could one possibly express joy in such a circumstance as his? To sing to distract yourself from boredom and misery, that I understood. To make tolerable an intolerable situation, that's what I'd promised myself to do. But to serenade the spirits as though giving joyful thanks?

If Cheng Yat admired such a spirit, I couldn't blame him. Then what did he need me for? It was too obvious: a blossom boy couldn't produce a son.

Po Tsai must have read my mind. I turned around and there he stood, bent over with hands on knees, his eyes catching mine.

"Big men always prefer the second wife," he said, then skipped away sobbing comically.

I held my hand over my mouth. Men marry the first wife for duty, the second for pleasure. Was that what the boy thought of me? Was it what Cheng Yat thought?

I returned to my place with the gun crew, mulling whether to ask Hawk Man what he thought, when Po Tsai's voice cut through the air again, this time from overhead: "Sails! Big fleet!"

Fifteen or more junks hugged the horizon, Kwangtung sails among them.

"Navy, do you think?" Hawk Man said. "Our twelve might frighten them off."

I cupped my hands around my eyes, unsure what to look for. "I've heard salt transports run in convoys."

A derisive snort behind me. The purser sniffed again as he passed. I didn't care what he thought. What mattered was whether Cheng Yat or the Taumuk would order guns and cannons readied. Though I didn't look forward to an actual engagement, I was eager to experience preparing and loading the big guns in the heat of a chase.

The largest out of what was now twenty-five ships altered course, clearly intending to cross our present track to windward. A long pennant snaked from its mainmast.

"Red flag! Now!" Cheng Yat called from the poop. "Gun master! Musket and pistol, powder loaded!"

"Your wish come true. There's our orders," Hawk Man told me before he ran off.

So, this was to be no battle. Po Tsai unfurled a red banner from the masthead. On the poop, Cheng Yat fired the pistol into the air. Hawk Man's musket blasted thick smoke. A pair of answering shots rumbled across the water.

"Who is it?" I said.

Melon Seed acted surprised. "You don't know? Cheng Chat. Captain's paternal cousin."

I was about to meet the family.

Cheng Yat had no such plans for me. The sampan pulled away through rough chop toward his cousin's heavily armed flagship.

"Don't be in such a hurry to meet him," Ah-Yi said while stitching an unfinished vest. "Or his wife. Sour old weasel."

I passed her a cutter. "They on good terms?"

"Who? Those cousins? Practically grew up together. Their fathers were brothers, rascal sea bandits just the same. Chat's family based on Tai Yue Shan island, Cheng Yat's over in Lei Yue Moon. Almost neighbors."

"Who's older?"

"Ah-Chat. Five, six years, I think." Ah-Yi leaned aside and whispered, "You've got the better looking of the lot. Aiya!" She plucked a needle from her thumb.

Cheng Yat returned at dusk and assembled the crew, then announced a raid on a salt port by the combined fleets—ours, his cousin's, and Wu's. Afterward, he passed me a packet, a gift from Cheng Chat's wife.

I opened it inside the cabin: an assortment of candied dried fruit. One nibble unleashed a rush of sweetness on my tongue and in my heart. It was an offer of connection, a welcome of sorts into the family.

Cheng Yat came in later than usual, offered quick bows to Tin Hau, slumped on the mat, and stripped off his tunic. I still didn't know how to approach him. There had been no more threats, no more raised voices since the night I'd claimed my place. Maybe that was what he'd been waiting for. His taciturn nature was how he acted with everyone. I had no choice but to accept that his stinginess with words was perhaps a grudging show of respect. But tonight, his brooding dimmed the space around him.

I offered him a dried melon wedge. He waved it away.

I turned up the lamp and waited for him to say something, but his mouth was more interested in nibbling a fingernail. I poured him the remnants of the wine jar, barely wetting his bowl. He swatted the bowl away, sending it rolling across the floor.

"Is it the raid? Something I should worry about?" I said.

He answered with a scolding look, reminding me without words to stay out of ship's business, then tore through his clothing basket, tossing garments right and left.

I picked up the clothes as fast as he threw them. "Damn you!" I said. "If I'm supposedly your wife, talk to me like one. What happened over there? What did he do to you?"

"Not your business." Finding his sleeping robe, he punched his arms into the sleeves, muttering, "Always has to be his idea."

"The raid?"

He slouched against the wall, head dropped, and arms folded around him like binding rope. "That too," he said.

"What else?"

He answered with a puff of wind. I finished packing the clothing basket and knelt in front of him.

"Old grudges?" I ventured.

"It's all past. Not important."

"The past is important."

"Not to me."

I'd seen bruises on his skin, but never like this in his soul. My hand rose by instinct toward his cheek, but I withdrew it in fear that a touch might shatter the fragility of the moment.

"Once I visited him in Tai Yue Shan. I was twelve." He paused, as though waiting for a signal. I nodded as gently as I could manage. "There was a fisherman, kept a raft tied way up this stream. One night, Chat convinced me to steal it, pole down to the bay, said he'd meet me with a net. When I rounded the last bend past the mangrove, there was Chat and the fisherman waiting. Never mind. Why am I telling you this?" He crawled to the mat and curled on his side.

Because he'd never told anyone, I wagered, and if I was quiet and patient the rest would froth to the surface. He proved me right.

"I got a beating, and Chat got the credit. He thought it a joke. I told his father. Woke up next morning, a dead cobra dangling over my bed."

"You were boys," I said.

But it clearly hadn't ended then. I knew it without setting eyes on the cousin: his fleet was larger, and Cheng Yat had gone to him rather than the other way around. This cousin had done something terrible to him, something worse than the story admitted. He'd made Cheng Yat look small. Even at this age, they *were* still boys.

"Close the lamp," he said.

He lay with his back to me and pulled on a light blanket. I doused the flame and settled behind him.

"Doesn't matter anymore," he mumbled. "Not a word out of you."

I rested a hand on his shoulder, then let it drift down onto his chest. In a way that this man might never understand, his telling me the tale had made him appear bigger.

I met Cheng Chat on the day before Mid-Autumn Day.

The tall figure in the shade of a rubber tree looked not just older than his cousin, but built of denser material, held to the earth by greater force, as if his standing too close to the gunwale might career a ship.

Both cousins had the same bony jaw and generous lips; both dressed all in black, plain cotton sailor's trousers and tunic. But there was no question which man emanated command like the lead dog in a pack. Yet, whatever charisma Cheng Chat may have possessed, Ah-Yi had been right: even Cheng Yat surpassed him in physical appeal.

Cheng Chat swept me once with his eyes. "So, you're the wife."

I offered a polite nod and inquired as to whether he'd eaten yet.

"Ate," he said, with the barest movement of his lips. He tapped Cheng Yat on the shoulder, and the two set off down the beach in silence. Lack of manners and speech obviously ran in the family.

I sat on a driftwood log watching sampans discharge captains and officers on the narrow beach. Wu-shek Yi offered me a passing nod as he caught up with the Cheng cousins as quickly as his fat legs could carry him.

This island was meant to be a rendezvous point, thirty *li* offshore from the target. Out here, the sun peeled open the sky, burning my eyes and shoulders and the pebbles under my feet. By tradition, the weather was supposed to turn on the evening of Mid-Autumn Day. I couldn't wait for relief in my life, if only just the temperature.

A single-mast skiff rounded the point and skidded nearly up to the beach. The deck was stacked with chickens in cages, presumably for the holiday feast. Its pilot was recognizable by his purple turban, unwinding over bare shoulders.

"The Rooster King returns!" Cheung Po Tsai splashed through the shallows, swinging two cages containing not hens but terrified cockerels shedding feathers in their wake.

The men wandered back to the beach, some of the younger officers helping to unload cages—every one of them holding a rooster—while Po Tsai returned hugging some parcels. Handing the largest to Cheng Chat, he said, "Wai, Old Uncle, lanterns for tonight." Another was for Cheng Yat.

When he ran to me, I expected one of his jokes. Instead he offered a package the size of my fist whose heaviness gave it away; it could only have been a tasty moon cake. He slipped something soft into my hand: I spied a folded silk handkerchief with flower embroidery. Clutching it in my fist so no one would see, the fabric burned between my fingers, sending fire up my arm into my face. The impropriety of such a gift from a boy to a grown woman. I tried to press it back in his hand, but he ran off again with a laugh.

Men had already started up a trail carved into the cliffs, each carrying a cage of cockerels. I was last to join the procession, weaving around others until I was behind Cheng Yat and Cheng Chat. Imagining a bloody sacrifice, I intended to ask where we and the roosters were going, but they were too busy listening to Cheung Po Tsai jabbering about his visit ashore. He'd spent the night in Tin-pak, the salt port we intended to raid the next morning. I gathered, from the tangled ribbons of words spewing from him, that he'd gone there for more than birds and festival lanterns.

"Full of misers and thieves. Aiya! Might as well rob me for what they charged for these cocks."

"Never mind," Cheng Chat said. "The barges. What about the salt barges?"

"Eighteen. I'm sure of it. Seemed full enough, though I didn't get close enough to peek under the canvas."

"Protection force?"

"Twelve old junks, crews up late drinking, ha! Practicing for the festival."

"The garrison?"

Po Tsai launched into a story in which he posed as a fisherman and befriended a pair of soldiers. "...look like farm boys, speak some dialect like they're swallowing frogs—"

"How many men?" Cheng Yat said.

"But you have to hear the story! Told them I had an order of fish for their commander, but I'd sneak them some—"

"Aiya!" Cheng Chat interrupted. "Your tongue is melting my ears, boy!"

Po Tsai laughed almost like one of his roosters. "A hundred forty-four men. Ha ha! So unlucky!"

"Unlucky they are indeed," Cheng Chat said.

The trail narrowed to a single-file walkway hewn into near-vertical rock. One misstep and a person would plunge onto wave-splashed boulders far below. Across the water, Tin-pak's walled garrison was faintly visible through the coastal haze. Our ships would strike at sunrise after a full night of festival feasting and drinking would have taken its toll on soldiers and residents alike.

Our walk ended at a whitewashed temple carved from a platform in the slope. While crewmen arranged the cages in the small forecourt, the men of rank burned incense and paper offerings inside.

"I'm surprised I haven't heard any womanly opinions about our mission," a high voice said from behind me. Wu-shek Yi stepped up beside me and planted incense sticks into a shrine in the rock. "Or have I missed the privilege of receiving your benign orders?"

"Benign is correct, sir. I advised Cheng Yat to place a ribbon around your neck so that no one confuses you with these poor cockerels and chops off your handsome head. But I see you prefer to take your chances."

"Ah ha ha!" His girlish laugh clawed my ears. "She's a clever one, but she doesn't know this place."

When the other sacrifices finished, everyone gathered around the birds while Cheng Chat droned an incantation. Then the cages were unlatched. Some roosters scratched and bobbed in the dirt, clucking haughtily, while others dashed into the bushes. A few stayed in their coops until men shook them out. Cages were discarded over the cliffs, and the birds roamed freely.

"They're getting away," I said.

Again, Wu laughed. "This is Cock Release Island, pretty one. Give a blessing, get a blessing. No killing in front of the Buddha."

He kicked a rooster off the temple steps. "We men of honor only liberate life. Ah ha ha!"

Back on the ship, I joined the women in hanging lanterns—round or square, made of paper or fish skin—in random arrangements of red, yellow, and white. Those Cheung Po Tsai had brought from Tin-pak were painted with words and patterns. Some unease lingered since the swimming incident, but the festival mood blew much of it away.

The Moon Festival had been my favorite celebration since I could remember—an explosion of colored lamps, candles and noise-making toys, summer's end fruits, and sticky candies. I never imagined a bandit ship might look so festive. But at sunset, when the entire deck would normally become a constellation of glowing lanterns and candles, ours all remained dark. No music or firecrackers either. Tonight we would stay hidden in advance of the morning's raid.

The sky turned the color of weak red tea. A fat orange moon peeked over the eastern tip of the island. We divided pomelos and starfruits among the children and ourselves, and for the first time, I felt a sense of community among this hodge-podge group of seamen and women.

The lanterns made a rustling sound. A light draft chilled my cheeks. Precisely on time, the seasons were changing, autumn's breath arriving to cool the fevers of the world.

The breeze picked up quickly, clouds raced past, and the moon winked in and out of sight. Swells splashed the hull, rocking the junk side to side. A melon spun across the deck.

A sudden gust whistled through lines, tearing free a red lantern and carrying it high into the night. Another followed as heavy clouds smothered the moon. Moments later, rain pummeled the deck while I helped rush the food and children to shelter below.

When I came back up, waves punched over the rails. I could barely see the deckhouse through the downpour. Cheng Yat shouted from the companionway—something I couldn't hear. But the whine of straining cables and the anchor winch's rattle made me quickly understand: nearly fifty junks were packed dangerously close together in the storm-wracked cove.

A wave cleared the sides, shrouding me in frigid water, my mouth and ears filled with brine. While men ran to fetch oars, the best I could do was get out of the way. I staggered up to the cabin and wrenched the door shut.

Rain and seawater poured through the porthole. I crawled against the tide sloshing across the floor, but each buck of the ship sent me sliding out of control. My knee sunk into something cold and meaty. A sacrificial chicken. I flung it aside, and rode the roll of the next swell, finally getting a grip on the porthole frame. I pulled myself upright.

And screamed.

In the faint light, it looked like a moving island. Another junk listed sideways, swept by wind and waves on a collision course directly toward us.

Lightning flashed, freezing stark images of men clinging to its gunwales, faces stretched in terror. Were they really just a few arm's lengths away? Thunder combusted the air. Two men dropped overboard just before—

A sickening crack.

The impact threw me across the room. My scalp struck something hard. In a flicker of lightning, the shrine leaned forward, about to crush me. I rolled aside, but a lurch of the ship flung me the other way. Wood and porcelain shattered beside my head.

The collision left the ship at a precarious tilt with nothing for me to cling to while I struggled to rise.

A series of lightning strokes offered me a clear study of the wreckage. The great goddess Tin Hau lay on her side, missing one arm, her narrow eyes, as usual, always, always fixed on me.

Cheng Yat counted twenty surviving ships; the Taumuk claimed twenty-one. What did it matter? By my count at sunrise, of the forty-eight junks we'd set out with, fifteen still floated, while five of those that had washed up on the beach looked recoverable.

But how many people would be? Bodies and debris littered the shallows. Incense smoke spiraled from every deck, some to the sea and sky spirits, but mostly to the dead.

A lot of good their spiritual offerings had done. Had yesterday's sacrificial chicken not been fresh enough or the wine too weak? Or did the merchants of Tin-pak, somehow alerted to the planned raid, pray to superior deities? Men were stupid to rely on the favors of gods. Prayers were made of air, and weather was nothing but wind and water.

Our enemy now was exhaustion. Even with survivors of wrecked vessels joining us to patch the damage and bail flooded holds, our junk still listed badly.

I fought a battle with a gash in my calf as I limped across the tilting deck with a full bailing bucket. I handed it off to another man and, not daring to rest in front of anyone—especially the Taumuk—immediately turned back to fetch a fresh bucket being raised through a hatch.

"I don't like them," the Taumuk said somewhere behind me.

The man in front of me stopped. He and I turned around to look. Three junks rounded the island's western point.

"We can handle a few fishermen," Cheng Yat said.

"If that's what they are." The Taumuk cast an accusing look to Cheung Po Tsai, knocking together the cracked foremast cowling. I shared the Taumuk's suspicion that perhaps something had slipped from the boy's big mouth while scouting in Tin-pak.

The approaching junks spread out, a maneuver that reminded me of fishermen spreading a net. Except there was no net.

Cheng Yat barked an order: "Heave cannons! We need to right this ship!"

A chain snapped. The deck lurched. I leapt away from a rolling pig cadaver. Someone caught me before I fell.

"Need your hands," Hawk Man said. He pressed me into a crush of people around the cannon closest to mid-deck.

"We can't," I said. I'd oiled and polished and pampered this gun myself as if it were a child. Hawk Man ignored me.

"Get a firm grip, children," he said. "Try not to hurt yourself. One... Two..."

I nudged between two men and slipped my arms under the barrel. Though the gun crew derided this cannon as just an old Chinese lump, it pained me to be part of pushing it overboard. How many days of my life would be discarded with it? Yes, I told myself, maybe I did feel that part of this ship belonged to me.

"Three!"

Pain shot through my leg as I lifted with all my strength, pock-marked metal digging into my flesh until I thought my arms and knees would snap. I felt the barrel budge, but the strain was too much for everyone. The next try gave us a loud crunch and the cannon tore off its mount. My arms felt as limp as a squid.

"One... Two... Hurl, children!"

Everyone thrusted sideways at once. Two thousand catties of precious iron teetered over the gunwale and disappeared into the murky water.

The ship rocked once or twice and settled. Standing was easier now; the deck had regained nearly half its balance.

It wasn't enough. A clap of gunfire, a shrill whistle—a man a few steps from me dropped like a rag, blood spewing from where his jaw had been.

"Braves!" someone screamed. One of the local ships passed our stern, its rails crowded with men in gray holding guns and every shape and length of blade. These were no fishermen but Punti militiamen out to kill pirates. The tilt of our deck made us easy targets.

The ensuing panic unnerved me as much as the approaching braves. I had nothing to defend myself with. The muskets were tucked away in storage; by the time I fetched and loaded one, it would be too late. There was nowhere to hide. Reason told me they weren't after the women, but a voice in my head screamed: *Death by a thousand cuts! Goatherd's slave!*

The only way out was to fling myself at their mercy.

Tell them: *I'm not one of these pirates. I'm a village girl. A captive.*

It was mostly true. I was no bandit. An outcast among water folk. Of no interest to them.

A bullet whistled past close enough to burn my cheek. Splinters burst around me. I dashed to the companion steps. I might hold them off until they'd satisfied their bloodlust by bolting myself in the cabin. As I ran upstairs, the voices dueled in my head.

They'll drag you to the nearest garrison to collect their reward.

Please! I'm not one of them!

Grappling hooks flew across. Angry gray-clad men swarmed over the gunwales. Hawk Man was passing guns down the line. Our men fired from the companionway as quickly as Hawk Man and Melon Seed were able to load fresh weapons. They could use help, but the way was too crowded for me to pass.

I was halfway to the cabin when a crewman in front of me let off a shot, engulfing me in thick, oily smoke. I couldn't hear, couldn't see, but

73

I felt a body drop from the poop deck overhead.

The gun smoke cleared quickly, revealing the man who'd just fired lying in a spreading pool of blood. A brawny Punti crouching over him turned his attention to me. He reared up, lifting a cutlass rippled with blood.

I stumbled back against the rail, seeking any sign of intention in his pox-scarred face—to capture me, to mount me? To murder?

Words formed in my throat—*I'm not one...*—but my tongue wouldn't say them. Somewhere in the middle of this fight something had shifted.

An animal scream from the companionway made me look without thinking. Hawk Man fell backward through a broken gap in the rail down to the deck below. A Punti brave leapt after him with a blade in each hand. My assailant, I noticed, was also watching the action. I cocked my leg and aimed straight for the groin.

His face puckered, his knees buckled. The cutlass dropped from his hand.

I was on my back, splinters scraping my scalp, the man back up with his hands around my throat—stinking breath, broken yellow teeth, a nose crooked from past fights. It was his eyes that frightened me—red and round and cold as a fish's.

The cutlass had to be somewhere nearby. I groped the space around me. If I could find it before he did...

But he had no need for it. He reached for his belt. A dagger appeared before my face.

I am going to die. If not moments from now, then at some village chief's or magistrate's command.

"I'm not one of them," I gasped through the hold on my throat, but he paid no attention. The dagger began a downward stroke.

I patted the space on my other side. Glimpses of gun smoke, crewmen herded onto the Punti ship.

"I'm just..."

The point of his blade pricked my chin. He slid his hand under my shoulders and lifted. He meant to carry me away.

Soldiers take turns. Fuck you when he tires of fucking his goats.

I groped around me. Nothing.

"I'm just a..."

My thumb met sharp metal. He figured out what I was doing;

letting go of my neck, he reached for the cutlass, but it was too late. My fingers found the hilt. Everything that every Punti had ever done to me, had ever said to me, had ever thought of me—everything they meant to do to me now, everything they were doing at this moment to the men and women I lived among on this cursed ship—coursed through my veins into my fingers. Of its own free will, the cutlass swung through the air.

"I'm just a Tanka whore, you bastard!"

He fell over, moaning, the blade lodged in his shoulder. I twisted it once, then pulled out the twice-blooded steel and ran.

I didn't stop to consider where I was running. I hardly knew where I was. No sound nor heat nor tilt of the ship, I ran alone through a silent theater, figures either side of me battling like puppets. For a moment I thought I had died and was hurtling into purgatory.

A familiar voice snapped me back into the world. Hawk Man called my name, or rather, wheezed it through a bleeding throat. His chest and belly striped with gashes, some so deep the muscles showed through. A Punti dragged him by the legs toward the side where no ship waited. He meant to toss the stricken Hawk Man into the sea.

I flew, I was told later, with the cry of a bird of prey. The Punti fell backward, his head struck the anchor winch. Hot blood coated my arm before I realized the cutlass was buried in his abdomen. I grasped the hilt with both fists and tore across his belly, feeling the drag of ripping flesh. The next plunge slipped neatly between his ribs and got stuck in the bones. The Punti bucked once and lay still.

Hawk Man writhed on the deck, each pained breath stretching the wounds in his chest. A spring of blood bubbled from above one knee. I tried stopping it with my hand, my sleeve, then remembered Cheung Po Tsai's handkerchief in my pocket. I tied off the tourniquet just as I felt myself slipping away.

My hand found his ankle. Its warmth, the twitching muscle, his stubborn pulse, and a coarse, but very much living, cough soothed me.

Cheng Yat was a blur through my barely open eyelids. His curses mixed with objects striking the floor.

"They took my chop! Those animals took my chop!"

The storage chest had been smashed open, its contents heaped around it. He swore again and kicked something aside.

I couldn't tell whether it was morning or evening, whether it had been a day or many days. I had no recollection of returning to the cabin or how long I'd been lying here. I only knew that my legs and shoulders were on fire, my head throbbed, and it hurt to open my eyes.

Something shattered against the wall.

"What the devil use do they have for my imperial chop?"

He must have meant the one in the yellow silk box. I'd never seen him even glance at it.

I tried to turn on my side, but my arm pained me. I tried to speak but gagged on a throat full of mucus. I coughed and tried again.

"They're gone?"

I meant the Punti, but he must have thought I meant his damned chop, which triggered more rage. He flung something at the wall near me.

"Here! They left your ugly red shoes you never wear!"

I squeezed my eyelids tight, but that didn't stop the tears. I was awake now and wishing I wasn't. the events played in the theater of my mind. The blade slipping in and out, in and out, like slicing meat, until his ribs refused to let it go. The final heave—I watched it again and again—the last gasp of a landed fish. His head slumped sideways, wide eyes staring down toward hell, their terrifying deadness my doing.

Had it really happened? Was I really awake? I couldn't distinguish dreams from memory.

A damp cloth met my forehead, liquid dribbled down my nose. I let in the world again. Cheng Yat knelt over me, regarding me with unusual tenderness. He dipped the cloth once more and wiped my cheeks. It smelled like tea.

"He's alive, you know," he said. "Hurt bad, but you saved him."

But I'd watched the Punti bastard—

It took me a moment to understand. The Hawk Man, he meant. I'd saved someone as well.

I held my breath, putting off the dreaded question. I swallowed and said, "Did I really kill a man?"

"The whole crew is talking about you. Those who saw it say they've never seen a woman so fierce."

"Answer me. Did I kill a man?"

Cheng Yat studied me the way a parent might consider a child while he wiped his mouth and chin. The cloth came away with a red smudge. He answered my question with a shrug.

"A lot of us did."

I curled up toward the wall, listening to him drop things back in the chest, then crack the seal from a jar of wine and drink himself to sleep.

Was that all a man's life meant? A shrug? The man had been a Punti, a snake, who'd tried to kill my friend. My heart felt nothing for taking his life, yet this coldness in my soul turned my stomach. Bile rose into my throat, choking me as I tried to swallow. There was no taking back what I'd done. Of all the actions I'd taken in my life, this one was irreversible, incurable, a venom which could never be expunged from my soul. Cheng Yat had recognized it and, by treating it so casually, had acknowledged that something inside me had shifted.

I was a killer. I was a pirate.

I was one of them now.

I woke to light rain breezing through the porthole. Dawn was breaking. Cheng Yat was already up, squatting in front of the damaged shrine.

A brute and a savage fighter, so worried about face, so greedy for respect that he cried louder over a brass seal than lost men and ships. Gods and prayers and guns and roosters had served this man poorly. He'd served himself as well as he knew how. Neither a good man nor an evil one, he wasn't fully the man he could be.

Was I the woman I could be? I'd always had a price but never been valued by anyone. I'd only ever belonged to anything because I'd been sold. Half my life I had dreamed of escape. Maybe it was time to finally embrace being part of something.

Being one of them.

I must have made noise when I sat up. The chanting paused. He turned his head.

"I want a wedding," I said.

He nodded once and returned to his prayers.

IX
Pirate

I was bedridden for days with fever and a thick bandage from shoulder to elbow. No matter what foods Ah-Yi brought, my body rejected all but the plainest gruel. I could say the same regarding the news which trickled in about the aftermath of the Tin-pak braves' attack.

They'd taken three of our remaining ships along with close to a hundred men and twelve women, besides those left behind for dead. Cheng Chat had sailed the next day while Wu's fleet and ours, plus five of Chat's ships, took refuge in a rocky bay, carrying out repairs with whatever materials we could scrounge.

"Eat this," Ah-Yi said, setting a bowl between my legs. "Could be your last chance of chicken for days."

"We're sailing? He didn't tell me."

"Nor anyone, until now. Eat."

The thought of leaving revived my appetite. The chicken was tender, the rice soft. "Did he mention where to?" I said.

"Tunghoi." Ah-Yi smiled as though I knew the place, though the name meant nothing to me. "Luichow? Don't know it? No matter. Nothing can prepare you for it."

"One thing I've learned is that I'm not prepared for anything."

"Isn't that what I've been telling you all along? Hee!"

"How is Hawk Man?" I said.

"Who?"

"The weapons master. Is he...?"

"Hawk Man, ha! That's the name for him!" Her face turned solemn. "Alive. Asks about you."

That was all I needed to hear. My legs were weak, but I made it down the stairs unaided, refusing all offers of help, and went direct to the galley where I asked for a bowl of fish congee and a flask of wine.

A powerful smell of rotting flesh rising from the forward hold would have turned me back if it hadn't been Hawk Man's room. Cockroaches scattered; a fly buzzed in my ear.

His chest was less bird-like now, shrunken and swathed in bloodstained muslin. The gash in his upper belly I remembered, but nothing prepared me for the sight of his leg, or what had been a leg, swollen into a black knobby maggots' nest, dripping fluid into a clay crock.

At the sight of me he drew a smile over his pain. I held up the wine flask.

"I figured you've had enough of herbal brews," I said.

"Save it for the living."

"Shut up. You're too stubborn to die. Or to refuse a drink." I tipped wine into his mouth and watched the lines on his face soften.

"Or a smoke." His voice gurgled, but it had life in it still. "Explains why I never had a wife."

"A handsome beast like you must have had plenty of girls."

A different kind of hurt eclipsed his face, one so deep that it couldn't have been physical. Had no woman ever wanted this homely but decent man? I didn't dare ask.

He tipped his head, signaling for more wine, and gulped greedily.

"That'll ease it. Now sit. Sit and listen because soon enough I'll have no one to chat with but the King of Hell." He stopped to take a breath. "Every man aboard boasts that he watched you plunge in that blade. Sure, whether they really saw it or not. The way they speak of you—"

His body suddenly clenched. His bad leg shook.

I sprang up, one hand on the ladder. "I'll get more wine."

The seizure ended. "No. Let me finish. Younger Sister, don't you see? If you'd only tame that demon's tongue of yours now and then, you might make something of yourself. Do not squander their respect, I say. You heard it from me, the Hawk. Now, if you wouldn't mind, I'm still half sober, which is half too much."

When I returned with the wine his eyes were shut, and his breathing a long rattle. After carefully sliding the blanket over his wounded leg, I sat beside him, dipped my fingers in the wine, and moistened his mouth. His throat whistled in his sleep.

"My friend," I whispered, wishing his eyes to stay closed, for he'd surely object to my tears. "My dear, dear friend."

I leaned over and kissed his lips, wishing him a loving wife in his dreams.

The coffin took spray over the bow each time the sampan bucked over a swell. One last taste of the sea before Hawk Man was laid to rest forever on a barren outcrop with only birds for neighbors. I clung to the casket that I'd helped build out of timber salvaged from the wreckage of Moon Festival night. He would have enjoyed the wit of it: a corpse sealed within a corpse.

A man leapt into the shallows and guided the sampan onto a pebbly beach. An earlier landing party had nearly finished digging the grave. It seemed a suitable feng shui spot: a sandy mound beyond the reach of waves, overlooking the sea forever.

Grateful to receive one of the few proper white mourning cloaks, I pulled the hood low to shield my eyes from the sun and my tears from those on either side. Cheng Yat led the procession around the coffin, trailed by the purser, chanting and striking a bell.

The empty grave was a plain hole in the ground, not some gateway to another world. I was leaving him behind, forever alone in a box on this unnamed little island, and that made me sadder still.

The last remains I'd grieved over—truly grieved—belonged to my mother. I'd been afraid to cry while my father raged about the expense—the grave diggers, the hired mourners, the offerings, all the sacrificial foods and wine—about how much fairer to the living to let the sea take her body and that of my brother. Finally his fisherman's superstitious fear of drowning had ensured his wife and son some dignity.

I joined the women and children folding paper into little models—ingots, boats, food, clothing—to be burned for the departed to use in the spirit world. I fashioned silvered paper into crude cannons for this man of weapons, to fire against his enemies among the ghosts. But what if there were no enemies, no Tankas and Puntis, no pirates, no navies in heaven? Maybe everyone there was flush with money, sea vessels, horses, and houses, just like the ones now rising in thick plumes of smoke. Maybe the spirit world was a prosperous and lively place, all fighting and struggle left behind here on the earth. Maybe that hole in the ground was a doorway to a better place.

But, just in case, I dropped eight shining paper cannons into the pyre.

Back on the ship, sails were patched, timber caulked, ballast reset.

Every conversation seemed to begin, "When we get to Tunghoi..."

Cheng Yat was uncharacteristically cheerful at the evening meal in the cabin, though still his usual taciturn self. Taking advantage of the mood, I asked for the fifth or sixth time, "What's in Tunghoi?"

"Ships. A harbor."

"Don't be flippant. Is this another raid? I hope you've thought this one out better."

He sucked greens from his bowl, something the cook had found on the island, and grinned. "I thought that by your reckoning I'm incapable of thinking."

"Since you mention it, I do reckon that. What plan do you have? All I see us doing is drifting, waiting for targets to happen our way."

The vegetable was bitter and stringy as a rat's tail. Cheng Yat frowned, though whether at the food or at me, I couldn't tell.

"Is that right? You have a bit to learn before you make such remarks."

"Then teach me! You never give me a straight answer to anything. You claim me as your wife—about time you treat me like one!"

He put down his bowl and slid closer. "You be the teacher. Instruct me how a man and wife should treat each other."

His smile unnerved me, so unlike his normal self, though spoiled by a green strand stuck in his teeth. I picked it off with the nail of my little finger. "First, the woman has to keep the man from looking ridiculous."

"Wah! She's reversing course! Stop making me look ridiculous? And I thought my prayers were useless."

"Quit changing the subject. I want to know where we're going. What's there? What is the target? Salt? Sugar? Soap? I want soap! I want to know how you plan to steal whatever it is without us being shot into pieces this time."

"Woman, you have always asked too many questions. It amuses me to see nothing has changed."

I slammed down my bowl and retreated to the porthole. The moon wasn't out yet, the stars obscured by haze. We'd just buried my friend, and Cheng Yat's loyal gun master, yet he was in a teasing mood. Nothing was clear anymore.

"Foo! I amuse you?"

I felt his heat; he'd snuck up behind me.

"You always have," he said.

"Fuck your old mother!"

"I was thinking of a different woman for that."

"Aiya!" I pounded his chest, which seemed to amuse him more. He caught my wrists before I could slap his face.

"I've never known a woman with such fire. If you ever started treating me with respect, I think I'd be disappointed."

"You want respect? Then give me answers! Aren't you angry at what happened at Tin-pak? Aren't you sad to bury your own men? Aren't you ashamed to live a life like bamboo splinters floating on the sea? Don't you want something more than this?"

"Gods save me, the woman of fire wins. I'll entertain you with answers. Will that please you? Yes, I'm angry! Is it possible to live this life without anger? Sadness? Shame? Never heard of them. This is the water world. We survive. What do I want, you ask? I'll show you."

He held my arms and guided me onto the sleeping mat.

"Tell me first what you want," he said.

"I want to know what's in Tunghoi."

"An old friend."

"Who?"

"What if I promise to answer all your questions after we arrive? What would you do for me?"

"Bastard."

"That's good. I want you angry right now. I want you very, very angry."

I hit him and pummeled him, which he made a show of enjoying. I, too, enjoyed seeing him laugh. Yet I was in mourning; I felt guilty about laughing with him, but layered on sadness made it feel that much more genuine, something bursting from me that compelled me to live.

He tugged at my clothes. I did what he wanted with all the pent-up longing for life in my soul.

X

Cheng Yat Sou

O ne afternoon—after how many days?—my eyes popped open, and everything was sharp and clear. I stepped out to the companion-way, arms and legs humming with pleasure as they carried me up the poop ladder. The air on top felt healing. If it weren't for a pinch in my heart from the memory of Hawk Man, the disasters might have faded from my mind.

We navigated a wide strait between tangled green wilderness to the west and, on the opposite shore, flat marshland patchworked with fish farms whose waters glinted red and gold in the lowering sun.

Ah-Yi leaned on the east-facing rail, for once not mending or sewing. She offered me an embarrassed smile as though I'd interrupted a dialogue in her head.

"Colors are different in this part of the world," she said.

I settled beside her, shielding my eyes against the glare. "How far to Tunghoi?"

"You're looking at it." She nodded toward the marshes.

It seemed a rather bleak place to inspire so much anticipation among the crew. The only signs of a community were a few stilt huts and occasional fish farmers poling bamboo rafts from which they hauled in nets. One woman lifted a basket and shouted our way.

"What did she say?" I asked.

"Think I understand their Luichow goose honking? Probably naming prices."

"I thought Tunghoi was a town."

"There! Like I just told you." Ah-Yi pointed to smoke columns rising beyond a promontory. "Hee! Arriving just in time for supper."

We rounded the cape into a long narrow harbor. My body buzzed with the same excitement I felt as a child when, once or twice a year, my father sailed us upriver to a trading port, though never one as grand as this. Now we entered a floating city choked with every size and shape of junks, barges, trawlers, and fast-boats, packed so tightly the only evidence that it was a body of water were the narrow lanes between, crawling with cowled ferries and rafts piled with goods. Merchants stood and waved as we passed, crying their wares.

This was not like the dense, teeming, haughty Kwangchow, nor any other port I'd witnessed on our journeys. This was the water world, the civilization I hadn't known I'd missed. Imagining the steamy aroma and slippery flavors of a real noodle shop nearly made me swoon.

I secured a seat at the front of the sampan, even before our ship's anchors were secured. Cheng Yat squeezed in beside me. Cheung Po Tsai slid the yuloh into the water; I had to restrain my tongue from shouting to hurry up and leave.

"Wait! Wait! Wait!" Ah-Yi plopped into the remaining seat, hugging a ceramic wine jar.

Po Tsai threaded us through alleys between ships, overlooked by curious children and dogs. The jetty looked like it had been tossed together by the tide—a rat's nest of planks, broken crates, and bamboo, sagging under a mob of onlookers. The crowd parted just enough for a white-haired man in a green robe to squeeze through.

"Is that the friend you mentioned?" I said. "What's his name?"

Cheng Yat shrugged. "He's the big man here. Everyone calls him Tunghoi Bat."

"You can call him Eleven Fingers Wu," Po Tsai said.

It was the first time I'd seen Cheng Yat get angry at the boy. "Don't you dare."

Po Tsai hitched a line to the jetty. The man in green steeped forward. "Wai! The wasps are swooping in!"

Cheng Yat leapt onto the dock and clasped shoulders with the man. Now I understood the nickname: his left hand had an extra little finger.

The rest of us trailed Tunghoi Bat and Cheng Yat through a warren of back lanes until we arrived at a wine shop perched over a narrow canal sparkling with the reflections of freshly kindled lanterns. Wu-shek Yi was already inside. Ah-Yi pointed me to a table where three young women, whom I guessed to be Wu's wives, giggled at my approach.

"So you're the—"

"Shh! Let her introduce herself!"

"Ah ha ha! She's too pretty to sit with us plain village girls."

My delight in meeting other women of my position swiftly evaporated in the crossfire of chatter about hairpins and ointments and cousins I'd never heard of. The food was far more interesting. Two little girls and the woman owner ran in and out of the kitchen, bearing dumplings and steaming plates of fish, pork, and rice. Rafts glided past below with lamps swaying from poles. It was heavenly after what we'd all been through and countless days at sea.

Men kept joining the feast, each treating Tunghoi Bat to a louder greeting than the last. I couldn't hear a word of what he and Cheng Yat were discussing, but their constant looks my way told me that I was one of the topics. Tunghoi Bat's glances at me were more assessing than friendly. He seemed a coarse man, with his crooked mouth and deep lines stitched across his face.

The last dish had been served, and the men started on the wine, their voices becoming louder and louder. Ah-Yi affected a yawn and patted my shoulder.

"There they go with the drinking. You know what they say—dogs make better companions than men because they wag their tails, not their tongues." She gestured that we should go. The Wu-shek Yi wives giggled and said goodbye.

As I stepped to the door, Cheng Yat did an odd thing: he smiled and waved goodbye.

Outside I asked Ah-Yi, "Why are we the only ones leaving? Where are we going?"

"Just a little tour of the town. Get some air."

The lanes and alleys were so dark, they swallowed the shadows. Few people were out. Noise and smoke poured from a gambling house.

"I get it that Tunghoi Bat runs this town," I said. "Is the whole place nothing but pirates?"

"Only when the fishing's poor," Ah-Yi said. "And have you ever heard a fisherman say the fishing's good? Hee!"

"I don't understand. If it's such common knowledge, why doesn't the navy come shut it down?"

"You're right—you don't understand." She laughed, rubbing her thumb and fingers together. "The great Emperor's admirals enjoy being paid to command nice-looking ships, not risking them getting scratched. Tunghoi Bat pays well. Hee hee!"

Back at the waterfront, boats still plied the harbor, coolies bore goods along the quay. The quay smelled of rotting sea life and piss.

"I suppose there isn't much to see," Ah-Yi said. "Anyway, you must be feeling tired."

"Not really."

"Or bored."

"I wasn't until we left."

"Or needing a cup of tea."

I stopped and put my foot on a mooring block. "Do you mind telling me what's going on?"

Someone whistled from the end of the jetty. Cheung Po Tsai nudged the sampan against a rickety stairway.

"Let's go," Ah-Yi said.

I gave up arguing and followed her into the boat, vowing to get an early start in the morning on my own. Po Tsai hummed a quiet melody; the dip of the yuloh echoed from surrounding ships. Reflections from deck lanterns mapped a dotted path through the water—not the path leading back to our junk.

"Aren't we going the wrong way?" I said.

"Making a delivery," Ah-Yi said. We fell into the deep shadow of an enormous vessel. Po Tsai twisted the yuloh and stopped us alongside. Ah-Yi hoisted the wine jar to a sailor leaning from the gunwale followed by a parcel I recognized as her sewing bag. With a sweeping hand gesture, she directed me to a rope ladder draped over the side.

"Tunghoi Bat's ship. We stay here," she said. "Don't look at me like that. Hee! Everyone knows you asked him for a wedding. We've just two days to get you ready."

A fortune teller once told me: "If there's a wave, there must be a wind."

His meaning had never been clear until now. One little wave couldn't exist without winds from every corner of the sky coming together in just the right way.

That was me right now.

All my life, I'd been tossed like a shard of driftwood, whipped by currents, smashed against boulders. But look at me now. Whatever had led me to this port, this ship, this cabin, to be fussed over and fitted with clothing for my wedding—My wedding! Such a thing had long dropped out of my dreams—whether it was the work of some god or a preordained happenstance of fate, it didn't matter. What mattered was that I was here now. What mattered was that I was getting something I'd asked for, for the first time in my life.

Tunghoi Bat's ship felt ancient, dark and musty. But it was easily half again as large as Cheng Yat's, the cabin tall enough to stand in without bumping my head on a beam. Today it was a palace of women.

A pretty young niece of Tunghoi Bat held a half-finished dress around me while Ah-Yi tsked and tittered behind my back. I was so delirious from lack of sleep the night before that I could barely stand. But stand I did, then sit, then stand again, while bright red and gold and yellow silks were stretched and folded and pinned and buttoned around my body's every turn and curve, including a few curves that weren't even there.

Occasionally I was given a glimpse in a copper mirror of a beautiful woman in beautiful dresses, served by busy, smiling helpers. I was a princess from a story.

In less than two days the entire water world of the great haven of Tunghoi would gather to watch me—me, Shek Yang!—marry my man.

For once in my life, the world revolved around me.

At daybreak I peeked through the cabin door. Men and women ran here and there, hoisting aboard roast pigs, baskets of lotus roots, fruits, mushrooms, wine. Men hammered together tables, hung banners, and swept trash. A crewman tripped when a goose nipped him; tangerines scattered across the deck.

The door slid shut in my face.

"Later, Elder Sister. They might see you." Tunghoi Bat's niece hid a giggle behind her hand.

I sipped tea on the mat, watching the girls lay out my outfits and listening to the bustle outside. Today I would assume an exalted place among these people, a princess of sorts in a kingdom that was still somewhat foreign to me. In fact, the concept of being part of any community was peculiar and new. The flower boats where I'd spent so many years had been a shifting world of friendships without cohesion, other than shared contempt for the job.

What would those girls say if they saw me now, waited on by bridesmaids? How many times had I listened to other girls plan their imaginary weddings? The dazzling silk gowns, the musicians, banquets of fifty tables—make that a hundred! How handsome he would be? How rich? Which of their customers might he be? The sea captain who boasted of three houses? The merchant who claimed to mingle with foreign devils in O Moon? Even I had entertained romantic dreams in the early years, until I understood that marriage was just a word men offered instead of a better tip. The real marriages I'd known were pragmatic unions, exchanging childbearing services for a roof.

I tried to convince myself that for me it was different. For most women, a proper marriage was the goal, the colorful, happy ending on the stage of their imaginations. It was the culmination of every feminine desire: a man, a home, a family. But not for me. Did it make me any less a woman that marriage and weddings and family carried no such meaning? For me, marriage represented a new beginning, a rudder—no, call it a platform—from which to launch a new life. Today I would be reborn.

Was Cheng Yat the man I would have chosen for such a life? My capture had been brutal, his conduct often coarse. Yet despite the unfairness I often felt, he had lately been treating me better than might be expected of a man. He said he'd been moved by my spirit. He'd praised my ferocity in battle. Was that why he'd granted my request for a wedding and even taken such care to surprise me? Was this how he thought he'd harness that fierce spirit and link it to his own? I liked to think so. Beyond the face it would gain us both, a proper wedding was a sure sign of commitment and respect.

The door slid aside for Ah-Yi and an armful of more garments than I might wear in a lifetime.

"Let's get you dressed."

I was forbidden to so much as twitch while my face was greased and painted; hair was washed, brushed, oiled, perfumed, twirled around bone hairpins, and woven through turtle shell combs and a mother-of-pearl fan. I was smothered in silk, robes tucked and smoothed. By the time the drumming started outside, my head was swirling and I wished for a nap.

"Wait, what's this?" I said. The bone buttons of my topcoat lacked the fresh sparkle of the rest of the outfit. They looked familiar.

Ah-Yi stood proudly. "Buttons from your yellow tunic, the one you had with you when—"

"No!" I twisted the top button, trying to free it from its loop.

Ah-Yi grabbed my hands. "Aiya! What are you doing? They started the drums."

"They're just going to have to wait until you replace these buttons."

"Are you damn crazy?"

Maybe I was, but I didn't care. These buttons were from my old life. I was a caterpillar becoming a butterfly. I needed to shed my whole skin.

"That life is finished. Throw them away!"

"Listen to this silly chicken!" Ah-Yi said, angry as I'd ever seen her. "I suppose you don't want these either."

A little girl knelt at my feet with a pair of shoes. I nearly choked on the lump in my throat. The red silk of my mother's wedding slippers shone like new, not a wrinkle or stray thread.

The girl hung her head like she was about to cry. I leaned over and stroked her hair.

"Of course I want these."

Nobody understood except me. These shoes were the last link to my days of innocence. Today I would begin a new life. Today I would bury the person I had been in between.

Ah-Yi tsk-tsked and told me not to move, working quickly to replace the buttons. The girl stretched the slippers over my feet, a snug fit but bearable.

My coterie of women stepped back to admire their work. "Such beauty will shame the birds from their branches," Ah-Yi said. Everybody laughed except me. I needed to see for myself.

Someone held up a hand mirror. I hardly recognized the goddess facing me, with rouged lips and painted brows, topped by a black cloud-scape of braids, spirals, and orbs, all held together with combs and beaded chains. Maybe it was the curve of the mirror, but I looked as tall as a ship in my shimmering red and ochre gown, embroidered with flowers so real I almost smelled their fragrance. I tried to picture my mother as a young bride. I wondered if she had also felt this beautiful, a beauty so potent it might last forever.

I presented myself outside on the companionway while my eyes adjusted to the sunlight and my ears to the gongs and drums. The main deck had been transformed into a banquet pavilion of round tables draped in red and topped with white dishes. Only women were present.

The heavy gown made the trip down the staircase both precarious and grand, while firecrackers played a fanfare on shore. At the head table, a gray-haired matron greeted me with hands clasped in front of her.

"We'll be cousins. But today I pretend to be your terrible mother-in-law," she said, though her playful words didn't match the lack of humor in her voice.

I dipped my head in mock fear, hoping to provoke a laugh.

"I'm Cheng Chat's number one wife," she said lightly, then turned her attention to the first course being delivered in a covered tureen.

I lingered with a smile frozen on my face. What was I supposed to do or say when such a prominent member of this society showed more interest in the soup than in the bride?

Other women were more polite, even eager to meet me, though all eyes seemed to be on the generous portions of food, little of which I was bound to enjoy. My job was to flit from table to table, absorbing a torrent of names which made me dizzy.

Ah-Yi's signal to return to the cabin came not a moment too soon.

"I thought this was the bride's day," I said. "I'll starve to death before it's over."

Two girls helped me out of the constricting robes and giggled at me sitting in my underthings attacking a bowl of leftover rice.

"Put that down. Eat less than a mouse," Ah-Yi said. "Then we practice."

"Again?" I burst into tears for no reason at all. I was happy, I was hungry, I was tense, I was free. So many names, so many things to remember. The look on Cheng Chat's wife's face, as though I were intruding on her territory. I felt crowded by all the people. I felt left out and alone.

Ah-Yi knelt in front of me and kissed my forehead. "My dear, dear little Yang. Your mother is here with us. I feel her spirit. Do you?"

I did, I was sure of it. I took a proffered handkerchief and wiped my cheeks.

Ah-Yi clapped. "Tear time over. Last chance to practice."

I changed into simple blue trousers and tunic. My attendants wrapped a red-fringed black sash around my waist. They all seemed to know the ceremony so well, whereas I didn't remember attending any water folk weddings before I was taken away. Would I ever stop being an outsider?

Someone knocked on the door: the show was ready to begin. A heavy black veil descended over my head.

I couldn't see a thing while the bridesmaids guided me to the deck chanting a sing-song tune. I couldn't see the stool I was meant to sit on and would have fallen if I hadn't been caught. Everybody thought this was hilarious. Without seeing their faces, I couldn't banish the thought that they were laughing out of ridicule for the bumbling newcomer.

A man's voice cut through the chatter.

"Everybody, listen! Quiet. Please, quiet. To ensure best fortune for the lovely bride, all spectators of the following ages must avert their eyes during the ceremony. Let me see..."

I heard papers crackle; people muttered and giggled. The man cleared his throat.

"If you're age twenty-two, forty-six, or seventy—are there any old grannies here?" He waited while the audience laughed. I wished I could have seen his mannerisms through the gauze. "I didn't think so. Well, if any of you young beauties is twenty-two, please turn away. If you're forty-six..." Here he paused. "Then I don't believe you! Ha ha! None of you ladies looks older than thirty. Especially my wife!"

A woman shouted, "That's right! Married the old bull when I was still in the womb!"

Even I was distracted enough to laugh.

"And now, seeing as men are forbidden from these proceedings, it is time for me to go where I'll be welcomed..." After a dramatic silence, he finished: "At the lip of a wine jar!" The women laughed. He slipped out, calling congratulations: *"Kung hei!"*

Someone folded back my veil. I held my hand over my mouth at the sight. Daylight was fading. The banquet setting was replaced by an open space covered in carpets. Long, red-draped tables lined both sides, each stacked with lacquered cases, silk-covered boxes, and bottles and flasks of all sizes. Multicolored streamers and lanterns dangled from a web of cords stretching from rail to rail, mast to mast. Every crate, every barrel, every gunwale, companionway, door frame, and step were occupied by a field of women, more than seemed possible for a single ship to bear.

In the center sat Cheng Chat's wife, her mouth puckered tightly into what she probably imagined to be a smile.

All those grinning, wide-eyed faces made me think of spectators at an execution. I shut my eyes and ordered the ugly voice inside me to shut up for once. This was all good, I reminded that voice. How had Cheng Yat arranged everything in two short days? This was for me, I reminded

93

the voice. It didn't matter what really went on inside those tittering heads. It made no difference what that old woman in the middle thought of me. I was about to become a wife, a respectable woman. I was about to become one of them, better than them. What was happening was unstoppable, and I would cope with the consequences later.

Ah-Yi, dressed the nicest I'd ever seen her in black embroidered silk, led me to a table flanked by bridesmaids holding enormous candles. Bowls filled with clear wine stood in the center. I selected the largest and carried it to a shrine beside the mainmast where I knelt in front of a red tablet representing the Cheng clan.

"Not yet," Ah-Yi hissed. I waited for two little girls to stretch a white sheet over my head. "So you're not exposed to the stars, remember?"

Why worry about stars? I thought. Let them call my mother in heaven to watch.

I raised the bowl three times to my new family, then emptied it into a jar at the base of the tablet. A strange feeling stirred in me, one that hadn't shown up during yesterday's rehearsals. I'd stopped believing in families the day I was sold away. I wondered what it would feel like to be part of a family again—like being born for the second time?

I repeated the gesture at a second shrine, in front of a scroll inscribed with my parents' names. While the white sheet again shielded me from heaven's eyes, I offered wine to my mother. *In my memory you never drank,* I thought. *Please make an exception now.* Then I offered to my father. No plea was needed.

The veil covered my face again, and I was back on the stool, peering down at my red slippers while a woman's gravelly voice droned on about lessons in obedience to father, husband, and son.

What if there were no sons? I'd spent half my life becoming expert at avoiding childbearing. No one needed to know my intentions to continue that same course.

The veil came off for the last time. Lanterns and torches cast circles of light across the deck. The bridesmaids, freshly changed into lime green silk, stood at the side, nodding a reminder at me. The final act was to begin. I rose to my feet.

One girl raised a neatly rolled new sleeping mat over her head and recited, "You'll never sleep in your maiden home again."

Another said, "Say farewell to your old life."

I froze. I'd been doing exactly that all day. But after all the preparations, repetitions, and sleeplessness for two nights running, I was about to humiliate myself. I'd forgotten my words.

Ah-Yi waved from the sidelines until she caught my attention. She held up four fingers.

Four. *Sei.*

Sounds like "die".

I remembered!

I raised a hand to my head and pretended to swoon. "I would rather say goodbye to the world of the living than to...ah..." I sorted the words in my head, "...than to leave the warm embrace of my family. Not a bridal bed should you prepare me, but rather a coffin."

A few muted laughs from the audience.

The bridesmaid from my ship danced toward me holding a ceramic flask over her head.

"But, sister, I have given you a drinking vessel so that we can picnic in the hills to celebrate your marriage." Placing the flask on the table, she shuffled away.

I had no trouble remembering now. I pretended to tear at my clothes.

"Let me trade these garments for burial clothes. I would die instead of leaving this cherished life of maidenhood behind."

This raised the biggest laugh of all. But it was friendly laughter. Maybe they weren't scorning me after all.

Another bridesmaid skipped forward, waving a clothing iron.

"But, sister, this I have given you to freshen your festive gowns for when we celebrate with your new husband."

Firecrackers exploded beside the ship. People screamed. A woman slipped off a platform onto other women below. This had not been part of rehearsals.

"Aiya! Too soon!" Ah-Yi said.

Cheng Chat's wife rose from her seat, her face burning like a lobster in a hot wok. She raised her skirts, tramped to the gunwale, and shrieked over the side: "You dog-faced idiot spawn of turtle pricks! I'll have your balls cut off and fed to crows just for that!"

I and the entire ship broke into hysterics. From that moment, I knew we'd be friends.

"Never mind! Never mind! Finish the show!" Ah-Yi waved a red scarf until everyone settled, then passed it to the bridesmaids. They

unrolled it to its full length and ran with it in a circle around me while I
spun in the other direction.

Everything became a blur of color: lanterns, banners, women's
outfits, the carpet below me, and the stars above. I flung out my arms,
spinning, while the bridesmaids sang and people clapped. I spun in
place, I spun in place. I was the moon at the center of the sky. I was
the dragon at the center of the sea.

This is the end. Shedding my old life.

I slowly came to a stop.

This is the beginning. Spinning into the new.

The scarf settled onto my shoulders, while the bridesmaids fixed
a green skirt around me. The same little girl helped me into my mother's
shoes, then took my hand and led me to the bow where a slipper boat
waited at the end of a gangway: the bridge from maidenhood to
marriage.

The two strongest bridesmaids lifted me. We all worried we'd end
up in the harbor as they carried me down the narrow plank, and we
laughed in relief when they finally deposited me on an ornamental stool
in the middle of the boat. Then they left.

The pressure of the last three days struck me all at once. My shoes
pinched. I had trouble sitting up straight. It took all my will to maintain
my composure in front of the women of Tunghoi waving from the
gunwales and cheering me, though I had trouble dismissing the notion
that they were putting on a show as part of the ritual.

The boat boy swung the yuloh, and we glided through the watery
corridor. For a few precious moments, I was alone and quiet, while a
single voice, the voice in my head, cried silently yet full-throated, for
the first time in my life, with joy. Red and gold reflections danced in the
water like fairies.

The marriage took place aboard Cheng Yat's—that is, aboard our—
junk. The concept of ours and us was as new and untested as everything
else that day.

The ceremony was thankfully brief: more firecrackers, a Taoist incantation, a short wait until Cheng Chat's wife arrived and settled
beside her husband to play parents to the newlyweds. Cheng Yat and
I knelt at their feet and served them ritual tea.

Then we stood up. I thought it was over.

It wasn't.

The air exploded with noise and smoke. Thousand-cracker strings hung from the mast tops writhed and buckled like fiery snakes, showering everyone with fountains of sparks and red paper shreds. Gongs clanged; drums boomed.

The pandemonium spread from ship to ship. Spitting firecrackers, stomping, ringing, beating pans echoed off hulls, filled the harbor, rumbled over the shores. Boys put on an impromptu dragon dance.

The noise faded. I heard my new name. A woman on a nearby ship cupped her hands around her mouth and called, "Cheng Yat Sou!"

Someone answered from several ships away. "Cheng Yat Sou!"

The calls spread from deck to deck, from one side of the water to the other, until they filled the whole harbor in a tumbling kind of unison.

"Cheng Yat! Cheng Yat Sou!"

"Cheng Yat Sou! Congratulations!"

I stepped onto a crate to better see the full view across the harbor and for the people to better see me. Every ship in Tunghoi was as bright as day under thousands of lanterns. Voices of men and women, shipmates and strangers, young and old, swirled through the air like an encircling wind, all proclaiming my new name.

"Cheng Yat Sou! Long life to Cheng Yat Sou!"

I slurped the words onto my tongue, swallowed them, inhaled them.

Cheng Yat climbed up beside me. With a hint of admiration—or was it something more?—in his eyes, he joined the call:

"Cheng Yat Sou!"

Cheng Yat's honored wife.

XI
Black Sails

I was late to meet Cheng Chat's wife. There was nothing I could do to hurry the sampan toward the wharf, short of taking up the yuloh myself.

I checked my hair for loose strands, straightened my collar. I had to appear my best for the first solo encounter with my intimidating new sister-in-law as well as my first excursion into Tunghoi since that first night. I was about to tour the town as the newest initiate into the ranks of the local elite.

I repeated the name aloud to myself: Cheng Yat Sou. I had achieved every woman's desire: to marry a man of position, a sea captain—a fleet captain—not as concubine, but Number One Wife. Shouldn't the sun shine brighter, the air taste sweeter? If I expected mountains of blossoms and music from heaven, I was brought back to reality as we approached the dock.

By daylight, the inner harbor revealed its true face: mud-colored water choked with rubbish and worse. Floating vendors and ferries cut in and out, narrowly avoiding collision, trading harsh words. The waterfront presented a colorless palette of gray bricks and sun-bleached timber.

I recognized Cheng Chat's wife waiting on the quay, dressed for cool weather in a knee-length padded tunic over a black skirt. With high cheeks and a face smooth as a plate, she might have been the wife of a prosperous merchant rather than a sailor who'd spent a lifetime at sea.

She greeted me cordially and led me into the narrow, winding innards of Tunghoi, speaking little except to complain about this shop or that hawker.

"This one's scales are fixed."—"That one sells old meat. Avoid him."—"Wai, Old Mok, anything fresh today? Ha! I almost believe you."—"And that rat over there—" She nodded toward a man tending a brazier in front of a sundry shop. "Wai! Tong-sang, how's business? This is Cheng Yat Sou. Don't you dare cheat her or I'll have your neck."

"Of course I know Cheng Yat Sou. *Kung hei!*" He waved me over. "Best price for you."

He sold me a roasted yam while Cheng Chat's wife visited a tea merchant across the lane. Its hot steam and bright orange flesh made a spot of sweet color against the narrow, dusty street. I wasn't sure what I'd expected to find in Tunghoi. It wasn't exactly a city of artisans, poets, and scholars. I suspected there wasn't a government yamen building, nor an official of any kind. It looked like just another tossed-together sea town, not one whose major enterprise was piracy, a haven for fugitives and outcasts, as though holding back a whispered secret which made it extraordinary in my limited view of the world.

I managed one delicious mouthful of yam when a gang of boys dashed around a corner straight into me, knocking the potato from my hand. One boy stepped on it and slipped backward onto the dirt. He looked up at me as if at his executioner, but I had to laugh at the sorry thing, his forehead comically shaven on just one side.

"Vermin!" A barber ran from the side alley waving a razor. "I finish the job—you pay me!"

The boy scrambled to his feet, not before the barber grabbed his queue and tugged him back. Then the barber abruptly froze, his gaze fixed somewhere in the distance. The boy wriggled free and chased after his friends.

Cheng Chat's wife stepped out of the tea shop holding a small parcel.

"My little indulgence. Do you—*Aiya!* No!" Gaping toward the harbor like the barber, she waved a fist. "Fuck your old mother, Chen Tin-bou!"

I saw nothing more unusual than a group of junks working their way through the anchorage, except that these looked like they'd cloaked themselves in their own shadows with striking black sails and hulls of the darkest wood.

Chat's wife hooked my arm and led me straight back toward the waterfront.

"Who is it?" I said.

"Black prick spawn of a turtle, that's who."

Half the town appeared to have gathered on the quay. Despite a passing shower, even coolies had set down their loads to stare at the black ships.

Chat's wife elbowed people aside until we reached the dock. She spat in the water, stuck fingers in her mouth and whistled like a man at a sampan waiting beside a pylon.

"Cheng Chat's junk?" the sampan girl said. My companion was obviously well-known here.

Without a nod, Cheng Chat's wife replied, "Fast and you might see a tip."

We settled under the boat's canopy and folded our legs out of the rain. I asked, "Are you going to tell me who is Chen the black turtle and why you're so anxious to see him?"

"See him? I want to rip his diseased tongue out before he talks to Ah-Chat. I'm not going back to Annam!"

It wasn't the first I'd heard of Annam, usually in background chatter, a faraway place many of the men had done some kind of business.

"What happened there?" I said.

Chat's wife eyed me suspiciously. "I don't believe it. He hasn't told you a thing?"

"He's a Cheng. They don't talk."

She laughed louder than the joke deserved. "Maybe I like you. You have to promise to be on my side."

"Maybe I will if I know what side you're talking about. This Chen is Annamese?"

"He's an ignorant running dog Chinese from Kwangshi who, by the look of it, still works for the Fatty Boy Emperor. You don't know what I'm talking about, do you?" She released an exasperated lungful of air. "You do know where Annam is, right? Miserable, hot kingdom with bad food, ruled by an inbred clan called the Tay-son. Thanks to us! That was a couple years ago. They had to crush a rebellion, so they pulled Chen Tin-bou off a fishing boat and put that dog in charge of their navy."

I understood hardly a word. "A Chinese fisherman? In charge of a navy? Why?"

"Maybe because we're smarter than Annamese? Even Chen, I'll grant him that. The way he tells it, he got himself shipwrecked on one of their beaches, and they immediately recognized his indisputable genius and asked him to form a navy."

The boat girl interrupted: "Chen Tin-bou talks big tales."

"Who asked you? Shut up and scull faster," Chat's wife said. "Anyway, the truth is that Annamese make great ships but terrible sailors. Chen needed seamen who knew how to fight."

"So I take it he recruited Cheng Chat?" I said.

"Didn't I say that? I suppose I didn't. Yes, him and everyone else who could work a sail. Chen came dangling money and big-sounding titles—like waving pork bones in front of hungry dogs. My dog-brain husband the bandit was suddenly a vice admiral. Even I was taken in by it at first.

"Then Chat brought in his cousin, your husband. Met some bad fighting, but after a year we had the rebels beat."

"He never told me. A whole year of fighting? But you won?"

She nodded. "Depends how you look at it. A year of warfare left the government bankrupt, if they ever had money in the first place. That's when they put us to work doing what we do best—raid ports across the border, hijack traders, smuggle rice and iron, things like that. We paid for their whole misbegotten country!"

"I don't get it," I said. "Sounds like you were still pirates, but handing over your money. Why bother staying?"

"That's why I like you. You're smart. Took the men a while to catch on. Of course, we got our cut, and we didn't necessarily declare all we took. We had nice ships. It was easy work. In Annamese waters we weren't outlaws—we were the law. Foo! There's the turtle's egg."

She spat in the direction of a dark mahogany junk which, up close, showed signs of multiple repairs and impending rot. Uniformed sailors with bowl-shaped haircuts milled around on deck. A strange feeling buzzed up my spine as we passed through its shadow. This ship had seen war, had commanded a navy. Chen's arrival seemed to herald some sort of grand adventure.

The ornate brass seal in Cheng Yat's trunk suddenly made sense to me. I felt guilty now for mocking his rage when it was stolen, though Chat's wife was intent on quashing any positive notions forming in my mind.

"Are you listening? As I was saying, the emperor died and who took his place? Can you believe his ten-year-old son's fat butt started staining the throne with his farts? Though it's really his uncle, the old emperor's brother, running things. Running treasure into his pockets is more like it.

"By then the rebels had their own navy, must have found a few good Chinese sailors. Anyone could see what was coming. I wanted to leave. I begged him to leave! But that emperor's uncle knows my husband too well. Promoted him to full admiral. He might have been a better one than Chen, but there was no chance to find out. Chen delivered us straight into an ambush. Chat's best friend Mok Kwun-fu..."

Her lips pinched together; her eyes went glossy.

"And his wife, a beautiful daughter..."

We came abreast of her ship. She clutched her tea packet to her chest and stepped out into the rain. "Twelve years there was enough, damn that cursed land. Let Chen Tin-bou die before I ever see his face again!"

Twelve years. Nearly as long as I'd been away.

Chat's wife and I ran across the rain-slick deck and up to the cabin, where the men looked up at our arrival. Chat's wife grinned like a goat.

"Uncle Tin-bou! What favorable wind whisked you our way?"

A tall, stoop-shouldered man with an unshaven mane of stringy white hair raised a cup to her. "Madam Cheng—"

"Save your toast," Cheng Chat's wife said. "Whatever you're here for, we're not joining." Then to Cheng Chat, "Let him finish his drink and get off my ship!"

Cheng Chat glared at his wife. Judging by the men's red faces and the stench of alcohol, they had already passed the first posts on the road to drunkenness.

Chen wasn't the monster in human flesh she had described, but he was still a typical man, drinking me in with his eyes while I sat on the mat behind Cheng Yat.

"I'll repeat for the ladies' benefit." Chen's cough came from deep in his throat. "We've regrouped and we're stronger than ever, have the Nguyen rebels pinned down in Phú Xuân. They're still no match for us at sea—we've close to two hundred new ships on the ramps. With experienced leadership, we'll crush them in little time."

"Go find your leadership among the fishes," Chat's wife said.

"Quiet, woman!" Cheng Chat said, then turned to Chen. "How much money?"

A high voice interrupted from the doorway: "Who needs money when I smell wine? Hope I'm not too late."

Wu-shek Yi brushed rain from his shoulders and squeezed his bulk beside Chen Tin-bou. "So, Old Chen, you're still among the living. What brings you? Your child master set to conquer China now?"

"Ah, Vice Admiral Who Pacifies the Sea! Conquer China? It would take two fleets just to encircle your vast gut."

Chen filled the men's cups from a jar with what looked like plum spirits. The way they tipped their heads back all at once reminded me of chickens drinking rain. As the talk continued, I noticed the only one who hadn't said a word was Cheng Yat, sitting there nibbling his fingernail like a child. I nudged him to stop.

Perhaps Chat's wife's story had colored my impression of Chen Tin-bou, but I sensed something transparently devious about him: the way he laughed, the way he filled the other men's cups higher than his own; he was a cat playing Old Uncle to the mice.

Then the cat pounced.

"Has it occurred to you that none of you men ever formally renounced your titles as officers of the Annamese Imperial Navy? Your lovely bronze seals are tucked away safe, am I right? You see? You're still officially under His Majesty's command."

"Very amusing." Wu-shek Yi said, examining his cup. "Maybe I haven't drunk enough to understand such nonsense."

Chen poured. "Ha, yes. To some it may seem funny. To others... well, it might be a bit much to call it treason if you don't return. Which is why we're offering—"

Chat's wife broke in. "No one is under your command on my ship! We're better off without you, so get youself—"

Cheng Chat struck her in the ribs with his elbow. At that moment I considered him far more hateful than Chen Tin-bou.

Before anyone could get in another word, Chen slammed down his cup. "Tell me, brothers. Do you think I can't see? Can't count? How many ships do you have between you? Where are the mountains of treasure you've amassed since you returned to your earthly paradise this side of the border? I search this room for men prosperous enough to refuse an emperor, but all I see is a flock of ravens contented to pick at scraps."

Cheng Chat, Cheng Yat, and Wu-shek Yi glanced at each other. At least Cheng Yat wasn't the only one whose tongue was tied. Chen's words, as insulting as they were, must have contained some bitter truth.

"Get this dog off my ship," Cheng Chat's wife growled.

"Woman, be nice to our guest," Cheng Chat said, laughing now. "Just old friends sharing drink and chatter. Nothing to it. Trust me, wife." He touched her shoulder, but she drew back.

"Should I? You all make me sick." Chat's wife tugged my sleeve. "We've smelled enough of this old hog's farts."

I wanted to stay and learn more, but her urging made it impossible for me not to follow.

The rain had softened to a fine mist. We stayed dry under an oiled tarpaulin at the tip of the bow, feet dangling over the water. The sky was clearing through a thicket of masts and cook fire smoke trails, just in time for sunset.

Chat's wife forced a laugh, but her voice carried a sneer. "I suppose it sounds so exotic, yes? All this talk of generals and emperors?"

How could I admit to this cynical woman the truth of her remark? Images of royalty strutting in brilliant silk robes through hallways lined with gold—I couldn't picture what a palace must look like—how do I compare these with the grime and pallor of a pirate junk?

The clouds retreated and let the stars come out. Water lapped the hull, dishes tinkled in nearby ships. A dog barked. Around me a city of junks huddled together so close I could probably leap from deck to deck all the way to Cheng Yat's—to *our*—ship. Soon the last repairs and restocking would be complete. Then which sea would we sail? Which horizon would we turn toward? Too much was happening too quickly to understand that this was really my life. How to make sense of this tingling in my gut? Was it actually possible I might become an admiral's wife?

"Was it so bad in Annam?" I said.

"I'll admit it was good, first few years at least—as long as we stayed out of their politics. We went on our raids, collected our rewards, ran into a few skirmishes. It was steady. Even learned to like some of the food, ha. Then the old emperor died, and it all turned to shit." She let out a deep breath. "Besides, by then, I'd had enough."

Egrets soared inland for the night. Bats fluttered around deck lanterns picking off bugs.

"You like this life," I said.

"Like?"

"So many years at sea, seeing the world, going where you want, taking what you want. You must like it."

Chat's wife grabbed a large-winged insect from the air and watched it struggle between her fingers before letting it go. "What does 'liking' have to do with anything? It's the life."

Those were the same words the other flower boat girls and I had often said to each other. We had no choice. Acceptance was the least painful path. Such was fate, as if invisible gods dictated everything. I'd never believed any of it. Some people's fate could change unexpectedly, like mine, not because of gods, but as a result of men's actions. No, I no longer believed in acceptance.

I kicked my legs in the empty air below me. "Number one wife, you said."

"When did I say such a thing?"

"Right before you declared yourself my mother-in-law for the day."

She shrugged. "He's no swan."

"Where are the others?"

Her look said it was none of my business. "Bottom of the sea, for all I care. I was the only one he properly married."

"How many?"

"Aiya! Think I keep count?" She waited for a sampan to pass below us, leaving a dark swath through the rippling moonlight. "Three."

"I don't see them here."

"Neither do I." She twisted around to face me, folded her arms across her chest. "All right, you want the story? Last one died a few years ago, giving child. First one died too, from poison food or something— no, not from me, much as I would have. The other he caught in bed with a sailor."

"And?"

"You don't want to hear."

I was scared to find out but assured her that I wasn't.

"Tied both with stones and—no." She looked away. A fishing junk crept by, a weak lantern illuminating a boy and his dog on a pile of nets. The boy waved at us. I waved back.

The men's voices carried over from the cabin, sounding like they were enjoying themselves a bit too much. Chat's wife tilted her head their way.

"Sometimes I understand," she said. "You know, that his best days

106

are behind him. I just wish he doesn't fall for Chen's nonsense all over again, running a fool's quest. You heard Wu in there, preening over his big fat title, Admiral-something. Chat's no better—loves all the pomp and wearing those long fancy titles like a woman strings beads in her hair. I've told him enough times, selling ourselves to them for money and mouth-farting honorifics is no better than whores spreading their—Oh oh oh oh! Kill me! Just kill me!" She slapped her own face over and over. "I never know when to shut up."

For someone so bold of tongue, she was uncharacteristically speechless with embarrassment. She was afraid she'd hurt my feelings! I think I loved her from that moment.

"We had ornamental titles too," I said with a little smile.

Chat's wife blinked, still too embarrassed to speak.

"On my last flower boat they made me call myself Precious Hairpin."

Chat's wife bit her lips. I could see she wanted to laugh.

"Better than the name I started with on the previous boat. Are you ready? Purple Cuckoo."

Her laughter exploded in my face while I ran through my other aliases over the years—Black Jade, Laughing Plum Blossom, and my favorite, Fragrant Peach.

"I want a title too! Give me one," she said.

"Mm. I don't know. If I assign you a pleasure girl name, that means you work for me, and then you have to..."

"He calls me whore often enough."

Now I was the one who couldn't stop laughing, even bumping my head on the winch. "Mm, mm, let me think...so young and pretty...oh, and you're new, so of course you're a virgin, right? You will be Lovable Cloud."

"I like Purple Cuckoo. The name is available, yes? Cuckoo! Cuckoo!"

"Fine. Welcome to the pleasure boat, Purple Cuckoo."

"Thank you, Precious Hairpin."

I shook my head. "New boat, new name, new hymen. I'll be Lovable Cloud. Now lie down and get to work!"

We laid back on the precariously narrow bow platform, calling names back and forth and swatting away insects as if they were part of the joke, until my lungs were too exhausted to laugh anymore. We both lay quietly for a while, watching the clouds pass, when the woman who had previously so intimidated me reached for my hand.

"Please call me Elder Sister," she said.

A door burst open in my heart. Words flooded from me, stories that I never would have told anyone, that had been left to fester in my gut: of my father's treachery, of the tawdriness of the flower boats, pompous and violent men and pitiless madams making me spit out my girlhood dreams like bitter seeds from a rotten fruit. She—my new Elder Sister— salted me with questions and brushed away tears. Our fingers entwined and never let go while we talked and talked until the middle of the night, until my body was melting from fatigue...or was it joy?

She got up to use the privy and didn't return.

Her voice pierced the darkness: "Bastard spawn of a pestilent toad!"

Light spilled from the open cabin door. Chat's wife pursued her staggering husband and Chen Tin-bou down the companionway steps. With one foot over the gunwale into his waiting sampan, Chen clasped Cheng Chat's shoulders. An agreement had been reached.

"Beast! We're not coming!" Chat's wife spat into the sampan, then lunged at Cheng Chat. "You filthy cat! Your promises are piss in a teapot! Hear that, Tin-bou? Whatever this wretch promised you is piss in your tea!"

Wu-shek Yi was so drunk he could barely waddle to the opposite gunwale. "I'll take my leave before I try any of that tea." He rolled rather than climbed into his boat.

Cheng Yat's shadow appeared tall in the doorway, and I knew this was something I wanted—to be somebody, the wife of an admiral. No, that wasn't it. I wanted to finish what I hadn't known I'd started when I left the flower boats, what had taken a new turn when I became Cheng Yat Sou: to run away from what I'd been and transform into something unimaginably new; if that meant leaving behind this whole cursed country, so much the better. I would take on a new identity—not an imaginary one like a Lovable Cloud, but a new me inside and out— protege of royalty, occupying new places, nourishing myself with new foods, speaking and thinking in a new language. All accomplished in a single step of saying yes to Chen Tin-bou. These thoughts filled my head but I hadn't had the spleen to confess to my Elder Sister. Someday I would. She would understand.

In the sampan back to our ship, Cheng Yat leaned on me like a limp squid. I didn't dare ask his contribution to whatever decision had been made, or whether his cousin had done the deciding for all.

"What title did he offer you?" I asked.

His head rolled lazily against my neck.

I helped him onto our junk, past the ever-busy fan-tan table, and up into the cabin where I left him fully dressed on the sleeping mat. Every part of my body was exhausted, but I knew I wouldn't sleep. I wrapped a blanket around my shoulders and climbed to the poop deck, sat back against the taffrail, and watched stars flit in and out of view.

"Heaven has a heart," I whispered. "And I have a friend."

XII
Borders

I missed her from the moment we sailed out of Tunghoi.
An oracle reading had promised auspicious sailing the next morning, so, despite heavy fog, rather than wait another eight days for the next alignment between spirits and sails, our fleets began the journey west.

The haze persisted all along the Luichow coast, clearing only for brief glimpses of mangrove swamps and little settlements which looked more and more ragged the farther south we sailed. Cheng Chat's squadron took the lead with ours in the middle and Wu-shek Yi in the rear. Chen Tin-bou went north in search of other recruits while Tunghoi Bat stayed home. Rarely did I catch a glimpse of the ship carrying my new friend. However far Annam might be, I was in a hurry for us to get there.

I found Ah-Yi stitching shoes beside the water tank.

"Seems this fog will never end," she said. "Nothing to see, nothing to do. I'll wager even making slippers might be a relief for somebody."

She pulled aside her sewing bag to make a place for me. Well, why not? Before I'd completely settled my legs, she filled my lap with mat cuts and fabric and a long needle that could have served as a battle weapon.

"Heel's the hardest, so best to start there," she said.

The old woman hummed while I mostly yelped. I must have put more holes in my finger than in the fabric. However ugly my stitches were, at least they held. "Such fun," I said.

"You're a worse liar than seamstress. Hee! Try this."

She showed me how to use the foreign thimble. At least I shed less blood while I worked on the instep.

"So... Cheng Yat had another wife once, didn't he?"

"Aiya! So that's what's on your mind. Almost had me fooled that you cared to sew. Almost."

"No. Yes. Ow!" The thimble popped off and the needle buried itself in my finger.

"Did you ask him?"

I nodded with my finger in my mouth.

"And?"

"He said, 'Ji-ji-ja-ja, useless talk.' Said the past is past, he doesn't waste breath on yesterday."

"Hee! That's him, all right. When the other fools honk like geese about this or that old raid or battle, have you ever heard him add a word?"

The old lady had a point. After the one time he'd told me that story about his boyhood, he'd never again spoken of his past without it being pried from him. I'd thought he was simply being stubborn.

"What can you tell me about her?"

"That thing in your hand looks less like a shoe than a mauled chicken. And that's all it's my business to tell you." She tied off a thread and smiled. "Maybe you should learn from your husband. You can't sail backward, so why worry about the waves behind you?"

I learned that we'd reached the end of the land while crouched over the privy with my trousers around my knees. Thousands of firecrackers blasted in every corner of our deck and on every ship within hearing. When I got over my shock, I understood: we were scaring off bad spirits before entering new waters.

When the noise subsided, I heard someone laugh nearby but couldn't locate the voice.

"Aiya! Cheng Yat Sou, not here!"

Cheung Po Tsai called from his perch over the mainmast. He had a clear view of my present activity, which now the whole crew knew about.

Even within the confines of the ship, I'd rarely crossed paths with Po Tsai since the wedding. If he was still pleasuring Cheng Yat, at least I wasn't aware of it.

"Turn your eyes away or I'll throw what I'm doing at you!" I answered back.

"Ai! Yang, not a joke! Bad luck to shit on what might be your grave!"

How dare he address me with such familiarity? I knew what I

wanted to shit on. But his superstitions were shared by the crew. I found a bucket in which to finish my business, so as not to offend whichever sea demons might still linger.

Almost immediately we were out of the fog and bucking on an angry sea. The land had shifted to our north, all wave-pounded boulders and jagged cliffs. This was Luichow's southeastern cape, entrance to the Hoinam Strait. For days I'd heard that name spoken with terror. It took little time to understand why.

I had never ridden a fiercer sea. For the next day and night every muscle of every sailor wrestled serpent-like currents, steering around hidden shoals while shifting winds traded punches at the sails. Whatever notion I had of lending my strength was lost in my own vomit while I huddled in the cabin. I'd never been seasick; I was nauseous from fear.

By the afternoon of the second day, the winds stabilized and we settled onto a steadier course. Cheng Yat staggered inside for the first time since we'd entered the strait. He thanked Tin Hau for sparing his crew, though he confided to her—or maybe to me—that a few bones had broken. He collapsed onto the mat.

I threw a blanket over him and thanked him for his seamanship, which deserved more credit for saving lives and ships than some lifeless statue. His snores said he hadn't heard a word.

I joined the bleary-eyed queue at the galley. In the west the clouds were breaking up into the bluest sky I'd ever seen. I carried my congee to my favorite spot by the spirit side rail. The vision before me made me lose my grip on the bowl.

The murky green waters we'd been sailing through ended abruptly in a line so straight it might have been drawn by a painter's hand, dividing it from a flat open sea of sparkling blue like liquid sapphire. I was truly crossing into another world.

"Is this Annam?" I asked.

Men around me stopped slurping their food and laughed. "Long way still. You going to eat that congee or bathe in it?"

Everything moved slowly on this side of the world. The coastline with its long white beaches stretched into eternity, unbroken by even a fishing hut. Seabirds hovered in the shore breeze, barely flapping their wings.

I asked Cheng Yat every day, "When do we get to Annam?" His answers were vague, meaningless.

"When you start seeing coconut trees, we're almost there," Cheung Po Tsai told me one day. He hadn't been with the fleets in Annam, so how could he possibly know?

"What do coconut trees look like, then?"

"Like hairy spiders with long limp pricks." He ran away giggling. One day I'd ask Cheng Yat to get rid of this irritating little fool.

Annam! The name tickled my tongue—exotic, whimsical, like something from a story. If only this long journey would end!

I saw my friend again for the first time in a bay on an empty stretch of coast where we'd stopped to fish and scavenge on shore. I didn't give Cheng Yat a choice: I was joining him on his cousin's ship.

Cheng Chat's wife slept tangled up in a thin blanket. I barely recognized the feisty woman who strode around Tunghoi spitting and cursing. Even in the dark cabin, her skin was pasty, her cheekbones like awnings over hollows etched in her face. The room smelled of medicinal herbs. Her eyes cracked open into half-moons.

"Younger Sister. Get me some water."

All I found to drink was cold herbal potion in a clay cook pot. She coughed and cleared her throat. "Foo! They've been pouring that bilge down my throat for days."

I went to the door and told a sailor to bring hot tea. When I turned around, she was sitting up.

"Where are we?" she said.

"That's what I wanted to ask. Are we close to Annam? No one seems to know."

"Wouldn't think so. I'd feel it in my gut."

I sat beside her and felt her brow. It was cool and moist. "Is that why you're ill?"

"It isn't a show, if that's what you're thinking. I get this way sometimes."

"I didn't mean—"

"Never mind," she said. "Ah, here's our tea. Boy! Bring melon seeds. I need to bite something."

Revived by tea and snacks, I spoke of the Hoinam Strait passage, the tedium of this leg of the voyage, but her responses were forced.

"Elder Sister, tell me," I said. "Let's talk like we did that night."

"Close the door."

I did as told.

114

"I never thought I'd be back here," she said. "I was sure we'd be headed for Tai Yue Shan, to live there like he promised." She told me tales of growing up on that mountainous island at the mouth of the delta, in a stilt house near a bay ringed by hills. Of how Chat's father had controlled the boat communities along the island's south side. How her own father ingratiated himself to the man—fishing for a big tortoise, he called it—lavishing gifts and flattery in order to arrange her marriage to Cheng Chat and thereby buy himself standing as a local chieftain.

"Fathers selling daughters," I remarked. We sipped tea in silence.

"He promised we'd go back there, build a house. I don't want our sons to be bandits."

"Where are your boys? I haven't met them."

"He's got them training on other ships." The bitterness choking her throat led to another coughing fit. I told her to lie down.

Someone knocked. A crewman stuck his head in. "Ah-Cheng Yat Sou, your husband says time you go back to your ship."

He was his usual moody self after a meeting with his cousin, refusing to speak until the sampan nearly touched our hull. "Raid tomorrow. Early start."

"Raid? I thought we were navy now, not pirates. Aren't we going to Annam?"

He stood to catch the line tossed from the ship.

"Answer me," I said. "You never answer my questions! Why another raid?"

He sniffed. "A well-mannered guest always brings gifts."

The raid on a salt port wasn't our first attack on ships at dock, but it was by far the largest and most dangerous I'd witnessed.

The action unfolded like one of those wide scroll paintings stretched across the walls of elite teahouses: countless junks and sampans, gunfire and smoke, and figures littering the water against the backdrop of a long, crooked bay. The target: eighteen salt barges.

A raid brought out something animal in Cheng Yat. Here, he was the attacker and he let down his defenses. That was the only way to explain why he so willingly answered my questions.

Why did only we and five other ships enter the bay? So they would think there were only six of us. Why were we taking their fire without firing back? So they would think we don't have the range. So they'll be tempted closer, right?

He got tired of answering my questions.

I was frightened. I couldn't wait for the skirmish to end. But I was learning. While cannonballs drowned out the screams of men, while ships on both sides took hits and traded flaming arrows, I was reminded of the games that old men played in Kwangchow parks. The barges stood like soldier pieces. The fishing boats were the generals. Our attacking junks tacked and weaved, like the crooked moves of horses.

"It's like elephant chess," I said.

Cheng Yat acknowledged me with a look I could only describe as dumbfounded, until a cannonball hissed into the water nearby and he ordered a retreat.

Their gunboats, which well outnumbered us, moved in for the kill. It was a lesson in strategy, in misleading the opponent and luring him to his own demise, as the defenders chased us past the mouth of the bay, directly into the sights of Cheng Chat's and Wu-shek Yi's waiting guns. We left with eighteen salt barges added to our fleet, a gift to split with our new employer.

Only later, after the celebrations, after we resumed the westward journey, did it strike me: Cheng Yat had been clever and extraordinarily brave; he'd pulled off a raid with precision and leadership. He had proven himself a pirate down to his bones. What would become of him—of us—when we ceased being bandits?

Ten days later, or maybe more, I stood out in the wind, combing my hair after a rinse with cold tea. The sky was dull gray. An early winter breeze chilled my scalp.

Melon Seed, who'd taken over as cannon master, whistled from the deck below.

"Cheng Yat Sou, see that?"

He pointed to a flat, muddy spit of land with what looked like a few ramshackle huts.

"That there's Annam."

XIII
Chiang Ping

A dockhand helped me up the slippery steps onto the wharf, then opened his palm for a tip: my introduction to the Annamese border town of Chiang Ping.

I'd expected to find a strange foreign version of the seedier sections of Kwangchow, all dark, dripping alleys crawling with unknown diseases and dangers. I wasn't prepared for the endless stretch of storefronts and warehouses which straddled the curving riverfront. The business of Chiang Ping was business, I'd been told, almost none being of the licit kind.

Cheng Chat's wife raced ahead, challenging me to keep pace in order to hear her identify the tide of people passing us on the street: big-chested Luzon men with childlike faces, Siamese with nut-brown skin and bowl-shaped hair, impossibly dark Melakans, stiff-backed men in Chinese merchants attire and unshaven scalps, whom she dismissed as Long Hairs: Chinese settlers who'd taken local wives and mannerisms. Almost lost in the crowd were Annamese men, identifiable by their loose-flowing hair. Where were all these people going in the middle of the day?

A group of young women strolled past in white, billowing two-piece gowns that were at once modest and shamelessly tantalizing.

"I want one of those," I said. "Bring me to a tailor."

Chat's wife pulled me to the side of the street, muttering obscenities about local girls as we sped up our walk. Cart pushers barked at us to get out of their way. Hawkers thrust jade combs and bracelets in my face, speaking a language both vaguely familiar and incomprehensible, like Cantonese as if spoken by cats.

"Fake," Chat's wife said. "If it's on Celestial Dynasty Street, you can guess it's rubbish." This appeared to be Chiang Ping's main thorough-fare; that left out a lot of merchandise.

She pointed us toward a side lane ahead.

"We just got here," I said. "I want to look around."

"Saving you the agony. You'll see. Taking you to heaven."

It seemed she meant it literally. We hiked up a steep lane of hard-packed dirt, lined with homes and small warehouses and a garbage-choked gutter. I insisted on stopping to let coolies pass, to catch my breath, and to make sense of all I was seeing.

From where I stood, Chiang Ping was less a town than a chaos of tiled and thatch-roofed buildings surrounding a snaking waterway, itself so choked with vessels it was near-impossible to tell where land stopped and river began. No wonder our ships hadn't attempted to dock here but rather between the islands west of the river's mouth.

Chat's wife harrumphed with impatience.

"How much farther?" I said.

"Soon. Past the bridge. Let's move."

She pushed her way through the crowd on the bridge, but I pre-ferred to stop a moment and admire an animal hawker bearing countless cages on bamboo poles, entertaining a swarm of excited children.

The bridge led into a busy market lane where I found Chat's wife arguing with a fruit seller in Cantonese. She bit a chunk off a pear and held it in his face. An Annamese woman with black teeth joined the hawker in shouting at Chat's wife until she threw a coin at them and walked away.

"Two cash for rotten pears!" she told me.

Shopkeepers waved from every doorway. "Pretty miss! Pretty miss! Special price for beauties!" I stopped at a porcelain shop filled with towers of colorful dishes. Chat's wife dragged me away.

"This is the place."

Clouds of perfume struck me before I even entered the door. The shop was stocked from floor to ceiling with soap: shelves sagging with blocks, fragrant balls arranged in baskets on the floor, and barrels in one corner overflowing with soap beans. Soap flakes crunched under my feet. A frail old man rose from a stool and greeted us in heavily accented Cantonese.

"Ah, pretty lady!" His teeth, like those of so many others, were nearly black from a lifetime of chewing betel nut. He ran a finger around his mouth. "Like lip oil? Have!"

He selected a bowl from a shelf and uncovered a lascivious red paste whose heavy florid aroma was something an aging courtesan might wear.

"Very fragrance!"

"I need soap," I said.

"Soap have many. Face. Hair. What for, I have."

"For her to smell better," Cheng Chat's wife cut in. "So her husband will want to make a baby."

"For washing clothes," I told him. One of the few good memories from my old life had been the scented gowns, a source of pleasure not just for the customers.

The old man scooped a handful of beans from a crock. "Best quality soap bean."

So waxy and soft between my fingers, I didn't hesitate. While he packaged my selection, I roamed the shop, drunk on the fragrance of shelves and buckets and baskets of soap, some cut into bricks, others shaped like birds, flowers, even gold ingots.

The proprietor crooked a finger at me. "Ah, beauty-beauty lady. Special for you. Like the Fragrant Concubine."

He held a fist-sized ivory colored ball under my nose. The mix of fragrances made me swoon: spicy ginger root and sweet white orchid flower.

The next one drowned my senses in pure rose essence.

"Fragrance from flower, transfer its soul to you."

I hoped that heaven would be as gratifying to the senses as this humble soap shop. Everywhere I turned, every shelf, every basket offered pleasure to my eyes, my nose, my fingers. I wanted to take home one of everything. I had reason to stay in Chiang Ping forever.

Sensing my indecision, he placed a butterfly-shaped wafer in my hand. "Must to have. Make face most softly. Man like kiss!"

"Not for her, then," Chat's wife said. "Already too many men want to kiss her."

The shopkeeper winked toward the back of the shop and whispered, "Pretty lady, maybe need."

There he unlatched a wooden cabinet and stood, pinching a tiny glass vial filled halfway with liquid silver. "From Holland ship. Best pure kind."

I'd never seen quicksilver before. One of the flower boat girls had boasted of owning a flask, calling it shinier than a sword and just as powerful. We all knew it as the contraceptive that only imperial concubines could afford. One tiny teardrop per day, and no need to swallow foul-tasting musk, roots, and lotus leaves. I'd begged her to let me try it, offering a full five days' earnings. Others had offered more, but the girl had refused to share, refused to even show it. When, later that year, she died from a mysterious ailment, all we found was an empty glass jar.

"How much?" I asked the soap shop owner.

"For beauty lady, five tael silver."

Cheng Chat's wife yanked me away. "Don't be stupid!"

I paid for five pieces of bathing soap and the soap beans, then she led me back out to the porcelain shop I'd stopped at before, but I had lost interest. My new friend was starting to unnerve me. She must have seen it too when I declined her suggestion to shop for fabrics despite her enthusiastic testimony about the colors and textures of Annamese silk.

"Are you tired? Those soap smells made me dizzy," she said. "This whole town makes me dizzy. I need a drink, and I know just the place you'll like."

"Only if you promise me heaven again."

"Judge for yourself."

We descended into the town through zigzag alleyways, past tailors and prayer paper shops and spice stalls that made me sneeze.

Then we were back on Celestial Dynasty Street, farther toward the big bend in the river than where we started. We crossed an open square in front of a temple, into a quiet section of the boulevard where she stopped me in front of a polished mahogany door flanked by translucent paper windows. The aroma of tea drenched the air even before we stepped inside.

The teahouse had the cool, secluded atmosphere of a private pavilion, all polished mahogany walls and furniture, under hooded lantern light. A few heads shifted as we stepped inside, before returning to their murmured conversations. This felt like where the rich of Chiang Ping would meet and make deals. I supposed that being wives of mercenary naval leaders earned us a seat among the elite.

We were greeted by a white-haired woman dressed in a flowing pink *áo dài,* the same billowing garment worn by the girls in the street, only hers shimmered with lofty elegance. Our table sat beside an opaque paper window. Passing figures outside moved like shadow puppets.

"Madam Le, my cousin Cheng Yat Sou," Cheng Chat's wife said, then switched to Annamese; one of the few words I made out was the one for tea. Madam Le showed teeth as black as the soap merchant's, then bowed and shuffled away.

"Welcome to the center of the world. For our kind, that is," Chat's wife said.

"You don't seem happy about it."

"Oh, Younger Sister, forgive me. I'm spoiling your fun."

"No. I'm just, well, happy to be here. Strange, you know, how much I feel at home."

"A nest of runaways, smugglers, and thieves. Not sure I'd call it home, though."

A man at another table nodded to her in a familiar way. He looked like he'd stepped off an opera stage, with a topknot of thick white hair and a padded blue gown that men only wore in old paintings. Chat's wife returned the greeting.

"You know him?" I said.

"A local broker. Buys from us sometimes."

"Looks like an actor or a clown."

"Not so loud." She leaned in and lowered her voice. "He's a Ming Heung. Confusing, I know. End of the last dynasty, Ming loyalists bolted to Annam to save their necks. A lot in this town. He's probably fourth generation, but they act like the Ming will come back, then they'll return to China. See? I told you, this place attracts freaks like maggots to rotten meat."

I resisted the urge to stare. Was there nothing ordinary in Chiang Ping? Even the tea was unusual.

Madam Le delivered two lidded bowls in which longan fruits embedded with lotus seeds bathed in pale, fragrant tea. She placed a dish of melon seeds between us.

"I can't drink this. It's too pretty," I said.

Chat's wife sipped hers. "Drink it. Where we're going, beauty is in short supply."

While my tongue reveled in the tangy sweetness, I asked myself, *Why go anywhere else?* This town had whispered to me even before I'd arrived; its voice had gotten louder the moment I stepped onto the quay. But now it sang out in intense flavors and fragrance and colors. From what little I'd seen so far, Chiang Ping reminded me of parts of Kwangchow; it was certainly no filthier. Yet it possessed something completely different than anything else in the world. A nest of runaways, smugglers, and thieves, she'd called it. Wasn't that me? With or without military titles, wasn't that us? *The center of the world for our kind.*

Its odd stew of people and languages and costumes, even its fake jade and rotten pears, were all new in a way I'd never experienced; a new concept of newness. Throughout my life, newness had always been something to fear—new boats, new masters, ugly new customers with sickening new needs. But here, newness held a promise. History didn't matter; here you could invent your own, like the Ming Heung over there, absorbed in some imagined past; like the Long Hairs who'd stopped being Chinese. Here I could cast away my clothes, my hair, my entire past, and construct a whole new person: an admiral's wife, a woman of standing. As long as Cheng Yat intended to stay.

"I hope we're not leaving too soon," I said.

"Whenever that dog prick Chen Tin-bou shows up, then south to where the real savages live."

I savored my tea while hers sat until it went cold. Her eyes darted around the room, every direction except at me. Something bothered her, and it wasn't Chen Tin-bou. Finally, she replaced the lid on her cup and, folding her hands on the table, stunned me with a piercing look.

"What were you thinking about in there? Quicksilver?"

A half-chewed lotus seed stuck to my tongue. Her tone of voice told me her view of the matter. She needn't say more, but she did.

"Married three months already," she said.

I gave her the tiniest shrug. "It's too soon, don't you think?"

"Too soon for what? He's thirty-six and no son. Why do you think a man his age takes a wife? If he wanted free fucks, he didn't need a ceremony."

I spit the seed onto the upturned tea lid. "I thought we're sisters. Now you're my mother-in-law?"

She feigned amusement, spinning her tea bowl cover between her fingers. "If a wife doesn't conceive, there's no telling what a man will do. Some of us are worried."

"Oh, really? Some of who? You realize I've spent every day of my life keeping babies out of this belly. I'm not sure I could get pregnant even if I wanted to." I cracked a melon seed between my teeth, as loud as I could for emphasis. "And I don't want to."

"Nonsense." Chat's wife replaced the cover and pushed her tea away, spilling a little over the edge. She covered her mouth with her hand, but I could see how her lip trembled. "I wish you could meet my boys. Twelve and thirteen, real men now, working on other ships. Too big to run to mother anymore." She dabbed her eyes. "I understand why you think like you do. Maybe I would too if I'd lived your life. But it's time you accepted that that life is over. You're a married woman now. Every woman wants children, whether they know it or not."

Of course I knew—no such desire lurked inside me, not in the deepest, darkest recesses of my being. What was childhood except hard work and fear and a spot of innocence that is scraped and pummeled and smacked away all too soon? What were children other than an ever-present burden and worry? Maybe it was true that many women desired children, but what difference did that make to me? I didn't doubt that my mother wanted me. But how had that made her life better? What had she accomplished by having a son when all he'd done is die in childbirth and take her with him? Where was the happiness? Mine had ended before it even began. I wished childhood on no one.

"I'm sorry," I said. "Maybe I'm not a normal woman. Maybe that's why I feel like I belong in this place. Nothing is normal here. Why have a child just so a man can toss them onto other men's ships? Or pawn them off to pay a gambling debt? Or live with a horrible mother like me who'd resent them to my grave? The kindest thing I can do for a child is never let it be born."

A cloud seemed to engulf her face and carry her to another world. She sat quietly until life returned to her eyes; she nodded faintly, like she'd made up her mind to confess.

"I had a younger sister. Inseparable. We played everywhere. I think we never stopped laughing and teasing. One day in her eighth year she woke up covered in spots and hot as cinders. Then, she was gone. Like that. My joy died with her, for so many years. It was born again when I cradled my first son in my arms."

She stirred the melon seeds with a trembling finger. "No, the kindest thing you can do is make another person's life worth living."

I didn't know how to respond. Of all the strange new notions that had struck me today, the strangest of all was the idea that one person can make another happy.

Chat's wife reached across the table with that cloudy look back in her eyes. "You were born in the Goat Year, the year my sister departed. I look at you and think she's returned to me. Younger Sister."

I took the extended fingers, kneaded the chill out of her flesh, but I had no words to offer her. Was she seeing me or her sister's ghost?

"I wish you'll join us when we go home," she said.

"Home? What do you mean?"

"Tai Yue Shan, like I told you. He promised me again. When this is all finished, this business in Annam, we'll build a house there as grand as any stinking merchant's. Our sons will be traders, not pirates."

"But don't you feel that this place is home? You said it yourself: we fit in here."

"I'll tell you something, Younger Sister." She opened her bowl and signaled for fresh boiled water. "You're new here. It's lively, I admit. And they do make nice tea. But Chiang Ping is the ugliest town in the world, a place fit only for the scum of land and sea. Is that all you want to be?"

"It's all I've ever been. Our men, too. They have good reason to stay."

Cheng Chat's wife sighed. "To fight, sure. Ah-Chat likes the action. Talks-talks-talks about the thrill of victory. But let me tell you..."

She cracked a seed between her teeth, sucked the kernel from the shell, dropped the husk, and licked her finger.

"Let me tell you. To live a life like ours..." She sighed. "And then to retire rich, have a home in one place, surrounded by family—and to end up alive. Alive!" She leaned forward until our noses nearly touched and whispered deep in her throat, "That's true victory."

XIV
Deluge

The rain started in earnest while we sipped tea at our regular table at Madam Le's. It had become a routine for Chat's wife and me: venture into Chiang Ping for shopping—one day fruits and spices, another day indulging in silk kerchiefs or polished wood combs, as much as our purses and discretion would allow—afterward, refreshing ourselves with tea and chatter. I applied myself to learning the Annamese words for everything, but I didn't know *thunderstorm*. I left it to Chat's wife to apologize to Madam Le for leaving our guava tea unfinished and dashing to the docks before all the sampans disappeared.

The sampan lady pointed at the sky, refusing the long journey to the Green Islands anchorage, until we tripled her fare. I crawled under the canopy and unfolded one end of the banana leaf wrapped around my parcel. Finding the herbs inside dry, I tucked it back together and clasped it between my knees.

"I shouldn't say anything," Chat's wife said.

"Then don't."

She obviously had guessed why I'd come into town earlier than her today but had said nothing until now, leading with a sigh that was becoming familiar. "I'm looking forward to being auntie to your sons. Patience, I suppose."

"Patience for ten thousand years."

Thunder rolled across the sky. Water dripped through a hundred holes in the matted canopy. I tucked the parcel under my tunic and smiled to change the topic back to the silks we'd been examining for winter robes. "I can't decide between the turquoise or the lapis color."

"Best to remain undecided until we find more generous husbands."

The boat woman dropped off Chat's wife, then pressed me for four times the fare until I threatened to send her back empty-handed.

By the time we reached my junk, I had to sprint through torrents sweeping like freshwater waves across our deck. What looked like the entire male crew huddled outside in the rain, making way for me as I passed.

"Cheng Yat Sou, have you eaten yet?"

"Cheng Yat Sou, good health!"

How cheerful they were. Today must have been pay day.

Inside the cabin, Cheng Yat sat among stacks of sycee silver ingots and baskets of copper cash coins, facing the fat purser, himself bent over a ledger. I hid behind a chest and changed into dry clothes, rolled my packet inside an old shirt, and buried it beneath a stack of beddings, always keeping one eye on Cheng Yat; he was too busy sorting money into pouches to have noticed.

"You sold the salt, then?" I said.

"Enough."

The purser opened the door a crack and called out a name. Moments later a crewman crouched at the threshold with open hands, into which the purser placed a pouch and a string of cash.

I slid beside Cheng Yat. The purser tilted the ledger away from me, as if I could read it. What if I could? What would I find in those pages?

"Where's the commander's name on that list?" I said.

"Never mind," Cheng Yat said.

"What do you mean, never mind? I just want to see the captain's share."

Cheng Yat looked at the purser and shrugged. He grabbed three pouches from the mound and dropped them in front of me. "Captain's share."

I weighed one in my hand. "That's all?"

Cheng Yat grunted and continued stuffing sycee into pouches.

I waddled over to the purser, imitating the last crewman's crouch, and opened my palms. "I'll take my share now."

The purser's eyes burned a hole in the ledger. He called the next name on his list. When he finished, I put out my hand again. "I want my share. I've worked like any man, haven't I?"

"Madam Cheng, if you'll please—"

"Sit down, wife," Cheng Yat said.

"What about the other women? Everyone works hard on this ship."

Cheng Yat held his temper for once. "We give the unmarried women—"

126

"Then I unmarry you until I get paid." I clenched my lips to show I was serious.

"I just gave you my share. Is that not enough? You want the whole ship? Now be quiet."

"I can't believe the captain gets only—"

"I said be quiet!"

"But don't you think—?"

I was interrupted by a furious knock at the door.

"Tell them to wait," I said. "We need to discuss—"

The pounding became more insistent. The door slid open before the purser could reach it. An unfamiliar sailor leaned his dripping head inside, panting heavily.

"Sorry, Captain. I'm from..." He took a deep breath and pointed away. "Captain Cheng Chat calls you. Fast-fast!"

Cheng Yat dropped the purse he was working on. "What happened?"

"Chen—" The sailor stopped himself, glancing at the purser, then at me. "May I speak in front of—"

"Speak!"

The sailor lowered his voice to a loud whisper. "Chen Tin-bou surrendered."

Of course I was not invited to join him for the crossing to his cousin's ship, nor did I ask, and not just because of the rain and lightning. I wasn't eager to learn the news.

No one on board knew what had happened, but I feared what it meant. Chen Tin-bou had led us to Annam. Though he hadn't actually led us; he had never shown up. Without him in charge, we would all scatter like ants. I watched the glamorous foreign life I'd already constructed for myself being washed away forever in these merciless rains.

The lightning and downpours didn't relent for another two days. I didn't blame Cheng Yat for not returning. Stepping outside for even a moment was like walking into a bombardment of stinging wet buckshot.

By the third day I was torturing myself with questions. He needed to come back. I needed to know. *When do we leave here? Are we returning to Tunghoi?* Maybe Cheng Chat's wife would get her wish, and we'd join them on Tai Yue Shan.

I had just replaced a wick in the cabin lamp when what I first took as thunder turned into heavy footsteps on the companionway.

The door flew open.

Cheng Yat threw himself into the room, leaving a stream of puddles behind as he bounded past me straight for the storage chest and dragged it from the wall. He shoved his arm behind it, then spun on his knees, heaving like a beast. In the weak light, his face flushed almost black, his eyes streaked red though I smelled no wine on his breath. He grabbed my slippers from the corner and shook them out before tossing them at the wall.

"Where is it?" He picked my coat from the floor, felt the pockets, then bunched it up and threw it at me. "Where the hell is it?"

I knew then that I'd been betrayed. Trying to be inconspicuous, I turned one foot toward the bed, but he understood. His eyes went straight to the target.

I'd purchased the pillow back in Tunghoi, palm thatch fastened around a stiff wooden frame. He and I lunged at the same time. It crackled but held my weight as I fell on it first. Cheng Yat shoved a knee into my back, twisting my arm behind me until I rolled sideways, clutching the pillow with my free arm. He let out a roar and yanked the pillow from my grip.

It didn't take him long to discover the flap I'd sewn into one end. He thrust his hand inside, pulled out a paper packet, and tore it open. Twigs, leaves, bark, and powder blew around the room, scattered by wind rushing through the open door.

He plucked out one packet after another and hurled them through the door where the wind broke them apart, dispersing their contents into the rainy night. At last he removed a bundle of dried lotus leaves, bit off a mouthful, chewed and spat the brown slimy mass onto the threshold.

"Is that enough?" he said. "Enough to kill a worthless girl? How much do you need to kill a boy?"

The remaining leaves flew from his hand. He dropped the empty pillow on the floor, stomped on it over and over, and kicked the shapeless tangle into the dark.

Then he went for me with a vicious kick in the ribs, but I refused him the satisfaction of showing pain.

"Slut! It's time you acted like a wife!"

He grabbed my hair and dragged me toward the mat. The only pain I felt was in my heart. Someone I'd considered a friend, who'd called me her sister, how could she be capable of such stinging betrayal? My hands balled into fists, but I was too weak to fight when he tugged down my trousers and forced my legs apart with his knees.

His full body weight pressed me down, constricting my lungs to desperate gasps of his sour, hot breath. He jerked and stung me, grunting in my face, but I felt only blackness in my heart and groin. Then he groaned one last time and rolled off, leaving a wet chill on my thighs.

I spent my last strength crawling to the door. The threshold was coated in a slimy mass of spat-out chewed lotus. I pressed my lips into it. My tongue raked the cracks and gutters for every sour lump, sucking and swallowing while rain gunned the back of my head. I showed him my slime-smeared lips, then licked them clean, grimacing at the bitter taste, his bitter face, my bitter heart.

"I hope I've killed your son," I said.

His hands went for my throat. My head smacked the floor. Acidic liquid spurted up my throat. I forced myself to swallow.

He pressed his face close to mine. "Then we just do it again, don't we?"

"Get off me."

"Remember you said you'd done your job? You wanted to be paid like the men? You lied! You haven't done the duty expected of a wife."

"Go put it in your little blossom boy's dirt hole."

His cheeks puffed; his eyes bulged. The lamplight tinted them animal-like yellow. Then he did the most unfathomable thing. His hands let go. He sat up.

And smiled. "Don't speak about my son like that."

A chill spread up my spine and through my arms and legs.

"I adopted Po Tsai. Made it official in front of the other men," Cheng Yat said. "You're his mother now."

Crawling face-up like a crab, I backed out the door, shaking my head. "Don't touch me," I said. "Get away. Don't touch."

I lay on the companionway, too spent to move despite the chilly downpour pounding my naked legs. He tossed my trousers at me. I flung them aside. Let the rain wash me clean.

A small object sailed through the doorway and landed with a metallic clank beside me.

"Seaman's share," he called as the door slid shut.

My trousers were so heavy with water I had to rest between pulling on each leg. Running down the steps left me breathless.

I would leave in the morning and disappear into Chiang Ping. The purse in my hand would support me for a while. What I needed was a place for tonight. The deck was empty, every hatch bolted shut against the weather.

I could stay with Ah-Yi, crowd into her bunk. I stood over her hold, prepared to knock, then decided against it. I didn't want to tell her the story. I didn't want to talk to anyone.

The galley hatch was firmly closed. I could possibly squeeze into the armory closet.

Leaning on the mainmast, all my dreams and doubts and anger swirled around me like the unending deluge. What would I do in Chiang Ping when the money ran out? I'd be just another exile among the flotsam and jetsam, fugitives and thieves. What skill could I fall back on to survive? I'd take my life before returning to my despicable former trade.

What had Ah-Yi said? *You can't sail backward.*

My back slid down the mast. I sat on the cowling, feet drowning in a puddle. I'd been a fool to think I could hide my precious antidote to motherhood forever. Now he'd found out in the worst possible way, at the cost of enormous face in front of his cousin and, even worse, men of lower rank.

No sailing backwards, but what was ahead? This was my life: wife of a glorified bandit. *I'm one of them now,* I'd told myself that night which seemed a lifetime ago. If that were so, if I were to survive in this world of pirates and mercenaries, I had to be more than a wife, more than a breeding cow. He wanted a son? Let him have that one, the one he takes to bed!

How stupid to think I could be just a wife! How stupid to depend on a man like Cheng Yat! How stupid to depend on any man!

I stood, extended my arm back, and threw the little purse over the bulwark. I was through with depending on Cheng Yat. I'd make that man depend on me!

I returned to the cabin and found Cheng Yat stretched out, asleep on the mat, while Cheung Po Tsai attended the shrine. I waited for the boy to complete his prayer, then wove every thread of composure into my voice.

"Please get out."

Po Tsai pulled a hat from the corner and bowed his head.

"Yes, dear Mother."

"I'm not—" I stopped my tongue. I'd never wanted a child, and here I supposedly had a grown son. Then let him obey me like one. "And never enter this cabin again."

I thought I heard him laugh to himself as he passed me on his way out the door.

XV
Poetry

I waited at the usual table beside the yellow paper window, waving away the mildew smell. The teahouse floor was damp and tracked with mud.

After ten days of relentless downpours, Chiang Ping reminded me of an aging whore who'd been washed free of makeup. Celestial Dynasty Street was ankle deep in mud, garbage, rat and dog carcasses, and things I didn't want to imagine. Goods were stacked out on the streets while shopkeepers salvaged inventories wrecked by the flooding. The whole town smelled of rot. Most distressing of all, everywhere were refugees from the surrounding countryside with hands out for food or money, mouths filled with stories of woe about homes, animals, and crops swept away by raging floods.

Some Ming Heung at a nearby table repeated a rumor that the Annamese emperor's brother's palace, somewhere near the capital, had collapsed under the heavenly onslaught of rain.

Cheng Chat's wife finally arrived, muttering apologies. I summoned the proprietor and attempted to order with my few words of Annamese.

"So clever," Madam Le said. "You speak so well." She touched my shoulder before moving to another customer.

Chat's wife's face looked swollen and tired, her head wrapped tightly in a red headscarf. She was in obvious bad humor—or was it guilt? I skipped the niceties.

"You told him."

"I heard what that brute did to you. I'm so sorry," she said. "But I didn't need to tell him."

"What do you mean, *didn't need to?*"

"Oh, please. Chiang Ping has no shortage of stabbing tongues who delight in reporting which herbs Cheng Yat's esteemed wife is seen buying."

"But you confirmed it to him. Yes or no?"

"Younger Sister, I never said a word to your husband."

"Don't call me that! You don't deserve to call me sister!"

Even Madam Le could see how deeply my remark stung; she served our tea and tactfully backed away. Chat's wife's hand trembled as she picked up the pot and leaned across the table to pour for me. That was when I noticed the lump protruding under her headscarf.

"Your turtle egg husband hit you?"

"He's frustrated," she said, with a lightness that didn't match the set of her face. "They elect him the new commander, and suddenly everyone expects him to know everything. Even he expects so. And the rain kept delaying his trip to the capital."

"That isn't why he beat you."

She studied the water stains on the window, then refilled her tea, though she'd only taken a sip. "My husband is very—how can I say?—opinionated."

"Of course I know." And I guessed by her manner that the opinions in question had something to do with me.

She blew steam from her cup. "He says you're trying to run your husband's business. His words, not mine."

"How dare he—"

"He isn't the only one, sister. Word spreads that you're trying to grab money, turn his men against him—"

"Lying ghosts! Who?"

"I'm sure you're aware of Leung's—your Taumuk's—hostility, it's no secret. Your husband's purser, too."

"They can go die!" I accidentally knocked over my teacup with an angry sweep of my hand. "Maybe I *should* run his business! He doesn't have the bladder to stand up to your pigeon-eyed husband!"

We looked away from each other while a servant wiped the table.

Chat's wife waved him away and said, "My husband merely remarked that you should put less effort into counting sycee and more into producing a son."

"Which is your opinion as well, yes? And it's just as much none of your business." It was hard enough dealing with Cheng Yat's temper. I wasn't about to take orders from other men, especially relayed through their wives. Damn every man in the world! And every woman too!

Younger Sister, I already told you, I didn't—"

"I'm not your sister! Your sister is dead!" I bolted from my chair, not caring about the eyes turning my way. "I know what you think, what everyone thinks—once a whore, always one, right? Only a whore beds men without spewing out babies."

"Enough! Sit down and stop embarrassing yourself. You don't know a word of what I think."

She pulled her headscarf back, revealing raw bald spots where hair had been torn from her scalp.

"Whatever my husband might accuse you of, I defend your name, even if it makes me bleed. Dear Younger Sister."

We held hands, exchanging hardly a word, for the whole return sampan journey. Newly arrived ships crowded the anchorage between Big and Small Green Islands. Wu-shek Yi was back from wherever he'd been. Another fleet at the north end surrounded a large junk flying black and white banners.

Chat's wife scowled at the sight.

"You know them?" I said.

She shrugged. "Sadly, I do."

"Friend or devil? Let me guess. The latter?"

"Kwok Podai. Our very own wise man. Or so he'll assure you."

The sampan coasted close to the beach. I dropped coins into the boat woman's hand and waded ashore. I sent men to unload the tung oil and rice I'd purchased in town. Cheng Chat's wife offered me a nod and a smile as the sampan pulled away.

Junks lay careened up and down the island's shore like beached whales. The air crackled with the clinking of chisels and hammers. Women sat shaving bamboo into fleece and stuffing it in baskets. I crossed a rock outcrop, shielding my face against stray fragments from men pulverizing oyster shells with sledgehammers. Farther along, men and women filled vats with shell dust and bamboo fleece, waiting for the oil I'd brought, to combine it all into *yau fui* for ships' caulking. Amidst the noise and activity, I heard a man call for his mother.

He meant me.

135

Cheung Po Tsai leaned on a hammer, bare chest shimmering with sweat, while the children swept his crushed shells into buckets. He waved and smiled my way. It was he who had just called me the thing that I certainly was not.

I sucked in my breath and said, "Where's our ship?"

He jerked a thumb, laughed, and returned to his work.

Our junk sprawled sideways on the sand, covered with men chiseling barnacles from the hull. Thick black smoke engulfed one end—rooting out wood worms. I hoped all my clothing had been properly moved.

I found Cheng Yat absorbed in inspecting the rudder and waited for him to notice me. Every word we'd exchanged these past few days had been about ship's business, which had kept us cordial at least.

"I got the oil," I finally said. "You were right about that dealer, a genuine rat. But about the price..."

I shook my purse so it jingled. "Saved us two whole taels. It pays to use the local devil's language."

He turned at the sound and raised his eyebrows in a show of being impressed. Faint praise was better than none, though a few words might have helped.

"You're very welcome. Where are we supposed to stay tonight?"

"We call on Kwok Podai." He pointed his nose across the anchorage. "He married my cousin. Let's see if you can act like a wife tonight."

Kwok Podai looked more like a scholar than a seaman in a full-length indigo robe, which shimmered as he welcomed us aboard with a formal bow. A square jaw and deep hooded brows were capped by a polished dome of scalp, though his queue fell long and loose and unbraided, like the tail of an untamed horse. But for all his singular appearance, his eyes took me in like any other man's.

He invited us to a round table mid-deck and offered me the stool closest to the mast.

"Madam Cheng, I believe this seat will best shelter you from the wind." It also just happened to place me directly facing him.

Kwok's wife Wong-yan, a slight crane-like woman who bore no resemblance to Cheng Yat despite being related, orbited the table, checking the food and replenishing drinks, performing the role of dutiful wife. The evening calm was disturbed only by the occasional buzz of a moth incinerating itself in a lantern flame.

I was pleased to discover that, like Cheng Yat, Kwok Podai didn't indulge in talk about past glories. Rather, he cut straight to business.

"More rumors are floating around this harbor than ships." He enunciated like an educated man. "It's difficult to believe that Chen Tin-bou would have tricked me into returning to his command and then turned around and surrendered to the authorities."

"Believe it," Cheng Yat said. "We're all fools. That's why we're friends. What I want to know is whether he took all our salaries with him."

Kwok refilled Cheng Yat's and his wine cups. "The same thought occurred to me. So, my friend, you still intend to serve the little emperor?"

"Let's see what Chat finds out in the capital. Maybe better off without the scoundrel Chen."

This was the first I'd heard such talk. The thought of staying lifted my spirits so much that I reached for my cup to celebrate. Kwok filled it to the brim, then raised his for a toast.

"Heaven and earth have always loved wine, so how could loving wine shame heaven?" he said. "Our poet Li Po made excuses for us all."

He drank and Cheng Yat and I followed. "To the new Annamese navy," Kwok said. "I believe it's your first time past the pillars, Madam Cheng?"

This strange man spoke in poetry and riddles.

"Never mind him," Cheng Yat said. "Talks of those pillars every time, but nobody's ever seen them."

"My friend, I never saw your lovely wife before, but I'm happy to say that she most definitely exists. What do you think, Madam Cheng? Do you have to see something with your own eyes to believe in its existence?"

"Since I have no idea what you're talking about, its existence doesn't concern me. Or should it?" I replied.

"Excellent answer. Perhaps I should explain. Legend has it that many centuries ago our General Ma Yuan erected a pair of bronze pillars to mark the boundary with Annam." Raising his arms to illustrate, he continued, "On our coming journey, we pass those pillars without knowing where they are, yet we sense the transition. Just as there are boundaries between you and myself which we don't see with our eyes, yet we know they're there."

Cheng Yat laughed. "You have that right. This one is harder than forged iron!"

I held my tongue, reminding myself to act civil in front of strangers. On first meeting, Kwok Podai seemed like a difficult man, charming yet pompous in the way he spouted words, though it was astonishing to meet a sea bandit who had anything to discuss besides the usual—that is, who had anything worth discussing at all. Still, underneath all the worldly talk, his message to me was quite plain: a tilt in his mouth and glimmer in his lively eyes that sent a signal straight to my groin.

The food was simple, scraped together, but satisfying. Kwok and Cheng Yat speculated about Chen Tin-bou and Annamese officials, which was lost on me. All I cared was that we would stay in Annam, assuming Cheng Chat's visit to the capital resulted in his appointment as Chen's replacement in command. But I couldn't think of Cheng Chat without thoughts intruding about his brutal treatment of his wife, all because of me. At the same time, my body remembered my husband's kicks and punches.

Meanwhile, I was a rabbit stalked by a tiger. The hunter, trying not to alarm his prey, stole glances, never lingering too long, but I knew. I studied Kwok: lanky and muscular, almost feline in his manner, eyes with a life of their own, a tongue that colored the air with words. His attentions made my cheeks burn, or was it the wine? I set down my half-empty cup and placed my hand over it when Kwok raised the wine flask.

He pretended surprise, then cleared his throat and recited like an actor:

> *I am drunk, long to sleep;*
> *Sir, go a little—*
> *Bring your zither, if you please,*
> *Early tomorrow.*

"One of Li Po's more amusing little gems," he added.

I covered my mouth too late to hide a giggle. He was making fun of me, yet what could be more ridiculous than a pirate reciting poetry?

A lantern stuttered and faded. While Kwok performed another verse about drinking, Wong-yan got up and refilled the lamp. She sat again, straight as before, surely aware of her husband's straying attention, but her only expression was a yawn hidden behind her hand.

"I suspect that our women are tired, or bored of our talk, or both," Kwok said.

He was partially right. I'd had a long day. In situations like this I was used to retiring alone while the men sat up drinking half the night.

"I find nothing boring about being entertained with poetry, but I'm certain you men have better things to discuss." I moved my stool back, signaling my intention to go. Kwok's wife was having trouble keeping her head up.

"Leave her," Kwok said. "Perhaps I can show you to your compartment?"

Cheng Yat pulled the wine flask closer, laughing when he nearly spilled it; even in the dim light his face glowed drunken red. "Bring another on your way back."

Kwok escorted me across the deck. In the dark, his ship looked of similar size to ours, maybe a bit larger, certainly less cluttered: crates lined the bulwarks, ropes neatly coiled.

He paused at a hatch which stood out as darker than the rest, some kind of polished wood. "Did you say you enjoy poetry? If you're still awake, you might be interested to see my library."

I'd never heard any person in my life mention a library, nor had I ever stepped inside one. But to discover one on a pirate ship? He must have noticed my surprise.

"Come, it's just here." He unhooked a lamp from the side rail, slid open the bolt and invited me to go first. I lost my footing on the ladder and stumbled backward against a bulkhead, though my head struck something soft. As Kwok descended with the lamp, light spread through the room, revealing walls lined top to bottom with books and scrolls.

"My humble sanctuary," he said.

That he could read was surprising in itself. I'd never met a literate boat person; that was why captains like Cheng Yat employed pursers. I had never even held a book. Without asking permission, I pulled one from a shelf. It was both heavier and more delicate than I'd imagined, a dense stack of paper sewn together along one edge.

"You've read all these?" I said.

"Sadly, yes. My library needs replenishment."

He hooked the lamp on the wall and invited me to sit on a polished bench in the center of the room. I opened the book at random across my lap, its paper soft yet as brittle as an old man's skin. An ink drawing filled one page: a mountain pagoda, surrounded by worm-like calligraphy. Several pages later, a drawing of a chrysanthemum nestled between blocks of text. I held it closer, trying to discern meaning from the printed words, but they may as well have been chicken scratches in the dirt.

"You know this poem?" Kwok said. Without me noticing, he'd sat beside me.

"Never read it before." I snapped the book shut.

"Hsieh Ling-yun, a landscape poem with a message: *Cherish transformation, mind will be unbound.* One of his last, written while exiled in Kwangchow. Do you know Kwangchow?"

My breath held still. What was the meaning of his remark? What did he know about me? I wondered which whisperings had reached his ears, and what that made me in his deeply piercing eyes.

"I've been to Kwangchow," I said, attempting an offhand tone. "Briefly. Smelly place."

"Ah, so have I. More than briefly. Perhaps we've seen each other before without realizing."

Cautiously, I said, "In a library?"

"Ha! The only library I ever saw was the one I practically lived in, belonging to my so-called master. If you had come to visit, I'd have remembered."

"So where might you have seen me?" I hoped that the soft light disguised my trembling.

"Nowhere, I'm afraid, unless you were in the habit of befriending street beggars, one of the jobs he assigned me. The only other times I left that dark hole were when I ran away."

"I'd wondered how a scholar ended up commanding a bandit— well, I really don't know what kind of ship this is."

"Bandit. Pirate. Scum floating on the sea. But no scholar. My father thought he'd turn me into one. Thought if I learned to read and write, I could escape a life of fishing like his and work as a clerk in the city. So, he indentured me to a drunken old scribe in Kwangchow, who treated me more as slave than student. In between begging coins for him and wiping up his piss, I managed to learn something before I ran away...But never mind my story, we all have our troubled pasts. This room around us, this orchard of poems, is my escape into a better world."

My gut twisted so hard it hurt. Another father selling away a child, although perhaps for a nobler purpose. What I might have done if I'd been sold to a scribe instead.

"How nice to have such an orchard," I said.

Kwok had opened the book to another page.

"Indeed. Here's a fruit you may know, quite famous, by Sit Tou. Tang poet? A thousand years old and resonates still. But a woman poet. More authentic, I propose, coming from your mouth." He offered me the book.

"So old, isn't it?" I said. "I'm not so fond of the past."

He regarded me as though he understood the double intention of my words, including the suggestion that our histories linked us. He replaced the book and returned to the bench with another.

"This will please you then. Quite new. Are there any contemporary poets you prefer?"

We held each other's gaze. Lamplight made his cheeks glow like a second set of eyes.

"Actually, I don't read poetry."

"Mm. I suppose scribblings on a page are no substitute for real human flesh and blood."

The room was heating up, whether from our close confinement or the rush of blood to my skin, I couldn't tell. With a slow blink, I turned my head aside.

"Perhaps you prefer stories." He left the bench and squatted in front of a low shelf, walking his fingers across similar-looking volumes, then pulled one free. He turned around, still in a crouch directly before me.

"This one's quite recent. *Dream of the Red Chamber.* Can't say I've finished it. Difficult to care about the pining of an idle rich boy. But if you'd care to—"

"No stories."

"I see. What do you read then?"

Enough with the teasing. This man was confident—overly so—he was eloquent and clever. But he was as slippery and transparent as water, in which it would be too easy to drown.

"I read men."

A single drop of sweat slithered down my neck. Dust sparkled in the lantern's glow like stars.

"I'm afraid to ask what you read in me," he said.

"You should be."

His mouth twitched, as though considering the thought, then formed a smile.

"I propose a trade. I teach you to read books. You teach me a woman's ways to read men."

"I wouldn't want to give away my secrets."

"Nor would I expect you to. Hence my proposing a fair trade. We can start with mine."

He returned to his place beside me on the bench, opening the book with one cover on his lap, the other on mine. It threatened to collapse into the gap between us. He slid closer until we nearly touched.

Kwok's finger traced a simple character of three vertical strokes. "Three lines, one curving aside at the end, like water rushing downstream. River."

He turned a few pages until he found what he wanted. "Three strokes again, all left to right. No, nothing to do with water. Number three."

His sleeve lightly brushed my hand when he imitated the lines of another word.

"Again, three strokes, tallest in the middle, all rooted on the ground. Mountain."

I leaned in to study the hook of the second stroke, but my head blocked the light. When I straightened up, his face was a finger's breadth away, half in the light, the other half a dark mask.

"Your turn," he said.

"My turn?"

"You said you read men." He opened his arms, letting the book drop. "Read me."

"For three words? Not a fair deal."

"A hard bargainer, I see. I'll have to work harder to earn it."

I stood on the edge of a precipice looking at a fire below. His slightest nudge might have sent me falling. I should have stopped here. I should have stood up and yawned and said it was time for me to go to my room, alone. For him to return to Cheng Yat and his wine.

The vessel shifted on a gentle swell, tipping his shoulder onto mine. We lingered a heartbeat too long, until I shifted away.

"Maybe now isn't a good time for lessons," I said.

"Maybe it isn't. But your presence brings to mind a poem. Will you allow me to share? No, I don't need a book. It's up here." He pointed to his brow.

"Another Tang poet, I'm afraid." He cleared his throat and recited:

It's dusk, my boat such tranquil silence,
mist rising over waters deep and still,
and to welcome a guest for the night,
there's evening wine, an autumn chill.

His voice leapt and swooped like swallows swooping and swirling through the confines of the room. My mother had told me simple stories, and I had watched street bards in Kwangchow parks. But never in my life had anyone read aloud just for me.

A master at the gate of Way, my visitor
arrives from exalted mountain peaks,
lofty cloudswept face raised all delight,
heart all sage clarity, spacious and free.

Our thoughts begin where words end.
Refining dark-enigma depths, we gaze
quiet mystery into each other and smile,
sharing the mind that's forgotten mind.

He finished. My mind hadn't understood every phrase, yet something inside me had shifted.

Who knew that words, through their sounds and textures, separate from their meaning, could stir a person's soul? How could it be that a poet dead for centuries could manipulate my heart through the tongue of this strange, handsome, dangerous man? What new course might I chart for myself if I knew how to read?

And how long had I been holding my breath?

I leaned back and steadied myself, inadvertently lowering a hand onto his.

The lamp light trembled, the room shimmered. A cool breeze filtered in. I felt another, heavier presence.

Overhead, framed through the dark hatchway, Cheng Yat's nose, cheeks, and forehead hovered like moths.

XVI
Ink

⸙⸙⸙⸙⸙⸙⸙⸙⸙

Cheng Yat said nothing about what he might have seen, or imagined, or could accuse me of. He said nothing to me at all in the days that followed except to talk about the careening and the rain—less frequent but still setting the work back. In turn, I told him about the growing numbers of refugees crowding into Chiang Ping and the rumors of fighting in the south. He kept his thoughts to himself whenever I mentioned Cheng Chat. The longer we waited for his cousin's return, the deeper the dread over what news he might bring from the capital, Thang Long: to go to battle or return to China. Either way, it meant leaving Chiang Ping.

He and Kwok Podai spoke of nothing else when the latter came to inspect our newly refloated junk. The topic upset me, and I was wary of Kwok's flirtations—and perhaps of my own response. I excused myself to the upper deck where the rain had subsided to an unnoticeable mist. My eyes scanned the ongoing boat works along the shore while my mind shuttled between Chiang Ping lanes filled with shops and *áo dài* girls and a dusty hold filled with books.

Kwok found me there, as if by chance. We exchanged observations about the weather, which prompted another poem—pale blue firmaments or something of the sort. He left me feeling like one of the breeze-stirred leaves in his verse.

What would he say if he saw me now, on the floor of a window-less room, holding a brush over ink-spattered paper? The Chinese monk who'd agreed to tutor me was the first teacher I'd ever had in my life, and possibly the worst, but I had no other choice. For a stiff extra fee, he agreed to keep our meetings secret.

"I'll let you get away with those *pit* strokes for today, but look at that vertical!" The skinny little man loomed over my shoulder. "Here, here, here, like crippled worms! Do a hundred more."

I slapped down the brush. "But it isn't even a word! I don't care how it looks. I just want to read—"

I stopped my mouth before I said "poetry". I'd risked enough by telling him that I wanted to read ship ledgers.

"Of course it isn't a word! How do expect to write words until you master your brush? If a tiger was clothed like a dog, would you praise it for its stripes?"

"I've never seen a tiger, so I wouldn't know."

"Exactly! Your strokes should all be tigers, so there's no mistaking them. And while you're reflecting on that, get to work with your ink stone. That...*fluid* you pretend to write with is so weak I could have it for tea."

After ten days with my alleged master, I could read precisely as many words and write far fewer. My progress might have been faster if I'd had the opportunity to practice. But where was I to spread paper and brushes on our ship without provoking Cheng Yat? Water folk didn't learn to read and write. Especially no woman would dare. Worse, a man—a commander—wouldn't tolerate a wife who outshone him. And even if he didn't object for those reasons, what if he suspected some deeper-held motive, one that might contain a granule of truth?

I finished my hundred practice strokes, received the monk's grudging approval, rolled my writing book around my brushes, and stuffed everything into my bag. After checking that the rain had stopped, I stepped outside into the sloping lane. Who was I fooling, at the old age of twenty-seven, thinking I could learn my strokes like a schoolboy? At the rate I was going, I would have to live to three hundred before I could read a simple New Year couplet.

A cold wind funneled up the passage, wrapping around my neck. I huddled over and quickened my pace. People filled Celestial Dynasty Street, taking advantage of the break in the weather. I decided to do the same: skip Madam Le's today and return to the ship before the next downpour. I hurried toward the docks at the head of the street, when I saw him.

Kwok was involved in an animated discussion with a knot of Chinese and Annamese men. Dressed again as half-sailor, half-scholar, with his neatly groomed, sculpted face, he was a swan among geese. He looked up. Our eyes met.

He nodded to his cohorts, gestured like he was excusing himself. The bag in my hand became heavy as iron. What if he could tell what was inside? What if he asked? If he insisted, would I show him? My work was too embarrassing. My motive too obvious. He'd invite me for practice. I might, in a moment of weakness, accept.

A hand grabbed my elbow from behind.

"Wah! Glad I saw you. Let's go!"

Cheung Po Tsai tugged me sideways.

"What are you doing?" I said.

"We have to get back. Hurry! Here, I'll take your bag."

He already had one handle. In my hurry to snatch it back, the latch popped open. The practice book uncurled; brushes clattered against each other. I clamped it shut, but too late. Would Kwok have spotted them from that far?

"Don't you dare tell anyone what's in my bag," I said. "What's your problem?"

"Oh, I thought you knew. Cheng Chat is back."

I let him lead me to the dock, turning my head once to shrug my eyes at Kwok.

The sampan left the river through a fresh rain while I hugged the bag close. My time in Chiang Ping had come to an end.

XVII
Cavalry

🙰

Two days later, two hundred ships followed Cheng Chat out of the anchorage. Destination: central Annam.

If this was war, then better we'd stayed in Chiang Ping. I thought we would end a month of uncertainty, rumors, and restlessness with a sense of head-held-high mission like those the men loved to boast about at countless drinking sessions back in Tunghoi. Instead, we were stuck with deck loads of frightened, seasick Annamese soldiers, many of them children, picked up in the port of Haiphong, to be ferried a thousand *li* down the coast for a mobilization that no one, even their clueless commanders, knew anything about. Three hundred mouths chewing betel nut day and night left our deck looking like a bloodier battlefield than any they might face.

Even Ah-Yi complained, "Filthy monkeys! All that betel rots their brains. Take days to scrape these decks clean."

I'd picked up enough unsavory Annamese to advise her, "You don't want to hear what they're saying about us."

Finally, in the middle of the sixth day, the Taumuk never sounded so happy as when he announced:

"Cast anchors! Lower sails! Get this stinking rabble off my ship!"

Sampans, pole boats, and bamboo rafts swarmed from shore to unload our human cargo. The disembarkation immediately fell into chaos. Soldiers pushed and shoved and leapt over the sides, some missing their targets, their heavy packs dragging them under the waves. It seemed almost a pleasure to drown in water as blue as painter's ink.

A long, curving beach of blinding white sand stretched from one end of the world to the other, fringed by an unending line of droop-headed coconut trees holding back vegetation so thick it seemed that nothing could penetrate it. My first sight of a jungle. Here and there, small clearings and canvas sheets indicated some sort of camp.

Cheng Yat was busy with the purser. I asked the Taumuk, "Where are we?"

"If I knew the name, I wouldn't be allowed to tell you. But I don't, so that makes things easy between us."

In the morning, while Cheng Yat put on his new uniform as Admiral of the Black Junks of the Imperial Annamese Navy, I stood at his back smoothing wrinkles in the silk.

"Woman, I'm not your child."

"Trying to help you look like an admiral, not a beggar."

His grunt bordered on amused. He must have been in good humor on his way to his first command conference. I hoped he appreciated my effort to be a proper admiral's wife.

Of course, there was no room for me in the sampan. I had to wait to join the cook and three empty oil casks on a hired ferry to shore.

Goods sellers surrounded us before our feet touched dry ground, offering fruits, hats, and coconut shell amulets. Word had obviously spread that thirty thousand fresh soldiers had arrived in the area. Probably every hawker and thief in central Annam had converged on this beach.

I followed the cook through a clearing in the trees and promptly lost him in a makeshift city of tents. Men, mostly young and displaying their brown bodies in little more than loincloths, moved in every direction, carrying buckets or sacks or heavy crates, stepping between groups tending cook fires or assembling weapons. Bright red betel spit flew from every direction. Here and there, a bullock dragged a cart, pigs and geese strained at harness straps, feral dogs ran in small packs. The sole difference between this encampment and a real city was that the only woman in sight was me.

Talk hushed as I passed; lewd comments followed in my wake. Realizing too late that a woman smartly dressed in snug red silk, passing alone through a military camp, was not a practical notion, I quickened my pace toward a canvas pavilion at a bend in the coast which I presumed to be the command center.

Two men blocked my way—one tall, the other shaped like a barrel—

and invited me in fake-polite Annamese to join them in their tent. I reached for a stone on the ground and, in my most practiced Annamese, invited them to go fuck their canine mothers.

I broke off in a run.

Uniformed sentries blocked me at the pavilion entrance. I tried elbowing my way through, barely able to stammer, "Admiral's wife."

A mousy little mustached official stuck his head out, regarding me as if I were something he'd spat out at lunch.

In mixed dialects, I said, "Let me in. Admiral Cheng Yat. His wife."

"I'm sorry, madam. They're quite busy."

Taking a chance with my Annamese, I smiled sweetly. "Is my friend the emperor inside? Please tell him Madam Cheng Yat is answering his summons."

His mustache twitched while he made up his mind. His head retreated. The flap opened for me.

The enclosed pavilion was hot and stuffy, meagerly lit by a single opening in the ceiling. Every man wore a uniform—black like Cheng Yat's for navy men. I guessed blue tunics indicated army. Two men were conspicuous in formal gowns of white and gold. These I took to be members of the Tay-son ruling clan, though neither was young enough to be the teenaged emperor. They stood with Cheng Chat, all three absorbed in a map on a table.

Another man in shimmering black said something to the royals, then turned his head. Kwok Podai smiled from across the room. I wasn't difficult to spot, a red plum in a jungle of blue and black. The two royals followed his look in my direction. I withstood their gaze until they turned back to the map.

Out of nowhere Cheng Yat sidestepped through the gathering and pulled me into a corner.

"You're not supposed to be here."

"You never said I shouldn't."

"I would think it's obvious. No women."

A bell rang. People drifted toward one end of the pavilion.

"I'll send someone to escort you back," Cheng Yat said.

"Send me a drink. I'm sweating in this heat."

Daylight abruptly flooded the tent. One entire wall rose like a curtain.

"Please go without a fuss," he said.

I waited for him to press through the crowd to rejoin the higher ranks, after which I found a place where I could see the view if I stood on my toes.

The sudden bright sunlight must have tricked my eyes. At the other end of a flat grassy clearing, an entire banana grove's enormous leaves flapped like chicken wings. The ground rumbled, sounds of wood splitting grew louder and louder. Whole banana trees fell aside.

Out came a creature I'd never believed real: unbelievably tall and round with a gray boulder for a head, wings for ears, and a swinging snake of a nose. Its back rose like a mountain peak, topped by a basket in which a person sat, tiny as a doll compared to its bearer. It only vaguely looked like the smooth jade elephants I'd seen in temples.

Another great beast followed, then another, draped in multi-colored cloaks, their tiny black eyes expressionless under thick hooded lids. A drummer sat on top of one, though his beat was barely distinguishable from the elephants' pounding steps. I stayed on my toes until my feet ached while an entire elephant army—I lost count at sixty—had trampled the bananas into mulch and formed lines in the field. Those with circular shields roped to their shoulders must have belonged to officers, I guessed.

At some sort of signal, two elephants on either side of a gap in the ranks raised their trunks and blew out a high-pitched, almost musical wail I could feel in my spine. This was not how I'd ever imagined an army would be. This was something monstrous and ancient.

I dropped back down onto the flats of my feet, thinking I'd seen it all, when the drumming resumed, and the elephants trumpeted again. I rose in time to see an enormous wrinkled brute which dwarfed the rest pass through the gap in the ranks, each leg guarded by a foot soldier bearing a shield. A helmeted figure stood rather than sat inside a ribbon-fringed mount, raising a sword to the sky. The rider shouted a command, the drumming ceased, and the huge elephant halted a few steps from the two royal attendees.

As if I weren't astonished enough, the elephant bent its front legs and bowed. The rider climbed from the basket, slid down the elephant's neck, and landed in full kowtow to the man in the yellow silk gown, whose hunched head protruding from a stiff brocaded collar made me think of a cobra.

I whispered to a uniformed official beside me, "Who's that man?"

The official cleared his throat. "The man in yellow is uncle to the emperor."

"No, I mean the...that other man, who just got off the elephant."

The official beside me laughed through his nose.

An army officer in front of me turned and whispered, "You don't know? That's General Xuan." Seeing my blank look, he explained in Cantonese: "Supreme Commander of the Army."

The audience parted to allow the emperor's uncle and General Xuan to come in out of the sun. And no wonder; it must have been excruciatingly hot for the general in that heavy armored jacket and tall pointed helmet.

The general moved toward the center of the pavilion with a confident, muscular stride, the way I imagined a lion might walk. He surveyed the room before stopping in front of the emperor's uncle. Embedded in the powerful helmet, the only discernible features were a pair of eyes. Was it my imagination, or had those eyes, for one brief moment, focused their fire on me?

The emperor's uncle clapped his hands. Three sentries rushed forward. Two removed the general's armor, then stepped aside to let the third remove the helmet.

My eyes stung as if someone had poked them. Of all the strange sights they had seen this unfathomable year, some terrifying and some beyond belief, this was the least fathomable of all.

The lord of the elephant cavalry, the supreme commanding general of the Annamese Empire, was a woman.

XVIII
Spirit River

I begged and cajoled Cheng Yat to arrange a meeting with the woman I dubbed the Elephant General in which I would be included. I wasn't sure what I would say to her, or whether we shared a common language, but even a polite greeting would allow me to breathe in the same air as a woman of unimaginable power and strength.

Every day I reminded him, and every day he reacted more angrily than the last.

"What should I tell her—on those rare times when we're under the same roof? That my wife has suggestions about strategy, supplies, or transport? Or maybe she'd be fascinated to hear your recommendations about scented soaps? Do you think we all sit around sipping tea?"

"Maybe you do! How would I know? All I see is how good I've made you look by working the wrinkles from your uniforms and polishing your buttons in this cursed heat, how hard I try to play the role of good little admiral's wife. I ask the least favor in return."

"You're out of line, woman," he said.

Then it was too late. The Grand Army and Navy of the Tay-son Empire broke camp and deployed south toward the Spirit River. That morning, as our ship left its anchorage, the trees had shuddered while a helmeted figure on a rattan throne led a procession of four-legged armored landships into the forest.

Days later, I stood on the poop deck, swatting away bugs in the middle of a muddy gray river, searching the jungled shore for any sign of an arriving brigade of thundering elephants.

The only things moving here at the Spirit River were men and weapons arrived day after day along the north bank, to be ferried across its broad expanse to the southern side. We were supposed to have encountered rebel fortifications along the south shore, but the only enemies to greet us were the fogbanks of insects which descended at dusk. And for me, the boredom. War, I discovered, is mostly waiting.

I watched yet another overloaded raft tip over and spill its human load: some swam to shore, others had to be dragged out, and the unlucky ones were sucked under with their heavy packs. This landscape eagerly devoured men.

Along the edge of the south shore encampment, an enclosed pavilion was being hastily erected for the Spring Festival banquet, what the Annamese called Tet. Rumor was that the emperor himself would make an appearance. Enormous bamboo frameworks were strung with heavy mats, colorful bunting and streamers, all strangely out of place between the dull river and prickly wilderness of the surrounding hills. It didn't belong here; the army didn't belong here. I had no role in this place. Only mosquitoes and snakes and tigers belonged.

A thud against the hull startled me from my reverie. Cheung Po Tsai climbed from a sampan with two other men, all straining on ropes to lift something heavy. A red scowling face rose over the side—a nearly life-sized statue of Kwan Yu, the god of war, taken from some temple, obviously. I thought we'd ceased being pirates in Annam.

I called down, "Isn't it bad luck to pray to a stolen god?"

Po Tsai raised his head without the usual mischievous grin. "Kwan Yu is happy to see action. Come. Pray with us."

He and his cohorts arranged the deity beside the deckhouse, complete with tallow candles and sacrificial fruit. Po Tsai seemed almost in a trance, kowtowing and reciting prayers. The sincerity of his devotion impressed me; I had never found it in myself to be so devoted to anyone, ethereal or real.

When his prayers finished, I walked downstairs. He startled, as though something about me disturbed him.

"Bring me ashore," I said.

"I don't think you should."

"Aiya! How dare—"

"I mean your hair. May I?"

He sprang to his feet and removed my hairclip. Using it as a comb, he gathered and arranged and put everything back together. I couldn't see what he was doing, but a woman across the deck nodded approval.

156

"There. Now you're the most beautiful woman in Annam, as befits you. Let's go," he said.

I had to admit, I felt a twinge of pleasure. What kind of young man besides a palace eunuch cared about a woman's grooming?

Soldiers crowded the Tet pavilion, transforming the space into a palace. Red fabric draped the walls. Festive lanterns hung from every beam. Massive scroll paintings were unrolled. On a raised platform that filled one end of the hall, women stitched yellow fabric to what appeared to be thrones. In the opposite corner, two men hunched over stacks of red paper, painting New Year epigrams, while assistants lay them out to dry across nearby tables.

I found Cheng Chat's wife among a clutch of women off to the side, my first sight of her since we'd reached the river. I stepped quickly to her, tempted to wrap my arms around my dearly missed friend. She dug a hand into an open sack and held it to me.

"Try some," she said. "They call it *mut*—Annam's great contribution to the world. The only one, as far as I'm concerned."

I set down my pile of clothes for this evening and accepted a handful of dried shredded fruits and coconuts. It was as tasty as she'd suggested.

"Ladies, I suggest you save that for tonight," a familiar voice said. I hadn't recognized Kwok Podai as one of the scribes. The other was an Annamese officer.

"I suggest you mind your own business," Chat's wife said, adding, "Why don't you write something for me?"

"I was just finishing." He laid a freshly painted, four-character epigram on an adjacent table, weighing down the corners with small stones. "For the honorable admiral's wife."

"I can imagine what you wrote for me. *Diseased cow wallow in bilge.*"

Kwok didn't take well to the joke. Maybe it was the scholar in him that valued truth in words at the expense of humor. He turned to me.

"Cheng Yat Sou, is there an epigram you prefer?"

"Anything. As long as it isn't a Tang poem." I added a smile. Another joke, but this one he accepted. The flames I remembered from his library returned to his eyes, kindling a circle of heat in my breast. He opened his mouth to speak but Cheng Chat's wife interrupted.

"I know! *Nin saang kwai ji.*" Every year a son.

"You write that, and I'll kill you both," I said.

"I certainly believe you capable of that," he said.

Kwok laid out a fresh paper and twirled his brush in the ink. As he lifted it to write, a commotion intruded at the entrance. A young Annamese soldier pushed open the flap and shouted excitedly. The Annamese officer beside Kwok stood to attention. Others rushed for the door.

"What did he say?" Chat's wife asked.

The Annamese officer scowled and said in broken Cantonese, "The scoundrel, who will punish, say, 'Pig coming. Emperor too.'"

The pavilion emptied. I could barely see through the onlookers lining the bank, but I heard shouts of excitement. A sampan nosed through a light mist, followed by a larger craft adorned with yellow imperial banners.

As the first boat was dragged onto the pebbles, the crowd parted to let through men bearing two enormous glistening roast pigs on shoulder poles. I tried not to think of how many days these had been traveling while feasted on by how many flies. The sweet, delicious smell in their wake called directly to my stomach.

A sedan chair was carried out to the royal barge, presumably to bear the emperor ashore, but his entourage was so hemmed in by spectators that I caught only the beat of drums and a glimpse of a yellow silk robe.

With nothing else to see, I made my way back toward the pavilion, only to find Kwok Podai in my way. With a slight bow, he offered me a rolled paper with both hands. As soon as I took it, he walked away.

I stood beside the pavilion, out of the wind, and unrolled the epigram. Whatever the words said, they were beautiful, a wild flowing script which leapt and twirled down the page like the passage of a butterfly. It was such a stylized manner of script; how could I ever train myself to read such language?

"Saw that ox hand that to you."

Before I could roll up the paper and hide it in my sleeve, Cheng Chat's wife grabbed it from my hand. She whistled at a man across a patch of grass whom I recognized as her ship's purser.

"No," I said, but she'd already held it up in his face.

"Read it," she said.

The purser blushed and looked at me, embarrassed. It was too late—he'd already seen it, and in any case, I was also curious to learn what it said. I gave him a nod.

It was my face's turn to redden as he softly recited the words.
Ching chuen seung jue.
Always remain young and beautiful.

I held Cheng Yat back at the pavilion gate with the excuse of straightening his collar and swatting fluff from his black naval tunic, but actually I wanted to give those entering before us a few moments to pass, so that our entrance would be that much more notable.

He returned my attentions by pointing to a stray thread in my waistcoat embroidery, which I smoothed down with a wet finger. I finally had an occasion to wear my formal robe of shimmering red silk which I'd had made in Chiang Ping, though now I worried that it was perhaps too feminine for my hoped-for encounter with General Xuan, the Elephant General.

"The other men better keep their eyes on the emperor and not on my wife," Cheng Yat said. He squeezed my hand. I squeezed his back.

Heads turned as we stepped through the doorway. I was sure we made a handsome couple, even among this well-dressed crowd. For the first time, I truly felt part of an elite as we passed tables occupied by officials and officers, some wearing robes of the royal court. Sentries in parade uniform stood along the walls between calligraphy and pennants. The pavilion had fully transitioned into a splendid banquet hall.

The admirals' table stood two places back from the podium and thrones. Wu-shek Yi and his wives took up a quarter of the table's circumference. Cheng Yat and I sat facing Kwok Podai and his nervous spouse. Cheng Chat arrived last, his wife nudging him aside so she could take the seat beside mine.

"I'm here, pretty woman. Who else you looking for?" she said.

I hadn't known I was so obvious. I stopped searching the room for General Xuan. I wasn't certain she was here; I'd neither seen nor heard any sign of elephants.

"Nobody," I said. "Just admiring the view."

"Well, I see nobody worth paying a copper's worth of attention to. The food better be good, at least."

Wu-shek Yi raised a hand to me. "Cheng Yat Sou! May I say that you look—"

"You look the other way, mister," Chat's wife cut in. "You already have enough chickens in your yard."

"I was going to say that Cheng Yat Sou looks nearly, but not quite, as beautiful as our commanding admiral's charming wife."

"That's better," Chat's wife said. And she did look good in the burgundy silk dress and white waistband I'd cajoled her into getting.

All conversation stopped when helmeted soldiers poured in, beating spears on the floor in a slow marching rhythm. I rose to my feet with everybody else, though my legs felt weak, knees trembling. It was almost too much to imagine. I, who had been a poor fisherman's daughter and common prostitute, and then a pirate, was about to find myself in the presence of an emperor.

A curtain behind the podium parted. Two figures in brilliant red and white robes stepped forward and settled into the side thrones. The older man I recognized as the emperor's uncle. The other was a teenage boy.

"Not the emperor," Chat's wife whispered. "That's the younger brother. Get ready to fake a kneel."

The pounding stopped. The royal guards shouldered their spears. Starting at the Annamese tables, the assembled guests dropped to their knees. As Chat's wife advised, I squatted as low as I could so as not to scuff my silk on the floor.

A moon-faced young man slowly emerged from behind the curtain. His shoulders sagged under a heavy blue gown with a golden sun embroidered across the chest. His look seemed gentle, distracted even. He settled into the high-backed throne, extended his arms to his subjects, and spoke so softly that I couldn't make out his words. But their meaning was clear. Everyone reclaimed their seats.

I remained standing just a little bit longer and was rewarded for my minor infraction. I spotted General Xuan seated in full dress uniform; even her hair braided and wrapped like the male officers at her table.

I knew my target for later, so I could now fix my full attention on Emperor Toan. Cheng Yat had said the boy was ten years old when he inherited the position after his father's death, which made him now not quite twenty. He occupied the stage like a nervous schoolboy, eyes darting to the ceiling and walls, while he recited a speech in a feathery voice. The interpreter, in a contrast that was almost funny, repeated everything in Cantonese at a yell.

This wasn't the gravity I'd expected of a royal audience. The boy emperor hesitated in the middle of sentences. Even if I couldn't understand his formal Annamese, it was clear he was slurring some words. His voice, the look in his eyes, took on a familiar glaze: this young man was an opium user.

I was participating in a comic opera: the awkward boy who ruled over millions, being fawned at with overdone obsequiousness by men decades his senior, who stood and applauded at each florid phrase.

"Joyful gratitude to our courageous heroes of the sea for their recent crushing victory..." I snuck a glance at General Xuan, just two tables away. She looked too bored and too intelligent not to understand what nonsense these words contained. A minor skirmish several days ago at the river's mouth hardly qualified as a crushing victory. But she applauded like the rest.

"The usurpers and their foreign barbarian masters are no match..." The emperor stared down at his hands as if he'd lost track of what he was saying.

I leaned over to Chat's wife. "Is he...?" But I held the question to myself. She had pure hate in her face.

The emperor's uncle took over in a deep voice: "They're no match for our great General of the Black Junks and Master of the Horses!"

Chat dipped his head modestly at the applause and his newly elevated title, his reward for a trivial action he'd barely been involved in. Beside me, Cheng Yat coughed inside his throat. Was he envious of his cousin, or embarrassed for him?

The emperor's uncle continued, "Soon we will have new cause for celebration when we retake our sacred ancient capital." He waited for the latest cheering to end, then added, "And our emperor will reunite with his precious empress."

"Empress?" I said.

Under cover of more applause, Cheng Chat's wife whispered, "When they fled the old capital, the deformed toad ran so fast he left wife number one behind. Pretty little thing. Better off without him."

The words from the podium faded. What had happened to that poor girl, abandoned to a violent enemy? What kind of people were we fighting for?

A man sprang up at a middle table.

"Emperor live ten thousand years!"

The room filled with more slogans, more cheers, from mouths stretched into impossible grins. I studied the boy on the throne, smothered in robes, inscrutable as a wooden puppet. Maybe this was an opera—not a comic one, but a tragedy.

Finally, the emperor's uncle led choruses of New Year greetings in Annamese and Cantonese.

"Chuk Mung Nam Moi!"

"Kung Hei Fat Choy!"

Then a curtain closed in front of the podium. Servants rushed into the dining hall with wine jars and steaming platters. The whole pavilion buzzed like a beehive. The food looked good, but I only picked at mine. I was eager for the meal to end, for the chance to mingle with General Xuan.

Cheng Chat was the hero of the moment, thanks to the royal endorsement. Chest spread wide inside his gleaming uniform, he was the picture of authority, a man at the height of his success, radiating power and masculinity. Someone, a high officer of some sort, beckoned him to another table to receive an extra round of congratulations.

As soon as Chat was out of hearing range, Kwok Podai spoke.

"Will someone kindly explain to me what we are here fighting for?"

I nearly coughed out some rice. Kwok dared to say what I was thinking.

Wu-shek Yi pointed his nose at Cheng Chat's back. "I know what he's fighting for."

Chat's wife sipped wine, looking at no one.

"As for why I'm fighting," Wu said, "for money, my friends, and little more. As we all are." Reaching his chopsticks across the table, he added, "And tonight for this sweet, tasty roast pork."

"I don't fight for money," Cheng Yat said.

"I see," said Wu. "So, you feel some loyalty to his royal juvenile majesty? Rather noble of you."

"Nothing noble about it. We fight here because it's all we know how to do. And we're good at it."

"You can speak for yourself," Kwok Podai said. "I'm with our fat colleague here. For me, I get paid whether I fight or not, unlike our usual activity back home. I was merely hoping there was more of a purpose to it."

"All of you, shut up!" Cheng Chat's wife banged her cup on the table. "You're all a bunch of crows, all you care about is shiny objects on your chests."

She stood and walked away.

At last the meal finished, freeing me to circulate among the other guests, exchanging polite New Year greetings and compliments about my husband. I lingered near a clutch of officers, including General Xuan. It took some time to summon my courage, but at a break in their conversation, I took a deep breath and insinuated myself in front of her.

I was surprised at how small she was, nearly four finger widths shorter than me. She had a round, weather-hardened face undisguised by makeup. I offered her a slight bow and we traded New Year wishes in Annamese: *"Chuk Mung Nam Moi."*

I felt as shy as a little girl. What words to offer to perhaps the most powerful woman in the world? Should I ask her when she'd begun riding elephants or maybe her mount's name?

My entire Annamese vocabulary suddenly evaporated like steam in a breeze. My mouth unhinged, but nothing came out. All I could think of was how to ask the price of pears.

The Elephant General smiled politely, but her eyes gave her away. If I had nothing to say, she was eager to return to the lively discussion going on beside her.

She broke the uncomfortable silence: "I'm sorry, I don't speak Chinese."

I stammered, "Good evening"—the only phrase that came to mind—then backed away into the crowd. I tried to keep my poise though my face burned, nodding curtly to each person I passed, until I slipped out the door into the hazy night.

I twisted and turned until late into the night, piecing together sentences in Annamese that I could have said, should have said, to General Xuan.

Greetings for Tet, General. I'm the wife of Admiral Cheng Yat.

May I invite you aboard our command ship, General? I'm afraid it isn't as colorful as a war elephant.

And the questions I really wanted to ask:

Good evening, General. How did you get to such a position?

Or: *Can you explain what we're fighting for?*

Why had we come here? To prop up an overgrown boy and his pompous uncle? How did these weak people command such intense loyalty? Maybe that was royalty's function—to dress in finery and lap up flattery like pampered pets while leaving the hard work and blood-shedding to real men like Cheng Yat and his cousin. And women like General Xuan.

The gap around the door blinked with light, followed by a far-off blast. I opened the porthole a crack.

Another flash lit up a patch of fog somewhere. Another bang, louder. The door rattled.

Cheng Yat rustled in the bed. "Hm?"

"New Year fireworks." I pulled on a quilted robe and stepped outside.

Hair whipped in my face. The wind had shifted to a cooler northerly. I searched the moonless night, tingling with sweet anticipation just like when I was a child, for each new wild burst of fire and color, chasing away the ghosts of the old year.

A hill south of the river filled with light and swiftly faded. Sky-rocket trails whistled across the sky, ending in a thunderous crack. A tent behind the beach exploded in flames.

My throat tore out the word: "Attack!"

Cheng Yat ran out shouting for the Taumuk, the cannon master, every man on deck.

Another spark somewhere in the hills, a burst, and a teeth-aching squeal. An enormous blast set more tents ablaze. Wind whipped the flames, casting a hellish glow over figures escaping down the beach.

I grabbed whatever I could to wear and ran down to the main deck. A few crewmen crawled from their holds with the sluggishness of men who'd welcomed the new year with a pipe. I found a single gunner standing helplessly beside a cannon.

I demanded to know where was Melon Seed, cannon master since Hawk Man's death. The gunner shook his head.

"I'll find him. You grab other men!" I shouted. Crossing the deck, I pointed two sailors to the ammunition hold but the Taumuk pulled them away.

"Need boatmen," he said. "Help evacuate the shore."

The futility of his effort was plain to see in the light of the spreading flames. Rafts sank beneath the weight of more bodies than they could bear. Overloaded sampans took on water while their occupants used the oars not to paddle but to beat back swimmers clambering over the gunwales.

I screamed back at the Taumuk, "We need gunners to—"

The shriek of another rocket. The banquet pavilion puffed out like it had swallowed the sun, then exploded in a dense fountain of smoke and embers.

I needed Melon Seed to take charge. Cheng Yat had found him first and was presently beating his head on the deck.

"Dog spore! I want cannons loaded and manned! I need muskets!"

Even in the weak light, the man's skin shone like wax, his opium stare focused on nothing. I added a kick of my own with, "Go die!"

A shell hit the water, spitting up a wave which capsized a raft heavy with soldiers. Our sampan pulled away toward shore. Cheng Yat gave me a look which I instantly understood: I was in charge of the artillery.

It had been nearly a year since I'd helped with the guns, and never once in battle. I tried to stave off panic by studying the incoming fire, remembering the things Hawk Man had taught me. Lack of moonlight made distances difficult to make out, but the shots were coming from two locations behind a low ridge line. I judged them to be at least two *li* beyond the shore. Yet from what little knowledge I had, such range was impossible.

"Foreign artillery," the gunner remarked. "Heard they got the white devils helping them."

Rebel fire tore apart the beach encampment. While our crew unrolled protective hides over the wales and plucked struggling men from the water, the gunner and I prepared our best cannon on the shore-facing side, a foreign-made monster that took a five-catty ball. It was inconceivable that we could shoot far enough to attack their positions. But we might be able to scare off an advance nearer to shore.

The gunner and I prepared the next cannon in line. The beach had descended into chaos. Men carried mats, boards, anything they thought might float, in an effort to cross the river.

The rebels' western gun went quiet for a long time.

"What do you think?" I asked the gunner, while the two of us alone wheeled the cannon back into place.

"Don't want to think. Don't exactly want to be here."

A red flash appeared in a different location. Louder this time. The whine of the projectile deeper. They'd moved in closer.

The shell smacked the water so close it lifted our bow clear of the river. I stumbled backward until my leg struck something hard. The deck plummeted; an explosive splash knocked me down. I spat water and tried to stagger up, but pain shot up my leg as if I'd been gored by lightning.

The shore camp was no longer the target.

We were.

With the support of a stray lanyard dangling from the mast I hoisted myself upright to see what was happening. The first hint of daylight had crept into the sky, enough to see details of the carnage on the beach, thick with broken tent poles and bodies.

A group of men emerged from a clearing beyond the beach, and I forgot my pain. They pulled behind them the strangest weapon I had ever seen: an impossibly short-barreled cannon cradled between enormous spoked wheels.

"What the devil?" someone said.

The Taumuk came over for a look. "Whatever it is, the bastards know how to shoot them."

I reached a hand to him. "Help me to the cannon."

He looked as if touching me was worse than being blown to pieces by the enemy. "I'll help you to the cabin."

"No! I'm needed at the guns."

He supported me across to the five-catty cannon. "Not a chance under heaven you'll strike them, but we've no other choice. Fire at will," he said and ran off to another chore.

"You heard him," I told the gunner. "Can we match their range?"

"Sure. If the powder's dry. If the ball's not corroded—"

"Shut up and tell me!"

"Can't get a point on them until we...aiya!"

The strange stubby gun again showed itself in action. It seemed impossible that a weapon could be primed, loaded, and fired that quickly.

The cannonball landed so close the timbers seemed to bend beneath me, but our ship didn't take the impact. The deckhouse on a junk not three lengths from us blew apart. The resulting swell tossed our ship, catapulting men and equipment overboard. In the sickening rain of timber and flesh which followed, I gave into fear and screamed.

The wounded junk spun free in the current. Someone yelled, "It's going to ram us!"

A few men ran to the bow with pikes, but there weren't enough of them to push off the wreck. It struck our bow with a hellish crunch, then scraped along the side, shearing off railings and the privy platform, before overturning and being swallowed by the current.

Cheng Yat ran over, his hair loose and wild. "Why aren't you shooting?"

166

"Look!" I pointed. The collision had turned us. Our cannons no longer aimed toward shore.

Cheng Yat ordered the pike men to maneuver us back into line, then yelled back at me, "Fire, damn you!"

"Damn you! Why aren't you getting us out of here?"

"It's my job to defend—"

"Defend what? That opium addict boy? By now he's gone or dead!"

"How dare you!"

"Defend your men! Defend your wife!"

A nearby junk fired a cannon toward shore. It was answered by a shot from the rebel mortar which fell short, but sent up a towering waterspout. Cheng Yat ran off, distracted by something else. Moments later I learned what it was as the cry traveled from man to man.

"Fireboats!"

Rafts covered with bonfires crept past a bend in the stream, carried by the current like a procession of floating lanterns, only large and deadly. One struck an anchored junk on its transom. In moments, the deckhouse went up in flames.

Crews on the upstream junks used pikes to repel the burning rafts, which now drifted on a collision course with us, their smoke already filling the air nearby.

"Haul up anchors!" Cheng Yat called. "Or just cut the damn lines!"

The gunner touched my arm. "Cheng Yat Sou! Look."

A second stubby cannon rolled in at the other end of the camp.

Winches rattled. The main sail lurched upward. And jammed. The junk listed and began a slow drift.

"Oars!" Cheng Yat said.

No one moved. Every oar and yuloh was on the ill-fated sampans.

All this time, exhausted stragglers pulled themselves up over the gunwales. The fireboats continued their silent march downstream, choking us in their smoke.

A familiar junk sailed between us and the shore. Kwok Podai stood ahead of the mainmast, shielding his eyes against the rising sun. He couldn't have seen me through the smoke and men around me. Or maybe he chose not to.

Never mind him. I had a clear, sunlit view of the mortar crew on shore, reloading their gun. They rotated it on its wheels until it pointed in direct line of sight...at me.

"We have to fire," I said.

"We're pointed too far right," the gunner replied.

I willed with all my might for our junk to rotate in the current. I yelled for someone to find a pike, turn the ship, but no one seemed to hear.

A sampan bore down on us, water spilling over the wales under the weight of its passengers. I leapt and waved my arms at them, directing them toward the bow. "Ram the ship!" I yelled. "Ram it!"

The gunner prepared the match.

Moving at a sluggish pace, the sampan struck—not hard, but enough.

The junk turned.

Just a little bit more...

"Do it," I said.

The match flared. The cannon blasted, crunching against its stops.

A flash from the shore gun was diminished by the sun. I almost believed it had no power.

Then the deck buckled.

A wall of heat slammed into me.

My feet touched the blood-red sky. The river sparkled above me like heaven. My mouth pried open. I screamed without sound.

Something punched my belly straight through to the bone.

The light, the guns, the smell of powder faded from my senses.

XIX
Sons

I remembered waking in darkness. Wrapped in blankets. The floor shifted. Timber groaned. We were sailing.

A great, enveloping pain welled up from my knees to my gut. I cried out.

A hand pried my jaw open. Bitter potion dribbled into my throat.

I stopped remembering.

Sunlight pierced my eyelids. I felt its warmth on my face while the rest of me shivered as if laid out in the coldest winter. I reached through the blanket to rub the dull ache in my leg, but my thigh recoiled at the touch.

The door creaked. I forced open my eyes. Ah-Yi came in with a gap-toothed smile and a bowl. She spooned watery congee into my mouth.

"How long—"

"Three days."

Ah-Yi said they'd found me wrapped around the mainmast before we slipped out of the river. A few of our crewmen had died. "You were among the lucky ones," she said.

I tried to sit up and look outside, but my muscles rebelled.

"We're in a cove somewhere," she said. "You're safe. Rest now."

Later—was it the same day?—a knock and the door creaked open. My mind was so foggy it took a while to recognize that it wasn't Ah-Yi with food or medicine but a crewman with hands full of tools. He nodded apologetically and crept to the corner shrine. He lifted Tin Hau from her perch and set the statue on the floor.

I propped myself on my elbows and tried to object, but my mouth was unable to form words.

"For repairs," he said. With a few swift blows, he transformed the base into a stack of boards and carried them out.

I fought the pain and forced myself upright, waited for the dizziness to subside, and limped out to the companionway. Thick haze blanketed everything. I could make out the bay and a fringe of vegetation. A few other junks rested nearby. Faint shadows faced inland which would have been west. Morning.

The main deck was covered with bandaged bodies neatly laid out as if for market. I was out of breath by the time I descended the stairs and found the Taumuk inspecting crewmen and women splinting broken battens.

"Where's Cheng Yat?" I said.

He ignored the question and passed a repaired batten to a man working on the mainsail, spread out beneath the mast.

My lungs felt like splintered glass as I filled them to raise my voice: "Where are we? Where's my husband?"

"You ask unanswerable questions."

The Taumuk kept his eyes on the repair crews. Lines of exhaustion seamed his face. How could he report his commander missing with such lack of concern? Where was Cheng Yat?

"He took a fast-boat, went searching for others. Where, I don't know," the Taumuk finally informed me.

He could have said that in the first place instead of making me squirm.

"How many ships did we lose?"

"You can count." He stalked away.

I disliked him more than ever. If I were in charge, he'd be first to be dismissed.

I counted the junks bobbing in the water, first from one rail, then the other. This couldn't be. Out of two hundred vessels which had sailed to Spirit River, only twelve remained? I'd seen Kwok Podai retreat with my own eyes, but his ship wasn't here. That meant more must be scattered along the coast. Cheng Yat was looking for them. He would bring them here.

He would find a healer to help me with my pain.

The cook handed me a bowl of still-warm congee with stringy

meat. In the back of the galley, rat carcasses hung from a beam. It didn't matter; meat was meat.

I'd consumed half the bowl when a cry sounded from the poop deck: "Boat coming!"

Where I'd hoped to find Cheng Yat, I spied only a *bau,* an Annamese style sampan with a single mat sail, coming from the south with men in Tay-son army colors. As they came alongside, one man stood up and clasped his hands in greeting, repeating the Annamese word for friends. He pleaded in rapid, nasal singsong. My basic Annamese was apparently better than the Taumuk's, so I attempted to translate:

"He says they're from a unit in, ah...somewhere north. Want us to bring them there."

An angry debate broke out among the crew about whether to share scarce rations with strangers. I held that we should offer them a bit of food and send them on their way. The Taumuk appeared to share my sentiment. He sent three crewmen into a hold.

It wasn't the food storage hold.

Our men returned with cutlasses in hands and daggers between their teeth.

"What the devil? These aren't enemies!" I tried to stop them, but my leg wouldn't let me run.

By then they'd leapt over the side, and my words were drowned in screams. My legs gave in to pain; my head hit the deck.

The Taumuk shrugged down at me. "Lost our sampan. We can use the boat."

The whole world stood still for days; even the pain in my legs lingered. Then sails appeared in the south, flushed red by the sun's last rays. Cheng Chat's naval banner fluttered from a pole where his foremast should have been. The mainsail was such a patchwork, it was a wonder it didn't shred to bits in the slightest wind.

Though there was no fast-boat among them, or other indication of Cheng Yat, still it offered some cheer. My friend was arriving to keep me company.

The Taumuk blocked me from the first boat across—no room for a passenger, he said, among the wild taro and green bananas scavenged from shore earlier that day.

The boat returned after dark with a sack of coconuts and the message that I was not welcome.

I tried pushing myself aboard the next crossing, this one bringing spare sail mats, but the Taumuk ordered a crewman to restrain me.

"Let go, you turtle shit!" I twisted in the man's grip and screamed at the Taumuk. "How dare you treat your commander's wife like this! When I tell Cheng Yat..."

"Admiral's orders." The Taumuk pointed to Cheng Chat's junk, but at the same time he looked pleased about it.

"Go die!" I said, elbowing the crewman in the chest. I sunk my teeth into his arm and broke free. Without another thought, I climbed onto the rail and jumped.

I'd forgotten to take a breath first. My arms and legs thrashed on their own until I broke the surface, coughing and retching and gasping for air. The yellow glow of a ship's lamp marked my target. Even with the cold water numbing me, my legs hurt too much to kick. I swam with arms only, barely keeping afloat until the strength drained out of me and I gulped more water than air. I considered turning back, when hands gripped my arms and pulled me up into the moving Annamese *bau*.

As it was on our ship, wounded bodies lay across Cheng Chat's deck like a haul of caught fish. I stepped between them in the dark, trying not to let my drenched clothing drip on anyone, and cautiously ascended the stairway with no light to see by nor any railing left to support me and my aching leg.

I didn't notice Cheng Chat until I nearly stumbled into him. He hunched on a stool in the middle of the companionway, twisting a brass pipe between his lips, staring into the void.

"Where is she?" I said.

His nose blew smoke, a curse without words.

I tried the cabin. It was latched from inside. I knocked and put on a cheerful tone. "Big sister!"

I waited, held my ear to the door, then pounded louder and called her again. I looked to Cheng Chat for a clue, but he only stared out at nothing.

At last I heard the latch move, then silence. I slid the door aside, each squeak and bump enunciating dread. Heavy incense smoke drifted through the gap. In the absolute darkness, glowing red cinder tips hovered like bat eyes.

A cold touch on my arm. I yelped. She caught me before I fell.

"You're shivering," said Cheng Chat's wife.

"I tried to swim here."

She tugged my sleeve. "You'll freeze. Take those off."

I struggled out of the clinging garments and pulled on the robe she tossed me, stumbled to the porthole, and tugged it open to flush out the smells of smoke and shit and rot. A sliver of moonlight illuminated an overturned chest, strewn clothing, and broken lamps. The mat was in shreds, pillows smashed. I guessed that they'd been fighting until I noticed the shrine. Two urns stood before it, each stuffed with bunches of smoldering sticks.

I had walked in on a funeral.

A little bird-like whimper in my ear: "They're gone."

I didn't want to ask. I didn't want to hear. The air turned to frost.

"They found Bo-yeung, my firstborn..." She choked on her words. I took her in my arms. She felt weak and frail like a hollowed-out tree that might crumble at the slightest touch.

"My firstborn," she blubbered.

I stroked her swollen face, her burning cheeks. She flinched at my touch.

He'd beaten her again.

She took a deep breath. "They found him dangling from a rope, his belly—"

"Don't," I whispered.

She pulled away from me, eyes bulging in horror. "My baby boy!"

"Are you sure it was him? Did you see him?"

"Of course not, stupid!" She dropped to her knees, hair flailing in her face like a demon. "You expect a mother to look at her dead child? Am I not already cursed enough?"

I urged her onto the remains of the sleeping mat. She covered her ears and kicked. "Stop cursing me!" I knelt beside and she pushed me away, saying "No!" Then she pressed my cheeks between her hands. "Sorry. I'm so sorry. I didn't yell at you. I didn't mean it."

I stroked her back until the crying subsided before I dared ask about her younger son.

She said in an eerie soft voice, "They hit the powder store. People saw his ship explode and burn."

"Maybe he got away."

"Don't try! Don't even try!" She clawed her face, rocking side to side. "I've seen his spirit. Both their spirits. A mother knows."

The air left the room as if ghosts sucked it up in the dark. I couldn't catch my breath. My whole body itched, even my eyes. A bitter taste gushed up my throat. I had to lie down if I didn't want to be sick.

I tried to embrace her again, but she pushed me away.

"Why didn't *he* die instead? Heartless gods! Bring my boys back! Take him instead!"

Her head hammered the floor. I pulled the grieving woman to me, stroked her, and held her tighter, trying to calm her, to calm myself.

She yelled toward the door as if expecting Cheng Chat to hear: "I told him not to come here! Curse this country! Curse that bastard! Got his glory and sent my sons to die. To die!"

She clamped her arms around me, crushing the wind from my pain-stricken lungs. "Don't die. Not you, too," she sobbed. "You're all I have left to love."

I rocked her in my arms, absorbing the spasms that rattled her, trying to squeeze out the pain. She pressed her cheek against mine and whimpered, "My baby."

For a brief instant, the baby was me.

XX
Cove

The sky through the porthole brightened and faded with hardly any notice; days passed lost to count. The moon completed a full cycle and half again. My pains subsided, my thoughts slipped away, while I nursed my friend through her grief.

Of all the experiences that were new to me of late—to find a home among outcasts, to sit in the presence of royalty and face a powerful woman, to be wounded in war—perhaps the most perplexing was this: to be needed by another person. Being blasted by a cannon shell, one either died or became crippled; the consequences were easy to predict. Not so when one was struck by love. I'd thought that being needed would fill a thirsty heart, but nothing was that clear. Love could be its own prison.

My life contracted into a narrow little sphere of feeding and bathing her, coaxing medicine down her throat, singing and wooing her into fits of restless sleep. The outside world intruded only when her husband entered the cabin, and then I had to rein her back when she reared up like a cobra.

Cheng Chat never spoke in my presence, but I suspected his sons were just two of a multitude of weights on his shoulders. He grieved in silence, brooding on the companionway with his pipe, a king without a kingdom, surveying the driftwood that had once been his proud navy.

I latched the door to mute the crumbling order, the fights and thievery I could hear and sense outside. When she slept, I sat at the porthole watching for sails that might be Cheng Yat. I left my friend's bedside whenever I heard a sampan touch the hull, thinking it might be him; it usually turned out to be food scrounged from shore—unripe bananas, a goat, sometimes a dog.

Two ships deserted one night. But every day new junks straggled in, missing sails and crewmen, sometimes with news, though never about him.

This whole new feeling of need weighed on my heart. Cheng Chat's wife, frowning now even in her sleep, had lost the two people she'd needed and felt needed by in return, leaving her with nothing—she had nothing left but a broken man. At least I had someone, but where was he? The longer his absence, the more the worry overflowed from my mind into my heart.

If he were here, he could assert leadership and restore discipline. I wanted someone familiar to talk to besides a hysterical woman, I told myself. But more than that—damn the bastard!—I missed my man.

Whatever gods he believed looked after him, please deliver Cheng Yat back to me.

One afternoon, I sat in the light from the porthole, grinding the last of the ship's dried seahorses into powder, a supposed cure for madness which hadn't yet lived up to its promise. Or maybe it had. Chat's wife rose from her bed as bright-eyed as if she'd woken from a good night's sleep. She cleared her lungs with a tremendous coughing fit and pointed. "Family shrine."

"What about a walk around the deck? It'll do you some good. It will do *me* some good," I said, trying my best to sound lighthearted.

Without a flicker of response, and still wearing her bed clothes, she shuffled to the door.

"Wait, first take your medicine," I said. She left before I had a chance to stir in the last precious few drops of wine.

I carried the bowl down into the small airless hold beside the mainmast set aside for the family spirits. Dust stirred by her movements sparkled in the light from the hatch. Wooden figurines lined the forward bulkhead, each representing a Cheng ancestor. At the far end stood two crude carvings, their wood still fresh, each of a boy riding a tiger.

A dirty white mourning cloak covered her from head to knees. She finished her bows to each of her sons, then dug deep into a pocket and pulled out slivers of dried fish. Now I knew why she'd refused to eat the night before. She portioned the fish into sacrificial bowls.

"No fruit today, Number One Son. Your favorite! No tasty pork, my darling youngest. I'm so sorry. I'm an unworthy mother." She beat her forehead on the floor.

I felt like grabbing her hood and pleading, *What about me? Don't you care about me? Please come back to me from the land of the dead!*

Maybe I'd never had a child, much less lost one, but I'd lost a mother. When did enough finally become enough and you understood that you can't sail backward? If only the dead could talk back, she might at least listen.

I knelt beside her, offered my three bows to the effigies, then handed her the seahorse medicine. "Drink, before it's cold."

Quick footsteps pounded the deck overhead. Excited voices worked their way through the walls.

With the flat of my hand I levered the bowl to her lips. "Drink!"

Half dribbled down her chin, but I couldn't care anymore, not after I heard the calls. I hurried up the ladder.

A large group of sails, maybe thirty or more, approached from the southwest. After nearly two months of living inside an endless funeral, my heart had never beat so happily to see a spot of crimson, barely visible at such a distance—the color of Cheng Yat's battle flag.

My heart shrunk at the sight of the scruffy ships he'd brought in. Where I'd hoped to see the reassembled fleet standing proudly in the cove, he'd rounded up a paltry twenty-five plus five or six disheveled Annamese fishing junks and traders.

Cheng Yat had aged ten years in the past forty-something days. New lines scored his face, his eyes sagged, hair covered his scalp like a ragged brush. A noticeably thinner Wu-shek Yi followed him on board.

I stepped toward him and opened my mouth to express relief at his return, but my words were overtaken by shouted abuse from the companionway.

"What the hell were you doing? You can't capture civilian vessels without authority!" This was the first I'd seen Cheng Chat speak or even move since I'd come here, and now he growled like he'd been woken from a bad dream.

Cheng Yat marched up the stairs, saying, "My men were starving!"

"Then let them starve like men! We're not fucking pirates anymore!"

Wu-shek Yi shot back, "Try convincing these villagers to feed their own navy. Sooner give you a pike through the skull than a chicken."

"Which villagers?" Chat shook a fist. "What did you do?"

Cheng Yat kept his eyes focused firmly on Chat. Never had I seen him so defiant toward the man.

"Tell me what you did!" Chat lunged and might have punched Cheng Yat if he hadn't grabbed his irate cousin by the collar. Chat had always been half a head taller than Cheng Yat, but now they faced one another nose to nose.

"Cousin, we filled sailors' bellies," Cheng Yat said. "If I have to choose between serving this...this empire, or serving my men, I choose my men."

Chat wilted onto his stool. "Any news of the emperor?"

"Rumors. Some rogue bargemen claim they saw the imperial retinue traveling north through the jungle."

"Or they could have been regular soldiers," Wu added. "Or a family of baboons."

I expected a new outburst, but Cheng Chat only shook his head. "So, this is what's left. No sign of any others? General Bo? Kwok Podai?"

Cheng Yat shrugged. "Lots of wrecks."

"I saw Kwok," I called to them, and described him fleeing the Spirit River at the height of the action. The men took this in without comment. Cheng Yat peeked into the cabin and signaled the other two men inside, then said to me, "Speak later. Meanwhile, keep *her* out of here."

Chat's wife was where I'd left her in the family shrine, rocking on her knees in front of her boys. She would heal—she was too strong not to—but her wound wasn't like mine. After forty days, I'd run out of medicine and songs and tricks for her. I left her with her ghosts and waited up on deck.

When the cabin door at last slid open, Cheng Yat came out first, walked straight to me, and led me by the arm to a quiet corner.

"What am I not supposed to hear?" I said. "What was the great admiral's pronouncement?"

"We wait for orders from the Imperial Court."

"You mean we sit here until we starve, waiting for your little emperor—"

"Woman—!"

"Look at him! Is he in any condition to lead? Did you say anything?"

Cheng Yat shook his head. "They're right what they say about you, always pushing your way into my business."

"Crazy! Why shouldn't it be my business? Didn't I fight? Didn't

I suffer wounds? Isn't it also my concern that this...this...navy, flotilla, motley wrecks—whatever you call it—is rotting here without a leader? He's failed! His time is over! You should take charge before somebody else does."

He knew I was right; it showed in his face. He said, more subdued now, "Chat's still in command."

"If you believe that, then I believe you're a coward! No! No no, I didn't mean that!" I threw my arms around him, not caring who saw. "Husband, please ignore my words."

To my surprise, he didn't pull away, though neither did he return the affection.

"Is that what you dragged me aside to tell me?" I said.

He wet his lips like he often did when he had something awkward to say. But whatever words had lined up on his tongue retreated at the sight of a living ghost.

Cheng Chat's wife staggered up the companionway, her mourning robe flapping on the stairs. Her husband was in the cabin; there would be screaming and hitting. Someone had to stop her.

Cheng Yat pulled me back. "She's an angry old woman," he said. "Never learned to accept fate, good or bad. You can't help her anymore."

How could I admit to him—how to admit to myself?—that he was right? That I felt helpless, futile, impotent to help my dearest friend? Nothing—not coddling, not prayers or effigies, not even seahorses or seagull bladders—could relieve the madness. In fact, my very sympathy might have fanned its flames. Just as an ill spirit had taken over the woman I adored, something opposite had entered the man who held me. A new stature, a sense of resolve, and something else.

"Let's go. A woman belongs with her husband."

Were these the clumsy words he'd meant to say? Did he see in my eyes that I'd missed him? That I'd learned in these past forty days how to give and give and give? What would it be like to receive?

"Did you miss me?" I said.

"You're my wife."

"Not what I asked. Did you miss me?"

He shook his head, eyes rolling halfway to heaven. "I *said* you're my wife. That's enough. You belong on my ship."

It wasn't enough. How long had I waited to hear that I was wanted? Forty days? Fourteen years? A lifetime?

"But you did miss me," I suggested.

"Aiya, woman! What's this question? Everywhere I take you, I put up with your mouth—in front of other captains, in front of emperors. I let you dirty yourself with guns, then I pay for your fine robes and flowery soaps. And what do I get? More questions! No man would put up with you like I do."

"Then you missed me!"

He threw up his hands and groaned.

"I missed you, too," I said.

He's been holding my arm the whole time. He squeezed it and let go.

I had barely slipped into the cabin to gather my few things when Cheng Chat's wife pounced and wrestled me to the floor.

"No! You can't leave me!"

How had she known? Could a woman who conversed with ghosts spy inside my mind? I turned our struggle into an embrace, squeezing her to me until I could barely breathe. "You'll be fine, treasure. You'll be fine."

"I've lost too much already!"

"You're not losing me." I kissed her cheek, tasted her tears, and ran my fingers through my friend's, my cousin's, my dearest one's white-streaked hair, over the bumps and scars hidden beneath. "My dear Elder Sister."

Her head pounded my chest. Her bitten-off fingernails scraped my neck. "He'll keep you from me! He'll beat you!"

"No, never, dear one. We'll meet again in Chiang Ping. Just you and me, shopping for silks and soaps and tasty snacks—and tea with sweet lotus seeds at Madam Le's. We'll laugh again! We'll be pretty again. My dear sister, I'll see you soon."

"No! No! No!" She tore herself from me, rolled to the wall and covered her face. "You're deserting me! No! No! No!"

She was a wild tempest of hands and elbows and feet. No matter what I said or how I reached out, she wouldn't let me touch her.

"Go!" she said, the cry of a wounded tigress drowning in a swamp. "Go, damn you! Go!"

I took a last look at an old white-haired woman in a white robe banging her head on bare timber, though I was no longer certain who she was weeping for—her sons, perhaps her real sister, or maybe her only friend. Her cries slashed the air like a rusty blade.

"Don't leave me! Don't leave me! Don't leave me!"

XXI
Pillars

We were leaving this wretched cove at last.

Rumors trickled in about Nguyen rebel black junk patrols, but without news or orders from the Imperial Court, the men decided to retreat north to seek instructions. We would separate into smaller squadrons and regroup in Halong Bay, downriver from the capital. If Halong Bay appeared too dangerous, we would gather in Chiang Ping.

I prayed for just enough danger in Halong Bay.

I watched Cheng Chat's departure with a lump in my chest. I would see her again. We would wander the lanes, resume our old ways. Life would be good again, she would see.

A day later, our five junks took a northeastern tack through high chop and blustery winds, intending to stay out of sight of the coast. What first appeared to be a squall on the southern horizon swooped in at full gale force. Waves and buckshot-like rain thrashed the ship, pitching the rails beneath the surface, while the wind threatened to sweep us into the Outer Ocean.

The storm left us within sight of an island to the northeast. The last of our five ships finally came to rest in a shallow bay as the sun dropped with exhaustion off the edge of the world.

In the morning, a shore party set out, returning later with yams and cassava as well as four men and a young woman. All were pockmarked with sores, the girl sprawled unconscious.

"Bring me drinking water," I said. "Are they locals? Did you get in a fight?" I asked one of our sailors.

"They're ours. Chinese," he replied.

They were from Kwok Podai's fleet. Like us, going north in a small group, they were the only survivors of an attack by rebel black junks and had been stranded on the island for the past month.

Ah-Yi and I moved the girl to the cabin, nursed her, and wiped her down with herbal potion. Her body was burned crimson and smelled of rot; clear fluid wept from a neck wound and between her legs. Only her eyes, open to slits, responded to our presence.

"What happened to you?" I asked.

She cleared her throat and spoke in a mousy voice so faint that I had to lean close to hear.

"They held me down. So many of them. They took turns—" She turned her head and retched the water she'd just swallowed. Coughs turned into convulsions; the trembling returned to her shoulder. When the fit subsided, she pointed weakly to the scar on her neck.

"Then they cut me."

"Let me get more clean water," I said and stumbled outside. It was my turn to vomit.

In the middle of the night, Cheung Po Tsai whispered through the doorway. "Lamps out. Now. Cheng Yat's order."

I snuffed the lantern and joined Po Tsai on the companionway. He signaled me to squat low and pointed.

A black silhouette of a ship crept across the mouth of the bay, then another. Four, five, six glided past. Fortunately, the moon was high behind the ridge, placing us in deep shadow. Not a breath, not a cough, could be heard until the ghostly patrol vanished into the night.

In the morning, the young woman was curled into a ball, stiff with death.

Po Tsai rowed us to the beach where he built a makeshift shrine from driftwood and stones while her companions and I dug the grave. The purser refused to come ashore to lead prayers. "Not ours," he'd said.

Back on the ship, I marched straight to Cheng Yat.

"I want out of this country of death."

He looked askance. "We all do."

On the fourth hot and stultifying day at the island, a single-mast skiff rounded the headland and immediately attempted to flee, but several musket shots changed its occupants' minds. Two men were taken aboard while their dog barked furiously. They claimed to be the island's caretakers, irate about their vegetable field and orchard that we'd successfully stripped bare. Cheng Yat interrogated them about rebel ship movements. They too hadn't spotted any black junks for several days.

Before he released them, Cheng Yat told them to wait. Po Tsai climbed out of a hold with an armful of strung coins. He dropped them into the skiff.

"We're not pirates," Cheng Yat explained.

One blinding hot day, after what seemed like months creeping up the coast, we rounded a long rocky island into a broad body of water as smooth and polished as a mirror, pinned to the earth by countless green craggy islets and backed by curtains of jade-colored hills. I leaned over the bow, entranced by my reflection.

"Halong Bay!" the Taumuk announced. Here the fleet had planned to regroup. Yet the only other vessels in sight were a couple of shrimp trawlers. Otherwise the bay was empty and silent. A row of three white stony crags jutting from the water reminded me of grave markers.

We crossed a channel between two islands into an inner section of bay. Here, several fishing boats bobbed in the surrounding waters, and people cast nets from shore, but no one turned at our entrance, as though we were invisible. A village straddled both sides of a narrow inlet on the northern side. There we would find food and possible news of our compatriots.

The approach was strewn with crags and boulders; forbidding defensive pikes protruded from the water. We came within shouting distance to a fishing couple on a bamboo raft. Po Tsai balanced on the rail, calling in broken Annamese: "Hello! Need pilot! Yes you show us go?"

The couple on the raft turned their heads long enough to cast hostile looks and returned to clearing their nets.

"We anchor here and take a boat in," Cheng Yat said.

For once, I wasn't eager to go ashore, but he needed me for my language skills. I accepted the dagger he handed to each of us and carefully tucked the sheath inside my tunic.

"How are we supposed to buy supplies without money?" I asked. Cheng Yat had exhausted our store of currency at each of the farms we'd raided along the way in his proud attempt to prove, like Cheng Chat had insisted, that we were still protectors of the Annamese Empire, and not common pirates.

"We don't need money," he said. "We're the navy."

Po Tsai tied up at the jetty and stayed with the sampan. I felt a hundred eyes follow me up the slippery stone steps behind Cheng Yat, the purser, and two other crewmen.

The waterfront was littered with nets and wood scraps, the ground slick with fish oil. Men loitered in shop doorways picking their teeth without a flicker of greeting, declining to step aside when we peered in at ship and fishing supplies. I finally asked a fat man in front of a carpenter shop where we might buy rice. He jerked a thumb. We followed it through a narrow alley into the market lane, filled with women shoppers in dark trousers and conical hats; not a pretty *áo dài* in sight. Here we passed tempting displays of fruits and summer squashes, pork sides and pungent shrimp paste. But unlike the markets of Chiang Ping, not a single vendor tried to hustle our business, no one waved us over, no one offered a buy-from-me grin.

Cheng Yat nodded toward a shop in the middle of the block, where a man in tattered blue shirt and trousers reclined among rice barrels and oil jugs. He lazily got up, clasped his hands in front of his chest and said in accented Cantonese, "You buy what?"

I did the talking in Annamese, listing quantities of rice, salt, oil, and vinegar. The shopkeeper nodded at each, then pointed out a basket of withered leafy vegetables. Without asking Cheng Yat, I added them to the order. A few curious locals gathered behind us to watch.

A woman came out from the shop holding an abacus. Beads clattered beneath her fingers. She announced the total.

Cheng Yat pulled his official chop from a pocket. "I will put my seal to this. The local government office will reimburse you." No translation was necessary.

"No can." The shopkeeper bared betel-blackened teeth. "Cash, silver, gold."

"I am Admiral Cheng of the Imperial Annamese Navy. My chop is valid."

The shopkeeper bit his lips like he was holding back a joke. I repeated as best as I could in Annamese.

The shopkeeper's wife laughed like a dog barking. The now substantial mob of bystanders joined in her merriment. Something wasn't right. I patted the dagger under my tunic.

"Annam no more!" a voice shouted from the crowd.

"What are you talking about?" I said.

The merchant's wife found this even funnier. "No more emperor," she said, flicking a finger across her neck. "Boy emperor put in cage, taken away."

I translated for Cheng Yat with a tremor in my voice, unsure that I'd heard right. I spun around at a tap on my shoulder. A tall, gangly man bared a mouth full of stained teeth.

"You don't know?" he stuttered in Cantonese. "Emperor, tie hands, feet." He imitated clamping irons around his wrists, then spread his legs and stretched his arms over his head. "One, two, three, four—" He said the next word in his own language, which I repeated in Cantonese: "Elephants."

He needn't have explained further. I didn't want to picture it. But he made certain that we did. He strained his arms upward with mock pain in his face. "Elephants walk. Emperor Toan one two three four pieces."

This raised a laugh from the encircling crowd.

"They're lying," Cheng Yat mumbled.

The tall man thrusted a finger at him. "I no lie! Tay-son finished! You Chinese finished! Here our country!"

An ugly murmur simmered around us. We were completely hemmed in. To reveal our weapons would have sealed our doom. The purser was visibly shaking. I tried to cover my fear as Cheng Yat stepped toward the merchant.

"Regardless of who's on the throne, I am still Admiral of the Navy. You must supply my ships."

The tall man translated for the Annamese listeners without disguising the sarcasm in his voice.

"No Tay-son. No navy. No army," the merchant said. "No admiral. No general."

The last word plucked a string in my gut. I blurted out, "General Xuan? The lady general?"

The tall man raised his voice over the hum of the crowd. "She wants to know about the lady general, the one who commands elephants!"

He lifted a large squash from a basket and held it in front of me. "Lady general head." He placed it on the ground and raised his foot over it. "Elephant," he said, patting his leg.

He stomped with his full strength. The squash exploded with a soft pop. He ground it with his heel into soft orange pulp while his onlookers laughed and hooted. I clenched my legs to keep from soiling myself.

The merchant's wife struck her fingers on Cheng Yat's chest. "Chinese no money, Chinese go! No more Tay-son. No more navy. No more Annam! New country now. Call Yuet—"

Her husband corrected her. "Vietnam."

"Time you Chinese leave," the squash executioner said.

A woman in the crowd echoed, "Go home China!"

"Chinese go home!" The throng squeezed in tighter.

"Vietnam! Chinese out! Vietnam! Chinese out!"

Pots banged in time with the chant. A young man waved a fishing knife. I clenched Cheng Yat's hand. I couldn't let his temper cause a situation we couldn't win. He put his arm around me and led me and the others through the mob.

"Vietnam! Chinese out! Chinese out! Chinese out!"

Something soft and rotten struck my neck. As we escaped toward the jetty, a shopkeeper waved.

"You buy something?"

At last, the familiar Green Islands hove into view. Chiang Ping was a short sail away. Wind whipped my hair; for the first time in months, all the weight lifted from me. I was returning home.

Whatever was happening elsewhere in the world, Chiang Ping remained a haven, an in-between realm, beholden to no authority. We could start over again here, stronger than before, with Cheng Yat taking a more active role, maybe usurping his cousin as the man in charge. I might open my own legitimate enterprise—a soap business!—and join the ranks of the prominent deal makers in the warehouses and tea rooms of this singular merchant society. My friend Cheng Chat's wife would join me—two strong women would be a match for any man.

All these thoughts poured into me as we neared the mud shoals at the river's mouth. Dogs prowled the flats.

The huts stood empty and void of people.

I smelled smoke.

We rounded the first bend. Almost instantly, the sails crackled. A hot wind swept the deck, burning my eyes. Grit dusted my lips. I wiped my face and found my hands smeared black. We passed into a shower of dry gray rain.

The riverfront was in ruins. All that was left of the enormous

186

fish market hall were blackened columns standing like dark sentinels. Once-familiar warehouses reduced to charcoal skeletons leaned precariously over the water.

Our ship nudged through oil and debris past a ghost city. Caved-in roofs, broken tiles. Those walls still standing showed telltale cavities where cannonballs had smashed through. Smoke columns crossed each other over the hillsides. The inner river, normally choking with vessels of every size and shape, was a watery graveyard of broken, smoldering hulls, and masts burned to black tapers. Some appeared almost familiar, like apparitions.

A muffled explosion came from somewhere on the north side followed by a white cloud of smoke. Tiles clattered to the ground. A wall collapsed with an almost human moan, though no actual human or even a dog appeared in the streets.

My home, my haven—my dream—had vanished in ugly black smoke. Where would I go now? What would I do? I needed to lean on something, but my eyes stung. I couldn't see. I stumbled around until I found Cheng Yat, leaning at a rail, stiff as an effigy, fixated on something farther up the shoreline. I spat on my fingers and wiped my eyes.

The main temple was shorn of its roof, its outer walls cracked but standing. Before it, a wooden pillar, like those used to hang firecracker strings for festivals, stood alone in the middle of the open square, a banner fluttering on top and a rope slapping its side.

Cheng Yat signaled to stop the ship. The hull grazed wood and bare stones. Sailors stood still as rocks, holding the mooring lines, but made no move to tie us ashore.

Sickness crept up my throat.

What had appeared to be a banner flying from the pillar was a turban unraveling in the wind. The rope swaying beneath was a man's queue dangling from a severed head—shriveled and black, but all too recognizable.

Cheng Chat stared into space through dark, empty sockets.

The whine of our hull scraping the wharf, the cries of the crew, and above all, the trumpeting moan like a wounded bull from Cheng Yat's throat, all blended into a solid, formless alarm. My head snapped right and left, searching the street, the alleys and doorways for another head, another body. But she wouldn't have mattered to those who composed this gruesome message.

"Get us out of here!" Cheng Yat shouted.

My legs melted. My knees dropped into the layer of ash that smeared the deck. Winches whined. Men shrieked orders; oars slapped the water. I pounded my head on the floor again and again while ash and bile coated my tongue and my breath caught in the constricted hole of my throat. I tried not to think of what they did to captive women, what they would do to my Elder Sister, if she was even still alive. I tried not to remember my final glimpse of her—with her purpling face, hands grasping the air, lips stretched and pleading—just as I now pleaded in return—to her, to Chiang Ping, to Madam Le and the soap seller and all the girls in their pretty *áo dài's* and all my pretty dreams:

"Don't leave me!"

嘉慶八年癸亥

PART II

—

Eighth Year

of the

Reign of Emperor

Ka-hing

—

1803

XXII
Hold

We were pirates again. Cheng Yat led a motley group of five junks, sometimes as many as twelve, drifting along the coasts and shipping lanes around the Pearl River delta. Nothing distinguished one ship seizure from another, one raided village from the next. Before I knew it, a year had passed since we'd fled the ruins of Chiang Ping.

As time went on, it became easier not to think about it, other than in my dreams where the faces of the dead shimmered like blue flames which couldn't be doused except with sleep or wine. I filled my days, like before, by maintaining the guns, though my spirit was lacking.

You can't sail backward. Wasn't that what Ah-Yi said? Then call it sailing nowhere; that's what we were doing. And that, for me, was enough. Vietnam had taught me the futility of wanting more. Wishes, I'd learned, can be deadly.

One chilly morning, we sailed up a wide estuary flanked by low curving hills. I had picked up my breakfast congee and prepared to return to the cabin when my heart started racing with a sense of danger. We were uncomfortably close to a hidden sandbar extending from the east bank. With the river running high and the sun in our eyes, no one could see it. But I knew it was there.

I knew this place.

The bowl fell from my hands.

A copse of trees on the western bend formed a shape as familiar as my own shadow. Dense mangroves spread from behind. Egrets rose from the trees, white ghosts against the pale sky.

I knew those birds, or at least their parents and their grandparents.

The helmsman swerved us around the sandbar just in time.

"No! Not that way," I said. I ran up the companionway and down to the rudder, to the bow, and finally found Cheng Yat squatting beside Cheung Po Tsai at the bow spirit shrine.

"You have to turn the ship around!" I said, louder than I should have.

He turned from whatever ritual they'd been performing and questioned me with an eyebrow.

"We can't pass the river bend. We can't go there!" I said.

Cheng Yat glanced at Po Tsai. "Did someone appoint a new captain to this ship?"

"Don't you see where we are?" I grabbed his shoulder, and this made him stand up angry. Po Tsai at least had the discretion to step aside.

"Of course I know where we are," Cheng Yat said.

A sampan emerged from behind the headland, close enough to notice a child crawl from the cowling. I would probably know his father, but I didn't want to see. Did Cheng Yat really recognize this place? Did he know its name? Has he never sensed another person's feelings, ones so strong that right now they could fly through the air like burning buckshot and shred his frigid heart?

"Maybe your father returned." One end of his mouth curled into a smile. "You can take your revenge."

Of course I'd thought about that a thousand times. I knew that if I found him, Cheng Yat would let me dictate whatever torment I wished upon the man. I could sit comfortably like a queen and watch him beg me for forgiveness as his brows and nose and fingers flew off one slice at a time.

Instead, I was the one begging. "Please! Don't take me to that place! Don't I have enough evil memories to last ten lifetimes? Besides..." I didn't finish the statement, but he must have understood the language in my eyes:

You know very well what else happened there. I don't want to start hating you again.

I called to the helmsman, "Turn us around!"

Cheng Yat seemed genuinely taken aback. He thought he was delivering me a surprise, but he simply didn't get it. I never wanted to step back into that life, even for half a heartbeat, not even to destroy them once and for all.

I scrambled down into the nearest storage hold where I fastened the hatch over me, muting the sounds and smells and the ghosts of Sun-wui. Hugging my knees in the darkness, I saw the clam girl's big eyes. What if we'd traded places? What if I'd been a step quicker and slipped inside the temple? Where would I be now? How a single moment can alter your life!

Shivering so hard I thought the whole ship might rattle apart, I heard an argument between Cheng Yat and Cheung Po Tsai.

"...no reason to go there now." I wondered what made Po Tsai care.

"Who gives orders on this ship? Not her. Not you."

We must have been close; I could hear birds whooping in the mangroves. I put one hand on the ladder. But no, I wouldn't allow myself to look. What if some local Punti recognized me when he saw my face and informed the whole village? "Shek Yang, the whore, remember? Turtle shit pirate now!"

The current shifted beneath me; the lower boom groaned like it did when it turned. We rumbled through that little line of turbulence where the inlet's smooth water met the rough and tumble of the wider channel. I'd bucked over that crease in the water a thousand times in my father's boat.

I counted ten massive beats of my heart to the place in the channel where, depending on the wind, we would turn to enter the sound.

Another ten beats passed, but the ship held course. We were passing Sun-wui. He'd neither stopped nor retreated. Nobody lost face.

I remained balled up like a hermit crab cringing in its shell until we were far beyond the boundaries of my ugly, shrunken memories.

Many nights later, the chill in my muscles and bones hadn't passed. I drank bitter medicine day and night, afraid I'd caught the coughing illness which had struck half the crew.

I moved to shut the porthole, but the purser made me leave it open for the light. The moon was nearly full, the sky clear and cold. I pulled a blanket tighter around my chest, inked my writing brush, and drew two horizontal lines in the top corner of my paper.

"Wrong order," the purser said.

I started over with a curt *pit* stroke. I hadn't planned to learn reading and writing again; merely seen an opportunity and seized it. I'd caught him pocketing silver that wasn't his and traded my silence in return for instruction.

I copied the word until it filled a full column.

"What did I tell you to write?" the purser said.

"Ox."

He grabbed the paper and shook it. Ink ran down the page, spoiling my work. "Then why did you write *noon?*"

"Give me. I'll get it right this time."

Someone rapped on the cabin door and cracked it open. A sailor peeked through. "Lamps out. Captain's order," he said, then told the purser, "Captain looking for you."

"What's happening?" I asked.

"Night raid," the crewman said, following the purser out.

I pulled on a heavy robe and stepped out to the companionway. The wind chafed my ears and made my head pound.

The men below spoke in whispers. Winches stayed silent as the sampan was lowered by hand. Lights in the distance hovered over their own faint reflections; shrimp boats, most likely, working through the night. I imagined the aroma of cooked shrimp that would welcome me in the morning, but the pleasure gave way to a sour taste in my throat. The junk dipped over a swell. My stomach seized in my chest.

I made it to the rail in time to vomit violently over the side.

A cold touch on my wrist. My eyes opened onto a figure who gradually focused into a spidery old man with a stringy white beard. My throat was so full of phlegm I had to swallow before I could speak.

"Who are you?"

Ah-Yi answered from somewhere behind him. "From the shrimp boat. Knows medicine."

Two fingers pressed my cheeks, stretching my lower lids so he could peer into my eyes. He told me to turn onto one side. "I need to examine your lower back and abdomen."

Ah-Yi answered for me. "She's no baby chicken. Go ahead."

His fingertips were like cold stone pestles. The cook stepped into the cabin and set down a crock, saying, "They want the medicine man."

"When he's ready," Ah-Yi said. "Get out. Your ugly face will only make her feel worse."

The old man rolled me onto my back and poked here and there across my belly, grunting even more than I was. He was beginning to frighten me.

"So?" I said. His face told me nothing, but Ah-Yi seemed strangely amused.

When he clamped his hands on my waist, I snapped, "Aren't you going to tell me what's wrong?"

"Shh! Stay still and I can inform you whether it's a boy or girl."

I didn't breathe for what seemed like two hundred years while his words soaked in. It wasn't possible. It couldn't happen to me. I had been so careful. Mostly.

"You're wrong! Get out of here! No, wait."

I pulled him by the sleeves and whispered, "Wolfbane. Can you get me?" Many girls I'd known had rid themselves of babies with this precious herb. All except one had recovered from its effects, and none of the creatures inside them. "Please, I'll pay. But you mustn't tell."

His eyes filled with disgust. He tugged himself from my grip and shuffled to the door.

"Wait," Ah-Yi said. "Boy or girl?"

He shrugged. "Maybe a sheep. Cries like her. *Myehh myehh.*"

"Call him back," I told Ah-Yi. But he was gone.

Cheng Yat stumbled in, smelling like he'd swallowed enough celebratory toasts to welcome a hundred sons. That and the pungent odor of boiling shrimp from the galley sent me to the porthole for a lengthy bout of retching.

He pulled me from the window with a huge sloppy grin. How was I supposed to tell him—to tell anyone—that I didn't want this child? How could I pretend to be happy? I didn't dare spoil his joy.

"Don't look horrified. It's me, your husband."

"Go away. I need to be alone."

"You'll have plenty of alone time. Now, we celebrate." He pressed a flask of wine to my lips and tried pouring it in. I shook my head so hard the bottle flew from his hand. He picked it up, took a swallow, then pried my jaw open and drowned my tongue in wine. "Drink! Be happy! You're giving me a son!"

The wine went quickly to work. Had the old man really said it would be a boy? Curse the old dog! It didn't matter anyway. Boy, girl, snake, or fox, I didn't want this thing inside me. I didn't want to blow up like a puffer fish. I'd almost forgotten that I once had dreams for myself, ones which would vanish forever in an instant within the cursed role of mother.

I might have had room in my belly, but there was no room in my heart for a child.

I barricaded myself in the cabin the next morning. I knew what was coming, and they wouldn't take me easily. A crewman, the cook, and finally Ah-Yi, tapped on the door, offering food. But no matter how hungry I was, I wasn't going to be tricked into opening the latch. Finally, though, I could no longer hold in the need to relieve myself—the kind that could not be easily capped in a jug. Waiting until I sensed no voices on the companionway, I crept outside as quietly as I could, padded to the privy and completed my business as quickly as my bowels would allow.

When I got up from behind the barrier, Cheng Yat stood waiting.

He led me like a condemned prisoner to a hold between the deckhouse and, of all places, the weapons magazine. The hatch stood open, gateway to my personal purgatory, the chamber meant to confine me, by tradition, from today until one month following the birth.

"I'm not living in there," I hissed through gritted teeth. It seemed the entire crew was on deck pretending to be busy with chores while their eyes and ears were all trained on the anticipated pyrotechnics from the captain's hot-tempered wife. Maybe he'd ordered them to be there, knowing that if I flouted tradition, they would blame me for cursing the ship.

"Don't give me a reason to fight you," he said under his breath.

Of course, he was right. It was a battle I would never win. I removed my arm from his grip and placed a foot on the ladder, saying loud enough for my audience, "Anyway, I'll be happy not to breathe in your filthy odor for a few months!"

There was more truth to my words than I'd expected. The hold was provisioned with a freshly woven mat and a blanket so new I wondered if it had been stored for just this purpose. Every surface of the room was newly caulked and smoothed. It was the cleanest and driest compartment in the entire ship. I teetered on the verge of gratitude until I quickly understood: no vapors were to be allowed in, so the baby wouldn't be born weak. It wasn't me he was thinking of. To hell with him and all of them and their stupid damned superstitions!

My clothing and personal items, all cleaned and polished, were delivered in a basket so new its fronds still showed some green. After I was given congee and water, I asked not to be disturbed.

I pushed aside a polished ceramic stool and sat on the floor, probing my belly for a lump, a seed, anything to indicate a thing growing inside me, but of course, it was too early for that. Nothing on the outside was different yet. What was the point of confining me so soon? Of tossing me into a crypt until I was ready to bear and be reborn? Yes, that was the feeling which burned like a lump of coal in my chest. I'd been buried alive.

For days I sat alone in the dark, my world reduced to sounds and touch. Every slight move of the ship, every chain screech or squeak of the rudder, came through my ears, buttocks, and back as though they were screaming at me. I started at each swell that batted the hull as if it would splash right through and drown me.

Food and water were delivered twice daily. I had the freedom to spend the days on deck if I chose, but other than runs to the privy when I could no longer hold it, I quickly got tired of people's attentions and advice.

Don't go up there. It's dangerous.

You'll catch cold. You'll catch fever.

You can't eat lamb. No crabs or shrimp. Melons, bananas, papayas, mangoes—forbidden to a pregnant woman!

Don't. Don't. Don't!

I wanted to scream, *I can take care of myself!*

Instead, I stayed put with my raging thoughts for company.

I tried to make sense of the changes that had come over me so suddenly. I was going to be a mother.

Mother.

Someone would call me mother.

Boy or girl? The old medicine man had never said, even to Cheng Yat. I would be revered among men and gods if I delivered a son. I would finally earn my special place among the society of sea bandits, mother to the precious male heir. And otherwise? I only had to recall the humiliations my mother endured to know that for a man like Cheng Yat, the sun and moon would collide and incinerate the world if I didn't deliver a boy, and I would be solely to blame, the unworthy wife, for violating the three obediences:

Obedience to father before marriage;
Obedience to husband after marriage;
Obedience to son after husband's death.

As if the husband's death is preordained. As if men could always sell and abduct me and violate me and then die on me.

I slapped the thing inside my belly.

I don't want you! I don't want you! I don't want you!

Boys could be ripped from my arms, thrown into battle—if they didn't run there of their own accord—and cast a mother's heart into insanity.

I don't want you!

Boys grew into men, who fought and drank, sold girls and stole women. My fist squeezed into my belly.

I don't want you!

I caught my wrist with my other hand and told myself to stop. I was teetering, spinning, although the ship was rock still. I breathed hard, in and out, until the storm in my head subsided.

Would I want you if you were a girl?

No daughter of mine would ever be wrested from me, not for all the money in the world, nor forced into marriage against her, or my, will. My daughter would learn guns and swords; if I couldn't find her an elephant to ride, I'd get her a horse or a donkey.

I leaned back and patted whoever lodged inside me.

If you must crawl from between these legs and enter this terrible world, at least let the gods make you a girl.

One morning I woke late, my mind clear as autumn air. The sick feelings had subsided. Only when I stood and stretched did the minor ache in my legs remind me that I was carrying a child. I craved light and fresh air—and food. I was as famished as a starving dog.

We appeared to be anchored off an uninhabited rocky coast with too many ships to be our squadron alone. The cook pressed a bowl of congee into my hands. I handed it back.

"Dried fish again? Every day, fish-fish-fish. Do we have any of those shrimps left?"

The cook smiled back. "Ah, Cheng Yat Sou, congratulations! But you know you're not supposed—"

"I don't care what I'm not supposed to eat! If the child comes out with ruddy skin because I eat shrimp—which I don't believe, by the way—that's the sacrifice she'll be honored to make for her mother. Throw in some black sesame at the same time!"

"We don't have black sesame, and you're also not—"

"Think I don't know that? What are you doing? Give me back the damned congee and fish!"

My conduct was rude, but I had the excuse: I was the fragile expectant mother, slightly crazed by pregnancy. Let them all suffer. The only one I could speak with truthfully was Ah-Yi. I found her surrounded by shoe-making scraps beside a bulwark.

She knew me by my shadow. Eyes on her hide-cutting, she declared, "Ah! Risen from the deep, at last. Just in time. Here." She handed me the carving knife and traced a finger along the pig skin in which she'd scored the rough shape of a shoe sole. "Hand's cramping. You finish it while I dig out something to show you."

I didn't have to make my usual excuses. I simply had to wait for her to realize her error—which didn't take long. She grabbed the knife from me in horror.

"Aiya! What are you doing? You're not supposed to touch blades."

She reached deep inside her bag and placed a tiny pair of shoes on my lap. "Yours. If you think them too plain, you can fill in the embroidery here and beside the heel."

They were not plain by any measure. Fruity red Vietnamese silk— so she'd been shopping back in Chiang Ping too!—bordered in yellow around the soles. The embroidery's intricate lines converged from back to front into laughing tiger heads across the toes. I held a hand over my mouth, struck by more than simply their beauty: I could imagine my child's tiny feet kicking inside them.

"They're...they're like precious jewels," I said.

"Ha! That's pouring on too much salt, but I do confess they're almost too cute to give up. Aiya! Your congee is hardening into glue. Eat! Eat!"

I slid the baby shoes into my vest pocket, so precious I felt as if I were stealing them, then attacked the lumpy gruel and now-flaccid fish jerky. Ah-Yi returned to work cutting soles, for adult shoes this time.

"Whose fleet is out there?" I said. "They can't all be ours."

"Don't remind me. You'll meet him sooner than you care to and wish you hadn't."

"Prepare me, then."

"Don't say I didn't warn you. Drooling old goat, General Bo."

"Please, no more generals!"

Ah-Yi softened the edge of the freshly cut pig skin between her teeth while speaking at the same time.

"I didn't understand a word," I said. "Can you stop working for one moment and tell me?"

"Hee! I said, it's one of those useless titles the Tay-son doled out. No, he wasn't with us—was part of the first campaign, before your time. But the old jackass gets livid if you forget to call him by his rank. Calls your husband Admiral to get him to play along with his game."

"Now you worry me. What game?"

"Nothing to worry about. They've been talking about a joint excursion. Pass me that wood block."

I passed it. "I presume that means a raid."

She hammered the sole around the edge, then plunged a threaded needle through the toe. "If you ask me, we can use some plunder to liven things up around here."

She didn't know how right she was. The past year had slipped by as if I'd slept through it. I couldn't stand another moment boxed in that dingy hold like a brooding chicken. I would become slave enough once the child was born.

Whatever this raid was, I had to be part of it.

Cheng Yat wasn't having it. He caught me talking to the cannon crew.

"Aiya! Away from those guns. You'll—"

"What? Harm the child? I would think you'd want him to get used to them, have him fondling blunderbusses while he sucks milk."

"Please, go inside." He seemed genuinely concerned. Did I detect feelings toward fatherhood?

"You walk me there and tell me about the raid."

We stood beside the hatch where he explained in his typically clipped manner. Our group and General Bo, whom I'd yet to meet, would sail by different routes and converge three days later near a salt port where we would attack from two directions. I found it difficult to share his enthusiasm. It was just another raid of an ugly little town to steal a load of salt, hardly a glittering prize.

"What makes you think he won't beat us to it?" I said.

"There you go again. Why don't you stick to things you know, like making babies?"

Another might have believed he was joking if they didn't realize that Cheng Yat was incapable of humor.

"I know as much about making babies as you do," I said. "Try asking me about breech loading mechanisms instead."

"Woman, you always do this! Twist my words and wring out your own meaning. Let me tell you, then—I'll do some twisting myself. If I supposedly know as much as you about being pregnant, then my words are as valid as yours. Am I right? And my words are: please go back into the hold where you and my child will be safe and clean. And let me take care of the business of stealing salt where at least I can claim slightly more experience than you."

"What about General Bo? Do you trust him?"

"We've known each other fifteen years."

"You didn't answer the question."

"Aiya! I hope my son doesn't drown me in questions all day like his mother!"

He walked away, leaving me at a loss for words. Cheng Yat had beaten me at my own argument. He had engaged me, truly engaged me, for perhaps the first time, not with his typical taciturn grunts and awkwardness, but by matching wits with me. What greater form of respect could a man offer a woman?

We waited at the rendezvous area three full days without sign of General Bo. Cheng Yat wouldn't talk about it. Everyone on board remained on edge. It was the new cook's assistant, a hulking, bearded bear of a man, who brought me the news along with evening rice: we would sail overnight and board the salt barges before sunrise.

No one had counted on a battle being underway when we arrived. The boom of cannons was heard long before the port itself was visible.

A hint of dawn colored the horizon. Cheng Yat dashed back and forth, yelling orders. My gut wanted to join the cannon crew in wiping down the guns, but naturally, this was forbidden, so I settled on an inverted oil cask and watched. We were close enough now to catch glimpses of ships in the light of gun flashes. From what I could tell, the barrage was one-sided. The battle was nearly finished. By the time we were close enough to consider taking part, the raiders were already leaving with two salt barges in tow.

It took all my will to not remind Cheng Yat of my suspicions toward his erstwhile brother-in-arms.

"So General Bo betrayed us and went in for the spoils?" I asked a passing crewman.

"He never showed up," he replied.

I frowned. "Then who—?"

"I don't know, Cheng-tai."

From the sound of it, Cheng Yat had figured it out, shouting, for all to hear, every name except the usurper's real one.

"Ox prick! Donkey shit! Fuck him for eighteen generations!" He took one last look through his spyglass before flinging it to the floor. No one dared approach close enough to retrieve it. I calmly walked over to pick it up. The glass had not shattered. I raised it to my eye.

One junk was familiar: larger and sleeker than the others; of dark, nearly black mahogany, though that may have been a trick of the morning twilight.

It slowly turned its stern our way while its sails filled toward the west. Across the transom were characters in blazoning red paint which, though unreadable to me, had burned themselves into my memory, reminders of its owner's love of words. It seemed like a lifetime ago when he'd written some words just for me, long lost somewhere in the madness:

Always remain young and beautiful.

I watched him through the spyglass, even as he gained distance and our ship turned south, relieved that Cheng Yat decided not to intercept. Relieved that Kwok Podai wouldn't see my swelling belly.

XXIII
Blockade

After months at sea, I should have been happy to stand on solid ground where at least I could walk without tumbling over my big round belly across a pitching deck. But this was Tunghoi. Here, I walked with a ghost.

She whispered in my ear when I passed the sweet potato hawker: "Pssh! Keep your eye on his thumbs that they don't touch the scale!"

And the seed merchant: "Fresh, she says? Maybe when I was a child."

More whispers: "Let's buy tea, Younger Sister."

Wherever I turned, I heard her throaty, lived-in voice: "My dear Younger Sister."

I tried to run from her, stumbling past hawkers and net makers, between coolies and drunken sailors, but still I couldn't spit out the memories that haunted my heart.

"I want a flower boat name too!" The voice laughed and laughed and laughed.

I nearly slipped in a puddle of mud, or something worse, in an alley taken over by dogs who barked furiously at the intruder.

All the men were there in the wine shop—Cheng Yat, Tunghoi Bat, Wu-shek Yi and his brothers, other captains and Taumuks—jolly and flush-faced with wine. I leaned on the door frame and caught my breath, afraid to look past them into the corner, to the table where she and I used to laugh and poke fun at our husbands.

But no ghost woman sat waiting for me. In her place, Wu's three wives and the wives of his brothers waved me over. The youngest was nearly as pregnant as I was. Even before my tea was poured, my ears throbbed with more than anyone ever needed to know about a cousin's husband's philandering and the price of preserved plums. Immediately, I planned my escape from these cackling creatures as primitive in their destiny as the geese they resembled.

"Seen the new village comb maker? You must!" Wu wife number two advised me.

"She's not thinking about combs," said wife three, the pregnant one, who couldn't have been older than sixteen. She placed a hand on my knee. "How's the baby?"

In fact, the little creature was kicking inside me. Even the fetus couldn't bear their chatter.

"Come to our village. We'll have our babies together."

"We'll be your midwives," said the fox-faced wife of...Wu-shek Sam? I couldn't keep them straight.

Another wife said, "She'll be your wet nurse. Breasts like a cow's!" The five sisters-in-law choked on their laughter.

I was saved by the proprietor's pigtailed daughter appearing with a plate of steamed fish, followed by her brother with spiced clams. It looked and smelled delicious, and everyone attacked with their chopsticks. But a few bites were enough for me. I had no appetite, either for food or the frothy gossip that consumed these women. More intriguing were the bits and pieces drifting from the men's table. Something about the provincial Governor-General killing himself. I slid my stool back to hear better.

"I swear, that's how I heard it," Tunghoi Bat said. "Shoved a snuff bottle down his own throat. Though my sources tell me he was pressing the Imperial Court for funds to build eighty new war junks to fight bandits, and the emperor turned him down. Long live the emperor, I say!"

"Maybe his wife did it," said Wu-shek Yi in his fluty voice. "That's why I treat mine like queens! Speaking of whom—I'd propose a drink to the ladies, but we're all dried up. Proprietor! More wine!"

It came quickly. Tunghoi Bat filled the cups. "To the mothers. A healthy son for Cheng Yat! May it be twin boys!"

"Or twin girls to serve my son," Wu-shek Yi said.

I pretended to be honored at their drunkenness in my name. But I wanted to hear more about the Governor-General. Rejected by the emperor, killing himself with a bottle. I thought such things happened only in operas. The question was, what occurs in the next act? Fortunately, Cheng Yat wondered the same.

"So, we get a new Governor-General," he said. "He'll want to prove himself like the last one, put on a show of fighting us scum of the sea for a month or two to prove his manhood."

"That is indeed the point, my fellows," said Tunghoi Bat. "I'm told it'll take at least a month for a successor to get here. Meanwhile, the whole Kwangtung and Kwangshi government hibernates, which offers us a rare opportunity."

"Who tells you all this?" Cheng Yat said.

"Ha! Same local *yamen* sesame seeds who tell me everything. No iron is so hard that it can't be melted down with a little *salary from the sea.*"

He paid. They spun stories. How were corruptible petty officials more reliable than a street bard? I held my tongue, waiting for someone else to speak up, but he anticipated the question.

"They'd better be telling the truth because what my source said next will interest you. Their office received a request for a naval escort for a convoy of deep ocean vessels from Luzon."

"—Yang, you listening? I heard you have the cutest baby shoes." Wu's second wife so startled me I didn't know what she meant at first.

"Show us," said one of the sisters-in-law.

"I thought you didn't sew. You've been keeping secrets!"

"Quiet," I said.

Indeed, everyone at both tables shut up.

"Sorry," I said to the men. "Please don't let us interrupt."

Tunghoi Bat cleared his throat. "Yes, well the ladies might wish to leave. We're talking boring business."

The Wu wives looked at each other like they might take up his suggestion.

"I'm staying," I said.

Tunghoi Bat wrinkled his nose as if I were a day-old fish, then turned back to the other men. "I was saying, there's been a request for an escort."

"So, we need to stay out of sight for a while," Wu-shek Yi said.

"On the contrary. Now is the time to act." Bat let the remark hang while he spooned spicy beans into a bowl with his six-fingered hand.

"In other words, you want us to pick a fight with the navy?" Wu-shek Yi said. "I think you may have raised a few toasts too many."

"You'll be the one raising toasts when I tell you. My trustworthy *yamen* fellow said he would have to requisition civilian vessels for such an escort but lacks the funds to do so. He worries that there may soon be no navy left to bother us. It seems our all-wise Celestial Emperor is more concerned with barbarian upstarts in the western deserts than in protecting a few coastal traders who are all dodging taxes anyway. Not only are they short on fighting ships, but I'm told that naval vessels destroyed in action are not being replaced. So, fellows, for the next month, our government is a big fat bear without a head to guide it nor claws to defend itself. If we were to join forces—"

"Join forces? Ha!" Wu-shek Yi said. "If the government's a bear, what are we? Five duck eggs don't make a goose and a hundred won't build a swan."

Cheng Yat slammed down his cup. "Exactly. Under whose leadership do we 'join forces'? Should I guess? Last time I let someone else take charge, I barely escaped with my balls."

"If you ask me—"

"No one asked, but we know the answer," Wu said. "We're sitting here drinking and talking stories, and suddenly you're leading a charge against the southern navy."

"More fighting? I'd rather stay here," Wu's first wife said.

"Might upset the babies," the pregnant one said.

"You still haven't shown us the shoes," said the middle wife.

"Will you shut up?" I said. Cheng Yat looked daggers at me. I didn't care. Bat's plan had merit. Every one of us certainly needed a boost to our coffers.

"How many ships do we have between us?" I said. "A hundred? A hundred and twenty? How many escorts could they send? Our hapless Governor-General swallowed a bottle because he couldn't raise eighty."

"Ah, the lady speaks," said Tunghoi Bat, his voice sharp as a bee sting, despite my supporting his idea.

Fatty Wu cut him off. "If she leads the charge, I might follow, just so I can watch her pretty behind."

Cheng Yat's teeth clenched so tight they could have ground stone into dust. Once again the wrong words had escaped my mouth, too late to snatch them back. He was now the patriarch of the Cheng clan, whose lineage could be traced back to the Ming patriot Cheng Singkung, while Tunghoi Bat was no more than a common fisherman with a deformity turned criminal, and Wu-shek Yi was Cheng Yat's former catamite. My remark about ship numbers had drawn attention to the fact that among the three fleets, Cheng Yat's was the smallest, at twenty-six junks. I'd cost my husband tremendous face.

We both were spared further embarrassment when a sailor burst into the wine shop. "Attack! Fishing boats shot at in the channel! Attack!"

Tables teetered. Wine cups smashed on the floor. Men and women alike stampeded out the door. Only we two pregnant ones lagged behind, supporting each other as we dragged our swollen bellies to the quay where we barely managed to squeeze onto the last available sampan.

Our deck was a riot of winches, ropes, sails hoisting, and of course, weapons being assembled, cleaned, and loaded. Women unrolled hides over the gunwales. I offered my help, but a strong hand wrenched me back.

Cheng Yat was red in the face. "You're trying to kill my child? Back to shore! Now!"

I was no weak little flower. Why shouldn't I work at a time like this? I wanted to tell him to get his hands off me, but there was something unusual about the set of his eyes, the tone of his voice. Something akin to fear. Not about the attack—he'd come through worse, always with courage. What I saw in him was fear for his unborn child. Inside this leathery man was a father waiting to be born.

I let it be known that I wouldn't fight him. "Go command your ships," I said.

It was too late for me to leave. The rudder was set. Anchors weighed. Sails filled. I helped myself up the stairway and stood outside the cabin, giving myself a clear view of our makeshift armada flowing out of the harbor, past the headland, into a stiff, angry wind.

And into a barrage of cannon bursts.

Thick gray gunpowder smoke masked the attackers until the breeze dispersed it. Sail markings identified them as naval ships. Shrouded in cannon smoke, they were impossible to count. Their shots made no sense. Tipping through swells with the wind across their beams, they couldn't hope to hit a target even if they were within range—which they weren't by a long measure. Their shots dunked into the water a full *li* short. Either their commanders were inexperienced or…

Suddenly, I understood. This naval force was sending us the message that they had ammunition to waste.

We were under siege.

Scouts reported warships up and down the channel, both east and west, though no one agreed on how many. All that mattered was that Tunghoi harbor was firmly locked in.

Cheng Yat returned from a morning filled with meetings exhausted, pale, and sweat-stained. His voice was raw; he'd been yelling.

"All ducks and no swan, like Wu said."

I called down for tea and ginger to soothe his throat, then sat still beside him and waited, my silence asking the questions.

"Wu wants to attack," he said. "Eleven Fingers wants us to sit here until the navy loses its nerve."

"And what do you want?"

The tea arrived. I filled the cups and dropped in ginger slivers. Cheng Yat blew on his tea longer than needed, as though considering my question.

"I want unity," he said. "Avoid a repeat of Spirit River."

My fear exactly, the one I'd been afraid to say out loud. Now that it was said, the ghost whispers returned to me as a multitude, screaming over each other, women and men, young boys and mothers.

"Not feeling well. Must be the baby," I told him.

Back in my hold, I rolled in sweat, pleading for this pregnancy to finish and normal life to resume. Not that life would ever have a chance of being normal with a child to care for. Thoughts of crying and feeding and cleaning and answering demand after demand kept me from sleeping to escape my present aches and pains. Then some new commotion broke out overhead, compelling me to climb up and see.

Cheung Po Tsai stood with his back to me, raining water like he'd gone swimming in his clothes. In front of him, three men, stripped to loincloths with their hands bound behind their backs, knelt in front of Cheng Yat.

"This one's the spy." Po Tsai kicked the fatter of the captives, a man with a flat northern face. From where I stood, the others looked more like fishermen or farmers than navy men.

"Where did you catch them?" Cheng Yat said.

"The rock cave behind the western headland—you know it?—

hiding in a boat, thought their fishermen's hats disguised them. Ha!"

One captive mumbled something. Cheng Yat made him repeat it.

"Said I'm just a fisherman. I've a wife, a son. I'll pay your ransom." He banged his forehead on the deck. Another man whimpered for mercy.

"You should have been catching fish instead of helping spies." Cheng Yat gave a silent order. Crewmen dragged the fishermen to the deckhouse. I couldn't watch, though I felt the chops reverberate through the ship.

The northerner neither moved nor showed any expression, even when Cheng Yat threatened him with a cutlass and demanded, "How many ships out there?"

Enraged at the spy's stony silence, Cheng Yat kicked him and shouted hoarsely, "How many?"

The northerner coughed up phlegm. Cheng Yat kneed him in the chin. The spy spat blood between Cheng Yat's feet, then spoke in accented Cantonese, "Curse you fucking pirate scum to hell's bottom realm!"

"Nail him!"

Two men held him upright with his back against the mast, while others tied his arms around it. Then a burly crewman hammered a spike through the spy's foot deep into the deck. His face reddened; his jaw clamped. He struggled to hold onto his dignity.

Just then Cheng Yat noticed me. "Go down. You'll curse my child!"

Wasn't the child already cursed to be born to a mother like me. Born into a world always in proximity to death? A superstitious world of *Don't eat this! Don't touch that! Don't wash these! Don't go here, or here, or here!*—awash with beliefs based on fear? Nobody could explain why a woman had to be quarantined throughout her pregnancy except that "it's tradition", and even the thought of violating tradition provoked horror. Let me give my child a lesson not to submit to the tyranny of tradition. I climbed all the way onto the deck and took my regular seat on an overturned oil cask. Let the poor baby get used to the sounds and the screams before he's out of the womb. Let him prepare to be born a pirate.

"I see you act tough like your elephant queen," Cheng Yat said. "Why sit way over there? Move her seat closer. Now! Beside me!"

Cheng Yat examined his cutlass while waiting for me to settle. I knew what was coming. I saw it in the set of his shoulder, the way his eyes sank into his skull, the tap-tap-tap of the blade on the deck.

Part of me wanted to run, leap into the water, and swim away until I reached shore or sank. I'd witnessed the Ten Thousand Cuts years ago in a Kwangchow square and had joined in the hateful lust of the crowd watching a criminal be sliced apart piece by tiny piece. It was too late to back out. I had to take his dare.

A crewman emptied a water bucket over the spy.

"Who's in command out there?" Cheng Yat said.

The prisoner gave away nothing; he appeared not even to breathe.

Cheng Yat pinched the man's eyebrow and held the cutlass over it like a butcher preparing to slice a chicken wing. "You heard me. Who is in command?"

The man slowly, deliberately, closed his eyes.

With one small motion, Cheng Yat sliced off the brow and flung it away like a bloody worm. The spy's jaw tightened, and his knees shook, but he denied his tormentor the satisfaction of seeing his pain, giving in only when Cheng Yat grabbed the other eyebrow. The man croaked, "Commander Suen."

"Again?" Cheng Yat said.

"Suen Chuen-mau."

"How many ships?"

The spy shook his head. The other eyebrow came off. At last, the man screamed.

The baby inside me flinched. It knew. I stroked my belly and silently apologized.

"I say it once more. How many ships? What kind of ordnance? What are his orders?"

The spy blinked away the blood dripping into his eyes and stared into Cheng Yat's. He spoke in Mandarin, the language of the government, in words common enough that anyone could understand.

"Orders to kill you filthy bandit spawn of pigs. Fuck your pig mother."

I turned away, tried to mute my ears, but the man's cries of agony could have pierced walls. I made the mistake of looking again. His nose was gone, uncapping a dark cavity of cartilage and blood. I must have nearly dropped off my seat. Hands behind me supported my arms and shoulders.

Cheng Yat turned around, his face red as fiery coal. "Bring her to me. Bring her here!"

The hands lifted me, nudging me forward.

"You! I told you not to watch. But you insisted! You insist to insert your nose into every business of this ship. Good! Take this!"

He held out his cutlass.

"You think you're smarter. You think you can do better? Oh, yes, I see you judge me. Show me, show us all, how brave and clever you are."

I took a step back, holding my belly, straining to calm the wrenching in my gut—was it the child's protest or my stomach about to snap?

"Never mind the baby," Cheng Yat said. "He can't see or hear." He pressed the blade's grip into my hand. "Chin or fingers next? Your choice!"

If this was meant to be a lesson in courage, he was mistaken. With my arm weighed down by the cutlass, I understood that slicing off a hand required no bravery on my part; what it needed was a reason. I felt no particular hatred for this man. Rather, I considered him pathetic, stubbornly valuing his pride over his life, fiercely loyal to some commander who'd sent him out to die. Cheng Yat expected the same of his crew, but that was the point: it was the soldier's job to kill or be killed, and not something that should arouse either pity or compassion. Still, I couldn't help thinking that this man roped to the mast, feet pinioned to the deck, trying to control the trembling from one end of his body to the other, was the most courageous one here.

Mutilation had extracted little information, and one more cut would make him faint dead away. I tried a different strategy. Laying the cutlass on the deck, I put on my best professional face from my old life.

"I'm about to become a mother. Do you have children?"

His mouth puckered into something resembling sadness.

"Answer a few questions, and I'll send you home. To your family. Your wife. Your beautiful sons and daughters."

Tears or sweat caught the light on his face. He wanted to trust me, or that was the impression I'd invented for myself.

Cheng Yat loomed forward and reached for the cutlass. The northerner coughed behind closed lips. He opened his mouth and coughed again, deliberately. A thick wad of blood-marbled phlegm struck between my feet.

I escaped to the hold, latching the hatch cover tightly to shut out light and sound. My back to the wall, I banged my feet against the floor, anything to drown the noise from outside. The chopping might have been my knuckles pummeling the bulkhead; the screams might have been cries from my throat. The baby twisted inside, sending pain to every point in my body. I grabbed my ankles, pulled my belly to my chest. The fetus struggled against me. *Yes! Fight me,* I told it. *Kick me, bite me—punish me for bringing you into this horrifying, painful, bloody world!*

Disgust washed over me, and at first, I didn't understand why. It wasn't the brutality of the Ten Thousand Cuts. I'd seen enough torment and dying in my time among the pirates, sometimes for no other reason than to steal a little boat. I myself had taken a man's life. Why should this execution bother me so?

The baby's kicking became unbearable. I stretched out on the floor and stroked my belly. *I'm sorry. I'm sorry. Don't blame me, please. Let's both have some peace.*

The silence struck me, not just inside the hold. Aside from the normal creaks and rocking, an almost reverent hush had overtaken the ship.

I wanted to cry at the utter stupid pointlessness of what had happened. What had we received in exchange for hacking a man to death other than a name and fresh blood soaking into the fibers of our ship?

Finally, I understood my disgust.

I'd have pried more information by simply having him alone in a room.

It took no more convincing to send myself ashore until the baby came. I was given a small one-room house in a dusty back lane and a servant named Siu-ting. She was a clever local Tunghoi girl of thirteen who kept the place tidy, prepared my meals, fanned me while I napped in the punishing summer heat, and put up with my moods.

Siu-ting was also my source of all the latest rumors: the navy was about to withdraw; the navy had expanded forces; the pirate leaders had prepared a common battle plan; the captains had come to blows in the wine shop and wrecked the tables; new food sources had been found. Though judging by the dwindling quality and quantity of items she brought from the market, that last rumor proved false enough to make all the other news suspect.

In the month that followed, I received frequent visits from the Wu wives, Ah-Yi, and other women. Cheung Po Tsai surprised me with a visit. Somewhere he'd found dried plums, which I greedily devoured. He even brought me a loose-fitting smock of cheerful blue fabric.

"Even a pregnant woman should look good," he said. "Especially one carrying my baby brother. Or sister. I'll take both, ha!"

The other men still considered my place of confinement off-limits. At least, that was Cheng Yat's excuse. He staggered in late one evening, sloppy with drink, wanting sex "with a real elephant woman." I threw him off.

"The baby's doing well, and the mother is coping. Thank you for asking," I said.

His eyes and mouth drooped like a confused puppy.

"Isn't that what you came here to find out? Do you care about this child? Because I'm trying very hard to," I told him.

"I came to pleasure you." His hands were all over me. Again, I pried him off.

"You want to give me pleasure? Show me you're happy about this thing you put inside me, so that maybe you can convince me to feel the same."

He stumbled outside, giving no clue of whether he had heard me.

One day I was alone, pacing in the dark and sweaty air, having shut the house tight against the aggressive flies. Someone knocked, then let herself in. I opened a window as much for the light as to freshen the air for my guest's benefit.

I had never warmed to Tunghoi Bat's wife: too convinced of the aristocracy of her position as wife of the local crime boss. She had dressed as if to remind me of that, in a patterned silk robe too formal for such a visit, her white hair bunched into a white ivory comb over a face so pale one would think she had just emerged from a cave.

"I've brought a little something for you," she said, setting a red paperboard box on the table and lifting the cover. Two compartments brimmed with melon seeds and boiled nuts. "Troublesome to find these days, as long as *they're* out there," she said, shrugging toward the harbor and the naval blockaders beyond. "But I well remember the cravings of a mother-to-be."

Expressing thanks, I offered her the stool while I sat on the edge of the raised platform bed. The nuts tasted stale, but the crispy melon seeds were a heavenly delight.

She smiled. "You must feel like you've come home."

"To be truthful, I'm not so quick anymore to call any place home."

"Don't be silly. You were married here. That makes it home enough. I feel practically like your mother."

Some mother! This was the first time in my memory that she and I had ever been alone together. I had a growing suspicion that her visit was motivated less out of motherly concern than to assert who was matriarch among the pirates since the passing of Cheng Chat and his wife.

"My dear, you look exhausted," she said. "Lie down. Don't be polite."

Her sympathy didn't match the coolness of her voice. Still, I was sore behind the ribs and even sitting up strained my back. I lay half-upright against a pile of cushions. "I sometimes curse Cheng Yat for doing this to me."

Bat's wife had a husky laugh. "I know what you mean. Believe me, you'll forget you ever had pain the moment you hold your son in your arms."

"I don't know that it's a son."

"Of course we all hope for one."

I sipped water from a bowl; it had an earthy tang. "Boy, girl, monkey, or pig, it's all the same to me."

"Wah! Bad luck to speak such nonsense. Boy or girl, either way you'll love it."

"Isn't it enough to give him a child? I'm expected to love it as well?" It was the question I kept asking myself. I gave her same answer I gave myself: "I'll be glad when it's out, so I can get back to ship's business."

"Oh, my dear." Bat's wife moved over and took my hand. "You can't be serious. That's no job for a woman. Maybe when you're older."

"Are you saying you have nothing to do with your husband's business?"

She pulled her hand away and looked at the wall, like she was holding back secrets. "I support my husband's enterprise. That's enough. When you're young, like you, the job of motherhood is taxing enough."

"I'm sorry, but that's all it is to me, a job I didn't ask for. I never decided to be a mother. Did you? But men expect sons."

"Maybe I'm more traditional than you, my dear, but it isn't something one thinks about, given the fact that one doesn't have a choice." Her mouth hung open, breathing back whatever words she had prepared next, though I could read her thoughts: *...unless one is a whore who takes* *bitter herbs.* She smiled with a shrug as if she hadn't meant such a thing at all. "Yes, it's a responsibility. But love for your baby—it takes you by surprise. You'll find out soon."

"Like my father. Loved me so much he sold me for a boat."

"Dear, you're confusing—"

"No, I'm not. I understand." I patted my bulge. "Hear that in there? Surprise me. Otherwise, I can always sell you."

Her face pinched in genuine pain. What had she expected, barging in and lecturing me? The way she put it, this "love" she spoke of was some kind of sickness that took hold of a body. My mother had certainly loved the little unborn boy who ultimately killed her. When Cheng Chat's wife lost her beloved boys, she became a wandering ghost. Motherly love was a fatal affliction.

Bat's wife refilled our bowls from the water jar and handed me one.

"Drink. I think the heat is driving you a bit mad," she said. "You might see me as a withered old lady, but at least I've known the love of a man and the love of a child."

"I should congratulate you, then."

"I apologize for coming here and disturbing you. Pregnancy does strange things to one's mind, so I'll forgive your bitterness. But you're lucky to have such a good man with a child on the way."

"I don't deny he's a good man. He's often kind, occasionally respectful, usually protective. I might even go so far as to say yes, I'm lucky in that sense. But to go any farther, then you're speaking of fairy tales."

"Oh, please, dear. Let's talk of something else." She offered me a handful of red seeds, but I waved them away.

"No. You brought up the subject of love. Maybe you're older than me and wiser, so teach me. Because love is something I've only ever seen in street operas. It's something faked by people in face paint. It's something poets scribble into words contrived to manipulate your heart. It's something I learned to fake on the flower boats. I'd have to fake it to claim that I love this thing inside me."

Her eyes squeezed into slits. She snapped the lid onto the box and stood to leave.

"You're a very sad woman," Bat's wife said. "But I don't pity you."

"Thank you. I don't want pity. I want water. Would you hand me that bowl before you go?"

Bat's wife's visit left me troubled, or rather, the things I had said did. For all Cheng Yat's moods and unpredictability, I'd come to understand him, and he'd come to understand me. I was indeed lucky to have such a man, even if I had a hard time confessing it to myself. And why had I mentioned poetry? What did I really know about poetry or its deliverer? The word itself frightened me as much as I was frightened of drowning.

But drown I did after Bat's wife left, this time in my own aches and sweat. No matter how many lumpy cushions propped my back, I couldn't bear to lie on the hard, wooden pallet while my huge belly made it painful to sit up. Flies buzzed around my face. I finished half the melon seeds, but they only made my stomach cry for something sweet—a melon or a sugar cane to chew. Where was the serving girl?

Hot sunlight poured through the window. I called out, "Siu-ting!"

If she didn't return soon, I would ask the next passerby to find me some fruit. I had coins. I had a position in this town. But no one walked past. The alley was lifeless, as if the entire population had fled.

If nobody was here, there was no risk to my modesty if I opened my tunic to let a puff of breeze cool my sweat. My breasts sang in relief to meet the open air. The baby stirred, poking a tiny foot or hand against my insides. Wincing, I felt for the place where it seemed to be pushing and pressed down with the flat of my hand.

The baby kicked.

It had to be a foot, a tiny human heel. Was it fighting to come out? Playing? Could it be a real, love-hungry child reaching for its mother?

Would he—would she—really love me? No one had loved me since the day my mother died, so why should they start now?

I pushed a finger into my belly, but nothing happened. I poked a different spot and was answered with a firm kick.

"Oh, you're a fighter, are you?" I said. I pushed again, digging deeper until it hurt. The baby struck back. "Yes! Be a fighter!" I patted my belly and laughed. I poked again and again and again. "Come on, fight! Fight me now! The only way you'll survive in this wretched world." Poke, poke, poke. "Fight! Fight! Fight!"

"Cheng Yat Sou, I couldn't find melons, and they're all out of chick—Aiya!"

I hadn't heard the door open. Siu-ting streaked across the room and seized my wrists, wrenched them away from my naked belly. I put up a weak resistance, but she pinned my hands to the bed plank,

218

breathing against my neck, a bird-like whistling sob. Something soft rolled off the bed onto the floor.

"I found you a tangerine."

It was my last fruit for a long time. The last of so many foods. The pains of pregnancy coupled with constant hunger—my body nearly bursting yet empty at the same time—I was heaving with impatience for it to be over.

One morning Siu-ting showed up with a handful of withered greens. "No fish today."

I slapped her so hard the vegetables spilled onto the dirty floor. "I want meat! Find me some meat!"

She rushed out the door in tears, leaving me alone again with my baby and my sweaty, filthy self. Food wasn't the only shortage I endured, but people as well. Everyone was hungry and exhausted, no one wanted to venture out in the smothering heat and stench to visit a crazed and short-tempered pregnant woman. I might as well have lived on the moon for all I saw of Cheng Yat. I desperately wanted to see him, if only to talk of the blockade.

It had gone on far too long. How many navy vessels were sealing us in? Rumors reported anywhere from fifty to a hundred and fifty heavily armed warships surrounded us, blocking the channel to north and south. Surely, we had the ships and men to resist them. But our only plan was to outlast them until their commander, missing the warm comforts of home and his concubines, decided he had fulfilled some imaginary goal and could report a victory over the bandits to the new Governor-General, which he in turn could relay to the capital as his grand first achievement in office.

The difference with our side was that we had no commander. We weren't a fighting force; we were three bands of thieves trapped like rats in a cage with no one to lead us out. Tunghoi Bat considered himself in charge simply because this was his base. Wu-shek Yi had the largest number of ships while Cheng Yat was heir to the oldest and most feared pirating dynasty in the region. Their petty jealousies left nobody as leader and no room for bold action. Everyone was tired of waiting for the blockade to end. I was tired of waiting for our men to agree on anything.

These were more than just idle thoughts borne of boredom. I was haunted by nightmares. This same morning, I jolted out of a dream of a smoldering town, blackened heads on pillars, whispering ghosts wandering the waterfront. Even thinking of it now made me shake so badly that my water bowl slipped from my hand and shattered on the floor. Struggling for breath, I leaned back against the wall, massaged the cramps in my calves, and let my mind again drift to Cheng Yat. I no longer blamed my husband for my condition, for his concerns and superstitions. He was living the only life he knew, as a bandit, as a man. Nobody made decisions for him, not anymore. Maybe this stalemate in Tunghoi harbor was just the opportunity to cultivate the leadership his late cousin once had. He needed my encouragement and support, and perhaps some goading. Otherwise my nightmares might come true. Never mind my condition, never mind the heat, I had to find him now.

I pulled slippers on over my swollen feet and stepped out the door, then hurried back in to grab my coin purse. I needed money to hire a sampan to bring me to the junk.

By the time I reached the market lane, my face burned under a merciless sun and my lungs couldn't take in enough air. The street was deserted, with not even a dog resting in the shade; they'd probably all been eaten. Walking three blocks left me struggling with each step, my back aching like a twig about to snap. Across the way, a temple's dark interior beckoned as a cool place to rest. I ducked under the outside canopy, dodging ash from hanging incense spirals, and entered the vestibule. A black-robed monk napped with his head on the table beside an offering bowl.

A few candles and oil flames cast shadows across the worship hall, lending drama to the towering red-faced effigy of Kwan Tai. I lit a fistful of incense sticks and planted them in urns around the room before finally sitting on a ceramic stool and fanning my face.

The air tasted like soot, but it was dry and cool. As my eyes adjusted to the dark, I noticed a bamboo cup filled with oracle sticks within reach. The last time I'd toyed with such things was years ago with other flower boat girls on a day's outing. We always made fun of such superstitions, but deep inside the others took them seriously, desperate for a magical way out. I reached for the cup, put it back, picked it up again, and rattled it. The monk in the vestibule released a throat-clearing snore.

I was ill at ease playing games with spirits, but before I could talk myself out of it, I was on my knees, shaking the cup forward and back until several sticks worked their way up and, at last, one toppled over the rim. The stick was old and worn, and I couldn't read the number. I nearly stuck it back in the cup but, reminding myself that this was just for fun, I dusted off my knees and brought it to the vestibule.

The monk was awake now, his eyes following me. I placed the stick in front of him. He tapped the rim of his offering bowl. I opened my purse and fished out two cash coins, then sat on the rickety three-legged stool facing him. He glanced at the number on the stick, tossed a pair of boat-shaped blocks on the table, then rifled through a box of paper fortunes. I regretted my impulse. A random stick, a toss of wood scraps, a piece of paper: this was how the gods spoke?

The monk's head rocked side to side while he studied the fortune. "Very good. Top top." He recited: "'Through harsh winter winds, revelries beyond the gate create envy, yet spring heralds shifts in affairs and sagacity brings renewal.'"

"Is there an interpretation?"

"Patience, please." He cleared his throat and continued reading: "'In the midst of chaos, seize opportunity; though the risks seem fraught with turbulence, practice wisdom and harmony will prevail.'"

"I don't understand."

"Shall I read it again?"

"No, I heard it the first time—something about chaos and seizing opportunity." Feeling a twinge of pain, I adjusted myself on the stool. "I'm a bandit's wife. We create chaos and seize money. How am I supposed to practice wisdom?"

"How would I know? It's only a fortune."

"I was hoping for some practical advice. Maybe you can explain further." I dropped another pair of coins into his bowl. He responded with an angry intake of breath.

"Madam, you've wet my floor."

A puddle surrounded my stool and flowed backward into the worship hall.

I ran the rest of the way to the waterfront, twisting my tunic under my belly as a makeshift sling. *Don't let the baby fall out!*

Sunlight blinded me. Pebbles stabbed through the soles of my slippers. I rounded the last corner. The harbor stretched out before me.

Empty.

Every ship was gone.

XXIV
Release

Afterward I remembered only pain and loud voices.
Like the sun in your eyes blanching everything white, the pain blinded my other senses: no sounds, no heat, nothing to see, only obliteration. I must have lost consciousness for a little while because a moment later, in place of pain my body felt like it had been trampled beneath giant feet—hurting to breathe, everything below was numb.

I was lying on the pallet in the plain little house while someone dabbed my legs with wet rags. People appeared to speak to me, but the words wouldn't compose themselves in my ears; it was noise, just noise—a cry, incomprehensible calls.

I looked to my side, and there was Ah-Yi with a bundle in her arms, and she was smiling while another woman swabbed the bundle with a cloth. I didn't know what it was. It had no features, just fabric.

Then a tiny hand poked out.

My child. It was moving.

We both had made it.

The baby's next cry returned to my senses.

I tried to talk. "Is it a—"

"Boy! Boy! Boy!" someone said. "Didn't you hear?"

They were wrong, they must be calling a servant. This child who had lived through so much pain, what else could it be but a girl?

Ah-Yi set the baby in the crook of my arm, where he tried out his tiny arms and legs. Was this really mine? I didn't remember it coming out. I'd missed the moment when this whole little body had emerged from my own.

He was strong, like I'd known my child would be. Some women

cleaned up, others stood around cooing and squealing each time the child moved or made a face.

My son.

I was too weak to lift him. Ah-Yi sat him on my chest while holding his big, round head.

"His father's lips," someone said.

"Mother's chin."

"Her ears."

I wondered where they saw this. Searching for an echo of myself in his face, I found only pink formless features under a tuft of intensely black hair and large pooling eyes which shut like fat clams as he let out a cry. Ah-Yi laid him gently to my breast. I held him there and felt him take his first meal.

My son.

I hugged the baby tighter as he chewed my nipple, waiting for that famous surge of motherly love. He was a soft, hot little creature attached to my breast, and nothing more, no matter how many times I silently mouthed the words:

My son.

Look at him, such tiny, fragile fingers. He can't support his head. Skin so red and raw.

What was I supposed to do?

My son.

I pity you. My son, I don't want to hurt you. But you came to me uninvited. You poor little baby, you have a terrible mother.

What about the father? Where was he?

"The ships. What happened to the ships?" I said.

Ah-Yi dabbed my cheeks with her fingers. "Don't cry, dear. This isn't the time to—"

"I'm not crying! Where is Cheng Yat? Where are all the ships?"

"Gone! The gutless turtles ran away," one of the Wu wives said. The others babbled over each other; not a single sensible word came through.

"Aiya! Will just one person please explain what happened?"

The baby started crying. Ah-Yi patted him until he settled back into feeding. "The navy ran, she meant. Not us."

"Only twelve of them," the eldest Wu wife added.

"I don't understand what you're talking about!" Only twelve retreated? What about the rest? I tried to sit up, nearly spilling the child, prompting shrieks from him and everyone around me, making me scream too.

Ah-Yi picked up the baby and scolded the rest of us to be quiet. Her rocking quickly calmed him. "Bunch of noisy hens, all of you," she said. "If you can keep your beaks shut, I'll tell the new mother what happened, then we'll all step out and let them have some peace."

A Wu wife opened her mouth to say something, until a withering look from Ah-Yi cut her off.

"The navy had just twelve ships, it turns out," Ah-Yi said. "They were clever at shifting them around. Kept us fooled, all right. Well, we can play tricks, too. Hee! Moved everything we could float out into the channel—junks, sampans, rafts—cleaned out the entire harbor, maybe two hundred craft. They were ready, though. Fired on us with all guns. I have to give them credit—they had their loading organized. Sent us quite a bombardment."

"How many did we lose?" I said.

"I'm not finished. Now, take this fellow back."

Now what? He seemed drowsy and uninterested in sucking milk. No instinct drove me. Nothing in his fat little form signaled for attention. I begged my heart to move me and guide me, but I was just so tired. Ah-Yi clicked her tongue and repositioned my arms around him.

"That's how to hold him. Hee! Stay still. This part of the story is where your husband comes in. Those navy guns are blasting us one after another—*Boom! Boom! Boom! Boom!*—we even took a few hits. Then Cheng Yat led the charge straight into their gunfire."

"Stop," I said. "Where's Cheng Yat? Was he hit? How many casualties?"

The baby hiccupped. Everyone laughed, whether at him or at my questions. Either way, I was infuriated.

"Dear, more blood was spilled in this room than out there. You ought to have seen—"

"Let me tell," said Wu's still-pregnant youngest wife.

"No, I'll tell," said the eldest. "Those navy turned their backsides and ran. Not that I was there. But my husband said their transoms looked just like dog bottoms with their tails tucked between their legs."

"What about Cheng Yat? Why isn't he here to see his child?" I wanted to see for myself whether he had it in him to be a father. And,

I didn't say out loud, I needed to sense whether he was the hero they had just claimed him to be.

He made his appearance that evening, after everyone but Siu-ting had left. The fumes in his breath gave him away: he'd been celebrating his newly elevated status as father of a coveted boy. The tiny bundle lay in his arms, eyes fixed on his father's face.

"See how he looks at me? So confident," Cheng Yat said. "A true warrior."

The word struck me like a bullet. Let him be brave, I thought. Let him be strong. But if at all possible, when one day he assumes the family criminal business, don't let him fight and die.

"I'm doing well," I said, making clear that he hadn't asked. "A few more days resting in bed, then I can move."

Cheng Yat held his son at a worrisome angle, head so far down that I worried he would slip to the floor. How dare he greet his child for the very first time in such condition. "Give him to me," I said.

"He wants to be with his father." He bounced the boy up and down like one might shake a rice sack.

There was no arguing with a drunk. I lied, "He's hungry."

I silently dismissed Siu-ting.

When she was gone, Cheng Yat took my hand between both of his. "I have a son," he said. Then he let go.

This was his way to thank me. Not a small word of praise after what I'd gone through for him. Some acknowledgment that it was I—me alone, after months of discomfort and half a year's isolation—who had given him what was supposed to be a man's crowning achievement? I felt sucked dry—my torso emptied and loose like a squashed bladder, my breasts aching from their unfamiliar job of gushing milk. My life itself, drained. Other than the new unasked-for role as mother, I was an empty vessel. The least he could do was fill it with a few warm words.

"I want to know what took you so long to see him, or his mother."

His back straightened in defense. "Do you know what I just put my men through?"

"I heard the whole story. I'm proud of what you did. But perhaps you could have put off some of the celebration and playing the hero to acknowledge your newborn son?"

"So now you're the caring mother and I'm the bad father? You're

226

the one who doesn't understand. Yes, maybe after I made those men go into what might have been, for all anyone knew, a massacre, maybe they needed me to share a little drink and play the hero for a short while before I could come here and play the father. Well, here I am."

We sat in silence for some time, listening to the baby snore lightly on my belly. Cheng Yat struggled to his feet, patted my head, and walked out.

The door's thud startled the baby into whimpering, then an extended wail. At least one of us had no shame to cry out loud.

As if childbirth wasn't messy enough, I was forbidden to clean my body or, worse, rinse my hair, for an entire month. Another unexplainable tradition I didn't dare violate. Stuffed back in the ship's hold, neither the baby nor I were allowed a moment of sunlight or fresh air. A pig lived in better conditions!

One day I couldn't stand it anymore. When Siu-ting brought rice and water, I grabbed the jar and poured it over my head, scrubbing and scratching the filth from my scalp until my hair was a tangled nest.

"Don't say a word," I warned the horrified girl.

Siu-ting was used to my fits by now. She checked the baby and wrinkled her nose, annoyed at me for again leaving the distasteful task to her. She removed his soiled cloth and rinsed his bottom—thank the gods at least that part was allowed to be washed!

"What day is this?" I asked.

"Day six."

Twenty-two days more. It may as well have been two thousand.

"If I was the empress, I'd make the men have to sit in their own filth and sticky hair for a month. No, make it two months!"

Siu-ting wrapped the boy in a fresh rag. "I hope you're empress before I have a baby."

After she left, I was too agitated to sleep, too exhausted to replenish the fluttering lamp. When the baby blubbered, my breasts responded as though they had ears, my arms pulled the little mouth to them without a thought on my part.

His little body was warm against mine, his toes tickled my belly. The gurgle in his throat as he sucked part of me into him was a happier sound than the wildest laugh. Tiny fingers found the back of my hand and pinched the loose skin, his way to express pleasure, I supposed.

"Don't worry, there's plenty to drink," I told him. "But you don't have to pinch so hard."

My throat quivered at the simplicity of his needs. So, this was the famous motherly instinct. Yet somehow it fell short of what I imagined to be love.

When he finished, I tried to play with him, but he fell right asleep, his head limp on my shoulder, leaving me alone with my thoughts, back to the day he was born.

That morning, the monk in the temple had read:

In chaos, seize opportunity;
Practice wisdom and harmony will prevail.

Cheng Yat had seized opportunity, led a coordinated force, the first since Vietnam, and with a simple, wise strategy, had restored order to Tunghoi and re-established at least temporary harmony among the pirate leaders.

But the oracle's words were for me, not him.

Moonlight through the open hatch cast a bright square onto the floor. I tried to picture myself in that square, a painting of my future.

I considered what I wanted to achieve, now that my place in the Cheng family was cemented forever by producing an heir. Now it was my turn. I tucked the baby into his bedding, then returned to my thoughts.

I wanted to be rich, of course, for a start. Money brought respect. Money brought power. But I would never achieve this if I let Cheng Yat continue to run things his way. He may have been brave in a fight, but he handled money like filling a mat basket with wine. Every incoming coin spent without planning, or gambled away, or stolen. He had all the strength and all the experience. Why, after so many years, were we still chasing every sad salt barge?

Then it struck me. He would never change. But I could.

I needed to have a say in managing the finances. I needed to be the one to make us seek bigger targets. I needed to put my voice inside his head, to make him want to be rich. I needed to be neither wife nor mother. I needed to become his guiding spirit.

I pondered where to begin, until the baby filled the room with a scream. He was hungry again. I unfastened my night robe and brought him to my breast. And then the idea struck me.

Even a tiny baby could open his mouth and with a single cry have someone a hundred times his size—or even a roomful of adults—under his complete control, delivering all the riches he desired straight to his mouth. The tiny infant latched to my chest had given me a lesson. Power came first. Power delivered wealth, not the other way around. Power came from neither strength nor size but from some other source. The goddess who wrote my fortune that day should grant me wisdom to discover that source.

Finally, the month was over, and I re-entered the world. But not before a desperately needed bath. I spent the entire morning behind a screen on the poop deck dousing my hair, my shoulders, chest, arms, and legs with bucket after bucket of water, while fondling the most precious gift ever known in this world, given by Wu-shek Yi's wives: a quail egg-sized piece of scented soap.

Ah-Yi had to practically drag me into my clothes and onto the sampan. "Aiya! Everyone's waiting for you."

The baby wailed the moment I carried him into the dark and smoky Tin Hau temple. No amount of rocking or humming would soothe him, and other women's cooing and tickling only made him louder. What a time to be hungry. He made do with sucking my finger, and I was free to proceed with the final birth ritual: his naming ceremony. A monk tapped a bell and the crowded worship hall went quiet.

Tin Hau in her red robe and jeweled headdress sat larger than life on the dais before me. As always, her eyes appeared to follow me as I stepped forward and bent slowly to my knees. I bowed three times with the baby in my arms, then raised him to the deity.

"Goddess of Heaven, I present you Cheng…"

I couldn't remember his name. I'd only learned it this morning, having heard it just once. I was tired, too distracted by the prospect of a bath. After a month alone with him, I'd only thought of him as *boy* or *Little Mosquito*.

I heard Ah-Yi clear her throat, and found her off to the side, tapping a clenched fist and pointing at me. Ah, yes, I remembered! Cheng Yat had honored me by uniting our family names in our son.

"I present you Cheng Ying-shek."

I kowtowed again to Tin Hau and lingered for a moment with my head to the floor, long enough to whisper for only the goddess to hear: "What do I do now?"

The rest of the day passed in a blur—chanting and firecrackers, the banquet at the wine shop, the predictable questions—"When does he get a brother?" All the exhausting months of pregnancy and isolation and drowning in my own thoughts had caught up with me.

Back on board, I handed the baby to Siu-ting. "His name's Ying-shek."

"I know, but—"

"Feed him rice water. I need to rest."

I hurried up to the cabin and threw myself on the old familiar mat. I'd been off in a foreign land and had finally returned home. I wanted nothing more than pure, uninterrupted sleep, but my head rattled with thoughts like birds in a cage, about motherhood and marriage and wealth and power. My breasts ached, so used to the baby sucking them dry.

A robe rolled up beside the trunk would make a soft pillow, which might help me sleep—until the color became clear in the moonlight: bright purple like a ripe plum.

The first boatload returned from the banquet. I stepped out onto the companionway and watched them board until I found the one I was looking for. Cheung Po Tsai saw me and waved.

"You're awake still! I want to see my little brother."

I tossed the robe down to him.

"He has a real son now," I said. "You're not needed here anymore."

XXV
Partners

The waters west of Crow Island were a fertile hunting ground for slow-moving coastal barges and ferries. By the end of summer, with my eyes over Cheng Yat's shoulder and my fingers on the purse, we were on our way to becoming rich, though not quickly enough, what with a fleet of thirty-eight ships sharing the spoils.

Mostly, I was too tired to enjoy it. Sleep was a memory; sore breasts, aching back, headaches, and exhaustion were constants. Child-rearing was a job for superhuman gods, not mere mortals. No wonder wealthy matrons in stories had households full of servants. As amusing as Ying-shek's baby gibberish and funny faces could be, I was lucky to have the nanny, Siu-ting, to pass him to when I needed to rest or think, though it was never long before he was hungry again.

One day the winds shifted, dry autumn northwesterlies ousted the summer inferno. My tiredness receded; the fog lifted from my mind. We'd had two good hauls in a row and were swimming in grains, abalone, and a passenger ferry's worth of silver. Cheng Yat was in an uncommonly good mood.

One morning, he postponed prayers so as not to disturb my sleep. He stopped Ah-Yi at the cabin door with her bowls of pork and ginger broth, instead delivering them himself to the "little mother". He even attempted jokes while we had our soup.

"Where's the little one? I thought you like having two Cheng men to boss around."

"I don't need to tell you which one smells worse and complains loudest," I said.

He actually laughed. This was a husband I hadn't seen before. He'd been more relaxed since the birth of his son and the productive summer. But here was a man who could accept a tease with a smile and reward me by stroking my cheek. I didn't want to spoil such a tender moment. But if not now, when? I knew now that Cheng Yat was capable of great kindness, but deep down, he was still the same man, as resistant as stone to change. Rather than regret this fact, I saw the moment as an opportunity. Soon enough the baby would arrive in search of my breast, Cheng Yat would step outside and be lost to his bandit business.

"Look at your hair," I said. "Like it's been coughed up by a cat. Stay there." I fetched my grooming box, knelt behind him, and combed oil through the tangles halfway down his back. "You never take care of your looks. Feel this." I guided his palm across the stubble of his scalp. "Maybe the next ship, you'll find a proper barber, not the butcher we have here."

"Why, when I have a pretty butcher like you?"

"Are you saying you'd trust me with a blade against your head?" I gave a little tug with the comb.

"Ha! Never. Then I might actually have to give in to your pestering."

"Crazy! Would I ever dream of pestering the hero of the siege of Tunghoi?"

"Now you're making fun of me."

"I will never make fun of you." I combed the hair into separate strands. "You made me proud, the way you shooed those navy bastards like frightened ducks. My husband defeated the great Mandarin admiral Suen Chuen-mau."

"I defeated a coward. No pride in that. Anyway, it wasn't just me."

"Hold still." I draped the first strand over my arm and combed out the next. "You led the attack, and everyone else followed."

"I happened to be in front."

"Everyone said it was your plan."

"Aiya! What are you up to?"

He tried to turn his head. I pinched his scalp to stay still and pulled the comb through the last bunch.

"Aiya yourself! What I'm up to is finishing your hair."

"When a woman heaps praise, it means she wants something. May as well say it."

"It isn't what I want. It's what you should want! Keep still." I dropped the comb and busied my fingers with braiding. "Look at what you achieved by fighting off the navy. Have they dared show a sail since? Look at you now. One successful raid after another, and top prices for our goods—or so your fat purser claims, if you trust that mangy dog. We're up to thirty-eight ships. Think what you could do with two hundred!"

"Mm, more flattery. And where do I find these two hundred ships?"

I yanked the braid tight. "Fatty Wu!" Yanked it again. "Eleven Fingers!" Tugged it straight. "General Bo! Kwok Podai! All the rest!"

"Stop."

"I am not going to stop!"

"I mean stop pulling my hair out, damn it. And stop telling me to steal my brothers' ships. For what reason?"

How to make him understand? These thoughts had been leaping around in my head for so long that they seemed obvious to me. I tied off the braid with a clean piece of twine.

"Remember that day Chen Tin-bou came to recruit you to Annam? Do you remember what he called you, all of you? No, you don't indulge in memories, do you? Well, let me remind you: 'Flocks of ravens content to pick at scraps.' Yes! And that's all those others will ever be—Wu and Eleven Fingers and the rest. Blobs of foam floating on the sea—drifting, drifting until something comes in their path, then skimming off what they can and not even knowing what to do with the damned money. That's what they are. Admit it! But I saw what you accomplished by making them work together." I let the finished plait drop against his back.

He turned around to face me lying on his side, propped on his elbow. "Old wife, I do have a memory, regardless of what you say. I remember Annam, or what is it now? Vietnam. Oh, we worked together. We called ourselves a navy, but we were just boats for hire. But when it came to a fight? Where was the working together? You're right, I don't remember that part. And things didn't work out very well for the top commander, or did you forget that?"

"That's because we were fighting for a lost cause that no one believed in."

"And the cause you're suggesting now?" he said.

"Money."

He let the word sink in. I knew him well enough to understand that he needed time to compose whatever thoughts would form his

233

response. But I couldn't stop myself.

"Try to imagine," I said. "Imagine if we all coordinated together, we could control the entire coast from Hoinam to Foochow! No one would dare oppose us—navy, merchants, no one—with one powerful man in the lead. Imagine the wealth! Imagine the power!"

"Don't you have enough?" he finally said. "Do I have to rub your face in that chest over there, full of silver? It's never enough for you!"

"What are you afraid of?"

"How dare! I risk my life so you can bathe in baubles and perfumes. And you use such language!"

"You think I care about perfumes? Are you even listening to me?"

He swatted loose hairs from his shoulder and made to leave. "I'm tired of talking about this."

A tap at the door. Ying-shek's whimpering came through. My real commander had arrived.

Cheng Yat patted my cheek. "Old wife, don't preach to me about who or what to command and I won't tell you which tit the baby should suck."

He took Ying-shek from the nanny, bounced him in his arms a few times, then handed him to me and left.

I didn't see him again for close to a month.

I was among the last to learn that he had returned.

Or that he had gathered other pirate leaders to pull off the greatest joint raid ever undertaken: the pillage of the foreign enclave at O Moon.

One cold and drizzly month into the Year of the Rat, I stood by the rail, clasping the baby bundled inside blankets, staring at the hazy outline of O Moon, a tiny spit of land overseen by a hilltop stone fort. I didn't know the difference between Portuguese or English or other barbarians. All I knew was that the foreign enclave's homes and warehouses were the source of legends, stuffed with exotic goods and piled with gold. And opium—foreign mud—that pinnacle source of ultimate wealth from the deepest springs of hell.

Today, aside from a single coolie pushing a cart along the waterfront, the place seemed deserted. Even the flag over the fort remained limp.

The plan was to starve the enclave into submission, though after ten days of surrounding them—our fleet on the peninsula's eastern side,

General Bo to the west, and Wu-shek Yi and his brothers commanding the southern channel between the settlement and Chicken's Neck Island—the blockade was starving us as well.

I felt its effects in my belly and breasts and, presently, in my arms. Ying-shek was growing quickly and constantly whimpering for food. I needed more than fish bait and worm-eaten cabbage leavings, but our forces had already stripped bare every farm, field, and fishpond on every island and settlement within reach. There was little left to feed ninety ships and upwards of four thousand crew, including a commander's mother and their child.

I didn't understand why we didn't simply send in thousands of men and take what we wanted. The Portuguese enclave was undefended by sea. Its only escape to the mainland was a single gate on a narrow isthmus, and our spies reported that the Portuguese fear of saboteurs had choked even that movement to a trickle. Other than their garrison, which rarely showed activity, the foreigners' only defense may have been their barbarian god. Cheung Po Tsai had made a daring foray into the enclave, disguised as a fisherman, and returned to report that O Moon "contains more priests than soldiers".

A cold gust scraped my face. Lined up on shore right in front of our eyes stood the prize: one warehouse after another, massive enough to hoard mountains of spices and towers of glittering goods from the ends of the world. And how many chests filled with rich, pungent balls of foreign mud?

"And sweet rice cakes for you, right, Little Mosquito?" I said, as though the baby had been reading my thoughts. He answered by squirming in his blankets.

"Yes, I know, I know. Nothing to see here, nothing to do. Let's find something to eat."

He appeared to understand, calming right away. When the cook shrugged that he had nothing to spare, Ying-shek cried out loud again. His comprehension of the world continued to surprise me.

"You're so smart, let's go find your father. Maybe he'll listen to you. He's tired of listening to me."

But Cheng Yat hadn't returned from his rounds of other ships. The cabin at least kept out the wind. I curled up with Ying-shek, cocooned together in blankets, and tried fruitlessly to rock us both to sleep.

At last I heard a sampan arrive. Someone pounded up the stairway at an eager gait. Cheng Yat smiled as soon as he came in the door and said, "I have a job for you."

This was something new. Since arriving at O Moon, he hadn't sought my advice, and as his mood fouled along with our circumstances, I had stopped offering any. Now he needed my help?

"Call Siu-ting," I said.

"No, you need the baby. We're meeting on Chicken's Neck to plan the next moves. Come, come."

"Then why would I need the—Aiya! No."

As soon as I stepped onto the companionway, I knew why. Two Wu wives crossed the deck, waving to me. Crewmen helped the three others off the sampan.

"I am not entertaining them!" I said.

Cheng Yat faced me with his back to them so the Wu women wouldn't hear. "I do my job, you do yours."

"My damned job is not to serve a gaggle of cackling geese."

"Spit all the vinegar you want, but you need to do this." He offered a friendly wave to the women, then pretended to fuss over the baby while he spoke quickly. "If these geese are even half as infuriatingly manipulative as you are..."

I couldn't believe it—he actually winked.

Then I understood. There had been grumbling that the blockade was falling apart. He needed allies, or at least informants, in the captains' beds, starting with the Wu brothers. It was rather brilliant of him.

"But if someone tosses them overboard, don't accuse me," I said.

The youngest had brought her new daughter, two months younger than mine. We placed them together in Ying-shek's padded basket in the middle of the cabin.

"Look at them together. So cute!"

"Wah! So handsome and pretty!"

Even I joined in. "They look alike. Who's the father?"

Everyone laughed. The eldest wife unwrapped a cloth and laid out nine or ten precious rice dumplings. I pinched off a piece and pressed it between Ying-shek's gums.

"Where did you find rice?" I said.

They glanced at each other, keeping secrets.

The wife of Wu-shi Tai, Wu's younger brother, said, "Just don't ask what's inside them."

The others cast her scolding looks. "Really. Don't ask," the eldest wife said.

Siu-ting brought boiled water. As stingy as I was about the ship's dwindling store of tea leaves, it was a fair exchange for whatever unmentionable delicacy they'd brought.

They did most of the talking while I pretended interest in other people's babies and what happened to this or that cousin in childbirth. The children, lucky for them, slept through it.

I had to steer them off this topic and get on with my mission. Food might be a way to start.

"I don't know how much longer I can stand it. Don't you dream of roast pork dumplings?"

"I know," said Number Three Wife, "I'm so tired of eating caterpillars. I mean—" She covered her mouth. I knew now what was crawling in my belly.

"Yesterday I swear they tried to serve a centipede in my congee!" said Wu-shek Sam's wife.

Wu-shek Yi's moon-faced youngest wife picked up her sniffling daughter and rocked her. "Anyway, my husband says we won't have to wait much longer."

"When did he say that?" I asked.

"This morning. He promised me spicy chicken when we get to Taiwan."

The others nodded as though this were common knowledge. Well, now it was.

Ying-shek belched. I joined the laughter, if only to cover my frustration. Men were generally easy to manipulate. A well-aimed pout and a few strokes of their vanity were often enough to snare them. Women, though, were devious creatures. Back on the flower boats I'd kept myself aloof from the other girls, never really understanding their little passions. Now I could only guess what moved such simple-minded fowl as these.

"Taiwan?" I said. "I've heard of it. Have you been? What color is the gold there?"

"What are you talking about, the gold?" said Wu's middle wife.

"Have you ever seen foreign gold? Not Spanish dollars, I mean their jewelry. I've seen it. It's a lighter color than ours. O Moon must be full of it. Thinking how it might look against my lovely fair skin," I said, holding up my less-than-fair wrist.

"Barbarian women there wear emeralds in their ears. Or so one of our spies claimed," the middle wife said.

"And their fabrics," I said. "The linens from their side of the world! I handled some once in Kwangchow—only the size of a scarf, but felt like baby's skin, so soft, not like this scratchy stuff on our backs. When we enter O Moon, that's the first thing I'm grabbing—going to make a hundred new sets of clothes!"

"I thought you can't sew."

"I'll pay a tailor with leftover gold."

"He'll sew mine with gold thread," said Wu-shek Sam's first wife.

"I wouldn't refuse some jewels in my ears," said Wu-shek Tai's.

"If your husband will let you," I said.

"Why shouldn't he let me?"

"You're going to Taiwan to eat chicken."

Wu-shek Yi's first wife waved a dismissive hand. "She's just trying to convince us to stay in this miserable blockade."

"Not at all," I said. "I wouldn't put up with another day of caterpillar dumplings for all the money and gold and jewels and pretty fabrics in the world. That Taiwan chicken certainly sounds far more tempting. I'll have to ask Cheng Yat if he's tried it."

Ying-shek waved his arms and legs; a bubble swelled from his lips. Wu-shek Sam's wife picked him up and bounced him in her arms. He chirped like a bird.

"You're clever like your mother," she said. "Pity that she thinks your father's in charge."

She handed him to me with a smile, and waved for the sampan.

We entered the twentieth day of the siege, the only sign of progress being the weather. The cold spell had broken, replaced by warm drizzle and low-hanging clouds. Here where the Pearl River made its last push into the sea, the currents and wind seemed allied with the defenders, trying to nudge us within range of the cannon shot occasionally lobbed our way. Hungry crewmen exhausted themselves at the sails and rudder just to stay in place.

Cheng Yat again cut rations in half. Leaks went without mending for lack of caulk; ropes lay tangled and frayed. More and more crew lay ill. Where were the bold moves he had promised? A thousand men could have charged the warehouses, taken their fill, and left. But Wu-shek Yi had refused to risk his men until the enclave surrendered. And so here we stood, playing a waiting game over which side would starve first.

There was no speaking to Cheng Yat about anything. He may have enlisted my service to drag other women into line—and hadn't they convinced their husbands to stay, thanks to me?—but there was no convincing him that I might have some other value on this ship. I would just have to prove it.

I woke early, waiting quietly on the mat until Cheng Yat finished prayers with his officers. Before the others left, I touched the purser on the arm and asked him to stay.

"Teach me to use an abacus."

His look could have sliced meat. He'd terminated our writing lessons long ago, and nothing had convinced him to resume. Maybe now he worried about being blackmailed into a new round of tutoring.

"Just once," I said with a smile. "It can't be that difficult."

Cheng Yat shrugged at him.

"Bring the ledger too," I said. "For practice."

He hadn't returned by the time a crewman brought watery broth for breakfast. "Must be polishing the grime from his beads," I said.

I'd already finished my meal when the purser stumbled in. He set the abacus on the floor. Beads clattered between his fingers while he rambled nonsense about earth and heaven. I put my hand over it to make him stop.

"Slow down, please. What are these?"

"Weren't you listening? These," he said, indicating a column of five beads below the divider, "are the earth rows. For single digits—one, two, three..."

I pointed to the pairs of beads above the divider. "Heaven rows, right?"

He nodded. "Each worth five. One down on top, one up below, makes six. Three up below, makes eight. Get it? Place the fingers so." He demonstrated how to count from one to ten. "Then we carry the numbers—"

"Wait. Are you going to let me try?"

He slid the abacus to me. Its wood was stained nearly black from years of use, the beads smooth and hard like river stones. I flicked them up and down in sequence, delighting in the sensation of each light, musical tap. On my second try, I reached number ten without mistake, flicking heaven and earth beads into place with a single satisfying click.

He taught me how to move past ten. I counted to fifty, more than once, to correct my management of the beads. It was as though my fingers were learning to dance. Once they stopped tripping over one another, it was remarkably easy. He dictated three-, four-, and five-digit numbers, which I managed a little bit faster each time. Cheng Yat nodded approval.

The purser took back the abacus. "Enough for today."

"You have somewhere to go?" I said. "I'm ready to add."

"No need to rush—"

"I said I'm ready to add."

He looked to Cheng Yat, who indicated he should continue. I'd never seen him use an abacus, had never asked whether he knew how.

The purser's fingers leapt all over the abacus like a crazed spider. Beads clattered angrily while he narrated his moves, never asking whether I understood.

I attempted some simple calculations but got stuck on four plus seven.

"Never mind. Next time," he said.

I hooked two fingers around the frame, and we engaged in a little tugging battle until he relented and showed me how to do it. I repeated the calculation, slapping the right beads into place with a crisp *tock*. Eleven.

I beamed with triumph at Cheng Yat. He returned a nod of pride.

"You've mastered it. Time for a rest," the purser said.

"First, I'd like to watch the true master. Show me how to add real figures."

"Next lesson."

I looked at Cheng Yat. "Wouldn't it be entertaining to see?" Without waiting for an answer, I told the purser, "I'm giving you a chance to show off."

He groaned in the back of his throat. "Give me some numbers."

"Let's make them real figures. Try some from the ledger."

He affected surprise, but his voice spoke suspicion. "As you like."

The ledger was less a book than a stack of papers bound on one edge with twine. The first page was crowded with words and figures in an incomprehensible scrawl, far from the tidy characters he'd tried to teach me. Even the numbers bore little resemblance to those I'd practiced. He recited aloud while his left hand moved down a column of figures, and his right translated them into movements of beads without his having to look. He announced the total, then pointed to the ledger, indicating that they matched.

"Impressive," I said. "It's as though your fingers have eyes."

"That comes with practice."

"Another."

"Just one more." He flipped to the next page.

"No, the latest one." I reached for the book. He slapped his hand down on the page. Again I turned to Cheng Yat. "The last raid before we came here, wasn't it the Hoinam trawler?"

"Mm. The trawler," Cheng Yat confirmed.

The purser flushed red, no choice but to flip to the last written entry.

I pointed at a word. "This must say sugar. Correct?"

The purser grunted again and racked the beads back to zero. "Three hundred eighty-five catties of sugar. Sold for four hundred cash. Comes to..." His fingers flung beads into place. "Two hundred thirty—"

"Wait," I said. "Too fast. Slowly, so I can watch."

He grunted and started over. "So. Three hundred eighty-five catties of sugar."

"Are you sure?"

"That's what's written. Of course I'm sure."

"Sorry. I thought we'd taken more."

Beads rattled under his fingers, though he wasn't moving them. "It's what was written. That's why we rely on ledgers and counting machines, not what we think we remember. Shall I continue?"

Cheng Yat cleared his throat. He was suddenly more alert.

"At four hundred cash," the purser said, shuffling beads more deliberately than before. "See? One hundred and fifty-four thousand cash, which we took in silver taels. This converts to..." The beads again clacked and rattled. "...two hundred thirty taels. Plus, we had—"

"Wait. You said it converts," I said. "At what rate?"

"We haven't come to division. Too advanced for a beginner. There's no point—"

"Entertain me."

Cheng Yat made a big shrug.

Again, the purser exaggerated a sigh. "Six hundred fifty cash per tael. It fluctuates, depending on the dealer."

"Never mind the fluctuations. Just show me dividing. Slowly, so I can try to understand."

Cheng Yat slid closer, eyes focused on the abacus.

"Ah, it's rather complicated," the purser said. "You haven't yet learned subtraction, which is essential."

"Just show me. Today is the introductory lesson." I delighted in seeing him flinch as I swept my fingers across the columns, clearing the beads to zero, then setting them to show one hundred fifty-four thousand. "Divided by? Maybe it's in here."

I had my other hand on the ledger when the purser grabbed it away and affected to study the page. "Six hundred and fifty, as I said."

Beads clattered furiously while he described the principles of division.

"Why did you clear the first column?" I said.

His fingers froze in place.

"It looked to me like a six in the first column. Two hundred thirty-six. But you cleared it at the very end."

He responded through pinched lips. "The figure isn't evenly divisible. I'll explain in another lesson."

He shook the abacus clear and tucked it and the ledger under his arm. "Now, I must attend the shore crew. They need disbursement for informants. With captain's leave, of course."

Cheng Yat waved him off.

"Thank you," I said. "A most interesting lesson."

The cabin door slid shut. The purser's footsteps faded down the companionway.

Cheng Yat took a deep breath and stared at the floor. "How did you know?"

"Know what?"

He looked up. "That he's been cheating me?"

"What made you ever believe he wasn't?"

I picked up our empty bowls and carried them outside.

Plucked from an afternoon nap by a distant thud of cannon fire—two, then three in a row.

I was out on deck in moments.

The fort seemed quiet. The only ships in sight were ours: a Tunghoi squadron to the north, and Wu-shek Yi's southward covering the channel. I couldn't place where the shots had come from.

Someone yelled. Others pointed. "Devil's navy!"

A black foreign ship with square white sails surged past the spit north of the enclave, firing from its bow. One of the Tunghoi junks jerked sideways. Our cannon crew scrambled to prepare the big guns. Half the powder would be caked and useless.

I spotted Siu-ting carrying the baby up the steps. He was screaming hysterically, upset by the commotion, and judging by the swelling of my breasts, he was probably hungry. I grabbed him and climbed to the poop deck for a clearer view.

The foreign ship was alone, its bowsprit jutting like a sword. With its slender hull and massive arrays of sails, it was as beautiful and toxic as a lionfish—lethal, in fact. I lost count at thirty cannons on one side, enough to maintain a continuous barrage all day.

The Tunghoi junks at the forefront of the attack dispersed without returning a single round, leaving their stricken brother behind, spewing smoke.

We were the next targets. The foreign ship tacked with startling speed, pointing a course obviously meant to cut off our escape to the east.

Ying-shek fidgeted madly in my arms. Some motherly instinct urged me to bring him to the confines of the cabin. Normally the poop deck was a safer place during an attack since most cannon fire, especially at this distance, targeted the main deck and waterline, though I couldn't be certain with the foreigner's high-placed weapons. If we were to die, let it be in the open.

Cheng Yat came up the ladder holding a pistol and ran straight to the transom.

"What the prick-eating devil is he doing?" He shot into the air and screamed. "The mother-buggering turtles!"

Ying-shek replied with a scream of his own. I felt like joining him.

Wu-shek Yi's fleet had sailed into open water, every last one with its transom facing us. I remembered his wife's quip about ships fleeing like puppies with their tails between their legs.

The foreign ship fired again, three more shots.

Cheng Yat hammered the rail with his pistol. He yelled over everyone's heads to the Taumuk who repeated the order to everyone below:

"Fill sails! Pull away east!"

Our bad luck continued. We caught a small convoy of traders, only find their cargo had been seized by another bandit group. Then a rogue Fukienese pirate gang, operating far outside their native waters, mistook us for a merchant fleet to the detriment of their ships and their commander's neck, though we lost several men in the fight.

Day after day, Cheng Yat raged and prayed. He blamed himself for failure in leadership. It wasn't so simple, I tried to tell him; we needed clearer organization and planning—but he always cut me off. Not my business.

One evening, I was changing Ying-shek's soiled wrap, when Cheng Yat came into the cabin in a fog of wine fumes and announced, "We're attacking the fort at Tin-pak. I have it worked out. A hundred men go ashore five *li* east—"

"No." I didn't look up. The child giggled.

"What did you say?"

"I said, no. You're not attacking any fort."

It was a stupid idea, and he should have known it. Ever since our audacious attempt on O Moon, every fort and garrison on the coast would be fully manned and on high alert. It was foolhardy to consider raiding a port, much less attacking its defenses. Maybe it was the drink talking? He leaned into my face until his breath could have melted my skin. "Did I hear somebody try to give me orders?"

I checked that Ying-shek's wrap was secure and set him on the mat. He'd been crawling for a number of days now, transforming from a sucking and defecating device into something more animal-like, delighting in his new skill.

"Did you hear what I said?" Cheng Yat aimed a slap at my leg, missed, and struck the floor. "Woman, answer! Are you trying to give me orders?"

Ying-shek stopped in his tracks, lip trembling, on the verge of crying.

"Keep your voice down," I said.

"Send him out of here! Call the idiot nanny."

"I will not. I want him to get a good look at his father, so he knows what not to become."

"Old wife, I haven't struck you in a very long time, and I hope that I don't need to."

"Go ahead. My face? Belly? Do it! Teach your son to beat up women and never look past the end of your nose. That's being a man. That's how to be a leader."

He watched his hands clench open and shut. "Women. Even when a man isn't guilty, he's guilty." Then he said to my face, "I don't know what wrong I've done you to earn such disrespect. Thanks to me, you have money, nice fabrics, your precious soaps. May I remind you that when I scraped you from the mud, you were nothing but a common prostitute?"

"And when I married you, you were an admiral."

He laughed, though the tone was bitter. "You can't forget that, can you? Ha! I have news: Annam no longer exists. Your little dream there is gone."

"What I can't forget is that the day your son was born, you led a great force which frightened away the imperial navy like nervous birds. I was so proud!"

Cheng Yat let out a breath, then we both watched Ying-shek explore the room until the boy lay on his side with the fingers of both hands shoved into his mouth.

"Look at you now," I said, quietly. "You had this grand scheme to starve O Moon into submission. But did you consider for a moment how, during the coldest time of year, you would feed your own crews? Then instead of seizing the opportunity to finish the task, some fat, squeaky-voiced former catamite of yours complains he's hungry and you roll up like a mealy bug?"

"If you'd played your part—"

"Don't you dare accuse me," I said. "It was clever, your idea. I did my part, and did it well. Was that your only plan, to let the women take over? That's the best idea you've had yet!"

"You shame me!"

"Fuck your old mother! You shame yourself!"

"Go back to your baby!"

He shoved me onto my back. I sprang up and knocked him over, pinned down his shoulders with both hands, and pressed my knee into his groin. "I am sick of this life. Sick. Finished with it. This life is dead." I ground my knee into him until he winced. "You have a choice. You can throw me out—and I'll make sure your son comes with me. Or you're going to make me your partner. And we make ourselves rich."

He squirmed under me with an unusual look bordering on fright, glancing toward the door to make sure no one could see.

"What craziness are you talking?" he said.

"If I weren't crazy, I'd leave this moment." How to tell him that I knew his business better than he did? That I was smarter than all of them? "What kind of life do we have? Petty bandits. Straying here and there, no destination. Grab a salt barge. Raid a village. Hope no one beats us to it. Kill and kill some more. If there's nothing to steal, we starve."

His breathing slowed. He spoke in a calmer tone. "And you think you know better?"

I released my grip and let him sit up. "No. I think together we would know better. You locked me in that putrid hold for half a year, and this is all I thought about. We need a greater force. We need to stop being a petty bandit gang and start operating like a business. Because it is a business, not the little boy's game you treat it as."

I poured out all the things I'd been forming in my mind these past months: the training we'd need, the equipment, the inventories and planning, the targeting of spoils, and finally, the alliances that would be necessary with other pirate gangs. He listened in silence until I finished, then finally nodded.

"I've thought some of the same things."

"And what have you done about it? Your cousin Chat was a leader. What about you? Sometimes I think you're afraid to lead. You're the head of the Cheng clan now."

"I know."

"You should be the most notorious, feared ruler of the Two-Kwang coast—so feared that men will come to you and offer their tribute without you lifting a hand. And be the wealthiest."

"Mm."

I narrowed my eyes at him the way his Tin Hau idol was looking down at me right now. "I want a partnership," I said. "I expect to be part of all planning and decisions."

He snorted. "Madwoman! What are you going to ask next? To be empress?"

"Maybe I am mad." I licked my lips and spoke slowly, enunciating each word. "Mad enough to make you the most feared, and richest, sea bandit on the China coast. The Emperor of the Sea, with me as empress.

246

Or I'll die trying."

Ying-shek had crawled to me unnoticed. He rested a hand on my ankle with his familiar cry that went straight to my breasts. I lifted him to me.

"I also want a wet nurse."

XXVI
Tai O

Our partnership worked. But no one could have guessed.

Of course, one needed only to step out on deck to see the results: over one hundred ships when gathered together. So many that Cheng Yat—that is, *we*—divided them into squadrons which expanded our reach beyond every horizon. All accomplished in under a year. Everyone praised him for his leadership, his strength, and his cunning. My role stayed hidden behind the cabin's closed door.

The cabin had become my secret world where I pondered the business, planned our targets and distributions, and managed his tantrums, without a word from my lips traveling beyond the threshold. This was our agreement.

My reward was meant to be in the ledgers, the proof of my success in the silks on my back, the jade on my wrist, the silver and gold that passed through my perfumed hands. But fabrics couldn't cheer, gold couldn't offer a thankful pat on the shoulder, a fine copper mirror showed my face only to me.

The more he treated me as a partner, the less I was treated as a wife. I set aside time for our child more than he did, though we were never a family. I hadn't thought that would bother me, but it did. A simple embrace for no other reason than that he was happy with me—for my work, for my mothering his son, it didn't matter—that would have pleased me ten thousand times more than another stolen sandalwood carving or silver-inlaid abacus. It wasn't kisses I wanted, and which he would never have given, but validation.

I could live with the secrecy. What I couldn't tolerate was the way that camouflaging my function limited my role in the enterprise. I needed more say in our dealings with buyers. It was time I came out into the open.

Which was why I sat at the front of a sampan, trying to contain my excitement, while Cheung Po Tsai weaved the little boat through the crowded waterways of Tai O, on the western tip of Tai Yue Shan.

Cheng Yat sat behind me looking tired, even worried. The center thwart sagged under the fat purser, lost in thought, guarding our bags of samples. Po Tsai, at the yuloh, sweetened the air with songs.

This city of canals bustling with commerce dazzled me. We weaved along the main waterway, between what seemed like half the junks and sampans and rafts in China. Rickety wooden houses lined both sides, perched high over the water on bamboo stilts. Children leaned out windows to toss coins at passing goods rafts and catch the treats tossed up to them with astonishing aim.

Po Tsai slowed the sampan to allow a rope-drawn ferry to cross the canal. "Pretty girls!" he called as a group of young Hakka women on the raft giggled and waved back.

He swung us into a crowded side channel, barely squeezing between houseboats and floating shops through opaque muddy water. An egret posed on a wooden piling until we veered too close and it lifted away.

Cheng Yat directed Po Tsai into an even narrower water alley, all the way to where the stilt houses gave way to a vast mangrove swamp.

"Is this where you always go?" I said.

"Old family friend. No more talk," Cheng Yat said, giving me a look that said the rest: *like you and I agreed.*

I followed them along a rickety raised walkway; in the mud below, red fiddler crabs scattered out of sight. We arrived at a forlorn fishing supply shop marked by a tangled pile of nets and a shapeless woman in a Hakka hat seated by the door.

Cheng Yat greeted her: *"Wai,* Yuen-tai, eaten yet?"

"Eaten, eaten—whatever that old glutton leaves for me." She rapped on the wall.

A man's head popped through the door, all teeth and lips. "Ah! Cheng Yat, my friend, long time! You're handsome as ever."

Cheng Yat clapped him on the shoulder. *"Lo Ban,* if your first words are such a lie, then I'm sure you plan to cheat me."

"I never cheat you—not while you're looking! Ha! You eaten yet?"

The shopkeeper pulled out stools, inviting us to sit.

"Eaten," Cheng Yat said. "I hope your health is good."

"Good, good." The shopkeeper bowed to me. "I'm Yuen. And you must be his daughter. Such a lovely young woman couldn't be this rascal's wife."

I kept my promise and, other than a thank you, smiled without comment, though it felt arrogant to do so. The man dressed more like a street coolie than a merchant. It was difficult to consider his dusty premises as a shop: a single round shrimp drying rack, ropes freckled with mold, a single tarnished compass. Clearly nothing legitimate had been traded here in years. I waited for him to look the other way, then discreetly dusted off my stool before sitting.

"Haven't I seen this young man before?" the merchant said. Po Tsai, having caught up with us after mooring the boat, wiped sweat from his forehead.

"Good memory. Was a boy then," Cheng Yat said. "You'll be doing business with Cheung Po Tsai before long."

"Good, good. What do you have for me?" Yuen's grin never left his face.

The purser unpacked a sack of samples onto a bench. Dealer Yuen weighed a Siamese bronze bowl in his hand. "How many you have?"

The purser checked his ledger. "Four hundred thirty-five."

Yuen held up a scale, placed the bowl on the pan, and adjusted weights along the markings on the beam. He flicked a finger on the rim, striking a dull tone. "Not much of a ring. Fifteen taels silver for the lot."

"Joking!" Cheng Yat said.

"I pay Spanish silver."

Cheng Yat glanced at the purser. We all knew our bottom price was twenty taels.

"Forty-five," Cheng Yat said.

"Oh, my friend, even I couldn't sell these at such a price," the dealer said. "Only foreigners buy such things, and they're as likely to melt them into bullets. Eighteen taels."

The purser shot back, "Forty."

Yuen clasped his chest. "Wah, you threaten my health with such talk. I give you twenty, half for any dented or cracked. I'm the loser here. But what's money among friends, ha?"

"For your health, then, I might consider thirty," Cheng Yat said.

"I might consider starving and selling the clothes off my children's backs to pay such a price for gaudy Siamese rubbish," Yuen said through his perpetual grin. "All right, twenty-five." He winked at me, the bastard, like he was showing off for a pretty girl. That did it. I wasn't going to stay quiet.

Cheng Yat raised an eyebrow. The purser reached for his brush. I was appalled. Had neither of them shopped in a town vegetable market before? Yuen was a smooth-talking storyteller; they were clumsy bears and no match for him.

I grabbed the bowl and held it to my face. "No. I'd rather keep them at that price. They're pretty."

Cheng Yat coughed inside his throat. If Yuen was angry, he kept it well-hidden. "Wah. The lady knows how to do business. Twenty-eight, lucky number. Not a bent cash more!"

The haggling continued over tea, dates, cotton, and a rare batch of tiger bones. I no longer made any pretense about being the wifely observer. Cheng Yat's face be damned, my role in this fleet would no longer remain a badly kept secret.

The men celebrated the deal over strong blue liquor. No amount of fluttering my fan relieved the heat and damp inside Yuen's shop. Outside, the sun baked the world. A flash of color past the doorway: a kingfisher darting into the mangrove.

"The lady needs refreshment too," Yuen said, offering a fresh bowl of wine, one drop of which could have ignited a forest.

I allowed myself a single polite sip. "Yuen *Lo Ban,* why do you buy from us?"

Cheng Yat nudged my leg. I nudged back.

"I mean, why don't you have your own fleet?"

Cheng Yat muttered apologies, but Yuen was amused, if not by the question, then by the idea of a woman asking such a thing. "Interesting question from an interesting lady." He waved over the piled-up samples. "I make good business. Why do I want to pay for ships and men? Too expensive, too much risk."

I knew I risked a fight later in the cabin if I didn't shut up, but the deal was over. Yuen was less guarded now, and I wanted to pluck what else I could. He fell for my warmest, most innocent smile. "Very smart man. So, we take the risk and you take..."

"My dear woman, for me plenty risk. Plenty expense." He made a big show of rubbing his fingers and thumb together, indicating bribes.

Cheng Yat tugged my arm. "Enough."

"No, I want to ask," I said, and I did: "I wonder, what if we were based in Tai O? Joint venture, I'm talking about. Share the risks, share the rewards. Elbow out competitors, build a strong enterprise." What I didn't add was something else high in my thoughts: we needed a base, and Tai Yue Shan fit all the criteria.

The purser tut-tutted.

Cheng Yat growled. "I said enough."

Yuen didn't seem to think so. This man loved to hear himself talk.

"Clever, clever lady. But maybe you don't know my trade. Think I buy only from you? Of course you don't. Why would I? If a man has many geese, why would he trade them for a single swan? Competition is good! Keeps prices in line, and I don't mean just for your lovely bowls."

"I'm sorry," Cheng Yat said.

"Why sorry? Your wife is a smart one. Too smart maybe, hah! Needs to understand the way things work." His eyes drilled into me: "See this shop? How much silver do you think I wrap in officials' palms in order to blind their eyes? You come here to sell to me a few times a year, no problem. But you want a base here? Wah! Imagine if, every day, Tai O swarmed with your bandit ships. Aiya! To buy that much blindness is rather beyond my means, madam. Beyond yours!"

He made it clear that the discussion was finished, at least the one I'd initiated. He had more to say, but not to me. After an uncomfortable silence, he refilled the bowls for Cheng Yat and himself, raised his, and said, "My friend, this may be the last drink we share."

"I'm sorry. I told her to stay out of my business."

His business?

"Nothing to do with her," Yuen said. "I intended to bring this up earlier, old friend. I regret to tell you that things between us might change."

"What are you talking about?"

"You see, there is a small matter...actually, not so small." He downed his wine and pushed the bowl aside. "Tai O merchants are red and green in the face lately. Some even talk of assembling our own fleet. Not like your lady proposes. For self-defense—from you."

"What the devil?" Cheng Yat said.

Yuen shook his head and sucked in his breath. "There are too many raids. Wait, before you say a word. I tell you this because you're an honorable man. I trust you. Just fifteen, sixteen days ago a local fisherman was accosted by a bandit group—not yours, I assume. Got their ransom, yet still they abducted three men and his niece, a pretty girl. Just two days later, different pirates seized his ship and demanded payment. His wife couldn't stop her tongue—as wives do, I fear. They cut down the poor woman and stole the man's catch."

"Wasn't us. I can't be responsible for—"

"Worse happened to a fellow trader—a rival, but I wouldn't wish on him what happened. Bought goods from a pirate named Lo. Do you know him?" Cheng Yat and the purser shrugged no. Yuen continued: "All straightforward, mind you. My friend arranged a resale to a super-cargo in Wong Po. Along the way, another gang hijacked his vessel, took everything on it, killed his captain. And then where do you think that dog spawn showed up to hawk his wares? At my friend's very shop! That thief earned a knife in his kidney, but the goods were never recovered. Heard enough? I've more stories, if you like."

Cheng Yat said nothing. These weren't our doing, but we knew such things were happening more frequently. Hadn't we ourselves fought off Fukienese bandits? An abundance of turtle hunters—us bandits—competing for a scarcity of eggs.

Yuen continued, "Things aren't like they were. There are too many pirates to keep track of, too many tumbling over each other to steal our goods. And, frankly, too many goods. It's affecting prices."

"Are you blaming me?" Cheng Yat said.

"I've known your family too long. No Cheng would ever stoop to cheating me, am I right?"

Cheng Yat sniffed.

"My friend, treachery is not in your character. Nor mine," Yuen said.

"Then why these stories?"

"I need you to spread the word." Yuen stood up unsteadily and pointed out the door. "You tell every thieving water rat between here and hell that if this doesn't stop, all of you will soon find it tougher to enter Tai O than to penetrate your granny's shriveled old cunt."

We fought like chickens and ducks on our way out of Tai O. He'd been shaken by Yuen's allegations, by the consequences his threats might have on our business. And he'd been shaken by my brazenly stepping into the bargaining. Whatever I suggested about his following Yuen's advice to warn the other pirates, he countered by telling me to take my own boat and be the messenger for my new partner Yuen. We argued until I ran out of wind and retreated alone to the poop deck.

The coast of Tai Yue Shan slid past—mountainous and barren, from here it looked inhospitable. This forbidding island was where Cheng Chat's wife had dreamed of spending her last days, in some secluded bay she'd described but never named. That was where we headed now, where the rest of our fleet waited for us. A place Cheng Yat had known as a child, whenever his father had brought him to visit his uncle and cousin—where, I was told, Cheng family graves dotted the hillsides. I knew its name now. A safe anchorage named Tung Chung.

We rounded the headland as the sun shrunk behind the steep hills, and I knew Tung Chung was a perfect haven for pirates. Walled in by steep hills, its entrance partly hidden from the sea by an islet just outside its mouth. Yet something was wrong here. The smell of what I'd taken for cook fire smoke grew into the unmistakable heavy odor of burnt timber. Further on, a blackened junk slumped in the water. Then another. Halfway across the bay, a rudder stood like a flag over a capsized hull.

The rest of the fleet was here, crowding the southern end of the water. A sampan rushed to meet us, one of Cheng Yat's squadron commanders shouting like a madman as he clambered over the rails. Yesterday, a different bandit group had attacked, catching them all by surprise.

"Who?" Cheng Yat said, almost a whisper.

Someone tossed up a sack from the sampan. The squadron commander lifted out a severed head by its queue. "Know him?"

Cheng Yat examined the shrunken face and shook his head. "Take him elsewhere. Bury him with respect. I don't want his ghost in my harbor."

Cheng Yat spent the rest of the evening praying alone at the cabin shrine, refusing visitors. I brought him food and tea, but he turned down both. He let me stay in the cabin—to watch, to sleep, but stopped me when I tried to speak.

At last, close to midnight, he extinguished the lamp and joined me on the sleeping mat. His skin was cold, his breathing labored. At last he released a drawn-out sigh and said, "Time to call a meeting of the chiefs."

XXVII
Gathering

Far up a steep hillside behind Tung Chung, summer was still a month away, yet the sun toasted my shoulders; even the stones in the footpath seemed to perspire.

"I need to rest." I sat on a boulder under a short, gnarled tree. Cheng Yat continued ahead. A local porter set down our satchels and joined me in the shade. The bay below sparkled in the sunlight.

"Is this where the emperor came?" I said.

"No, not this place. Other side of the island."

The knowledge disappointed me. Cheng Chat's wife had told me a legend about the last Song Emperor, only eight years old, fleeing the Mongols all the way to Tai Yue Shan with his court. Tung Chung seemed like the ideal defense: its entrance restricted by little Chek Lap Kok island; the bay surrounded by fields and paddies, ringed by steep barren mountains. No wonder Cheng Yat intended to make this his permanent base. A base for more than our own fleet, I reminded him.

The bay had transformed into a forest of masts. Our fleet's more than one hundred ships took the best anchorage, the south end closest to the village. Wu-shek Yi and his brothers packed the waters to the west. I recognized General Bo's ships by a white streamer on his foremast. Cheng Lau-tong, another veteran of the first Annam campaign, was also somewhere out there. Nearly every day, more junks filed in: little gangs of two or three, or fishermen dreaming of riches. Some came from as far as Hoinam, responding to Cheng Yat's call up and down the coast: a pirate syndicate was to be born.

Responding to Cheng Yat's whistle from farther ahead, the porter led me onto a crumbling trail over a sheer drop. My heart only stopped racing when we reached a landing hewn into the slope. A small village of arch-roofed shrines clung to the mountainside: the Cheng family tombs. The porter laid his satchels on the ground. Before he left, he motioned me aside.

"The Song boy emperor? Bad luck, I think, to talk about," he said softly, casting a wary eye at Cheng Yat. "Came to the island to rule. He and his dynasty both died."

Cheng Yat finished clearing weeds around one crypt, then unpacked offerings from a sack and arranged them in front of Cheng Chat's memorial stone. I did the same for Cheng Chat's wife. I still remembered her face, the way her voice cracked a little each time she spoke of returning here to live in peace.

A dark cloud passed overhead. A sudden breeze stirred up dust. We let it blow the heat from our bodies. Below, two local shrimp trawlers entered the bay.

"They'll never listen to me," Cheng Yat said.

"Listen to yourself first," I told him. "If a tiger had that attitude, it wouldn't frighten a mouse."

"Very encouraging."

"Just feed them the plan as if they're already hungry for it." I chopped one hand with the other for emphasis. "Territories. Protection fees. Shares. Passes—"

"Aiya! Not now! Haven't you lectured me enough?"

A raindrop splashed at my feet. I thought coming up here to tend his cousin's tomb would embolden him, that Cheng Chat's spirit might magically take hold. Leaving me to take care of the planning and finances, my husband would be free to concentrate on his talents. He had proven himself a fine commander, with a subtle sense of strategy and a predator's instinct for when to strike and, perhaps rarer, when to back away. But I worried that his tight-lipped clumsiness of speech hurt his potential as a leader.

"Maybe I should do the speaking?" I said.

"Maybe you should. This is all your idea, a woman's idea. Women like to talk."

I took his tease with a little smile. Imagining, refining, and putting into cohesive form the principles for a pirate confederation had been a mutual effort which we'd discussed, fought over, and finally agreed upon over the past month. But the difficulties of composing a plan that would transform the entire China coast were simple compared to the task of training Cheng Yat to speak in coherent sentences.

His chin pointed to the harbor. A group of ships rounded the western point, one flying a long, scalloped yellow banner. Tunghoi Bat was arriving. Cheng Yat glanced at the clouds. We hurried down the path while a light drizzle fell around us.

We separated at the bottom of the hill—he back to the ship, me toward the main village, joining the crowd scurrying down the muddy market lane to get out of the thickening rain.

This village was homely, like any other coastal settlement. The people were the usual mix of Punti, Hakka, and water folk. It had none of the color or vibrancy of nearby Tai O. But that didn't mean it couldn't be built into a bandit capital—a place I could try to call home.

With thousands of visiting seamen to entertain, every hovel had turned into a makeshift tavern, gambling den, or who knew what else, but all I wanted was something to eat. A fat rumble of thunder sent me hurrying through the nearest doorway.

The air was thick with curses and the clatter of fan-tan tokens. Lit only by the weak light through the door and a glowing coal stove, I couldn't see what was on offer but was drawn inside by the comforting aroma of freshly boiled noodles. An overturned crate served as my table. A girl of around ten approached with the weariness of an older woman and took my order: boiled pork dumplings and a fried radish cake. I also asked for a lamp.

Rain spattered through the doorway. Somewhere in the corner a loud drunk accused every last native of western Luichow of being a savage dog-fucking card cheat. His target condemned the entire population of Tai Pang Wan to fuck their ancient grandmothers in the fourth pit of hell. A table capsized. Bowls smashed. This pieced together, sweaty village was to be the base for the grand alliance we had planned?

Nothing ever would live up to my dreamy memories of Chiang Ping, where I sipped pretty teas with the friend I'd just honored on the hill, my dear sister, gone for nearly three years, leaving a hole in my heart that had yet to be filled.

The girl brought my dumplings. They were mouth-burning hot and delicious. I tried to focus my thoughts on Cheng Yat's and my plan for a system of organized extortion spanning the coast, but my mind kept filling with ghosts.

A dark figure filled the doorway, shaking water from his robe. He stepped in my direction, a familiar bounce in his stride. Cheung Po Tsai dragged a stool to my table.

"Rains any harder, I might grow fins. Lucky me finding you here."

The serving girl hooked a lamp to the wall, then brought a platter with two glistening white radish cakes.

"I'll have the same," Po Tsai said. "My old mother here will pay."

"I'm not his mother." I blew on a dumpling pinched between my chopsticks.

Po Tsai tore off a corner of radish cake and stuffed it in his mouth. "I'll pay you back."

Lamplight danced on his face. Eighteen now, I had to admit he was a handsome young man with a mischievous tilt to his brows who ought to have been married by now. I would speak to Cheng Yat about finding him a wife. And setting him up on another ship.

"How do you like this?" He stood and spread his arms so the light caught his tunic: a garish shade of purple one would expect on an opera stage. A pair of elaborately embroidered dragons faced one another across the chest.

"Let me see." I rubbed the fabric between my fingers. Good quality Hangchow silk. "Lovely. Which woman did you steal it from?"

"Steal? Ha! Not this. The fabric is from those three barges, remember? Just picked it up from the tailor."

The girl delivered his food. After swapping our plates of radish cakes, he popped a whole dumpling into his mouth and made a face. "Hot!"

He swallowed, fanned his bowl, then propped his head on his other hand. "Not-my-mother Cheng Yat Sou, why don't you like me?"

How could a man his age be so innocent? I preferred not to be drawn into such a conversation. "Maybe because you dip into your captain's treasury to throw money at tailors."

"I would never. Never, never, never. I will never betray Cheng Yat. Or you."

"Yet you have money for tailors? I know how much you're paid."

"Too little, right? Ha! But do you see me tossing coins into gambling baskets like those monkeys over there? I don't drink wine, never smoked foreign mud. Don't even know how to pay for a woman." He leaned across the table and whispered like he had a secret to share. "A man who doesn't squirt his money out his eel or squander it on games or drink or foreign mud—well, that man can afford fine things, right?"

"So, you squander it to dress like an emperor."

"Why not?" Po Tsai sat up, delighted at the remark. "The emperor and I both have to piss, and we both have to wear clothes."

"You think the emperor eats plain radish cakes?"

He pushed his plate aside. "You're right. If he doesn't eat such lowly food, then neither do I!"

"I thought you don't throw money away?"

"It isn't my money. Didn't you say you were paying?" He leaned back and let out a hearty laugh, then stuffed an entire radish cake in his mouth. "See? I'm responsible with your money, if not mine."

I couldn't stop myself from laughing.

"But you didn't answer my question," he said.

I'd forgotten what he'd asked—oh yes, something about why I didn't like him. It was a foolish question, and as he propped himself on the table like a bemused cat, I thought it one not worth a reply. I busied myself cutting the last radish cake with my chopsticks, until his next remark made me drop a piece on the floor.

"Ah-Yang—may I call you that?—I've been thinking. All those men you were with, did you love any of them?"

"This has gone too far. Finish eating and, and…"

"Yes, I'll go. But you haven't answered any of my questions."

I almost said, *I'm your mother!* Instead: "Do you like girls? Have you loved any?"

He laughed, giving no clue to the answer. With his looks and his impish charm, half the young women in China would have thrown themselves at him. Even I had trouble distinguishing this beautiful young man from the monkey-like child who had formed my first impression. He may have been a catamite once, but that didn't make him less of a man. Or did it? Had his mention of emperors been a hint? Maybe he preferred the passion of the cut sleeve, seeing himself as Tung Hsien, attendant and lover to Emperor Ai.

He licked his fingers and called the serving girl over. "One more radish cake. This time, I pay." He smiled again. "You don't answer my questions, I don't answer yours. Just like a married couple."

"Since we are clearly not a married couple, let's start by you answering me. What happened to your father?"

His easy demeanor dropped; his shoulders tightened. He aged five years in front of my eyes. I'd touched on something difficult.

"I've heard your story a hundred times," I said. "Out fishing with your father, taken by Cheng Yat. But nothing about your father. Did he get away?"

The radish cakes came, but he nudged the platter aside, eyes fixed on an empty place on the table. "I thought you knew," he finally said, all humor wiped from his voice. "But I forgot, you weren't there."

"What happened?"

I sensed his discomfort in the way his eyes turned aside, then drilled into mine. "I think my father was a good man in the end. They tried to send him off, but he clung to the rail and fought his way on board. Then they offered him money to buy me, and he accepted. So, they filled a sack with coins and ingots—it was a lot, quite heavy. He took the sack and then—*pa!*—he swung it at Cheng Yat and missed, broke another man's nose."

"And then?"

"I think you can guess the rest of the story. I also can only guess."

"You didn't look?"

"By then, they tied me in the cabin."

"But how can you—" I couldn't complete the question. How could he be so cheerful all the time, as though he'd been born to sail with bandits? How could he have so willingly submitted to becoming Cheng Yat's young lover and seem to enjoy it? But he guessed my meaning.

"How could you marry him?" he said.

Of course, he was right. We had both made the best of our circumstances. We were both survivors. We'd been rivals for our abductor's affections when we might as easily have been conspirators against him. We were the same, yet so different.

He took a bite of radish cake, then reposed on his stool with the ease and confidence of a virile young tiger at the beginning of the world. He observed me differently in the undulating lamplight, not as prey or rival, but the way a tiger might regard his mate. His cheeks were more pronounced, his jaw sharper. Without his ever-present grin, he was more tiger than man, more man than boy, younger than me by only one year more than I was to Cheng Yat. I had a burning urge to sweep him into my arms and offer comfort that he hadn't asked for. Or maybe to receive comfort for something we didn't necessarily share. At the same time, I felt awkward, plain, and old.

"How do you not hate him?" I said.

He shrugged. "I never see you pray. Maybe that's why you ask such a thing."

"I stopped believing—if I ever did to begin with—before I can remember." I took a piece of radish cake. It had gone cold and lost its flavor.

"I believe in everything," Po Tsai said. "If this god won't help you, another one will. I saw a foreigners' temple in O Moon. I didn't go inside. But maybe I could believe in their gods too." He turned his head. "Stopped raining."

He stood and brushed himself off. "You worry Father loves me more than you." A statement, not a question.

The stool quaked under me. My breath came quick and shallow.

"He doesn't, you know," Po Tsai said. The purple silk shimmered like fire as he bowed. I clasped my hands to hide their shaking.

He gave me a last, oddly searching, look before he ducked out into the street.

The harbor was so full one couldn't see the headlands through the masts. It was hard to believe there were that many junks in the sea, any trees left to mount sails for the commercial ships upon which we preyed. Yet two months since the first arrivals, only six fleets besides ours had arrived, eating and drinking Tung Chung dry. Never mind, Cheng Yat kept telling me, those who didn't take part would regret it. His patience at an end, he consulted the oracles for the next auspicious date. The conference convened on the seventh day of the sixth month of the year.

My first mistake was to keep things relaxed, like any normal captain's gathering. I made sure the cabin was generously stocked with wine. I dressed so as not to draw attention from Cheng Yat: tidy dark gray tunic and trousers, hair bundled with a simple pin. I would join him to greet the men as they came aboard, then I would retreat and let him run things like a meeting of old friends. How much I needed to learn about leadership.

Wu-shek Yi, his brother, and a cousin showed up early with General Bo, followed by a gray-haired fleet leader, Cheng Lau-tong, all immediately indulging their interest in our store of wine. Next to arrive was a big-chested man whose bulging eyes crawled all over me.

"Looks like it was worth sailing halfway across the world after all. Name's Chin if it pleases you, but everyone calls me Son of a Frog."

"Master Frog." I forced a smile, thinking frogs are easy to catch.

Kwok Podai greeted me as if I hadn't been avoiding him since his arrival three days ago. Three years since that terrible night at Spirit River, his face was rougher, his hair had strands of white, but those eyes still speared me in a way that was as fresh as yesterday.

"Madam Cheng, your beauty should amaze the birds."

"And your mouth is slick with fragrant oil."

Tunghoi Bat appeared last, clearly by design, with little more than a perfunctory nod as he strode past me to take command of the drinking.

Cheng Yat called the commanders into the cabin. It was his show now. I would keep my mouth shut in the corner. The error of my promise soon unfolded.

Tunghoi Bat took control from the start as if he was the convener. "A bigger set of scoundrels than I've seen together in years. Let's get this over with—I'm not here to enjoy your weather."

"You've enjoyed his wine, though," Wu-shek Yi said.

Cheng Yat cleared his throat and prepared to stand, as I'd encouraged him to, but he apparently thought better of it and simply clapped for attention.

"I remember as a child, when a fishing boat returned with a good catch, next day all the other junks sailed for that same ground. Everyone came back with half-empty holds, some with gashed hulls when the competition came too close. Afterward every family hated each other for days."

He paused, long enough for me to worry that the effort of stringing so many words together had already tied him in knots.

Finally, he continued: "That's us. Fighting over the same fish, stealing each other's catch."

Tunghoi Bat broke in, "If you're accusing me of stealing your catch—"

"I accuse all of us! Myself included!" Cheng Yat said. "We all know, every man here, that we're too often getting in each other's way, looting each other's territory—"

"What territory?" Kwok Podai sniffed. "I've seen no walls in the sea, no map with your name on it, or mine."

I smiled to myself. I'd anticipated such a question, though I'd expected it from Tunghoi Bat. All the better that it came from Kwok because the response I'd rehearsed with Cheng Yat so many times suited Kwok's own logic.

"Maybe that's what we need," Cheng Yat said. "Maps and walls known only to us. How many times have you taken a trader that another robbed three days before? Or a month passes without a single barge in sea lanes that used to run like rivers of salt? We're stealing from each other and scaring all the traders out of the sea."

"It happens, but so what?" said Tunghoi Bat. "Is that why you called us together? To warn us all to stay out of your—what did you call it—territory?"

This was where Cheng Yat was supposed to launch his argument for an alliance. But everyone was talking in each other's faces. Only Wu-shek Yi's squeal penetrated the noise.

"Friends! Friends! Let me say something, please, friends, please. This is all a bit ridiculous. Yes, thank you. Quiet for a moment. My dear old colleague Cheng, if I follow your meaning, the next time I spot a lovely prize bobbing in front of me, I should invite their skipper to tea and ask him, 'Honored captain, may I have the pleasure of plundering your ship's bowels—unless of course one of my esteemed colleagues has already taken your silver and raped your daughters within the past, say, three months?'"

Laughter turned into a shouting match. Cheng Yat was too busy arguing with Wu to bring the meeting back to order. I wanted to stand up and announce an adjournment until tomorrow, but nothing would have undermined Cheng Yat more. Instead I kept my silence, studying each man in turn for how he might be influenced. General Bo, Cheng Lau-tong, and Son of a Frog, the three with the smallest fleets, had the most to gain from an alliance. The real battle was to win over Wu and Kwok. Tunghoi Bat, I sensed all along, was thinking about how to insinuate himself as leader.

The light faded quickly under a heavy dark cloud. Raindrops tapped the hull. Maybe Cheng Yat had been right: these crude old sailors couldn't see beyond the ends of their stubby noses to grasp the need for a few simple rules that would benefit them all. It was his job— *our* job—to make them see the goal like a sail beckoning on the horizon.

Cheng Yat finally pounded the floor for attention. "One man at a time!"

It should have started with him, but he let Kwok Podai speak.

"It seems to me that the problem is our own success," Kwok began. "The emperor, in his enthusiasm to fight foreign armies, has left the entire coast to fend for itself, while we have enjoyed the benefit of his neglect. As a result, our own fleets have grown while the world itself has not expanded. I suppose it was inevitable that our little ventures occasionally overlap. But has it done us any harm? I don't see a man among us who's starving."

"Agreed," General Bo said. "I steal here, you pilfer there, they lose cargo either way. Makes no difference to them the name of the thief. Now, if you're talking about joint raids—"

"No!" Cheng Yat stood, finally. "We're here to establish an alliance!"

That shut them up. Tunghoi Bat look set to hijack the silence, but Cheng Yat beat him to it. This had turned out to be the wrong way to hold a conference, but at least Cheng Yat was wresting back control and returning to our practiced points.

"An alliance," he repeated. He beat a hand against his palm with each phrase, as I silently mouthed along. "Set territories. Rights of passage. Protection fees. Cooperation instead of chaos. Quiet! Let me finish. This isn't about joint campaigns, or sharing each other's spoils, and it has nothing to do with friendship," his last remark directed at Tunghoi Bat. "It's about business. We need a set of rules and territories that we all agree on and all profit from."

Wu laughed. "Rules? Territories? What, like provinces? You're proposing a sea bandit empire? Who gets to be emperor? Not that I care, so long as I'm in charge of the imperial concubines."

This prompted a crossfire of sarcastic shouts, like dogs barking at cows. He'd lost control again. It occurred to me that he had run out of replies and was unable to rein in the chaos. It was my turn to panic—which explained my next move.

I stuck fingers in my mouth and whistled, the way Cheng Chat's wife used to. Every one of them stopped mid-sentence and stared at me.

"A pirate confederation!" I said. "It's time you shut up with the jokes. We propose a confederation. Separate fleets, separate areas of control, following a common set of rules and agreements. Any man who doesn't join be damned. And that's all I have to say."

I leaned back into the shadows, having said too much. I shouldn't have said *we*—I should have said *he*. But Cheng Yat went on as though my outburst had been part of the plan, though I would pay for this later, I could be sure. He laid out the proposal: each of the seven fleets represented at the meeting would work its own exclusive section of the coast. Merchant ships robbed in one territory would be issued documents which granted unhindered transit through other fleets' waters. Any rogues or upstart bandits from outside the confederation would be eliminated with the cooperation of all.

The men paid attention with uncharacteristic quiet until Cheng Yat voiced his most radical proposal.

"A system of protection passes granting ships total immunity from plunder. Income from these passes is divided among the fleets."

A thunderbolt echoed in the hills. Rain sprayed through the porthole until I forced it shut. With uncanny timing, the torrent rattled the ship on all sides, making further discussion impossible. Cheng Yat cracked open a jar of wine. All nodded at the suggestion to talk again tomorrow.

I knelt in the corner wringing my wet sleeves into a bucket when in the corner of my eye, I caught a small movement. Kwok Podai held up a fist, meant for me. He wiggled his pointing finger downward, like an elephant's trunk.

Cheng Yat spent the evening in a sulk, biting his fingers and praying at the shrine, or at least pretended to pray, until I couldn't stand it anymore.

"Are we going to go over what to say tomorrow?"

He pretended to ignore me. "I told you they wouldn't take it seriously."

"They took it the way stupid men always take in new ideas, one drip at a time through the pin holes in their brains. Let it seep in overnight."

"And what if I'm not convinced myself?" He spun around to face me, more animated now than he'd been during the meeting. "All we really need is an agreement to keep the Tai O bloodsuckers happy. But that's not enough for you! The great Cheng Yat Sou wants to be queen of the sea. Maybe even I don't understand what you want."

"What I want is for you! For everyone on this ship! For the tillermen and the gunners and even old Ah-Yi. I want us to be something more than…than…a flock among flocks of crows."

"Those 'crows' are my friends. I've sailed with them, fought beside them. Some of them I trained myself and sent into the world, and look how far they've come. Can't you understand? I want to be their comrade, not their lord! But you—all you talk about is power and glory. Maybe that's how women think. Maybe you should set up your own women's confederation."

I didn't think he even believed himself. Behind his frustration, I could hear how much he wanted this alliance. I knew this was a man who didn't back out of a fight. But this was a fight with weapons none of us truly understood. "The world is changing," I told him. "Look out there and see it: A new Governor-General. More foreigners in these waters. More of us! The business is changing. There's more goods and more money, so it's pulling in interest from outside. The Fukienese are sniffing around. The triads are stretching their fingers offshore. Or am I wrong? Tell me it's all in my imagination."

He didn't have an answer. I followed him around the room while he searched the wine jars for leftovers.

"We can't go back to the way things were before Annam," I said. "That way vanished a long time ago. We need to change, or we'll be swallowed up. If we do it with cunning and strength, we'll come out on top. *You* will be on top!"

"So, nothing of this is for you? That's the best joke I've heard all day. I'm tired of talking. I want to sleep." He found some remnant wine in a jar and tipped it into his mouth.

"Put down that wine! We need to prepare for tomorrow."

To spite me, he sucked the last drops and licked the rim.

"When will you have enough? You wanted a wedding, you wanted to rub against royalty, you wanted a hundred ships. I gave you everything you asked! And what do I get? Your mouth! I won't have you shaming me in front of everyone!"

"How could I possibly shame you? Why would I do such a thing? You should have seen yourself. You did good. You did very good! Those men respect you. That's why they responded so powerfully. I was so proud." My smile threw him off guard. I wrapped my arms around him. "My dear husband, I've never seen you turn around in the middle of a battle. And you're going to win tomorrow because tomorrow, we'll be smarter. And *you* will have *your* confederation."

I let go and went to the door. The rain had passed. A fresh wind brushed my face. I called down to a sailor on deck: "Send up the purser. Tell him to bring plenty of ink and paper."

XXVIII
Haven Hollow

This was how to host a conference: Cheng Yat in his modified naval uniform and me in sober black silk with red trim. Mid-deck, a table arranged for tea beneath a taut canopy. Today there would be no nonsense.

I circled the table, handing each man a stack of papers covered in elegant script, each with an official red chop.

Wu-shek Yi fanned his stack out on the table. "Are we playing some betting game?"

Kwok Podai, of course, could read them, eyebrows raised, impressed. "They're protection passes. Grant the bearer, his ship, crew and specified cargo unhindered passage from port to port. This one's for salt, this is for lumber. One for passengers. Interesting." He tidied his pile. "But nothing especially new. We've always extracted tribute from local shipping."

"What's new," Cheng Yat said, "is that if you sell a man such a pass and he displays it to me, I also have to honor it, as must each man here and every one of his ships and crews."

"So, Kwok plucks a petal and nobody else can sniff the flower," Tunghoi Bat said.

Even I joined in the laughter, relieved that our ploy had worked. His uniform, the pavilion, something they could hold in their hands—it was a performance. Cheng Yat explained about setting fixed rates for each commodity, fee collection, and distribution of income among the fleets. He might have been more forceful, but he did the job, floundering on only a few details, such as the price of a salt pass. But we were prepared: the supportive wife's hand on his shoulder, five little finger taps…

"Fifty," he said. "Fifty taels protection fee for every hundred sacks of salt, for one voyage. For lumber—"

Wu-shek Yi coughed. "My good friend, I could get six, ten times as much by seizing the damned salt! Why should I—"

"Because you'll get more by not seizing it, if you start looking past the end of your stubby nose."

My error was to partake of the tea, which was beginning to take its toll. Kwok Podai watched me. Had he noticed my fidgeting? His mouth like a brush stroke, eyes filled with the same questions as that night in his library. I replied with a little twitch of my brow. Let him believe in possibility for now.

"No one will accept it," Tunghoi Bat said. "If I were a merchant I'd rather take my chances."

"If you were a merchant, your customers would have strangled you by now," said Wu-shek Yi.

Cheng Yat grunted. "I'll repeat myself. Try to pay attention. If merchants and carriers trust that they won't be attacked—nothing stolen, no lives taken—then they'll fill their holds higher, more ships will sail. The more ships and goods, the more revenue for them, the more for us. No risk, no fighting, we all grow as fat as our friend Wu."

Son of a Frog sat up from a slouch. "Why would the government put up with it? Letting us control the sea lanes, collecting what amounts to taxes. They'll come at us with all guns firing."

Kwok was quick to answer. "On the contrary, my friend. The scheme is quite brilliant and, in fact, well-timed. We have another new Governor-General, in case you didn't know. Na Yin-sing apparently arrives with a reputation as a suppressor of rebels, no?" He looked to Tunghoi Bat, who nodded confirmation.

"But only on land, not at sea," Kwok continued. "He has no ships, and the army is controlled from the capital. Considering the repeated failures of his predecessors to contain us, I believe he would welcome the opportunity to claim credit for the pacification of the southern coast."

With the tide of argument in our favor, I took the opportunity to escape to the privy. Squatting behind the barrier, I couldn't stop worrying: was Cheng Yat stumbling over his words right now? I reminded myself to trust him. He knew what he wanted, what we both wanted. Never mind the details, or his wooden way with speech. What he lacked in eloquence he made up for with conviction. He was bringing them around to the pass system. A full confederation was one step away.

They argued well into the afternoon—how to set territories, how to share spoils among different-sized fleets, and what to do with outsiders who didn't join. Tunghoi Bat won the contest for the amount of blather spewed, but it was clear that they all were coming around to the idea of an alliance.

We'd accomplished what we'd wanted that day. The most crucial decision was left for later: the leadership.

After all the tension and the day's heat, I was desperate for a nap, but even this had to be postponed. While the other men meandered to the rail to hail their sampans, Kwok Podai lingered under the canopy until we were alone.

"Enjoy the meeting?" he said. "I liked your performance best." He tapped a finger in the air at shoulder height.

"He needed a few reminders, trivial details. I take it you're aligned with his plans."

Wind rustled the canopy, letting sunlight through the gaps. I stepped toward a fisherman's hat leaning against the gunwale. He grabbed the hat before me and placed it on my head as though it were a crown.

"You're very clever, Madam Cheng."

His words hung between us like droplets suspended in air. "I thought your beloved literature was filled with clever women, Captain Kwok. Please, you can quit your flattery. The confederacy is entirely my husband's idea."

"Is that right?"

"Why are you so surprised?" I said.

He rested an elbow on the rail, studying me. "Everything about you surprises me, Yang."

Such familiarity disarmed me. His smile came from somewhere deep, his dark eyes crackled with a force that rooted me in place. I imagined myself in that cramped dusty room, rows and rows of books looming over me, pressing us together. I squeezed my eyes shut and turned away.

"Nothing to be surprised about. Like any woman, all I'm interested in is a place to call home, and to peacefully grow rich."

"This place? Tung Chung? Rather a bleak spot to call home."

"Is there no place you consider home?"

He dismissed the question with a sniff. "Truth be told, home is a concept that I only find in books."

"Ones written five thousand years ago."

He threw back his head and laughed. A few people turned their heads our way. I looked toward Cheng Yat, but he was too involved in bidding farewell to the others to pay attention to us.

"You and I are more alike than you believe," Kwok said. "I see it in all your—of course, I mean Cheng Yat's—talk of territories and bases. People like us don't have homes. At best we seek a protective haven until circumstances change. Why deny it? It's in our nature. In fact, you remind me of the woman in—"

"The poem?" I was still familiar with that sideways glance of his.

"A poem that could have been written specifically for you."

My heart skipped. I wanted to hear, but I didn't want to let myself. Cheng Yat glanced over. I turned to step away, but then Kwok's deep voice wafted over me like a cloud of rich steaming broth.

> *Fair is the pine grove and the mountain stream*
> *That gathers to the valley far below,*
> *The black-winged junks on the dim sea reach, adream,*
> *The pale blue firmament o'er banks of snow.*
> *And her, more fair, more supple smooth than jade,*
> *Gleaming among the dark red woods I follow:*
> *Now lingering, now as a bird afraid*
> *Of pirate wings she seeks the haven hollow...*

While his words said one thing, he spoke something different with his eyes, a message which burrowed into the lower reaches of my being. It was the wrong message at the wrong time; yet wasn't it true that sometimes the wrong message is the one we most want to hear?

"Lovely, but I'm not some twittering bird. I've changed. I'm not looking to hide in some haven, and I'm certainly not afraid of any pirate men, wings or no wings."

"In that case, Cheng Yat Sou, you haven't changed one bit."

Neither have you, I thought. Confusing me, making me crazy with the twists and turns of his words.

"Thank you for your eloquent support of my husband's proposal. I hope you'll also see the wisdom of installing him as confederation leader."

"And I was going to propose someone more fearless to lead us. A certain woman, perhaps."

I straightened. A notion so fanciful that I hadn't dared to voice it even in the privacy of my own thoughts. I had to end this conversation now; there were too many things I might say, do, or even think which I might regret for a lifetime.

"Kwok Podai, you're very clever with words," I said. "But words can misfire if you aren't careful."

It took another two days to refine the details of the confederation framework, agree on fleet colors, and decide the leadership that all knew was a foregone conclusion. Then three different monks from three separate temples met to decide the most auspicious time for a union, giving us five days to celebrate and draft the final pact.

At dawn on the fifteenth day of the sixth month of the Year of the Wood Ox, Cheung Po Tsai unfurled a banner from the tip of our mainmast. A long red wedge with a white scalloped fringe flapped in the breeze, the symbol of the soon-to-be legendary Red Flag Fleet.

Every ship in the harbor followed suit, hundreds of banners snapping in the wind:

Blue flags topped the masts of Wu-shek Yi's fleet.

Yellow marked Tunghoi Bat.

Son of a Frog flew green and General Bo white.

Cheng Lau-tong's were banded white and red.

Kwok Podai's black-flag fleet fired cannons from the far end of the bay. Firecrackers erupted on every deck, reverberating through the hills while smoke obscured the sun.

The Confederation of the Colored Flags was born.

The leaders assembled at a pavilion set up on shore, bringing wives and Taumuks, scribes and lucky brushes. At last, at the peak of the day, Cheng Yat's purser declared that the Ox Hour had arrived. A poll among the men affirmed Cheng Yat as the Confederation's *Dai Lo Ban*. Then, with little fanfare, each fleet leader approached a document that only one among them could read, and affixed his seal.

Cheng Yat surprised me by insisting on returning early from the celebrations. He seemed to be in a giddy mood I didn't recognize, neither drunk nor sober. The moment the cabin door shut, he maneuvered me onto the mat with a look on his face I'd never seen before. This was a new man, one who'd found words, who had finally found his place in the world. He was reeling with happiness.

I embraced his passion and returned it with fervor. We were playing at love while both knew it was something else. We were celebrating a triumph, an alliance, and devouring each other the way we would now devour the world.

The Pirate Pact

*W*e seven signatories to this pact—Cheng Yat, Mak Yau-kam known as Wu-shek Yi, Ng Chi-ching known as Tunghoi Bat, Lei Sheung-ching called Son of a Frog, Cheng Lau-tong, Kwok Podai and Leung Bo—have discussed among ourselves and agreed to these rules.

If laws are not severe, and evil modes never abolished, then commercial trade can not occur. Today we have fulfilled the grand achievement of joining forces and setting out this pact. Since we are of a single will, it does not matter whether each fleet's strength is great or small or the abilities of its men the same. We must exhibit compassion and not cling to petty enmities. Thus, these documents shall be distributed to every flagship and each regulation impartially enforced.

1. We have agreed that our seagoing vessels, large and small, will be arranged in seven branches named Heaven, Earth, Black, Yellow, Universe, Cosmos, and Vast. Each vessel must record its commander's nickname in a register. Each must inscribe its branch name and registration number on the bow and must fly its branch's banner on the foremast.

2. Each branch has its own banner. As soon as it is discovered that any ship falsely displays another branch's flag or color, the junk and its weapons become the property of the whole group. The commander who has intentionally deceived the confederation will have his fate decided by the group.

3. If a boat hinders a vessel holding one of our safe conduct passes and damages it, sells its cargo, or robs it of money and clothes, the value of the plunder must be estimated and the victim reimbursed.

The offending vessel's weapons and anchors will be confiscated and the commander will suffer punishment commensurate with the case. If the offending vessel cannot pay the compensation, then the amount will be deducted from its branch's future shares.

4. When attacking a merchant ship not possessing a pass, its entire captured cargo belongs to the junk which strikes first. If another seizes it by force from the original captor, he must compensate the initial captor with a sum double the original worth. Those who disobey will suffer attack from the entire group.

5. No matter which branch's boats wrongly detain a junk with a pass, those who witness the action and apprehend the offender will be rewarded with one hundred silver dollars. If any of our brothers is wounded in the action, the entire group will be responsible for his medical care. Furthermore, the group will demand of the culprit to pay him a reward. Those who are present at such an event but sit on the side and take no action will be punished as accomplices.

6. If any vessels sail without permission into seas and harbors to rob, irrespective of any documents or currency in their possession, they and their accompanying boats will be seized and burned, their weapons confiscated, and their commanders executed.

7. If any merchants on land or sea have been the enemies of any one of us, and neither hide nor disguise themselves, and are bold enough to openly do business, we must restrain our personal anger, though we may be displeased. We cannot use our power as a pretext to seize or harm them or to kidnap their kith and kin on the grounds that they are our enemies. Any violation will be treated as a crime of false implication.

8. If a flagship has a matter to discuss with another flagship or the whole group, it should hoist a flag on its mainmast, and the bosses of each branch should come to confer. If a branch commander has an order to transmit to his own boats, he should hoist the flag on the third mast, upon which all junks must assemble and hear the orders. Any who do not assemble will be held in contempt and punished accordingly.

By order of our Dai Lo Ban, this pact shall be copied to each flagship so that it can be respectfully obeyed.

Written by Secretary Ng Sheung-tak in the Ka-hing Reign, Tenth Year, Sixth Month

嘉慶十年乙丑

PART III

—

Tenth Year

of the

Reign of Emperor

Ka-hing

—

1805

XXIX
Confederation

The end of summer was a fruitful time to cruise the tributaries of the lower Pearl River. Harvests had been good this year. The last of the coastal traders from the south were completing their journeys. Meanwhile, the foreigners in O Moon prepared for their annual trading season upriver in Kwangchow, which meant increased traffic in goods ships and barges, and ferries stuffed with merchants and their silver.

Yet something felt wrong this morning. A light southwesterly wind nudged us along the delta's western shore. The sky was jewel bright. Soon I recognized what unsettled me: I smelled smoke—not just burnt wood but the faint, sour tinge of scorched flesh.

Setting aside my breakfast bowl, I got up and watched black plumes rising from the western shore. Rounding a bend, we came upon devastation.

Squat figures picked over a landscape of blackened stone hearths that was once a village. The work, no doubt, of one of our squadrons, evidence that the pass system was still not finding the welcome we'd expected. Riverside village chieftains had been resistant to the notion of handing over rice or pigs in return for ink marks on paper they couldn't read.

We sailed past a littered shore. Navigating around a sandbar brought our ship close enough to identify the debris as not driftwood, but the contents of people's homes salvaged from the fires. A woman crouched beside the water with a baby strapped to her back, a fishing line in her fist; the basket beside her looked empty. I could see the whites of her eyes peering through tangled hair, staring at me full of hatred. How to respond? Turn my head in shame? Nod in sympathy? The poor young farm wife, consigned to a life of mud and dung, had lost even that—though just a few years ago this same Punti woman would have happily insulted me in the street.

Cheung Po Tsai whispered over my shoulder, "Kill a chicken to frighten the monkeys."

We anchored below a market town at the confluence of two rivers. Cheng Yat ordered the squadron to remain on alert while he and I went ashore, accompanied by a platoon of bodyguards. All dressed alike in black with identical scabbards and swords, the guards were as much for our safety as for show. We were about to make first contact with our land-based counterparts in crime, the Three Harmonies Society, one of the more powerful triad societies controlling this region of the delta.

A red tiled building as large as a warehouse dominated the waterfront, with only a single visible entrance. A dour doorman looked us up and down. Today no one would mistake me for a consort or even a wife. I was dressed for business in an indigo gown and vest, embroidered around the sleeves and collar with gilded thread. Cheng Yat, for his part, wore a black jacket with red cuffs to mark his fleet color and a badge across his chest combining the colors of every fleet, plus his best black silk turban. The doorman took Cheng Yat's coin. As if by magic, a curtain parted.

Cheng Yat and I, with two of our bodyguards, followed a heavily muscled man across an enormous smoke-filled hall crammed with gambling tables and braying, spitting men. Something crashed: A lamp went out. A scream cut the air as if someone had been stabbed. Employees in blue vests pushed past.

I cupped a hand to my ear, asking Cheng Yat to repeat whatever he'd just said that had been swallowed by the melee.

He pointed his chin somewhere. "I said you can wait out here. See? There's a women's table."

In a corner, a cluster of grease-painted girls laughed together.

"Very funny." I frowned a warning: this was no place for jokes. The triad boss had changed the meeting date three times, a tactic smacking of insult. The Three Harmonies Society was far from the only gang operating in the Pearl River delta while Cheng Yat came as Dai Lo Ban of the powerful Confederation of the Flags.

He glanced me a reminder: I was here to observe; I should confine my comments to niceties. He'd been living up to his promise to treat me as a partner, but even I acknowledged some limits were necessary. Our escort knocked at a door in the back wall, exchanged a few words with someone, and motioned us inside. Our guards were to wait for us outside the door.

The sweet smell of opium infused the air. Though the room was dimly lit, its intense colors could have outshone the sun. The walls groaned with huge gaudy paintings and gold calligraphy on bright red silk scrolls. A rose stone lion stood sentry to one side. Almost lost in the shadow of a rosewood bunk, a man reclined on his side, his bare belly protruding from a yellow silk robe embroidered as though the tailor feared to leave out a single color that existed in the world. If this was Boss Yip, then a more insulting welcome to his maritime counterpart was hard to imagine.

"Commander Cheng. Have you eaten?" He cleared his throat and emptied it into a spittoon. "Ai! Where's that boy? Ah-Lam, get out here! Sweeties for my guests!"

Another door opened, and out stepped a slender young man made up like a woman, all blushes and blues, gliding across the room in a shimmering azure robe, offering glimpses of flesh beneath. The boy placed bowls of candied plums and lotus seeds on low table.

Cheng Yat and I seated ourselves on a pair of ornate ceramic stools. "Master Yip, a pleasure to meet you," Cheng Yat offered.

"I heard your wife is lovely, but no one warned me that she rivals the Four Great Beauties."

"Master Yip," I said, vowing to myself that, if our business relationship commenced, beauty would be one of the last things he associated me with.

"Call me Three Fingers." He extended a hand. Fat jeweled rings adorned his two inner fingers next to stumps where the last two should be. His grin could have earned him the name Twelve Teeth. "Finally, I meet the notorious Captain Cheng. Tell me about your family. I hear you have a son."

"I have a son. Two years old and already a bit of a boss."

"Splendid, splendid! Bring the boy along next time. Ha, I hope you noticed that I'm extending you an invitation."

I didn't know what to make of his accusatory undertone. As far as I knew, Cheng Yat had never met this man before, invited or not. In fact, Yip had been the one to postpone our current visit.

"Pardon me?" Cheng Yat said.

"I'm talking about you kindly staying out of my territory."

"If you're talking about the river trade—"

"Of course, I should have expected such an ingenious man to play innocent. But please, eat, eat. Ah-Lam, get your hands off me and bring tea."

Once the boy left, Yip propped his head on his hand. His voice turned nasty. "Tell me about your little raid at Chih-ao. Did that go well?"

My gut clenched. It had happened a month ago, soon after the Confederation conference. One of our Red Flag squadrons had sailed up a tributary to a small fort where they set fire to the barracks and stripped the garrison of cannons and powder. The soldiers had fled. No lives were lost—an inconsequential raid. Why mention it?

"I hear talk that our esteemed Governor-General Na is unhappy about this little incident and is aching to take it out on me. But what can he do? The Manchus run the army, not him. And the local commanders receive enough—shall we call them favors?—from me that they would be inclined to do as I ask. What I'm saying, Commander Cheng, is that your fellows might not be so fortunate next time."

We heard the boy returning. Yip's tone turned cheerful again. "In future such, ah, terrestrial adventures would be best left to those who run the territory, don't you think?"

"We've always desired cooperation. That's what I'm here for," Cheng Yat said.

"Yes, of course, so rude of me to speak first." The fat man struggled to raise himself. The boy set down the tea set, rushed to Yip's side, and maneuvered his legs until he sat fully upright. "So, Big Boss Cheng, what do you have for me today? A client wants bird nests. I can fetch you an excellent price."

"I think you know why I'm here," Cheng Yat said.

"No bird nests? Truly a shame. But please, eat, eat."

I tried a lotus seed; its sweetness stung my tongue. Everything about this man dripped with excess.

The boy, Ah-Lam, treated us to a full tea ritual, warming the tiny cups and discarding the first serving as elegantly as a teahouse mistress. He served each of us and retreated behind his door.

Cheng Yat removed a protection pass from an inner pocket. "I wonder whether you've seen one yet."

Yip held the document close to his face with his good hand,

pretending to read, though giving himself away by lingering over the wrong places. As Cheng Yat explained to him, these passes extended unhindered unloading and overland transport of a ship's cargo—that is, protection from Yip's thugs at the docks, something we could sell at a higher price with his cooperation and splitting shares.

"First time I've held one, but of course I know the details." Yip put down the paper and gulped a full cup of tea. "I speak only for the Three Harmonies Society. We're prepared to honor your passes for a one-third cut."

Cheng Yat pressed his fingers together. "We offer a generous tenth share."

"Wah, my honorable comrade, why so stingy? I hear your passes have been slow to be embraced. We have our own ways of influencing shipping owners. That makes us rather vital to your enterprise, does it not?"

"One-tenth," Cheng Yat said, "plus exclusive first option on any goods seized from noncomplying vessels between O Moon and Wong Po."

"We have that anyway, whether you claim to bestow it or not."

Yip and Cheng Yat argued back and forth as politely as befit two criminal chiefs. Yip had been clever in raising the raid at Chih-ao, putting us on the defensive. Nevertheless, our pass system ensured a greater flow of goods and money through his eight remaining fingers.

Yip clapped for the boy. Ah-Lam returned with a lacquered box which he gingerly opened on the table. After assembling a delicate porcelain pipe, he laid out a spirit lamp and various tiny brass bowls and picks. Finally, he lifted the lid from a small round container and kneaded its black pasty contents between slender fingers.

"I need a reason to celebrate," Yip said. "So let's call it one-sixth and put our seals to the deal."

I glanced sideways at Cheng Yat. This was higher than we'd settled on as our fallback offer.

"I see the lady doesn't like it," Yip laughed. "Well, you can't argue with women! All right, my friend, we'll agree on one-eighth, lucky number, or...?"

Cheng Yat looked to me, then back at Yip and nodded.

"Very good!" Yip said. "One-eighth of pass fees from any vessels landing in my territory. Shall we smoke on the deal?"

Three Fingers watched the opium ball sizzling over the lamp. I coughed lightly—a warning. Cheng Yat dismissed me with a wave. The boy tapped the smoldering bead into the pipe bowl for Three Fingers to suck in with a long, hissing breath. He raised his feet onto the platform and lay on his side. "Please, do me the honor." Blue wisps fled his nose and throat as he spoke.

I flashed Cheng Yat another warning, but he leaned over and took a few rapid puffs from the pipe. The boy moved like a dancer around the table, willowy fingers unwrapping a plum candy with a delicate, fondling motion, and extended it to me. When I declined, he tucked it between his teeth and lay beside Yip, feeding him the fruit from his own mouth.

We stepped outside into a cool drizzle which cleansed the film of smoke and decadence from my face.

"That man is a fat cow," Cheng Yat said.

"A clever, conniving cow," I said. "A rich and successful one, but poor in taste."

Cheng Yat laughed. "Listen to you! The sea princess talking about taste! Did you see that boy? He could teach a woman like you a few things about how to dress."

"Oh, you like the pretty little blossom boy? Good for you. I'll turn my eyes and let you have him next time. What I want is to be in on Yip's damned opium."

Something felt wrong. I glanced back at the gambling hall. It hadn't occurred to me immediately, but the guards we'd stationed there were nowhere to be seen. Farther down the waterfront, some sort of commotion was going on. There were men who looked like ours in a heated exchange with a small but growing crowd. It didn't look like a fight. We quickened our steps.

A sailor I didn't recognize ran toward us. Only then did I notice a fast-boat moored nearby. A blue banner drooped from its mast.

"Lucky chance to find you here, Commander Cheng! We've been searching—"

"What is it?" Cheng Yat said.

The sailor caught his breath. The way others regarded him, he must have been the fast-boat's captain. "My commander, Captain Wu-shek Yi—"

"I know who your commander is."

"Sent us to find you. Requires your presence."

"Why? Speak already!"

The crowd had shifted to surround us. "Then you don't know yet."

The young captain raised his voice to be heard. "Cheng Lau-tong quit the Confederation. Surrendered to the authorities."

Everyone had a story about why Cheng Lau-tong quit:
Half his face torn off in a skirmish.
Tired old dog returned to fishing.
Sold out to the damned navy.
I know him—he's no traitor.
No, I know him! Never trusted the old snake.
Winded old fool.
Hunt him down.

We found ourselves again back in the wine shop in Tunghoi—by agreement, Confederation conferences would alternate between Tunghoi Bat's western base and ours in Tung Chung to the east. The fleet leaders seemed happier to bicker than to form a coherent response. The loss of Cheng Lau-tong's ten ships hardly mattered to the Confederation, but as one of the founding signatories, his treachery—if that's what it was—knocked a crack into a still-fragile alliance.

I shared my concerns with Cheng Yat on the sampan to shore: "I don't think he'll fight for the navy."

His brow pinched.

"I just have a sense," I said.

"A woman's sense. Hmf. Women follow women's sense; pigs follow pig sense."

"Don't patronize me. I've met the man. Lau-tong is no traitor."

"There, you see? Your woman's sense is no sense. He surrendered, yet he's no traitor. Pff!"

"I think he's tired." I turned my back to him and faced the approaching quay. "He's fifty years old. Maybe he chose to return to his village and leave the sea behind."

"Or maybe right now, he's leading a naval force up the coast, meaning to blow a hole in my head—and yours."

I flipped round and poked his chest. "Are you stupid? Why would they need him to lead them? That's what worries me."

"More woman's sense?"

"Maybe *you* need some woman's sense! Or any kind of sense. Unless they're unbelievably stupid, the mandarins know that the surrender of a fleet commander means the rest of the Confederation leaders are likely to gather. And where more likely than here?"

"You're thinking like a worried old lady. Haven't they learned already that they can't touch us in Tunghoi? Think about it—the new Governor-General barely warmed his seat, not likely to take a risk that might paint him like a fool. Besides, they wouldn't dare approach in this weather."

On the last point, he may have been correct. I'd tasted it in the air since we'd arrived two days ago. This morning, long swells rolled through the anchorage; fish leapt on either side of us; the air was as thick as oil.

Of course, we couldn't avoid this meeting. He had to reconfirm everyone's commitment to the Confederation. The risk needed to be taken.

Now, seated in the wine shop, fanned by empty words, I settled into my unease. Storms were coming, and not just from the sky.

In the middle of the night, canvas slapped the hull. Thunder rumbled in the distance. I nuzzled into Cheng Yat's back. At least Tunghoi offered proper shelter in a typhoon.

A knock on the cabin door, tiny but insistent. I sensed the rough sway of the ship, the pounding of the storm.

The knock again. Too regular to be debris tossed by the wind. I crawled over and raised the latch.

Two-year-old Ying-shek stood at attention in his tiny blue sleeping suit, eyes wide, drool dangling from his lip. He was alone.

"Where's Siu-ting?" I said.

I ushered him through the door and held his hands. His whole body shook. Something had frightened him.

"What? What happened to her?"

I knew the answer from the way he pouted and tucked his head to his chest, a child vowed to secrecy. The nanny had dropped a few hints during the voyage to Tunghoi, her home village, after all. The rotten girl must have run off!

A crash of thunder.

"Ma!" Ying-shek fell at me; the heat of his body burned through my robe.

A memory popped into my head: maybe six years old, out in the fishing sampan with my father, seeing lightning strike the hills. I cried with terror and threw myself at him, but he offered neither a hand nor a word to comfort me. *Only lightning,* he said, *be strong.*

I held my boy in my arms and rocked him sideways until he calmed a little. Was this how a real mother did it?

Another thunderclap, clearer this time.

"Let's go have a look, see if it's anything to be scared of," I said.

He shook his head. He tried pushing out of my grasp. But I had a sense of something and carried him out to the companionway. On the deck below, men ran and shouted. There was no rain, no lightning. Fat pink-gray clouds streaked across the sky, but nothing signaled a storm.

What I'd mistaken for thunder was followed by another burst, then a telltale, barely audible whistle. At the headland by the mouth of the bay, the old customs house exploded.

I needed to find out what was happening, but now he wouldn't let me go. Ying-shek's fingers pinched my arms, his sobs penetrated my chest. I'd never faced such a situation; his nanny had been his caretaker. Should I make him watch and learn to *be strong,* or let him think I could make it all go away? Little Yang in the sampan had wanted to hide in her father's arms. Fighting back panic, I carried Ying-shek back inside and shut the cabin door.

I carried him around the room, bouncing him in my arms, stroking his back, trying to calm him at each cannon burst, each sudden gust, the snap of sails in the wind. "Please don't cry. Please don't cry."

A loud thud and the floor tilted, sucking the strength from my knees. My legs flared with pain; the ghost of a memory of Spirit River. But it was just the rudder dropping into place.

This time he didn't cry. I thought my comforting was working until I felt a warm spot on my chest. A dark stain formed on Ying-shek's trousers. I hugged him with a sudden burst of feeling. The poor, frightened boy had been trying to hold back his tears for me.

I laid him on the mat, stripped off his clothes, and wiped him. An old tunic of Cheng Yat's made do as a makeshift robe. He smiled at me as if he knew how ridiculous he looked in his father's oversized shirt. The simple act of changing his clothes almost made me forget why we were inside and what was happening out there.

When the next explosion sent shivers through the hull, I knew things were not going well. I needed to go outside and see the situation. I needed to load guns, check muskets, and make sure everyone was doing their jobs. But I couldn't possibly throw myself into battle with a terrified infant in my arms. My whole body protested the feeling of not taking part, and I silently cursed the nanny for deserting him—for deserting me!

He seemed calm enough; now it was my turn. I lay beside him and stroked his thick, shiny hair. His face was like a shifting image—there was Cheng Yat's long chin and high cheeks, then he turned slightly and looked just like...but how well did I know my own face? In him, I saw echoes of my mother's wide-set eyes and a nose like a bone button.

"Ma." He touched my cheek, and my soul broke open.

Hadn't she told me about this, my long-departed friend? That moment when you feel a child's need and respond with...what? Was it motherly instinct, or a need of my own? This heart that pumped against my breast, these fingers that tugged my robe, those lips, that chin, they had once been inside me. Here in the middle of a fight, with ammunition raining down and waves pounding, here in this little cabin sealed off from the light, I was seeing my son for the very first time.

And then he surprised me. He squirmed out of my embrace and walked on unsteady legs to the porthole. He wanted to have a look at the battle.

"My big man, brave like your Ba."

What I meant was that he was more like me, not letting anyone hold him back.

I dragged the panel open and boosted him on my knee, both of us squinting against the wind's punches. We were within less than a *li* of the outer channel. Navy gunboats blocking the headlands far outnumbered those which had tried to fool us during the blockade when Ying-shek was born. Who knew how many more backed them up in the open waters?

Soldiers had taken the northern headland, firing muskets from behind the ruins of the customs house. Both sides traded cannon fire that seemed never to end, until one of our ships faltered. The stricken junk listed into the water while flames shot up its mast. Men leapt overboard into the turbulent chop.

I tried to tear the boy away, but he clung to the porthole frame without taking his eyes off the action. I wondered how much such a young child could understand. Did he have any idea know how bad our position was?

The gunboats were all upwind, giving them the advantage both in attack position and range of weapons, while the weather itself backed them. The clouds were darker, fatter, woolier. In the northeast, lightning flashed in a black sky. A shell splashed close by, rattling the entire ship. In seas like these, such close shots from a bucking vessel were less a matter of aim than of chance. Then rain struck like bullets, and the boy hid his face against my collar. I called my own retreat back into the cabin.

"Don't worry. Your Ba will save us," I said, wanting to convince us both. What was Cheng Yat's plan this time, or did he even have one?

I tried to distract us both by tossing together leftover scraps into a semblance of a meal. While my heart pounded and breath caught at every violent noise raging outside the walls, Ying-shek seemed fascinated by my actions with cold rice and meat. What thoughts navigated inside this child's mind? His mother preparing food for the first time in his experience was of greater impact than the incomprehensible notion of looming death. I made a face at the unappetizing mess. He imitated me and giggled. I couldn't help myself; in the midst of battle and storm, we laughed together.

I was cleaning up when Cheng Yat stumbled into the cabin, leaving a trail of water toward the wooden chest.

"The gods don't favor us," he said.

"Don't you dare say such a thing!" If the gods controlled the weather, they were equally brutal to both sides. The rest was not a matter of divine assistance but of organization and preparedness, and the navy had proven our lack of both.

Cheng Yat rummaged in the chest until he found what he wanted: an old pistol that he rarely used.

"What's that for?" I asked.

"The others are plugged—wet powder."

"I mean, what are you using it for?" Surely, he didn't intend to sink a ship with that.

"Never mind! We're running for it!"

"We're *what?*"

"The storm. Running the storm. Aiya! There's a dry powder sack in here somewhere."

"Are you crazy? Outrunning this blow in open water?"

His hand shook as he funneled powder into the breech. "I didn't say outrun. We're running *into* the storm."

"Faat din! Now I know you're crazy!"

"Suppose I am." He loaded a ball and checked his weapon. Outside, more gun bursts. Or was it actual thunder and lightning now?

"What makes you think they won't turn and pursue us?"

He shrugged. "Because they're not crazy."

I followed him to the door, meaning to say something, but it was too late. Moments later I heard him fire into the air. Someone hoisted a banner at the foremast. Our ship turned into the wind.

I dashed back inside and grabbed Ying-shek. Could he possibly understand the danger his father had just placed us in? I couldn't shelter him anymore, not at the cost of blinding myself to my own possible doom.

"We're stepping outside," I told him. "Can you be brave?"

Despite his grunts and squirming against pelleting rain, I clutched the frame of the open doorway with one hand, holding him tight against me with the other.

Down below, men strained at the tiller, coaxing the protesting vessel like a beast against its will. Swells crashed over the bow. Smoke mushroomed from our guns. Other Confederation ships followed on either side, creeping forward over waters resembling a field of glass shards. Lightning flashed, closer now, thunder competed with cannons.

Out in the open sea, we climbed and dipped over liquid mountains and valleys. Our bodies were struck by saltwater bullets. The boy struggled against my grip.

"I'm not letting go of you," I said.

Ying-shek forced his way around in my arms. He wasn't trying to escape. He wanted to face forward.

We passed the wreckage of the customs house and cleared the headland into the channel, toward the source of the wind. The navy's front line turned aside, cannons silenced, probably too wet to fire. Only one enemy stood before us. We were face-to-face with the wrath of the gods.

I glanced down to see how the boy was taking it. Ying-shek betrayed no expression as his father's ship passed through curtains of freezing rain into the looming heart of the storm.

"You're a better man than most," I said aloud, intending my remark for Cheng Yat, but Ying-shek turned at my words with a curiously stern set to his jaw. I suppose I meant him, too.

XXX
Shadow

A cove somewhere on the Luichow coast had transformed into a boat city in hell. Staved-in hulls and crippled masts slumped in pools of debris that continued to wash up days after the typhoon. Alert to the likelihood of another ambush, only the most critically damaged ships lay careened on shore, even though in the past twelve or thirteen days, not a single navy ship had been sighted. They were probably licking their own wounds.

Ying-shek followed me everywhere, all the time, like a shadow, clinging to my legs whenever I stood still—that is, when he wasn't climbing over cannons or shimmying like a monkey up and down ladders, though always with an eye on me. I couldn't have a moment alone on the privy without him crying for me. Yet when Ah-Yi took him one morning while I lay ill, I felt his absence.

One evening, Cheng Yat stumbled in, reeking of drink and streaked with grime from whatever repair he'd been overseeing. Refusing food, he tore off his turban and went straight to the Tin Hau shrine when he noticed Ying-shek stacking wooden blocks in the corner.

The boy arranged them in a rough arrow shape and showed his father. "Boat-boat." Ying-shek's high spirits banged on the door of his father's thick-as-mud gloom.

"He can't stay here anymore," Cheng Yat said.

"He's our son."

He said nothing. Maybe he heard my insincerity. I knew who I was, and though it sometimes pained me to admit, if I was a parent at all, it was to the fleet. Ships, cargo, and passes were my babies. The previous arrangement of daily visits had worked well for me. Ying-shek needed a nanny.

Some of Cheng Yat's incense sticks scattered onto the floor. His hands trembled as he picked them up.

"Ten thousand prayers aren't enough," he said. "The gods don't favor me."

"Shh! Your men might hear!"

What he said, though, rang true. The navy may not have shot us out of the water, but in proving the Confederation's lack of preparedness, they'd dealt Cheng Yat a tremendous loss of face.

"Don't be a stupid egg," I said. "We lost what? Seven, maybe eight ships. And you talk as if they beat us? The fact is that they didn't destroy us, even with the advantage of surprise, even with the weather in their favor. You faced them like a man against turtles—tell me who were the victors? Not them! By the gods, you led us straight into a typhoon! Don't you think, just maybe, your goddess here sent it in order to save us? Tell that to your men!"

A small voice in the corner said, "Stupid egg," followed by a giggle. A clatter of blocks, then again, "Stupid egg!"

It took every bit of my will not to laugh.

"Get him out," Cheng Yat said.

"He's your son."

"He doesn't belong in here. Where's the nanny?" He grabbed at Ying-shek's sleeve, but the boy squirmed free and tossed a block at him.

"No go!"

Excellent! Some spleen in the child. Cheng Yat got up as though to strike him, but I got between them. "He needs to spend time with his father. Do you realize—"

"Oh, and suddenly you're the devoted mother? Yes, I'd like to see that instead of playing with ledgers and pretending you run this fleet!"

He pressed around me and dragged over the frightened child. "Here, mother! Give him to the nanny and bring some wine on the way back."

Ying-shek's heart beat as fast as a bird's. I tried to calm him, but the ferocity of my strokes made him squirm and hug a pair of blocks. "You're drunk. The little *chau mui* ran off! We'll find a replacement in Tunghoi."

"We're not going back there. Not yet."

"Are you serious? You're afraid to go back?"

Cheng Yat returned to the shrine with his back to me.

"I want to know what you're talking about," I said.

294

He mumbled something that sounded like *revenge.*

"What did you say?"

He ignored me and rummaged under the altar. I grabbed a block from Ying-shek's hands and threw it at Cheng Yat, hard enough to know it didn't come from his son.

"Tell me!" I said.

"Why do you need to know?"

"Because you promised." I yanked his arm, spilling oil from the flask in his hand. "Partners, remember?"

"So now you're an admiral too?"

"I'm your wife. I'm your partner. Or have you forgotten? Without me, there'd be no Confederation!"

"All right! Shut up and listen then. A little raid on Tin-pak port. Must be overloaded with salt barges delayed by the weather."

"So, we sell them passes?"

"No. Not this time. We show the government dogs how undefeated we are. Satisfied...partner?"

There was no use arguing with him in his current state. Let him beg his porcelain goddess for favors. He'd get none from me.

Ying-shek slinked into the corner, hidden in shadow except for his eyes, which stared unblinking at his parents. I made a place for him at the foot of the sleeping mat.

In the middle of the night I felt a tiny arm hooked over my waist.

Every day, the boy gave me lessons in power. No matter what raged outside—noisy repairs or fighting or weather—he needed feeding and bathing and minding to keep him from falling or choking or soiling himself. The more we got used to each other, the more he resisted my training, a true man in the making.

At breakfast I quietly ate my congee while Ying-shek sat as usual, with hands folded in his lap like a tiny monk.

"I'm not feeding you anymore," I said. "Whatever that maid did, you're on your own now. Here." I placed the spoon in his hand and closed his fingers around it. I took another spoonful of my own, blew on it, and put it in my mouth, then another and another, until my bowl was nearly empty. "Together. Let's do it. One, two, three..."

He finally gave in and, mimicking me, filled his spoon and blew on it so hard that gruel spilled over the side.

"Now eat."

He took a tiny, hesitant sip.

"Good boy! That wasn't so difficult, was it?"

With a rap on the open doorway, Cheung Po Tsai ducked inside, dressed in his usual violet and a coal-gray turban. "Baby brother!" He crouched beside Ying-shek and patted his head. "Have to get you a man's turban."

"If he's your brother, you can take him this morning," I said.

"Gladly," Po lifted the boy into his lap. "Want to join your *Gogo* on my new ship?"

"My new ship!" The boy tugged Po's ear.

"Ha! Sailor, show respect for your captain."

He pulled out a copper coin and flipped it in the air, then placed it in the boy's hand. "Ha. Now you can play fan-tan like a man." He taught Ying-shek to flip the coin while directing his speech to me. "I came to say goodbye. Tomorrow, I command my own junk."

"What are you talking about?"

"Know the fast-boat with the short mainsail over there? Lost their captain in the fight? Cheng Yat appointed me!"

Each time Ying-shek dropped the coin, Po laughed and stooped to retrieve it. His rapport with the child was natural, endearing, the way I imagined a real uncle would act. Or a father. If only the boy had a father like this. If only I'd had such a father. Or such a husband. Ai! How could I have such a thought? Po Tsai had bloomed into a supremely confident young man, powerful as a horse, with a taut body and a face that would weaken any woman. I hardly remembered the enmity I'd once felt. I would miss his presence on my ship.

"Well, Captain Cheung Po Tsai, all you need now is a wife."

"Ha! Never. Then I'd have to share my beautiful clothes!" Po Tsai lifted Ying-shek and spun him in the air. "You're a bird now! A magpie—no, an eagle!" He set him down and patted the boy, then as suddenly as he'd appeared, he ran off. "Bye, big man!"

Ying-shek watched him go, then looked at the floor.

"You can fetch the coin yourself," I said.

I knew that Cheng Yat's raid on Tin-pak would commence in the early morning hours, but nevertheless, the first cannon shot startled me awake so suddenly that I momentarily forgot where I was. Floorboards hummed; an offering bowl fell with a crash. I sat up quickly, my first instinct to shield and comfort the child, but there was no whimper, no tiny figure scrambling to find me.

Ying-shek lay motionless at the foot of the mat.

"No!" I swept him into my arms. Had he been struck by a stray splinter, knocked out by the concussion?

He opened one sleepy eye. He'd slept through it! Another cannon shot pressed the air. Ying-shek reached around my neck and dozed on my shoulder. It took me a long time to calm myself, while I wrestled with the horror I'd just felt. This wasn't about need or desire or power. It was something I couldn't yet quite understand.

Ying-shek snored through the next explosion. The sounds of battle had become routine to him.

Outside, dawn burned a hole in the clouds, illuminating row after row of salt barges. Cheng Yat had guessed correctly. But why open with a fight? We could have avoided the heavy bombardment from the local garrison if we had snuck in and commandeered a few barges before dawn—we could have been well on our way before they could muster a defense. Instead he seemed bent on all-out war. He hadn't consulted me. And no wonder: such tactics went entirely against the principles of the Confederation. Take their cargo, sell them passes, but fight only in defense or when it served to enrich us. For Cheng Yat, this attack on Tin-pak wasn't about business; it was about his cursed need for revenge.

There was no speaking to him, no convincing or pleading, not with him busy screaming at the gunners, and the boy fidgeting to be fed.

By the time Ying-shek finished his congee, we were sailing east. Neither we nor the defenders scored a direct hit, and not a single grain of salt was taken. The humiliation Cheng Yat had come to inflict became his own.

I stopped him before he reached the companionway stairs.

"Enough, please," I said.

"I don't need to hear this now."

"You need to hear it! We're in no shape for more fights. It's time we—"

"They're in no shape either. They were ready for us, that's all. They won't be so prepared in Hing-ping. No fort."

"Stop this! Let them think they won. Let them get lazy again. Your men need a rest. *I* need a rest! Let's go back to Tunghoi or straight to

Tung Chung—"

"'Let them think they won. Let them think they won.' Crazy! Only a woman would spout such rubbish. No! I need to let them know they lost!"

There was no fort in Hing-ping, like he'd said. But news traveled faster on land than on water. When we reached his new target just ten *li* up the coast, the salt ships themselves were armed. Our sampans returned bearing wounded and dead.

That night, we sat out another gale. Cheng Yat refused to speak and glared at his son who played in the corner with his blocks, pretending they were ships, making shooting noises with his tongue.

By midday, the weather settled and we returned to Hing-ping. Let Cheng Yat have his fight, his taste of blood. Let him earn face in front of the pack since that's what we were: a pack of wolves. When the hunt was over, we could finally sail for Tung Chung, back to the business we started.

I carried Ying-shek up to the poop deck, intending to distract him with toys, but he scrambled to the rail and raised his arms to me. Though I was exhausted, I gave in and picked him up. "See? The red flags are ours. Blue are Uncle Fatty. Here come the green flags. Do you know their commander's name? Son of a Frog."

"Frog!"

A group of Green Flag junks sailed in close to the salt barges, trading cannon fire as they passed. Fresh winds quickly cleared the smoke, without visible damage on either side. Yellow Flag ships made the next pass. Ying-shek clapped his hands when the smoke cleared. Two Yellow Flag ships suffered shredded sails, another's foremast had collapsed, while one salt barge listed.

"These aren't toy boats," I said. He seemed to understand; his face turned sober as the skirmishes continued.

Staring toward the sun hurt my eyes and the boy's weight strained my arms. I was ready to place him inside, when Ying-shek pointed. "*Gogo!*" His target was a Red Flag unit assembling in the west.

"*Gogo! Gogo!*" he said again. *Elder brother,* his name for Cheung Po Tsai. What made him think his *Gogo* was on one of those ships? But of course he was. All of a sudden, I was wide awake—and afraid.

The Red Flag squadron arced single file into the bay, guns thundering in rapid sequence, all the while taking fire in return. The boy struggled and cried in my arms. I realized how tightly I was squeezing him.

A loud crack crossed the water, followed by a shattering explosion. Flaming balls of smoke erupted from the lead Red Flag junk, casting burning fragments into the air and over the side. No, not fragments; those were pieces of men.

Ying-shek screamed and fell from my arms. I screamed too. I grabbed him off the deck and hastened down the ladder. Let him witness other men dying. Not his *Gogo*. Not my Cheung Po Tsai.

The moon passed half a cycle before Cheng Yat amounted enough small victories in his spree of revenge that he could return to Tunghoi with face intact. Unable to wait a moment longer to get off the ship, I bribed Ying-shek with a promise of sweets to stay aboard with Ah-Yi for the day.

On the sampan I kept my mouth shut while Cheng Yat boasted to the others on board.

"A shame we lost so many men. But it was no victory for that shit-devil Governor-General or his navy!"

Of course that's what you think. My lips moved without speaking. *Because that's what I beat into your soft skull last night to stop you from taking a drunken leap overboard.*

Fifteen days of raids, skirmishes, and bad weather had cost us twenty-six ships and hundreds of men killed or captured. In turn we'd torched the fort at Lung-men and nearly a hundred vessels. But we'd come away with nothing. Let Cheng Yat call it a victory. I was sure that at this moment Governor-General Na was composing self-lauding reports for the exalted emperor.

At the dock I reminded Cheng Yat: "Tell Po Tsai to go see your son. The boy's still crazy with worry."

It was my turn to undertake a mission. Winding my way through Tunghoi's lanes, I stopped to buy soap and the promised fruit candies, then left the village along a footpath around a mangrove swamp, across a stream, and into a cluster of fishermen's stilt huts hovering high over the mud. I'd been told which dwelling to look for but would have recognized it even without directions by the look of despair from the woman in the doorway. I waited at the bottom of the entry ladder until a man emerged, hands clasped in welcome, though his voice was unsmiling. "Please enter, please enter."

Their home was a single cluttered room smelling of fish, though they'd made attempted respectability by rolling out clean mats. A girl, tall for a twelve-year-old, stood clinging to a wooden bunk, unable to disguise her trembling.

I held my breath a moment, taken aback by her eyes, large and moist like a cow's.

"What's her name?" I said.

The mother hid her mouth behind her hand. "Ping."

I wanted it over with. I presented a heavy sack. "Forty taels. Count."

The father waved his hand in a face-saving refusal. I set the sack behind him and watched him relax. He urged the girl to step toward me. A squeak escaped the mother's throat.

The girl descended the ladder after me, looking neither back at her parents nor at me. I slowed my pace on the way to the ship to make sure she followed.

I pointed out the hold she would live in, then led her up the companion ladder. Ying-shek burst happily from the cabin and plucked the seed candy from my hand.

"This is your new nanny, Ah-Ping."

My voice cracked a little. I'd put myself through all the preparatory talk—*Now you'll have two mothers. Someone to play with you whenever you want. You'll be safer having someone with you all the time*—but I couldn't bring myself to say a thing. It wasn't as though I were abandoning him. What made me feel that way? *Your Ma needs to work so you can have nice things*—that might at least have approached the truth.

"I'll play with you every day like always. But you live with Ping."

"Ma!" He dropped the candy and clung to me. I patted his head and squeezed his shoulders. He would just be down the stairs on the same ship. I'd see him every day—if I wasn't on a business junket. If I wasn't meeting agents or buyers or spies. I needed the freedom to do my work. I needed to be myself again.

I needed to feel his hot breath on my neck.

I knew how hard this would be for him. I hadn't figured on how hard it would be for me.

I knelt and kissed his forehead, then put his hand in Ping's. He cried all the way down the companionway. His sorrow carried from the hold.

"I'm not fit to be a mother," I whispered. The last word stuck in my throat.

XXXI
Proclamation

Combing my hair out on the companionway, I relished the pleasant chill in the air, the much-awaited change in the weather in time for the Mid-Autumn Festival. Something broke the surface ten lengths off the spirit side. Then another, and three more. It was another happy sign: a family of pink dolphins—it wouldn't be long before we arrived in Tung Chung, after a difficult, storm-wracked journey.

The rugged coast of Tai Yue Shan formed through the haze; the familiar headland appeared straight ahead. The sheer mountains framing the bay, tides blanketing the mudflats, eagles and kites circling lazily over Chek Lap Kok—despite the cool wind, my chest tingled with warmth: I was beginning to think of Tung Chung as home.

It wasn't the triumphant homecoming Cheng Yat had imagined for himself, nor had I for that matter. The shell we'd wrapped ourselves in—of dominance over ships, over men, over the southern China seas—had been bruised.

Coming into the anchorage, my eyes found the hillside clearing where Cheng Chat's wife's crypt, if not her body, was rooted into the rock. If I believed in spirits, then I might have believed that hers looked across the bay at me, her Younger Sister, claimant to her role as matriarch of the pirates.

I had a sudden urge to pay quick respects before we anchored. Dust chafed my nose the moment I opened the hold for the family shrine. Inside was so dark, it was hard to tell which wooden slab represented Cheng Chat or his wife. Groping in the corner for a kindling stone, I was astonished when my hand landed on what felt like a book. In the light from the hatch, I recognized it as a ledger. I slipped it into my tunic and, foregoing candles or incense, mumbled a prayer and a promise—I would do better, I would be the tiller guiding my husband, I would stand in the way of anything that might harm our child—before I hurried back to the cabin.

Between my limited reading skills and the purser's cryptic swirls, I understood little except that the ledger's entries seemed recent. What was it doing inside the shrine? But I was already late; it could be studied another day. I wrapped it in an old robe, tucked it inside my clothing chest, and stepped outside in time for the shore ferry.

People's loud chatter on the boat irritated me. I had no compelling reason to go into the village. After months cooped up on the ship, I had an urge for wide-open space. After everyone disembarked at the dock, I offered the boat woman a few coins to carry me to the opposite shore.

The tidal mud, thick like thick sauce, swallowed my feet. Mudskippers wriggled out of my way. A city of birds hunted among the shore weeds: ducks and grebes, curlews and moorhens, egrets and herons. Towering, awkward spoonbills dug crabs with their paddle-shaped beaks. My father once told me they flew in from the top of the world, the sure sign that summer was ending.

The thought of him brought a sour taste into my cheeks. I dipped my hands in the water and splashed my face. I hadn't thought of him in a year, maybe two. Why now had this memory risen inside me? Why today, when I had better, nicer things to consider? Maybe it was time to track him down, show him how far I'd left behind his filth-ridden, miserable little world. *Do you need more money? Here, a fistful of silver ingots...or do you prefer gold?* Then shove them into his throat and laugh while his body jerked and his face went black as a spoonbill's.

Following the shore back toward the village, I was surprised by the sight of Cheng Yat and Kwok Podai sitting behind the beach under an awning at a cooked-food stall. Judging by their jovial manner, I guessed they were discussing marriage conditions. Kwok's cousin, a young ship's captain, was arranged to marry the daughter of Cheng Yat's deceased youngest brother. A girl stood nearby; that must have been her. She looked fifteen, head modestly lowered, hands clasped in front, but she couldn't hide the tense set of her shoulders.

Kwok stood at my approach. "Ah! Here she is, my soon-to-be... what's the word for aunt of the bride of the groom's paternal elder cousin?"

"No idea," I said.

"There must be a word for it." Kwok's eyes swept me as if his lashes were fingers as long as his arms. "Let's just say you and I are at last related by marriage."

His words struck me dumb, but Cheng Yat only laughed. "Old Kwok wants relations with every beautiful woman on the China coast, though not necessarily involving marriage."

"I don't have to listen to your filthy talk." I took the girl's arm and led her to a driftwood log in the shade of a tree. Cheng Yat's niece had a boyish chest and a round, sweet face that promised to bloom into womanly beauty as she got older, if she wasn't worn out by ship's chores or childbearing by then. She sat sideways to me and hung her head, timid as a baby mouse in my presence. Of course I understood. I'd once felt the same in front of another matriarch prior to my own wedding.

"You know how many girls all over China will envy your marriage?" I said.

She cocked her head as though she was being mocked.

"It's true," I said. "Not because of his looks, though I'm sure he's handsomer than mine. And I wouldn't know about his prick." The girl blushed and swallowed a laugh. I tapped her knee. "It's what he doesn't have that makes him such an enviable catch."

The young bride's expression changed to worry. "What doesn't he have?"

"A mother!"

The girl covered her mouth and giggled. "Even the emperor's wife has a mother-in-law, isn't that so?"

"Right! The empress herself will be jealous!"

The girl became twice as pretty when she laughed.

We talked at some length about her father who, despite the Cheng family heritage, had remained a fisherman in Lei Yue Moon until he had died during his single brief stint as a pirate. While we spoke of our favorite foods and the roaming life of a sea captain's wife, a lone fast-boat out in the bay tacked toward our part of the beach and slowed to a stop. A violet-robed figure waved at the railing. Before the bow scraped mud, Cheung Po Tsai was splashing through the shallows.

He stopped for a moment to shield his eyes. A smile split his face, and, heels kicking up sand, he raced in a new direction—not toward Cheng Yat, who had risen to greet him, but to me. One arm clutched a sack to his chest, the other pivoted like a bird's wing, like some hero out of legend returning from his quest.

Po Tsai dropped his sack and, grasping me by the shoulders, planted a firm kiss first on one cheek, then the other.

I was so taken aback that I forgot to breathe. What did he mean by this brazen act in full view of the world? Such spleen! My face burned all over except for the wet spots on my cheeks.

He pulled back with a crooked grin that suggested it was just a spot of mischief. "That's how foreigners do it in O Moon."

"Do what?" I said. Perhaps it was done in private between lovers, but I was his—I didn't know anymore, now that he was a fully grown and fiercely independent man—his colleague?

"Really. They greet each other like that: kiss-kiss. Women to women, men to women, right out in the open, in front of everyone!" Po Tsai left me for the men's table and helped himself to tea.

"Because their women are all prostitutes," Kwok said.

Po Tsai laughed. "Barbarian women are too ugly to be prostitutes. Even their men think so—it's why they have Chinese mistresses."

"I wouldn't let a foreign man greet me that way," Cheng Yat's niece said. "Their beards must scratch!"

While Kwok Podai laughed with the rest of us, his eyes stabbed Po Tsai with contempt, or, I hesitated to admit, jealousy. And perhaps with reason. While my husband looked on bemused, and the man who made no secret of his intentions glowered, I was aware only of the lingering imprint of a younger man's lips on my skin.

Po Tsai himself broke my spell by waving me over to the table where he had unloaded his sack. "Treats for my little brother. And one for you."

He presented me a paper box whose contents rattled. "Go ahead. Try one."

Inside were little round cakes. I said I'd save them for later, but he insisted I try one nibble. It tasted like sawdust mixed with beach sand and went down my throat like caulking putty.

"This is what foreigners call cakes?" I said. "I've had enough of barbarian ways for one day."

"What did you really bring?" Cheng Yat said.

"Cakes not good enough? All right, then. Gold will have to do."

He plunked two heavy silk pouches on the table. Cheng Yat

removed the bindings from one and shook out its contents with a look that turned to displeasure. I caught a gold coin before it rolled off the edge. An embossed eagle with an open beak: Spanish gold. Altogether, only seven—a paltry sum for nearly two months of protection pass revenue from the foreign enclave.

"Believe me, I asked him. Liu swore that's all there is," Po Tsai said. "Told me, 'It isn't easy selling cakes to foreigners.'" Liu was the Red Flag Fleet's agent in O Moon, on the strength of his ability to speak the foreigners' tongue. Honesty remained to be seen.

Kwok Podai echoed my thought, at least I thought so. He spilled gold and silver from the other pouch onto his palm, but his eyes turned aside to Po Tsai. "How much do we trust him?"

I couldn't tell whether he meant the O Moon agent or Cheung Po Tsai himself. Why was he picking on him? Because Po Tsai had kissed my cheeks, as if I would ever allow it again? As if I were available to any other man than my husband? Silly, childish envy. However, I couldn't say anything, not even a joke, and risk stirring him up. The wedding was more than a bond among families; it forged the Red and Black links in the chain that bound the Confederation.

Perhaps Cheng Yat also caught a sense of this when he said, "I trust my men until they give me reason not to."

"I hope you'll trust me with this other matter. I found them posted everywhere." Po Tsai reached inside his sleeve with an actor's flourish and produced a rolled paper, which he offered with a tiny bow to Kwok Podai. "Maybe honorable old uncle can read it."

Kwok unrolled it across the table. The paper was ripped around the edges; shards of dried paste crackled from the back. Printed words filled the upper half while handwriting covered the bottom; in between were two grand-looking red chops. Kwok frowned as he looked it over.

"Aloud, please," Cheng Yat said.

"An amnesty proclamation from the government, bribing our men into mutiny." Kwok took a deep breath and cleared his throat. "A decree of pardon and peace.' Such nonsense! 'Any man pressed into service with sea bandits is exhorted to return to allegiance. All ordinary sailors who have done service with pirates, whether or not of their own will, shall be entitled to surrender with impunity. Captains who submit with their full crew and vessels shall earn the greatest lenience from just punishment. Moreover...' Ha! You'll like this: '...any man who should present the severed head or ears of a pirate captain or ship's officer shall thereby demonstrate his atonement and earn himself greater reward.'"

He ran his finger down neat columns of characters. "Lists of where and to whom to surrender. It bears the official seal of Kwangtung and Kwangshi Governor-General Na Yin-sing."

"That's it?" Cheng Yat said.

Although I couldn't read it, I understood that he had only recited the upper half of the page, the section with block characters. "It's all about what they expect and not what they offer," I said.

Kwok nodded confirmation. "I would guess that's all the Governor-General wants the palace to see on their official copy. Certainly, the emperor would never authorize the additional incentives which Na's minions have handwritten beneath."

He recited a detailed list of conditions and rewards. Each man who returned to allegiance would receive ten silver taels, plus the choice either of a position in the army or a road pass to return to their home village. Helmsmen, artillery men, and other skilled crewmen would be retained by the navy while captains and Taumuks deemed innocent of major crimes would be offered commissioned ranks.

"Nothing about women?" I said.

Kwok spun the broadsheet around as if I could read it, his finger pressed beside a column of words. "Indeed, he saved you for last. You're to be settled ashore under the benevolent protection of the local authorities."

"Kept as whores, in other words. Or sold to Mohammedan traders perhaps?" I looked to Cheng Yat, but he paid me no attention. Rather, he swept the poster from the table.

"Ten measly taels? Anyone who'd sell themselves for that isn't worth keeping as crew."

"I say we take up the offer," Po Tsai said. "Every man collects his ten taels, then heads right back to their ships. Ha!"

"I'll earn more by slicing off your plump little ears." Kwok Podai said while he stood up to leave. "I've a wedding to plan. Good day."

I hardly slept that night, what with Cheng Yat constantly getting up to relieve himself and pace the room. I told him to get some sleep, but he growled back about Governor Na's proclamation.

This was the first time the government fought us not with guns but with words and money. Most of the older generation among our crews, the veterans of Vietnam and before, were too loyal and too clever to trust any government's promise. I was less certain about the new people flocking to join the Confederation. They were crude men, desperate men, superstitious to the core. Fugitives, castaways, fishermen too lazy to fish. Such men responded only to greed and fear.

Governor Na's was a cunning move. It required a cunning response. Cheng Yat wanted to increase crewmen's pay. That might work in the short term, at least until the Governor-General raised his bid. Better to cultivate a sense of loyalty and obedience that couldn't be strained by a tempting offer of cash in exchange for treason. We needed to expunge potential traitors before they could do us harm. And I knew just where to start.

In the morning I pretended to fix a vest button while the men conducted prayers. While Cheng Yat and the Taumuk bowed and chanted, more than once I noticed the purser glance around the cabin. The Taumuk left promptly after the final offering, but the purser lingered.

"Looking for something?" I said.

He feigned innocence, though his body tension said otherwise.

"Could be this?" I slid to the chest and fished out the ledger. "I wondered why we hadn't seen a recent accounting. I'm sure you're relieved I found it. Strange, though, where I found it—among the refuse pile in the family shrine."

Cheng Yat stopped tidying the shrine and turned around, blinking.

The purser sat with his hands in his lap as though imitating a black-frocked monk.

"That ocean trader, our biggest haul in years, remember?" I directed my words to Cheng Yat. "As I recall, we took over four hundred catties of abalone. Four hundred twelve, I think was the number. Do you remember?"

"Enough," the purser said.

I raised my eyebrows to Cheng Yat.

"Over four hundred, that's all I remember," he replied.

"As I thought. So I corrected it..."—I opened the ledger, flipped a few pages, and pointed to a scribbled figure, overwritten in my crude scrawl—"...here."

I hadn't been certain that the unreadable squiggles had stood for abalone, but the purser confirmed it with his next words.

"My figures reflect the final count."

"Oh, the *final* count, as recorded, is three hundred eighty. So over thirty catties unaccounted for? Spoiled maybe? Eaten by rats? Well, if you say so." I tapped a line halfway down the page, where I'd made another correction. "This says swallow's nests, yes? Two thousand—"

"That's enough!" Cheng Yat raised a hand as if to strike me.

I didn't flinch. "Fine!" I flung the ledger to the floor in front of him. A page flew loose. "Read it yourself. If you're able."

Cheng Yat quietly ordered the purser to collect the ledger and leave. Then he latched the door and turned on me. "How dare you—"

"He's back to falsifying figures! What? You don't remember? His manipulations with sugar prices he thought you'd never notice because you can't read or use an abacus?"

"I said enough!"

"How long has this been going on?" I said. "If I were Dai Lo Ban—"

"You're not Dai Lo Ban and never will be! That man has loyally served me since long before I scraped you out of the mud."

"You call that loyal, stealing from right under your nose? Didn't you say only yesterday that you trust a man until he gives you reason not to? Didn't I just show you thirty catties of reasons, and how many before that? The man has no more loyalty than a worm! He should be flogged in front of the whole—"

"Woman, shut your lips and listen for once. Was this the first time you exposed his cheating? Of course it wasn't. I remember your clever little demonstration with the abacus. You think I didn't know about this long before? You think I'm so blind or stupid! You think your husband is weak! Oh, don't deny it. Yes, you're so smart, learning to read a few words. You think you understand men just because you know how to make them dance for your pretty smile. But you've learned nothing about how to lead them."

"Then you're blinder than I thought. But how do you lead? By letting men eat from your bowl and then flip it in your face?"

Cheng Yat gnawed a finger like he was tearing off a strip of meat. "Let me tell you something, wife. You want an answer to this dog of a Governor by breeding loyalty among my men? Well, that will never happen if we do it your way. No, shut up and listen for once! You're clever indeed, but you've not spent a lifetime commanding boatloads of seamen. Most men are beasts—you can buy their service with rewards or bribes, and if they try something..." He drew a finger across his throat. "No loss to anyone. But a man like that, the man you just shamed— unexpendable, and he knows it! Let such a man skim a little for himself, and you have one who would lay down his life rather than let you fail— because he would fail with you." He paused, letting it sink in. "So, advise me, woman, how to choose between abalone and loyalty?"

He turned back to his shrine and let me simmer in my defeat. My taciturn, goat-stubborn husband had given me a lesson in leadership, and I was too proud to admit it.

The harbor filled for the wedding between the Red and the Black. Banquet tables lined the shore. Blind musicians struck melodies; firecrackers filled in at the breaks. Tung Chung quickly drank itself dry.

When the young couple knelt at our feet, I thought I'd lighten the occasion with a quip about being a stand-in mother-in-law, but changed my mind when I saw what dignity Cheng Yat brought to the role: jaw clenched, skin taut across his cheeks; he looked like an artist's living portrait. How did this young couple regard us? Did I look as regal as Cheng Chat's wife had appeared on my wedding day?

A lavish private banquet took place on Kwok Podai's junk, seasoned by music and fireworks. For one precious evening, I could set aside all the worries and threats, the arguments over strategy—and indeed, even the gains and triumphs—that had consumed me these past several months. I drank to the groom, drank to the bride, drank to whatever slurred pronouncements from guests even drunker than I was.

I congratulated Kwok Podai and may have even asked him to recite a poem for the occasion, but whether he did or not, my attention was taken by the younger women twittering around Cheung Po Tsai. He wore an uncharacteristically subdued gray tunic, its uppermost clasp left undone in a rakish, deliberate manner. I marched over between his admirers, clutched his shoulders and planted a foreign-style kiss on both of his cheeks.

I later recalled a yelling match between Cheung Po Tsai and Kwok Podai, which I may or may not have become embroiled in; Cheng Yat pulling me away; collapsing in the cabin laughing at nothing; his turban wrapped around my hand like a mitten.

Back in our cabin, Cheng Yat carried me to the mat, but not in a gentle way. I slipped out of my clothes and wrapped my hands around his neck. I wanted nothing more at that moment than to have him against me, skin on skin. I'd give him the Sky-Soaring Butterfly, riding him on top.

He pulled away. "You were disgraceful tonight."

"What are you talking about?"

"Don't play innocent. Every man I know devours you with their eyes, but only Cheung Po Tsai receives your kisses like from a common—"

"What are you implying? If you think—"

"I'm implying nothing. I'm saying it aloud." He threw the blanket over me and crossed to the corner where he kept his wine. "Old habits are hard to break."

This stung deep. I turned my back to him and licked my lips, seeking a trace of Po Tsai's skin.

XXXII
Barbarian

I shielded myself from icy spray, picturing someplace before a crackling fire behind solid dry walls. But my eyes found only restless whitecaps on a gray sea, another island faint in the distance.

It was the part of the business that satisfied me the most and that I enjoyed the least. Goods flooded in—salt, rice, fabrics, timber, spices, either stolen or bartered for passes—increasing the need for storage places beyond the knowledge of authorities and rogues. As we neared the island, I implored the gods to present us with a cave or an abandoned stone hut, something suitably secure, so that we might call this expedition complete and return home.

If I had ever thought prosperity would make life easier, I was mistaken. The Confederation had not merely achieved success but had succumbed to it. After three months in force, the Governor-General's amnesty proclamation had accomplished the opposite of what he'd intended. Although a handful of ships and crew had surrendered, the decree had exposed the government's weakness while growing acceptance of the protection pass system made it clear that the dominant force on the coast was the Confederation of the Colored Flags.

Between confiscated ships and fishermen and traders flocking to us with dreams of easy riches, the Red Flag Fleet alone had grown to three hundred vessels. Simply feeding our fleet, now a staggering twenty thousand mouths, was a logistical quagmire, which I took upon myself to untangle. We needed constant supplies of food, medicines, blankets, and rope. All I ever seemed to do was work. As uncomfortable as this latest expedition had been, at least it gave me a chance to rest. Plus, it was important that I was involved in every decision about every location to hide our precious cargoes, not to mention committing each place to memory...as a precaution.

The closer we came to the island, the more temperamental the crosswinds, tossing up swells steeper than cliffs. Cheng Yat ordered the Taumuk to abandon the approach and divert to Chicken's Neck Island. We entered the sheltered anchorage at sunset, joining a host of other Red Flag ships, including, at the far end, what appeared to be Cheung Po Tsai's junk.

"Please no visits tonight," I told Cheng Yat. "Feeling exhausted."

One of the ship's women brewed me a tonic which sat foul on my tongue and stomach.

"Hot wine will do better," I said.

A small flask filled me with a pleasant glow. I curled into a welcome sleep.

A commotion outside roused me. The sun had long risen. I pulled on an extra robe and stepped outside.

This was the first I'd seen Po Tsai in nearly two months. His stance seemed to claim a wider presence in this world; his face was a sculpted jewel. I raised a hand in greeting, but he and Cheng Yat were busy raising their voices at something. Beneath the stairs huddled the object of their—and the entire crew's—attention.

It was the first real foreigner I'd ever seen close-up. The thick, tangled hair was the proper color for a fox, not a human being. Its cheeks and chin were covered in a mossy layer of the same hue. How could any creature be born with such a nose, a craggy red rudder arching from the brow? But most startling were the ghostly gray-blue eyes, as if they'd bled away all color.

The stranger hunched beneath the slant of the stairs like a cornered animal, but not a frightened one. His shivering wasn't from fear but because he wore nothing but trousers and a rough cotton shirt in freezing weather. Behind him huddled six other creatures of another strange race, with dense blue-black hair and smooth, expressionless faces the color of too strong dark tea.

"Where are they from?" I said.

Po Tsai noticed me at last and grinned. "Caught hem in a skiff making for O Moon. This one, Red Fur, tried to swim off. Ha! Hooked him like a fish."

"No, I mean what land?"

"Guessing English, at least the red one. Reckon from that foreign trader, didn't you see? Anchored over by Three Corner Island. But the beasts aren't talking."

Cheng Yat nudged the red-haired one with his foot. "You. From where? What cargo?"

The foreigner reared back and spat out a word which sounded like a Cantonese good luck blessing. But the growl in his voice and his hateful glare implied that his language held an entirely different meaning for the word *fook*.

Some of our crewmen imitated the foreigner's words: *"Fook yiu! Fook yiu!* Ha! Ha!" The way they pronounced *yiu* gave it a nasty meaning in Cantonese, possibly not far removed from the foreigner's.

"Where the devil is Ah-Fai?" Cheng Yat said. "Aiya! Finally!"

A sailor climbed aboard, tall and skinny with a plum birthmark across half his face. I knew him vaguely as a cook on one of the other junks who'd grown up in O Moon, so he possibly understood some of the foreign devils' tongue. He addressed a few halting phrases to the red-haired one, who mumbled a clipped reply.

"Speaking English," Ah-Fai explained. "Wants his jacket back."

Cheng Yat purpled. "I didn't ask what he wants! What cargo is their ship carrying?"

Ah-Fai relayed the question as best he could, multiple times, but the reply was always the same. "He insists on his jacket."

Po Tsai pushed Ah-Fai aside and kicked the Englishman in the hip. "How many guns on your ship? Guns." He pointed at a cannon and, getting no reaction, fired an imaginary musket. The foreigner recoiled, then checked himself and addressed the dark men behind him. They whispered among themselves before the red-hair spoke.

Ah-Fai translated: "He says twenty cannons. Bigger than ours. Newer. Hundred fifty crew."

I almost laughed at their crude bluff. That sounded like a warship, not a trader.

A gust whistled, sprinkling the deck with a light drizzle. Red Hair hugged his knees to his chest. I felt a twinge of pity.

Cheng Yat walked away. "Let the devils shiver until they're prepared to speak the truth. I need hot tea."

Cold rain drove me inside, wrapped in blankets, though never enough to stop the shivering. The foreigner captives, especially Red Hair, unsettled me. They were strange, volatile creatures who could bring a generous ransom or might as easily attract trouble. I wanted them off my ship as soon as possible.

Ah-Yi entered with a pot of tonic brew, which at least warmed me while at the same time turning my stomach. She settled behind me and combed oil into my hair.

"This weather is killing me," I said.

"The weather is killing your hair, not your body." She clicked her tongue. "So dry, you don't take care."

"I need new soap."

"What you need is common sense and chicken fat. Stop moving! You care more about money these days than about your hair, let me sell it to a wig maker. Get good price in Kwangchow."

I flicked my head, laughing off her remark. I was proud of my thick, black tresses without a strand of white. No one needed to tell me how attractive I still was at the advanced age of thirty-one, not like so many other women who dried out from work and mothering. Maybe my skin didn't have the silken luster of a young girl anymore, but neither was my face covered in lines, other than a few beside my eyes, finer than moth wing veins. Though Ah-Yi was right; at this age I needed to pay closer attention to my hair and skin if I wanted to stay this way. And I would, when the weather warmed up, when I recovered from this grippe.

A tap at the door, a girl delivered a plate of fried radish cakes. Streaked with pork and browned around the edges, but curiously, they had no flavor. I took another piece and another, but the sensation was like swallowing paste.

"Tastes like heaven," Ah-Yi said.

My stomach folded in half. I made it to the porthole in time to feed my meal to the fishes.

Ah-Yi offered me a cup of boiled water, but not without a knowing smirk. "When was your last 'red tea'?"

"Shut up." How could she tell? It had been two months since I'd last bled.

"I had a sense when I came in. Now I'm certain."

"I said shut your lips! It's all the pressure lately, and the cold!" I flung the comb at her. "It's the foreign devils! Brought their strange diseases on board! I'm ill!"

The latch rattled. This time Ying-shek walked in. The nanny hesitated in the doorway. "His visiting time, missy. Should I take him?"

"No. Come here, Little Mosquito. Your naughty old auntie is just leaving."

I flashed a look at Ah-Yi: *Don't you dare say a word!*

"Big boy, brought your play sticks? Wonderful. Sit on my lap, let's build something."

Ah-Yi returned later with hot fish-and-ginger broth and dried salted plums. Anyone who had seen her carrying them to me would know exactly what they implied.

The broth soothed my throat, raw from singing childhood songs to Ying-shek. I told him his mother was tired, which was the truth, and sent him along with Ah-Yi.

A light doze was the best I could manage with the discomfort in my abdomen, but I must have appeared deeply asleep when Cheng Yat and Cheung Po Tsai came into the cabin and launched into a hushed argument.

"Three thousand and not a copper scrap less," Po Tsai said. They were discussing the ransom.

"Not for a plain sailor, even a barbarian. Anyway, the blackies are slaves. Five hundred taels and be gone with them."

"Shall I remind you who captured the bastards? I should set the price."

"No, you should listen! This isn't some boy's adventure game."

Po Tsai chuckled. "Ah, so I'm man enough to command a ship, but a boy when it comes to—"

"You'll be a man when you quit parading girls through your bed and marry one."

My eyes popped wide. Girls? It was the first I'd heard of this; I hadn't seen him in months, plus it was none of my business, of course. But I desperately wanted to know who. I must have made a sound, because Po Tsai turned his head to me.

"You awake?"

"I wasn't." I pretended to yawn. "Until you dragged your mouths in here."

They mumbled apologies and left. But now I couldn't sleep; I had trouble catching my breath. I imagined a young woman lying naked beside him. I told myself I was pleased for him.

"Probably cheap little fish ball girls," I mouthed to the wall.

In the morning, I awoke hungry as a goat. The air was chilly, but my shivers had gone. Nothing was wrong with me after all! I finished a full serving of fish congee and asked for a second. Much to my surprise, Cheung Po Tsai came through the doorway with a steaming bowl in his hands.

"Feeling better? Wah, still cold out there." After a few spoonfuls, he reached into his coat and held out a fist. "Something else to cheer you up."

He shook his fist until I extended my hand. Shiny gold pieces dropped onto my palm, fatter than coins but too light to be gold. On closer inspection, each had a little loop on the back. I understood: these were brass coat buttons, though not Chinese in style. I offered them back. "Give the man his coat."

"Feeling pity for the creature?"

"Feeling sorry for us. He'll die and then be worth nothing."

"Ha! Ha! Always pragmatic, you." He pressed a button into my palm and closed my hand around it. His fingers were thick and callused but warm. "He can sacrifice one."

I pulled my hand from his and spun the little golden knob on the floor like a toy. Po Tsai watched, delighted.

"Eat, eat, before it's cold," he said. "Miss me?"

"Maybe. Too busy to notice," I teased. "You seem to be doing well commanding your own ship."

"Fun, but *aiya!* Too many decisions! Sometimes I just want to climb a mast and sing like in the old days."

Old days? That was a laugh. He was hardly twenty. "You can sing from the helm and order your men to listen under threat of having to endure your jokes instead."

"Oh, what a cruel person you are!"

I took another few servings of congee and set it aside. "Thank you. I was so hungry," I said. "Now, please excuse me so I can dress for the day."

He broke into a grin and patted my knee. "Wai! When this cold front passes, I'm sailing upriver. You should come with me!"

"Mm. That would be..." Awkward, I almost said. *What about these girls you've been bedding? How would they like you bringing your adoptive mother for the ride?* He looked at me with such innocence that I was loath to disappoint him—and frankly, myself—but I couldn't possibly be seen doing such a thing.

I patted my chest. "Watching my health. Thank you, Ah-Po Tsai. Some other time."

The red-haired foreigner started screaming again with a voice that sounded like he'd swallowed gravel. I was losing my patience, not with him but with Po Tsai for provoking him. For the sake of everyone, I wished he'd return the vulgar man's jacket. But when I stepped outside for a look, he was standing below in a blue-black coat, which he held closed in his fist due to its lack of buttons. A couple of our gunners held him by the arms while another waved a gun in his face. They looked ready to break his bones, demanding he teach them how to restore and work a foreign-made musket that had been rusting in our magazine for a year. Though he must have understood based on their actions, his refusal to cooperate was equally clear.

Where were Po Tsai or Cheng Yat? It wouldn't do us good to cripple a captive any more than it would to water a barrel of salt. He was inventory.

I stepped back inside to put on an overcoat and fix a turban on my head. By the time I came down on deck, the foreigner was back beneath the companion stairs, surrounded by his black-faced shipmates. Someone, as a joke, had pasted a New Year lucky *fook* character on the deckhouse wall above them.

The Englishman appeared rougher than the day before, his skin blotched red and his scraggly beard peppered with dried food or mucus. I tried to imagine how he might look in his normal life, properly groomed, standing tall in his trim wool coat. Would such a man be considered handsome by his peers? His eyes were turned purposely away, by which I knew he was aware of my studying him.

I felt a twinge of sorrow for the man. Hadn't I twice been taken against my will? Hadn't I too felt like a desperate caged animal? I tried to imagine what it might be like to reverse places with him, to travel to the opposite end of the world and fall captive in a place where everyone had fox fur hair and noses big enough to steer a boat, where men kissed any woman on the street, and everyone spoke an incomprehensible garble. Might they consider my black hair and smooth features ugly? Would they ridicule my speech? Did foreigners live in a society like ours, have the same morals and feelings as normal civilized people? Was there a red-haired woman in a far corner of the world who pined for this strange, tattered man?

I squatted to his level and tried to catch his eye. I remembered too how it had felt to receive kindness in captivity.

"What is your name?" I said.

He glanced at me without moving his head, but his lips drooped in disdain.

I kept my voice gentle. "What...is...your...family name?"

"He name Turner," a voice behind said. One of the dark-skinned men grinned my way, showing a fine, full set of teeth.

"You speak the language?" I said.

He rocked his head side to side, still with that clenched smile. "Little-little."

Had anyone known this? I wondered why he hadn't spoken earlier. I asked his name. His face lit up with understanding. He introduced each of his companions in a torrent of syllables I couldn't make sense of.

I gestured toward the red hair. I'd already forgotten the name. "Sorry. His name again?"

"Turner."

"Tah-nah," I repeated.

That glance again. A cat caught in a trap.

"Tah-nah—I hope you can return home soon."

I turned my eyes to the dark man to translate. I shouldn't have looked away.

The red foreigner spat. Maybe aimed at me, maybe not. The wind gave it speed. Phlegm exploded on my robe.

The barbarian! The filthy, uncivilized barbarian! No, they weren't like us at all—beasts, not people! No worthier of human kindness than a snake. Tapping my chest repeatedly, I cursed in his senseless, ugly language, flinging him his favorite word:

"Fook! Fook! Fook!"

Now he looked at me and laughed, baring his teeth into a face-splitting leer while vigorously rubbing his crotch.

I ran up to the cabin, tore off the soiled robe and threw it out the porthole, followed by the half-digested remnants of my midday meal.

I blamed the red devil for the return of my sickness. Yes, I'd missed my bleeding for two months. But I'd been drinking my herbs; it would not have been the first time they caused me to skip a cycle. In any case, the discomfort and nausea had only risen since the foreigners appeared. They were a curse! What foul foreign plague had spewed through the air, through my clothing, through my skin, mouth, and eyes? The affliction robbed me of rest—one moment tearing off covers, another moment not even ten blankets were enough—hot, cold, hot, cold, day and night the same. Only water could pass my throat without protest from my gut. My only recourse was to lay still.

Just the thought of Tah-nah brought a sour taste to my throat. He didn't belong here, not on my deck, not in our seas, not in China. I wanted them off my ship!

The door latch clicked; wood slid aside.

I screamed—long, loud, bouncing off the walls and ceiling.

In came a huge creature with a dark round face encircled by thick black beard. An enormous fist raised a heavy staff.

I grasped for anything within reach that might serve as a weapon. A bowl. I would fling it at the monster's head. I would—

Ah-Yi rushed inside. "Calm down! He's a doctor."

A foreign devil doctor? He looked like anything but. His body was as round as his head, his nose as round as his body. Black eyes hid beneath tangled black brows. Yet despite his monstrous appearance, his manner exuded calm. The thing in his hand turned out to be a bamboo tube.

Ah-Yi addressed the intruder: "Go. She's no coward, just a bit crazy."

"Hah? He understands the language?" I said.

The strange new foreigner smiled through the curtain of his mustache. "Only little." His voice was deep as a bull's.

"He's with the others?" I said.

Ah-Yi shook her head. "Tai Pao-fuk's squadron just came in, had him for months. His medicine is queer, but they say it works."

The foreign doctor waited patiently until we'd finished speaking, then tapped his wrist and extended his hand. It took a moment to understand that he wanted to take my pulse. I held out my arm just enough for his fingertips to contact my wrist. To be spat at by one foreigner and now have my hand held by another, what strangeness had entered my life?

He pointed to his eyes, then showed me his tongue and said, "May I?"

He examined my tongue, studied my eyes, then sat on his haunches and waved Ah-Yi to my side. In simple language he instructed her to poke me in various places while he inquired about any pain. He turned completely around when he made Ah-Yi probe the lowest regions of my torso. What a contrast to the so-called doctors who used to examine the flower boat girls, unashamedly inserting anything and everything into our most private places.

"England man?" I asked him.

"Hayastan. You Chinese say *Ah-me-ni-ah*." His tangled eyebrows huddled together. Seeing that the word was unfamiliar to me, he drew my attention to the floor, tapping first to my right. "China." Then to my left. "England." Finally, he tapped in the middle, in front of my knees, and said with a laugh, "Ah-me-ni-ah."

What a contrast from the nettlesome Tah-nah. This foreigner belied his size with gentleness and civility. I felt better already—until he handed me a rice bowl and said, "You pee."

"What?" Ah-Yi and I said in unison. Did he know what he was saying? Surely, he'd mispronounced another word.

"Pee." He pointed into the bowl. "Pssss..."

"You're joking. Piss in a rice bowl?" I said.

The doctor smiled like he'd heard the response before. "Not for drink." He moved into the corner, turned his back, and cupped his hands over his ears.

I looked to Ah-Yi for guidance. For a woman of my position to urinate into a rice bowl! In front of not just a stranger, but a man, a foreigner—a captive!

"Finish?" he said.

"No!"

Ah-Yi's shrug was no help. I took a deep breath. The doctor from Ah-me-ni-ah had succeeded in gaining my trust, but this? Nevertheless, now I was curious. What secrets might he find in a stinky bowl of pee? I managed to dribble a modest half bowl. When I was decent again, Ah-Yi rapped the floor.

The doctor returned to his former position, uncapped his bamboo tube, and explained, "Is wine." He measured some into the bowl, swirled the liquids together, and examined it in the light from the porthole. This was a story to tell, I thought, expecting any moment to see him dip a finger in and taste it. Fortunately, he did not, instead tipping the contents out the porthole, then squatted beside me and patted my hand.

"You are healthy," he said. "Inside healthy child."

Ah-Yi clapped her hands, but I just stared at nothing: dust flakes sparkling in the light. The doctor sealed his wine tube, offered a goodbye, and left the cabin on his own.

I heaved the wet bowl at the wall, where it shattered in pieces.

"Please go out," I told Ah-Yi. "No, don't bother to clean up."

I could deny it no longer. More confinement. More pain. Another young life feeding on my body, my time, my soul. To have it confirmed by this alien alchemy imbued it with an odd, otherworldly spell.

I rushed to the porthole, leaning out so far, I had to check myself from falling, and shrieked long and high at seabirds and the battering waves, screamed at the reddening clouds until my throat chafed. Then I slid back inside and collapsed on the mat, feeling strangely, emphatically calm.

When I declared my refusal to spend another half year inside a musty hold, Cheng Yat merely nodded. Maybe he felt the same as I did—surprised yet not surprised, but neither did I sense any joy. When had it happened? When had I had the opportunity or the energy to even talk to Cheng Yat after dark, much less make love with him? I couldn't remember the last time. Or maybe I could? I'd swallowed my potion which had never failed me. Or had I been too preoccupied to remember? I was always so cursed busy!

The sick feelings subsided over the next month, and I was normal again except for the first hints of stretching across my belly. I took up my lists and ledgers. Life and work resumed.

One evening Cheng Yat came in with a little smile that told me he brought news. For once I didn't care. Let him come out with whatever it was without waiting for me to prompt him.

Finally, he said it. "You'll be rid of the foreign devils soon."

"Oh?"

"Word from O Moon. The Chinese merchant society offered to pay for their release."

"Good. Though I don't see how it's any of their business."

"They want favors from the English."

That made sense, I supposed. "They're paying the ten thousand taels we called for?"

"They offered," Cheng Yat said. "But now we're asking thirty."

I felt a cramp, my first in days. "Crazy! You can't do that! I want them gone!"

"Calm yourself. It's only a negotiating position. Wait until you hear the other news."

I waited.

"Na is out as Governor-General. Disgraced. Dismissed by the emperor himself!"

To this, I only nodded. He circled around to look at me. "I thought you'd be at least, well, amused."

"Do you have anything else to tell me?"

"That's all." He unwrapped his turban and rummaged in the chest, unloading stacks of papers.

"Leung Po-bo stopped by this morning to congratulate me," I said.

He removed a few boxes and finally found what he was looking for: his personal seal for protection passes.

"So did your niece," I said tartly. "And some captains' wives. Word gets around."

Cheng Yat repacked the chest and fumbled with the rusty latch. "What about the red-fur foreign devil? Did he congratulate you too? Why do I need to hear this?"

"Because it seems strange that the wife of the Dai Lo Ban of the Confederation is expecting a child and only the great man himself shows no interest."

His face fell. His jaw moved like the old Cheng Yat, tongue too tangled for words.

"All we ever talk about is business-business-business, work-work-work. I'm about to be a mother again. How nice it would be to hear a peep of acknowledgment from the father?"

He gave me the oddest look, one that shifted between anger and guilt. I dropped onto the mat and turned my back on him.

"You don't have to say anything. Take your precious seal and go."

He didn't move. His breathing became louder, faster. I expected an eruption. Instead, a quiet accusation: "Am I not doing a proper job in mimicking your contempt for your own children?"

He went on, his voice breaking like an undammed river of sadness: "You don't remember the first time, do you? You were always so angry!

You hated that baby inside you, and I felt your hatred blow in my face like a burning hot wind. I thought if this time I let out even a hiccup of joy or blow a fart that sounds like *son,* you'll rush out and fling yourself into the sea."

Had I really been such a monster? If I kept my mouth quiet now, would he come out with the words? I wanted to hear him express the wonder of being a father again, even if he insisted on it being a boy. That he looked forward to having a family with me, so that even I might be swayed into wanting the same.

"I'm sorry," I said.

I turned around. His eyes glowed like black pearls. "You make me crazy sometimes. I never know how to speak to you," he said.

"Try. Try now."

"How to try? Tell me. I don't have fancy words or poetry."

"I don't need poems."

"How much I've come to respect you," he said. "No, that's—*aiya!* You know how bad I am with words that you haven't put in my mouth. There! That's what I mean. How much I've come to depend on you! Without you, I'd be—"

"What?" I turned over and invited him to lie beside me.

"A common crow, remember? Scavenging for scraps." We both smiled briefly.

My turn. "And without you..."

Without him, what? I didn't want to say it—*I would still be a whore in the mud*—the words were too ugly. Without him, I wouldn't be a wealthy woman. Without him, I wouldn't hold power over the lives of twenty thousand others. To speak such things aloud would seem somehow to trivialize them.

Without him, I would be on my own, responsible for myself, never having known...

The answer struck me right between my eyes.

"Without you, I would never have truly known a man."

He nodded, grateful that I didn't press him to say what was so difficult for him to express.

"What words do I say now?" he asked. "Congratulations? No. Maybe..." He stroked my midriff, then his hand moved up my side, tickling my skin with broken calluses. "Thank you for bearing my child—my children."

That was good enough. The lantern flickered and weakened, reducing his face to cheeks, lips, and eyes.

"Go finish your passes," I said.

"Those can wait." His hand slid inside my night robe. I opened my arms to him just as the lamp flame surrendered its fight with the darkness.

Not once had either of us mentioned the word *love*. Not that either he or I would have expected it. Nothing expected, nothing false spoken: maybe that was a small portion of this thing called love. A small portion was enough for now.

I woke up late, roused again from sleep by now-familiar rough voices down below.

The first thing I noticed was Cheung Po Tsai's junk tied to our beam. The dark men were herded onto his deck like a flock of sheep. The red-haired one, Tah-nah, raised a nasty racket of *fook's* and *dam's* as a gang of Po Tsai's sailors hoisted him over the rails.

XXXIII
Invincible

No one ever told me how different pregnancies could be. This time the discomforts were fewer, but I was always tired. Maybe it was the mid-winter cold, maybe the work, or both.

Our ships scurried from place to place collecting protection fees throughout the delta, taking advantage of the coming new year when everyone was eager to settle debts. Smothered in blankets, surrounded by mountains of bullion, ledgers, and receipts, it was easy to forget the soreness in my back and thighs. But a fortune teller warned Cheng Yat that if I didn't rest, it could bring worse weather and misfortune. Even the baby growing inside me seemed to protest. I had no choice but to entrust everything to the pursers.

The oracle proved correct. Immediately after the Spring Festival, the winter monsoon relented, and so did the remainder of my pains.

The idleness allowed me to spend more time with Ying-shek, a chance to fulfill my motherly responsibilities. Soon his younger sibling would demand all my attention, and I would return to my regular activities.

It was the first warm day of the year. I suggested to Ying-shek that we should go outside in the sun. Seeing my four-year-old trying to act grown up and help his wobbly-legged mother cross the cabin moved me so much that I forgot to duck, and I bumped my head on the door frame.

"Sit, Ah-Ma. I make it better," he said.

I did as he suggested. He held my cheeks and kissed the tender spot on my forehead. He was a good child, perhaps too good for this kind of life. I owed it to him, to his unborn sibling, and to myself and Cheng

Yat, if not the Confederation, to imagine new ways of maintaining our wealth and power while reducing the uncertainty and danger.

The place to start was right here—this fraying old junk with a cabin in which I couldn't stand up straight when we could easily afford to build something more befitting a fleet commander.

Lingting Island drifted past as we sailed downstream into the open delta. Ying-shek and I tossed stale rice into the air, laughing at the seagulls who swooped down for the treat, rarely missing a catch.

Someone called out, "Mandarins!"

At least twenty naval junks emerged from behind Lingting. Nothing to be concerned about; I continued feeding the gulls. Both sides would follow the same playacting that had already become routine. The navy gunners would wait until we were out of range, then fire a few haphazard shots. Our ships would make a show of changing course. Navy commanders would submit a report that they'd attacked nasty pirates. Gratuities would find their way into the proper hands. Nobody got hurt, no ships damaged, everyone back to their business.

Except this time the government ships pursued their business a bit too accurately. A ball splashed down close enough to rattle the deck.

"Let's go inside until it's over," I told Ying-shek.

Thus, I missed our first battle with government forces in more than a year. I tracked the action by the sounds of the guns and turns of our ship. Ying-shek sat stiffly at my side. Maybe it was the nearly forgotten tension of fighting at sea, but cramps took over my body. I had to lie down. I wondered whether the tiny creature inside me could hear and sense the danger.

I wondered too why we were fighting. Why were we in this position, putting the Confederation leader and his son and all our ledgers and much of our gold, not to mention the leader's wife, in danger? All we'd been doing was peddling passes, a job that could have been left to subordinates. The Confederation chief and his command ship had no reason anymore to participate in routine raids. He had to start acting more like an overlord and less like a common bandit.

"Get me a rag," I asked Ying-shek. "Dip it in cold tea." He insisted on being the one to wipe my face and belly. Yes, he was a good child. I didn't want him to fight battles when he grew up.

I was dozing when Cheng Yat came in, searching for his favorite cutlass. I knew what that meant. I didn't intend to watch.

"Did you see that? We're unbeatable!" he said.

In all, twenty-eight government ships were captured, their officers disemboweled, and eight thousand sailors given the choice of death or enlisting with the Red Flag Fleet. Yet the incident disturbed me. Not only did it indicate the government was back on the offensive, but our ships had been caught unprepared and overconfident against an evenly matched, well-armed force.

We had been lucky this time, not unbeatable.

We were also rich, very rich. The Red Flag Fleet—indeed, the entire Confederation—was sailing on a sea of money.

Sometimes I had to stop myself, find something to lean on, and catch my breath.

Rich.

To reach into a coffer and scoop out handfuls of gold.

Rich.

At the click of my fingers, men, women, and girls lined up to serve me.

Rich! Rich! Rich!

I'd thought that power came before wealth, but it turned out they were two sides of one coin. Wealth was the gateway to another world, beyond indulgence. Wealth was more potent than guns or armies or lofty titles bestowed by emperors. Wealth offered me power over my destiny in ways that gunpowder never could. What was stopping me from wielding that power? Deep inside I was still the squashed little whore, scared that any moment the money flow might stop, frightened that every spent copper postponed my freedom.

Wasn't I free now? What was I doing stashing wealth in caves? It was about time to put some to use to buy a better life.

We were back in Tung Chung. A warm spring shower curtained the bay. Cheng Yat and I enjoyed a rare midday meal together in the cabin: spiced pork dumplings over fragrant white rice.

"Imagine a cabin you can stand in without hitting your head," I said.

He fed himself a dumpling and licked sauce from his chopsticks.

"The leader of the Confederation of the Flags should sail something grander than this old junk," I said.

Now he regarded me with the wariness of a cat.

I set down my bowl. "I want a new ship."

"What's wrong with this one?"

"Here's what." I raised a foot and pointed to a map of scars and callused skin. "Splinters. Deck worms. Here's what else." I dug a fingernail into a dark spot on a floor plank. It came out like a farmer's spade, flaked with black rot. "Have you looked at the main deck recently? The cannon treads have practically bitten through. The muck in the holds—you could grow yams!"

"Time for careening," he said. "A good smoke out, scraping and caulking. I'll get the carpenters—"

"A hundred carpenters couldn't transform this old bucket into a ship befitting your status. What do you think it looks like, meeting men like Three Fingers with this sorry stack of timber? Look where we're sitting—we're living like fishermen! Don't you want more room?"

"I have enough room."

"Enough room for everyone to have to hear your foolishness."

He was the first man I'd ever met who didn't leap at every chance to possess something bigger, newer, more powerful. Sometimes humility was far from a virtue. Not that he was really humble, with all the "I'm unbeatable" nonsense he spewed at anyone who listened.

Cheng Yat had to give up these minor skirmishes, these little raids. Did Three Fingers Yip the triad boss stand in the street peddling foreign mud? Did the Governor-General of the Two-Kwang Provinces knock on doors to collect taxes? Cheng Yat had to finally shed the role of pirate captain and start regarding himself as pirate king.

"Why are you so stingy with yourself? We have enough money to build the most magnificent command ship anyone has ever seen," I said.

"Woman, how many ships in my fleet? Three hundred forty, fifty? And how many have I ever paid for? Maybe you should get out your abacus and add these numbers: zero plus zero."

"What good is having money if you don't—"

"Stop now! I've told you many times! This ship has supported me half my life. It's brought me good luck...if you count my catching you as good luck. Well, believe it or not, I do." He patted the floor like he would a faithful dog. "How many fights has my trusty companion here been through? Why would I need something else? My little boat is indestructible."

He shoved another dumpling in his mouth. "Like me."

And then he was away again on some new treasure hunt. There was no point in arguing nor in joining him, so I took over an empty house in the village with the boy and his nanny Ah-Ping. The sky fell down day after day, transforming the lanes into rivers of effluent-rich mud.

I accepted the boredom and discomfort, and drifted into long periods of reflection. The Confederation was moving in the direction I wanted, thanks to my constant presence at the proverbial helm—Cheng Yat would call it nagging. The protection pass system was becoming an entrenched part of doing business. Harvests were plentiful. Trade was expanding. If only Cheng Yat would see it for what it was: banditry had become simply one part of a greater operation, no longer the central focus. The sooner he finally realized this—but one thing at a time. First, I had to convince him to build a new command ship. He would come around. I knew this man deeply.

For all the disagreements between us, there was no fight there anymore. We argued like working partners, or the way I imagined well-matched husbands and wives aired their differences. I sometimes wondered if this was what love really was—nothing at all to do with passion or sex, and everything to do with calm acceptance on level terms.

This child growing inside me seemed to link us, more so than the first. I might not have chosen a second pregnancy, but after the initial shock subsided and after Cheng Yat's confession to me, I accepted this new life inside me. In return, the baby gave me barely any trouble, not a kicker and fighter like the first one. But even he had grown into a sweet child, sitting now on the floor beside me, cheerfully playing with brushes and ink. In a year or two, I would hire a scribe to teach him to read and write, but for now Ying-shek was content painting crude pictures of boats and fish. I envied him for that; such simple contentment I wanted for myself. All I needed was just a little more, not so very much to ask.

On one of the rare dry days, I sent Ying-shek with the nanny to shop for fruits and treats. Sooner than I expected their return, I heard his little feet kicking off mud at the door. He burst into my room with a big four-year-old's smile stained red by something sticky sweet. "Ah-Ma! Ship! Come see! Come!"

I rolled up my trousers and followed the stream of people to the waterfront. A fine drizzle shrouded the bay like a fog. At first, I thought it was a trick of the light. A warship nearly double ours in length, with masts taller than any I'd ever known, glided through the harbor while reefing its sails and turned slowly to a stop. I counted ten cannon slots along one side. The Confederation command banner flopped in the light breeze.

I whistled for a sampan.

The vessel was so large it had steps mounted on the outer hull. These led to a deck that seemed as large as a village. Ying-shek ran around yipping like a happy puppy.

Cheng Yat waited beside the mainmast with arms folded across his chest.

"Is this what you wanted?" he said.

I followed him around broken hatches, a dangerously fissured mast, up rotting companionway steps—all I could think of was the months of repair work that would be needed. But it had a fine cabin: I could barely reach the ceiling with an upstretched hand; such a luxury! I rummaged through storage chests, finding little of interest, while half-listening to his narrative of its capture. An engagement near Shuang Chuan Island, finding Black Flag ships under siege by nearly a hundred navy ships. Two days of battle, losing, winning, surrounding, destroying.

"I know you don't want me fighting, but I saw this ship and I thought of you."

One other word stood out, which gave me a cold chill every time.

"Invincible."

When he stepped out of earshot, I gave my first order on the new command ship of the Confederation of the Flags: scrape the deck clean of bloodstains, a grim reminder of how vincible was its previous commander.

I submerged myself into the warship's renovation, planning and supervising every detail. Each space, every bulkhead, would be patched, polished, and put to pragmatic use. Sailors' bunks were jettisoned and quarters restructured with proper partitions for families. Holds were converted to counting rooms; one became an archive for ledgers. I sent men to Kwangchow to fill a ship with the finest paint; others scoured the island for the tallest, straightest trees to replace every mast. Ah-Yi led an army of women in weaving mats and sewing sails while carpenters whittled dragon scale patterns into new hardwood rails. Sawdust permanently flecked my hair. Oil stained my hands brown. But my spirit soared with the hard-earned joy of seeing my personal creation take form. In a lifetime aboard ships, from my father's junk to the flower boats to Cheng Yat's aging hulk, I'd never been given the choice to live there or not. This was the first vessel I had ever decided for myself to live on, and I would make it serve my purpose.

Tearing out bulkheads and building furniture into the structure, the cabin became a parlor fit for an aristocrat. Dominating the side wall was my specially commissioned gift to Cheng Yat: a bejeweled, nearly life-sized figure of Tin Hau. The goddess's eyes, like those of her predecessor, seemed to follow me wherever I moved. But there was something judgmental in this one's glance. Maybe she challenged me to accept the existence of a spirit inside her pearl-flecked porcelain frame. Or maybe, more likely, it was an illusion, like everything supernatural. My prayer was only that Cheng Yat would like it.

I worked whole days aboard, and as my belly swelled, I spent nights in my luxurious new cabin. Although Cheng Yat could be talked into inspecting the Confederation's new flagship, he wouldn't sleep aboard—because the date was inauspicious, because of a fortune stick reading, or some business he had aboard his old junk—each time a different explanation. But I suspected the real reason was that he wasn't ready to be seen giving himself up to a woman's accomplishment, one he had almost nothing to do with.

At last, near the end of summer, the soul plank was hammered onto the bow. A chicken was sacrificed; the work was finished. A deafening barrage of firecrackers scared the old spirits away.

Even then, Cheng Yat postponed adopting the grand new ship as his own. His excuse this time: "I don't want to disturb you until the baby is born."

"Look at this ship! There's enough space; you couldn't disturb a hundred mothers," I told him.

"All the same..."

"I thought you wanted this. I put in so much work."

"You wanted it. I delivered."

Men! Stubborn as buffaloes, happy to roll in mud. Never mind, I needn't wait for him. Ying-shek and Ah-Ping moved in. Ah-Yi was glad for the spacious hold, which she insisted on sharing with three other widows. I would make this ship my home and office, the headquarters of the Confederation of the Flags. Let him have his musty old junk until it fell apart and he had to swim through the murk and crawl aboard.

Cheung Po Tsai had no such reservations. He inspected every corner, praising my attention to detail, down to the joists and tackle. He was more striking than ever in a shimmering blue tunic, his scalp pink from a fresh shave. He brought steamed buns for a treat.

"Look at you," he said. "Last time I saw you, you were like Sheung O come down from the moon. Now you look like the moon itself!"

"Don't disrespect a pregnant woman. About time you had a wife and son of your own." I sunk my teeth into a bun. Despite its having gone cold, the savory pork glided down my throat, bringing pleasure the whole way.

"I'd rather have a ship like this than a wife," Po Tsai said.

"Ha. I understand. But I don't understand why Cheng Yat is so—how to say it?—*hesitant* to take it over."

He looked around, drumming his fingers on his lap. "Are you telling the truth? You really don't know?"

"Why? Did he say something to you?"

"He didn't. But he doesn't have to. Ah-Yang, it's a beautiful ship. You did a wonderful job with it. But this trader isn't from the water world. Yes, I mean it. The people who built it aren't our people. It was commissioned by merchant owners who probably set foot on it only once. Captained and crewed by hired sailors. Yes, it floats and has sails, and carried huge loads across the ocean to worlds you and I have never dreamed of going. But this...this *vehicle* never belonged to anyone or any place."

"Excuse me. In case you hadn't noticed, it does now," I said.

"It does. And it needs time to build up its spiritual force."

"What are you talking about? I made sure it has all the proper shrines—an enormous Tin Hau in the cabin, another for the crew. We've the Bow Spirit, Sky Spirit, Hoi Hau, Kwan Tai—I don't even know the names of all of them—even a local shrine for Hau Wong. You could spend all day worshiping here. All new and fresh!"

"That's the problem," he said. "You threw away the old shrines."

"Oh, please! A shrine is a shrine. If you're going to worship some invisible being, isn't it better to have one that isn't chipped and rotting?"

"Aiya!" Po Tsai walked to the cabin shrine. He ran his hand over the goddess's lacquered sheen. "Think of how many people died when this ship was taken."

"Of course I did! We scraped blood from the planks. We did every purification rite and more! You weren't here—this cabin was thick with monks. There were so many firecrackers I thought they'd blow holes in the deck."

"All supervised by Cheng Yat Sou...who doesn't believe in spirits."

I didn't see what difference it made. Maybe my skepticism made the demons and ghosts feel that much less welcome. "I participated in all the worship rituals," I said.

"Aiya, Yang, haven't you ever learned? It isn't about worship. It's about reverence."

"There's a difference?"

"There is a difference."

Something inside me resented being lectured to by this pretty young man. But he looked so serious. He rummaged for a flint and kindled an oil lamp in front of Tin Hau. "Reverence isn't something you do. It's what you feel in your heart. When you became master of this ship, all you felt was how big it was and how many rooms you could give it, am I correct? If any spiritual beings were present here, I'd wager they were brought aboard by the crew, given a home here, absorbed their prayers. Then you discarded them without a thought while hollowing out everything else. What you have now is a big, empty vessel."

"I confess! You're right! I don't believe in those things! You'd think that a handsome, rock-sturdy, seaworthy vessel would be worthy of all the 'reverence' you need, rather than clinging to some rotting near-carcass of a junk."

I sat on the newly woven carpet in the center of the floor and surveyed my big, bright, beautiful, and, according to Po and apparently Cheng Yat, soulless cabin.

"I'll take it if he doesn't want it," Po said.

I made it clear that I was in no mood for his jokes. "He's just being a stubborn, pig-headed old egg."

"Maybe that's why you're suited to each other. You're the stubbornest woman I've ever seen. No, I mean well! Nobody else could have accomplished what you've done here."

"I thought you just condemned it for being a big, hollow, pile of timber."

He settled beside me, playfully bumping shoulders. "Only trying to convince you to give it to me."

"Leave the subject," I said. "I'm pregnant and tired and my legs ache."

A sunbeam through the window set the air aflame with sparkling dust, a sight which would have cheered me before our conversation. Maybe he was right. Maybe this whole ambitious project had been misguided—maybe I'd been wrong every step of the way—attempting to impose grandeur on a man who'd never sought it. Yet the ship was what it was. I'd fashioned it to have everything a great commander needed. If it was missing some ethereal element, I would sow the seeds of infusion myself when I gave birth to my second child in this room. Let a new life begin here. No one could then accuse it of lacking spirit.

Po brought a cushion for my back, crawled to my outstretched feet, and lifted one by the heel.

"May I? I learned something. Let me try it on you."

"Will it hurt?"

He laughed. "Only if I'm bad at it."

He folded down my toes and held my leg above the ankle while he twisted the foot this way and that. Then he jabbed his thumb into spots on the tough underside. It was painful at the beginning, but soon I felt a warm tingle in my chest as though I was bathing in hot water. I also felt a surge of hunger and stuffed half the remaining bun in my mouth.

He switched to the other foot.

"Nice?"

I nodded. "You learned this from one of your girls?"

"I don't know who you mean."

"Don't lie to me, Cheung Po Tsai."

"No lie? Your feet need cleaning. Ha ha! I learned from a doctor in O Moon. Wah, that reminds me, almost forgot to tell you: we finally unloaded the foreign devils."

I pulled my foot from his hand. "Ai! Why did you ruin my day reminding me about them? How much?"

"Two thousand eight hundred in coin, three chests of opium— aiya! Wipe your chin."

Before I had a chance to do so, he ran a finger under my lip, held it up to show me the swath of sauce, then put it in his mouth and sucked it clean. He didn't notice that some had dribbled onto his lip. My face burned, but not only because of his action.

"Opium?" I said. If there was one more thing I desired, it was to enter into this trade.

"You want? I'll give you in exchange for this ship."

"You drive a hard bargain."

"So do you, Ah-Yang. Maybe why your husband is afraid of you. Ha! But I'm not." He squatted and spoke to my belly. "Hello, little baby brother or sister. Ha! Lucky you, spending so much time inside this lady's womb."

The innuendo wasn't lost on me. I slapped his cheek, meaning to be playful, but hard enough to leave a red mark and a look of surprise on both our faces.

My time came on the hottest day of the summer.

The new flagship's cabin had been prepared in advance. But no matter how many comforts surrounded me, the past few months of work had wrung out my body like an old rag. I thought the pain and contractions would be familiar, but they were no easier than the first time. I pushed and twisted; midwives squeezed. They stuck wood between my jaws to stop me from biting off my tongue. Still, the strong-willed child refused to greet the world. Right around sunset, in one blinding burst of hot shredding pain, it finally slipped through and filled the cabin with its cries.

Let it be a girl, I thought. *One who'll grow up to be strong.*

"A big mouth like the mother's!" Ah-Yi said.

"Give me," I said. "No, don't bother cleaning. Give me my baby."

A slippery red form slid into my arms, a healthy young penis pointing at the sky. Another boy. A playmate for his brother. Healthy and active.

I guided the tiny lips to my breast, but he wasn't interested in eating. Wide round eyes fixed on mine. I stroked his wet black hair.

"Maybe I'll try harder this time," I whispered to my newborn son. "I...I promise." An inky wave of exhaustion washed over me. Before losing consciousness, I heard Ah-Yi say, "Call the father."

On the day of the naming, the largest banner I'd ever seen unfurled from the main mast of the Confederation's new flagship. So heavily embroidered with dragons and symbols, it barely launched in the passive wind.

Cheng Yat named his new son Hung-shek: Hero of Stone. He was a fat little baby, content to feed day and night, but timid as well. He cried easily, and I spent many nights bouncing him in my arms. Once more I faced the challenge: how to open my heart to a creature who didn't seem fully formed, who hadn't even had a name until today? I tried, like I'd promised myself. I held him and sang to him until sometimes he purred like a kitten. Even Cheng Yat, on his daily visits, liked to carry him around the room. But wherever I turned, I found Ying-shek's eyes fixed on the new intruder in his life as though he were a bug that deserved squashing. Arrogant, drunken sea captains jockeying for power I could manage. But a jealous boy was beyond any skill I possessed.

Following the ceremony, I left the baby with Ah-Ping and led Ying-shek up to the poop deck.

"You're my boy, my number one son," I tried to reassure him, but I guessed he sensed the desperation in my voice. His silence cut like a knife.

"Look at all those ships," I said. Hundreds of vessels crowded the inner harbor—red flags, blue, white, yellow, green, and black. This boy whose shoulder I hugged, who would inherit this massive assemblage of power someday, glanced around without expression, then broke away and ran to the back rail.

In the corner where the parapet met the transom, a lone magpie bowed and flicked its tail. Ying-shek smiled for the first time in days. As he scampered close, the magpie flew off.

The last guests finally boarded their sampans long after dark. The cleaning crew took over the deck. I hooked my arm in my husband's.

"Stay. You promised."

Ying-shek went off with the nanny. I carried the baby, Hung-shek, to the cabin and tucked him in to sleep in his corner. The day's heat lingered in the room.

Cheng Yat had too much to drink. I led him to the large padded sleeping mat, peeled off his outer garments, and changed myself into a light robe. I kindled a single lantern which cast a yellow sheen across the floor.

We sat quietly for a while. Then he took my hand.

"Thank you, wife."

This was something new. "For what?" I asked gently.

"This," he said. "This ship. Two fine sons. This, this...this Confederation."

"You're drunk."

"No. Maybe. Doesn't matter. You're my wife, my partner. Sometimes you're even right."

"You're my husband." I raised his hand to my lips and kissed the thick skin of his knuckles. "This is our home now."

"Mm."

"New son. New ship," I whispered. "New start for everything, the Confederation, for us."

The cleaning crew's noise and banter died down. A splash and the swish of a sampan pulling away. The ship settled into silence. Cheng Yat lay down and let out a deep breath.

"You're not telling me something," I said.

He turned on his side. "One last trip in the trusty old junk."

"But you promised!"

"I did, but—"

"Where?"

"Time for a duty visit to Tunghoi."

"In that old thing? This is your chance to show off the new ship!"

I tried to disguise my disappointment while in my heart I understood. His ship had been his most faithful companion. Like a cherished old dog, he wanted to favor it with one final glory.

He touched a finger to my lips. "When we come back. I swear to the gods."

He was soon snoring, curled beside me like a trusting child. I checked the baby, then I lay back down beside Cheng Yat and stared out through the porthole.

I needed patience. Patience for one more trip in the old junk. Patience for a needy baby. Patience toward my eldest son, maybe learning to open my heart. No time for regrets. You can't sail backward. Time to surge forward and catch the soaring winds.

In a corner of the sky, the high clouds parted.

"Soon I'll have everything," I whispered to the lady in the moon.

XXXIV
Following Ghost

One hot, windless day, a crewman named Shiu filled a burlap sack with chains and ballast stones, roped it to his chest, and leapt overboard.

I reached the rail as the first air bubbles broke the surface, ruffling the otherwise flat, leaden sea. Ripples broke against the hull, each in the same spot as its predecessor. The ship hadn't drifted even a finger's width.

Crewmen swore at the drowned man for cursing the ship with a following ghost. They eyed each other, wondering who might next succumb to madness on the flat, dead sea.

A sail batten creaked.

Every head twisted upward, eyes begging for a sign of wind—a ruffle in the sailcloth, a swinging thread. The mainsail sagged like an old man's belly, and every banner hung limp.

Cheng Yat watched from the upper deck but turned aside when he noticed me spying him. His stupid pride, I thought.

The trip to Tunghoi had been a waste of time: accounts were balanced, silver exchanged; in all, a mere half a day's work by a roomful of pursers. Predictably, the meeting was followed by ten days of drinking. Cheng Yat, Tunghoi Bat, Wu-shek Yi, and Son of a Frog practically lived in the wine shop while the back lanes overflowed with sailors following their example.

Despite my boredom, I was glad we'd left the boys behind in Tung Chung with their platoon of nannies and wet nurses, prompted by my selfish want to be free from children for just a few days. The longer we remained in Tunghoi, the more my growing sense of foreboding had confirmed my decision.

The skies there had been a rich late autumn blue, the air sharp and clear like panes of glass. Deep in my gut, something about the light disturbed me. When I met Cheng Yat during a rare moment of coherence, he told me he'd noticed it too. The air tasted sour, he'd said.

Then Wu talked Cheng Yat into a joint raid on a foreign ship. We spent days pitching in rough seas south of Hoinam Island. By the time we finally began the home journey, even a child could have seen ominous signs in the chalky white sky. Now it was my turn to urge for a delay in leaving, and Wu backed me up, but Cheng Yat had made up his mind to outrun the weather. It was just the autumn change in winds, already overdue.

He opted for a direct route across open ocean rather than the usual course along the arc of the coast. A punchy southwesterly on the first day offered good progress, but no sooner had we lost sight of land than the wind sputtered out like a dying candle. The twelve ships in our group spread out so as not to steal one another's wind. Day and night, men coaxed the sails like delicate butterfly wings, trimming each batten by hair's widths to eke power from the least whisper of air. Our crews set adrift gilt paper boats as offerings to the wind, until we ran out of paper. The heavens held their breath.

Even the fish knew what was coming and had retreated to such depths that rations were cut.

By the third hot, windless day, the only stirring in the world was between men. The deck seemed too small for forty-odd crew, people bumping and pushing, growling at one another to get out of the way. Fights broke out at the fan-tan table; a basket of coins was tossed overboard. Cheng Yat placed a ban on games.

And now here I stood, bearing his wrath because of one angry remark the night before, still feeling his slap on my cheek. But I'd been right: he should have turned back that first day, but he would rather risk twelve ships and five hundred crew than risk losing face.

Up on the poop deck, where I should have met a breeze, the air was thick as syrup. I watched Cheng Yat, the Taumuk, and other crewmen feed offerings into a shrine; smoke rose straight into the sky without so much as a curl. The sea spread flat, unbroken by even a single whitecap.

After prayers Cheng Yat came up the ladder and, seeing me, stalked to the opposite rail, but we both fixed on the same object: a gray-green smudge on the horizon.

I asked, "What do you think?" I had to repeat myself before he mumbled an answer: "Dragon or tiger, take your choice."

Clouds herald dragons, gales foretell tigers, the old seaman's saying went. What kind of storm lurked there, behind the edge of the world—the crushing swagger of the dragon or the tiger's frenzy? What difference would it make?

"It's too late in the season for typhoons," I said.

"Tell that to the Sky Spirits. You're the only one not praying."

"So this is my fault? Your fickle gods need to hear a woman's voice? Fine, I'll pray. Give me something to burn."

His eyes shrunk into the shadow of his brow. "Burn your precious opium. If we hadn't wasted five days chasing—"

"What in demon's hell are you talking about? If you hadn't—" I clenched my mouth shut. The only good that had come of ambushing the foreign trader was forty chests of opium, which we'd split with Wu. As delighted as I'd been at the haul, he could hardly accuse the hunt of being my idea. I reminded myself that Cheng Yat's temper had little to do with me, that everyone on board felt the strain. I walked over beside him and laid a hand on his shoulder. "You need to rest. We'll fight this."

"Why don't you fight it, oh great Queen of the Sea? You seem to know it all." He jerked free of my hand and stormed away.

Was that really how he thought of me, of trying to be the boss? Maybe I should be! It was his decisions that placed us in jeopardy, and now things looked to become worse. Surely, I couldn't mismanage things any more than he had!

Back on deck people looked aside as I passed. I didn't care what they'd heard, whether they blamed me or Cheng Yat for their predicament; I wanted to escape everyone at that moment. I dragged open the center hold hatch and let myself down to inspect my treasure.

I squeezed between stacks of opium chests, jiggled the bar lock I knew to be loose, and lifted a heavy lid. A sweet earthy aroma enveloped me. My fingers swept across neatly packed orbs encased in rough, twiggy plaster, larger than cannonballs yet bearing greater power: the power to seize men's souls—and their purses.

I slid to the floor and leaned against the bulkhead. How soothing it felt: opium-scented air swirling around me, the breath and voice of money. This was only the beginning. Three Fingers Yip and his triads would no longer be the sole purveyors of illicit foreign mud. The

341

Confederation would grab a steady piece of the trade. I imagined floating opium parlors. I imagined myself riding an ornate sedan chair past black-robed officials and fat compradors kneeling to me and beating their foreheads on the cobblestones.

I laughed. So funny! I would be the richest woman in China. No more old, rotting junks. I would live in a palace; my boys would grow up as princes. I would laugh in the faces of every person I'd ever known. Sea Queen? No, I would be the Opium Queen!

I laughed.

I imagined.

Sharp rattling startled me awake, like iron pellets striking the hull. In complete darkness, I forgot where I was until I felt a wooden chest beside me. Opium fumes must have lulled me into sleep.

Someone had shut the hatch overhead. I felt my way to the ladder and was halfway up when my feet left wood and I might have been airborne if I hadn't clenched the top rung in my fists. The ship had dropped into what must have been an unimaginably deep trough.

I had to pry the latch open. Rain hammered my face and whipped my hair. Woolly clouds reduced the sun to an orange smudge. Greenish black liquid mountains rolled across the world. They'd reefed the mainsail, while the front appeared ready to burst. I heard the Taumuk's voice shouting but couldn't make out his words through the wind. A line of tillermen coerced the rudder to one side and fastened it into place. Winches spun. Ropes cried.

The ship reared back to face heaven. I hung on, riding the swell up over the summit, ready for the inevitable plunge to come.

Then the wave collapsed on top of me and hammered me back into the hold.

A sharp edge of something sliced into my hip. My head struck wood. I sat up, coughing and spitting out water, while a waterfall drained down inside. I looked around and screamed.

The opium!

The bottom chest was half submerged. I had to get out of here. I had to seal the hatch.

We leaned into the next swell, the mass of water shifting around my feet. At last I pulled myself onto the deck, then held on for my life as the ship pitched nearly sideways over the ridge and careened downward until snapping upright in the bottom of the next gloomy trough. I yanked the hatch into place. I needed men to bail the hold before the next upheaval. The wind out-shouted my cries for help.

Cheng Yat stood at the bow, reduced to a black and silver figure from an ink painting. The next swell loomed over like a giant claw. I ran to him against the wind and the spray and the tilt of the deck.

"I need men to bail!" I said. He appeared not to hear.

"A flooded hold!" I yelled. "The opium!"

"Fuck the opium—" A thunderbolt obliterated the rest of his words.

Fat clouds and sheets of rain snuffed out the remaining twilight. I couldn't see a thing, stumbling from handhold to handhold across the deck, tripping over a rope when the ship heeled through yet another swell, jabbed in the ribs by someone running past. I fought my way up the companionway stairs and crawled the rest of the way into the shelter of the cabin.

Rain pounded the hull with the force of a hundred fists. I raised the wick in the lantern and went cold at what the light revealed. The Tin Hau shrine lay on its side among incense and broken bowls. The pedestal was empty, the goddess sprawled halfway across the floor. I crawled toward the dethroned idol, when my knee came down on something hard. A scream launched from my belly and trumpeted out my throat. Tin Hau's arm lay on the floor, now cracked in half beneath my shin.

I had to put everything back together. Cheng Yat would see this as the worst of all omens, if he didn't blame me for it first. My first attempt to right the shrine sent me rolling across the floor, but finally I maneuvered it into place against the wall. I strained every last muscle in my body lifting the figure of Tin Hau. She was cold and slippery, like carrying a corpse.

The idol finally back on her pedestal, I pushed the impossibly heavy chest against the shrine as a buttress, then collapsed on the floor, gulping to catch my breath, clasping the goddess's broken limb in one arm, the other outstretched to steady myself against the violent sway of the ship. Perhaps I could use belts and turban cloth to attach the arm, just so Cheng Yat wouldn't immediately notice. I struggled onto my knees and reached for the chest's latch.

I flew against the opposite wall. The lantern lifted from its hook and crashed down, exploding into orange flames. The ship was spinning, tossing things around the room. A stream of burning oil snaked across the floor, popping and bursting as it consumed mats and fabric. I beat the blaze with a blanket, but it spread too quickly, fingers of flame now branching in every direction, smoke chafing my eyes and throat. I felt my way to the porthole and yanked the cover aside. The first burst of air engorged the fire, then water poured in and steam mixed with smoke. I rolled to the doorway and with my last remnant of strength, opened it to the wind and rain and saltwater spray.

The shrine had withstood the onslaught and was safe from fire. I bowed to the goddess of fishermen, the protector of seafarers. I wasn't ready for death. I was too young. I had too many things unfinished. *Don't punish me.* I beat my head on the floor and pleaded, "Let me live. Please save me! Please give me a sign. Show me in your eyes that I'll survive."

I abandoned my prayers when, in the flash of a lightning bolt, Tin Hau's blank stare passed over me with utter indifference.

Her eyes had always had an unearthly quality, seeming to bore knowingly into mine, wherever I happened to move in the room. But now she didn't look at me. Her chipped white face stared blankly at nothing. This porcelain sculpture with the living eyes appeared to have died.

I sat up quickly and clenched my fists together. I begged.
You can't die.
What was I saying?
Were you ever alive? Can I have been so wrong to not believe in you?
Was this what Po Tsai had been talking about—the reverence, the infusion of spirits? Had I been blind to it all along? Without them, what was this ship but a fragile construction of wood, tossed and beaten on a wrathful sea?

I tried to talk myself out of fear. I'd lived through typhoons before, though never this violent, never this far out to sea, so far from shelter. What choice did I have but to trust in the history and spirits that strengthened every timber?

Cheng Yat and his best sailors could save this ship—*would* save this ship. But who would save my precious opium?

All night the storm smacked us like a spiteful beast toying with its prey. Yet the ship still held, and I endured within the armor of the cabin walls and its now-closed door, sucking in air flavored with burnt oil and fabric. As light crept through the cracks, I convinced myself that we would survive. The ship had always come through. It was a good ship—yes, a lucky ship, like Cheng Yat had said—in the hands of a powerful sailor who understood the sea.

Our cargo was a different question. The hold where the opium was stored had taken on water from the start. Someone had to check what was salvageable, so that this entire trip would not end up a waste.

The cabin door flew open at the first touch of the latch. Rain whistled crossways; wind tugged at my clothes. The deck was stripped clean. Even the cannons were gone, whether deliberately or taken by the waves. A splintered stub remained of the foremast. Only the tiller crew remained on deck, fighting to orient the rudder through peaks and valleys of furious water. In the false calm at the bottom of a trough, I nearly fell from the companionway stairs; the vessel leaned like a cripple.

The hatch cover was swollen shut. I waved over a passing sailor and together we pried it open. The flooding exceeded my worst premonition. Every opium chest but one was drowned. What was more, the water-logged hold unbalanced the ship. The good chest needed saving, the rest needed to be flung overboard and the compartment bailed.

"Get men to help," I ordered.

Cheng Yat appeared beside me with a rope. He looped a length around my waist, shouting in my ear, "What the hell are you doing? Get back to the cabin!"

"We have to move—"

A wave as tall as the mainmast stretched overhead, then spanked down and knocked the air from my lungs. When the flood receded, I found myself tangled in ropes against a winch, vomiting water. I scrambled toward the opium hold until Cheng Yat yanked me back.

"We have to toss cargo! Bail the hold!" I screamed.

"Let the men do it! Get away from here!"

"We can save one chest!"

"Crazy! Get back to the cabin!"

He led me by the rope until the junk rose sideways over a precipice and spun down the other side, plowing into the bottom through a gusher of foam. The tiller sprang sideways, batting a man into the gunwale. Cheng Yat released me and ran through hard-hitting spray toward the tiller crew.

345

The crewman I'd sent for help returned with two others. Together they dropped into the flooded hold and levered the dry opium chest up through the hatch, where I and another man lifted it free. If we could save just this one, I thought, it would bring in enough money to justify the danger, and I'd make sure these men each received a generous reward.

I pointed. "To the cabin."

They protested, indicating the companionway, and I understood the danger of hauling the heavy chest up the slippery, canting steps.

"Lash it to the bulwarks," I said. At least then it wouldn't be underwater.

"But the captain—"

"I speak for him!"

A man ran off and returned with a coil of rope. Under my direction, we ran lines through scupper holes and railings and bound the chest to the gunwale.

The remaining chests were so heavy with water that by the time two had been lifted and cast overboard, the men were retching from exhaustion. Clouds thick as felt snuffed the light. The wind's fury doubled and blew out what remained of the sun. We were in a towering gray-green room surrounded on all sides with water. An anchor tumbled past, broke through a railing and vanished. The air smelled sour.

The exhausted sailors succeeded in lifting another chest onto the deck, when Cheng Yat grabbed one by the neck, shouting, "All crew at the mainsail! Launch a sea anchor!" His eyes bulged, cheeks were drawn in, like a skull filmed with skin.

His eye fell on the chest secured to the gunwale.

"We need rope," he said.

"Not my opium!"

Others unraveled the bindings and left the chest bound by one narrow twine. Another tilt sent it sliding across the deck. Sickness filled my gut as it smacked the opposite gunwale. Men clung to the mast, slashing the sail bindings, while others strapped rope around both ends of the boom, fixing the other end of each line to the farthest aft rails, transforming the sail into a gigantic kite.

The next swell rose from the sea, its spine whipped into scallops like scales on a dragon's back.

Cheng Yat howled, "Out of the way!"

The sail began to unfurl. I dropped to the deck as the wind caught it, yanking it high overhead, a wounded bird riddled with holes. Then it pitched downward and plummeted into the sea. The junk reared up, the bow swung, a beast fighting its reins. It settled into the slant of the oncoming wave and pierced the crest in two. We sliced straight down the other side. The bow scooped the trough bottom with a terrifying slurp, before the ship righted with barely a tilt. I breathed again. The sea anchor had done its job to stabilize the ship.

On the way up the next swell, confidence gave way to panic. The sail had entangled with the rudder. Men dashed to the rails, tugged ropes, screamed for help. The air around me crackled with the strain, as if the deck might fold over and collapse in on itself.

And then, suddenly, the pressure let go. The air was sucked from my lungs and ears. Wind and rain evaporated. My head might burst into a thousand pieces. The ship held still as though poised in empty space.

Then a sound—inaudible, but a hum of sorts—spread throughout the hull. I felt it in the soles of my feet, now vibrating my bones, gathering force from the surrounding water, like a leviathan rising beneath us from the ocean depths. The water glowed as if from some ghostly light. I smelled fear on the deck, felt static tingling in the air.

I had never been more afraid.

The water around us popped. Something from a narcotic dream: giant droplets shot upward, then joined into heads of water taller than the bulwarks, then even higher, taller than the mast. They collided and sparred with each other and burst apart like spumes from a thousand whales. It was no sea I had ever seen in any dream or nightmare. It was the dragon who lived beneath the sea gone mad.

A hand struck my shoulder. Cheng Yat yelled words I could not hear.

The dragon arched its back. The sea around us brightened, lurched upward, slinging the ship to the sky while my guts fell away. The watery summit on which we rode burst all at once into thick white froth. My eye caught the cabin door swinging free. I wanted to run, but my legs refused to move. The hum in the deck shook my legs, rattled my knees. I turned to Cheng Yat for help, but he had joined the tiller men trying to yank the rudder free.

The sky spun—slowly, slowly, gradually gaining momentum. Or was it the sea? The water drew white circles around us.

"More men!" Cheng Yat screamed.

The deck pitched aside with such force that splinters sprouted from the boards. Just as suddenly as it had stopped, the wind returned with such vengeance it tried to drag my head from my neck. I clung to a peg while spray washed over me, the hum now a ratcheting I felt in my ribs. I heard a sharp crack.

Above me on the slanting deck, the opium chest toppled over and continued, tumbling side over side.

Directly toward Cheng Yat.

My scream rose through my belly, into my lungs and throat, piercing the storm, the waves, the hidden sun. His back was turned. He didn't see it coming until at the final moment he looked toward me. His legs bent to leap away, but the deck was too far skewed, too wet. The opium chest bounced over a peg, suspended in the air, then crushed my husband against the gunwale as it split open and spewed its molten contents around him.

I scraped forward on my knees, reaching for him. He was still alive, twisting and fighting his forward slide toward the gap in the rail left behind by the opium chest.

Everything let go. The sea, the ship, the air groaned, a mournful voice from the abyss. The wave folded in on us. I was spinning inside a hellish pit of bile green sea.

His arm stretched to me, then his feet left the deck. I watched my husband rise like a spirit and shrink to a black smudge which vanished into the dark funneling void.

My world flipped over.

Sound and light, wind and rain, thought and feeling ceased.

Thick cold filled my throat, engorged my lungs. Ten thousand bubbles like falling stars.

I saw a woman's body floating free in space, familiar of form and shoulders and head.

It was me. From somewhere outside of me, I watched Shek Yang cease to struggle.

I watched myself drown.

I saw my hands open, my arms and legs spread wide like a cross.

A lamenting voice called to me, on and on, almost singing.

Don't let go. Open your mouth. Let life in.

Again, I heard my name. A different name, but clearer. A real voice. "Cheng Yat Sou!"

My ears swelled with sound—crashing waves, wind whistling,

wood grinding against wood. Voices and more voices. Light returned.

Something hard pressed my chest. Water spewed from my throat. I retched and retched again. Chilling cold spread outward from my heart into every arm and leg.

"Ah-Cheng Yat Sou!"

I turned my head and ventured open my eyes. A young sailor knelt beside me. Behind him, two men paddled furiously with short oars, and beyond them a woman hunched over the side. I was on a sampan, spread across a thwart. I recognized some of our crew.

"The captain?" Pain stabbed my throat as I spoke.

"Only us," the young sailor said.

I forced myself up. Searched the boat. Behind me a prone figure with a gaping wound in his side. I scanned the sea around us. Only pieces of broken wood. And us.

The sampan lifted through another swell while the oarsmen chopped the water to keep us upright. On the way down the precipice, the little boat struck something with a hollow thump. I raised myself onto my elbows to see.

Scraping against the sampan's hull was an empty opium chest, missing its cover. An oarsman nudged it away with his paddle. The crate rose on one end, and in a move which mimicked a mournful bow, dunked into the sea, leaving only bubbles.

In the split moment before it vanished, it looked like a coffin.

嘉慶十二年丁卯

PART IV

—

Twelfth Year

of the

Reign of Emperor

Ka-hing

—

1807

XXXV
Ceremonies

The storm returned each time I shut my eyes.

Woolen clouds smother the world. Pounding rain. Waves crashing like breaking glass. The deck tips. The opium chest slides down, down, down... crushing my man.

Lying in my dry, empty cabin back in Tung Chung, each tiny sob triggered violent coughs that I felt in my ribs.

Tumbling in a black void. Cheng Yat reaches for me. I try to reach back. He's sucked into the spinning abyss.

In my waking dreams, I leapt after him, like a modern-day Zhu Yingtai. But no butterflies emerged, only new marks on my scalp as I banged my head on the floor to strike out the memory and the shame.

The opium chest wouldn't have been there if not for my foolish greed. I had murdered my husband. For such a crime, the sea had not even surrendered his body back to me. He returned only as a ghost in the never-ending storm behind my eyes.

How long had I been stuck in this living death? A few days? A month? My eyes focused on a neatly folded stack of white mourning robes, and I remembered. Today was the three-times-seventh day since his passing. I had to get up and dress for the ceremony.

I raised myself on one elbow, gritting against the twist in my spine. Fire bolts shot up my arm, which at least blocked the tormenting itch, as if scorpions had burrowed inside the tourniquet. Waiting for the ache to subside, I faced the Tin Hau shrine I'd had built for him. An empty statue, signifying nothing, its precious wood and jewels now concealed under blue mourning cloth.

He'd gotten his wish: he had never wanted to move onto this big ship with its hollow pretensions. He had spent only a single night here. Not a single timber bore the scuff of his boot or a scratch of his blade. Not even a whisper of his spirit infused its decks.

I sat up all the way and again waited for the pain to fade.

Yes, he'd received his wish in a terrible way, just as I'd gotten mine: I was free now.

After all, what kind of husband had he been? Taking me against my will into a life of violence and war. Short-tempered, stingy with words and affection. But he'd praised my spirit; he had offered me respect. We had been truer partners than I thought a man and woman could be. What kind of wife had I been to him? Manipulative, insolent, even cold. But I'd given him physical pleasures and brought him two sons. And I had believed in him, made him the success he might never have become without me. Whatever soul he had allowed another to touch, I had touched it.

Now none of it mattered. I was free. We both were—he to roam and plunder the heavens, me to bear the consequences of my unprepared freedom.

A tap at the door. Probably the priests come to escort me. I pulled on the heavy white trousers and top, but my arms hurt too much to slip on the outer robe. I would ask them for help.

Instead of priests, a sailor and his wife knelt in the doorway. They bowed deeply.

I recognized him: one of Wu-shek Yi's captains who must have just arrived in Tung Chung. The man mumbled his sympathy and regrets. I hardly listened, their words little different than the others who'd called on me day after day.

The woman said, "Wish the Widow Cheng eternal life."

I nodded thanks and handed each a *white gold* envelope containing a copper coin.

Widow Cheng.

The name was as good as a prison sentence. Widows had no place in the water world—at best they were figureheads to be pitied; at worst, shunted below like Ah-Yi, called upon to patch men's shoes. All the work I'd done to build the Confederation, and to build this ship, meant nothing against the weight of tradition. I was entitled to cling to my status as commander's wife until the final ceremony on the six-times-seventh day, when Cheng Yat's soul was ordained to enter heaven, after which I had no more value than yesterday's rice. I wiped my eyes on my clean white sleeve. Was I mourning the loss of a man's life or the loss of my own?

"Ah-Ma."

I rubbed my face once more and forced a smile. Ying-shek stood in the entrance, stiff and solemn in his new blue silk tunic and trousers. He lowered his head, fighting a touch of quiver in his lips. A hug would have hurt my arm and ribs and might have shamed him in his obvious effort to play the man. The nanny, Ah-Ping, stood behind him with baby Hung-shek suspended in a back sling. My two boys, my two poor boys, whose mother's heart was too hollowed-out right now for either of them.

"You look very handsome," I said. "You father will be proud of you when he passes on his way into heaven."

Ying-shek's brow knitted into crevasses, the uncanny image of his father. "Am I the new captain?"

"Oh, my big boy. Not yet."

"Why not?" He backed away and wrapped his arms around the nanny's knees. What could I say that he would understand?

In the sampan to shore, I handed him a bundle of *white gold* envelopes, reminding him to hand one to every mourner. "That's a big man's job, to respect your father."

The funeral pavilion was on the beach outside the village. At my insistence, its towering bamboo latticework was paneled with sailcloth and arrayed with banners in every color of the Confederation fleets. The chanting grew louder the closer we came until I couldn't hear anything else. I pulled Ying-shek's mourning cloak over his outfit, fitted my own white hood, and crossed the pebbly sand with my son. The platform was already packed with mourners and priests. Wu-shek Yi stood with General Bo. Closer to the main podium, Kwok Podai offered me a suitably somber bow. But the one I most expected remained conspicuously absent. Twenty-one days and still no sign of Cheung Po Tsai. To miss this important ceremony was unlike him, the epitome of disrespect. Worse, I felt abandoned by the one person with whom I'd shared Cheng Yat.

I was swept into a crush of droning monks and nuns, one gray-robed shaven head the same as the next. My arm itched so badly, I wanted to chew off the wrappings, while my back felt like shredded cane. During the interminable ceremony, I tried to disguise the discomfort, torn between genuine desire to honor Cheng Yat and impatience with the tedious, repetitive rituals, none of which would make a speck of difference to him in the afterlife.

At last, I was permitted to move, leading mourners in circles around the coffin, a purely symbolic empty box; his actual body was among the fishes along with most of his crew. Then more kneeling, standing, offerings, incense, and chants until I was ready to faint and all I could think of was food. But first, I had to feed rice and wine to a life-sized paper effigy which bore little resemblance to my husband. Around him sat piles of chicken and fruits and cakes which made my stomach rumble, but those were reserved for Cheng Yat. If they remained untouched by tomorrow, that meant his ghost hadn't lingered and he was settled comfortably in the spirit world.

Then it was the turn of the eldest son. I urged Ying-shek forward. He seemed frightened to stand so close to the coffin but relaxed when a priest handed him an empty drinking bowl. I had gone through this ritual with him on the sampan, and he was eager to perform his role.

"Add water," he told the priest. "My Ba needs water."

Many of the assembled mourners laughed. Ying-shek's eyes filled with tears.

I leaned in and reminded him gently, "Not here. He'll use this to drink water in the spirit world."

The priest mimed smashing the bowl. Ying-shek looked at me. I nodded. He raised the bowl with both hands above his head and threw it with all his strength next to the head of the coffin, dodging the shards which flew at his feet.

For the first time since the storm, my heart felt full. I scooped my son into my arms. "You did a good job, my big, big boy. Your father is happy with you. Now he'll never be thirsty when he walks beside the gods."

After a dignified interval, I excused myself back to the ship where the children and I ate rice together before they went off with Ah-Ping. Though a sore back and arm tempted me to lie down, I couldn't afford to waste time. After sending a crewman to summon the purser, I changed into a modest black robe, fixed my face and hair, and waited.

He announced himself at the door sometime later, offering the faintest of bows, his annoying little mouse-tail queue swinging at his neck.

"I see Ying-shek takes his role as master of the Cheng clan quite seriously," he said.

"Did he give you a *white gold?*"

He lifted the corner of an envelope from inside his coat.

"I'm surprised your pockets aren't full of them," I said.

"You think shameful thoughts of me. The only thing I carry is my sincere sadness at your loss, indeed everyone's loss. Your sorrow is mine."

"Your condolences are accepted." I fought back a yawn, but then decided to let it show. "As is your resignation."

"I'm...ah...not sure I heard you."

"Your esteemed service is henceforth no longer required."

He blinked as if to clear dust from his eyes. "Cheng Yat Sou, with all respect, your husband always valued—"

"My husband is no longer in charge." I wondered if he noticed my trembling hands.

"Regretfully true," he said. "In the meantime, my loyalty remains with the Red Flag Fleet."

"You may take your loyalty elsewhere, along with your clothing and other possessions. You are no longer employed by this fleet."

"By whose authority? If a successor to Cheng Yat was appointed, no one has told me."

"I thought you're a man of faith. Until a higher power decrees otherwise, the authority is mine."

We faced each other across the room. His round head reminded me of a tea pot coming to a boil. That smug indifference hadn't changed since the first day I'd seen him. Even after all these years, to him I had never ceased to be the outsider, the intruder, the conniving upstart. And to me, he had never stopped being the common crow among eagles.

"With respect, I refuse to accept the rash remarks of a grief-stricken widow." He turned his back to me, an insult he would never have inflicted on a man. "My deepest sympathies for your loss, madam. But now I must return to my work. I'm quite busy preparing the books for Commander Cheng's successor, whoever that may be."

I waited until he reached the doorway and spoke to his back, "There are a thousand men in this harbor, any one of whom would slit your throat and chop you into twenty-four pieces if I asked them. Can you say the same for yourself?"

I flung a *white gold* packet. It landed with a rattle at his feet, its meaning unspoken but clear. He already had a mourning envelope for Cheng Yat. This one was for the death of his position with the Confederation of the Flags.

"Please deliver me whatever ledgers are in your possession and vacate this ship—no, this harbor—by sunset."

I retrieved the abandoned white envelope from the empty doorway. I knew then that he would obey. I had asserted power—as *myself*, not as wife or deputy—the power of command, through my own unbridled force of will.

At last, I lay on the sleeping mat with a floating feeling, as if a fist had let go of my heart.

I needed to be left alone to think without hearing that dreadful name from the endless stream of well-wishers: Widow Cheng. Also, I needed medicine. My back was on fire while I wanted to gnaw the bandage from my arm and scratch the itch down to the bone.

Ordering no further visitors that day, I sent men to summon the village herbalist—who normally refused to call on ships—with clear instructions that if he didn't come immediately, they were to abduct him at knife point.

The doctor showed up with a basket of herbs and salves. He sliced off the bandage, rubbed in a chalky ointment which miraculously soothed the itch, and pronounced that I no longer needed a splint. I recognized only half of what he measured into a boiling pot—*dong quai,* ginseng, dried plums, goji berries—along with bark and branches and crumbled stones, and finally a piece of chicken. My stomach tried to reject the resulting, unimaginably foul concoction, but there was no question that it soothed the pain. He left with the promise to deliver a full medicinal course later that day and ordered me to rest. I sighed. As if rest were possible.

When the door later slid aside on its polished track, my tongue recoiled, expecting the herbalist and an even worse tasting brew. Instead, Wu-shek Yi's bulky figure pressed into the room.

"Didn't anyone tell you I'm not taking visitors?" I said.

"They did. I come as a mere courier boy. I believe you were expecting these." He placed a sachet of herbs on the cooking table.

I couldn't look at Wu-shek Yi without blame. If he'd never talked Cheng Yat into ambushing that foreign ship; if he hadn't delayed our departure by six days…

It wouldn't have been difficult to read my thoughts. Wu settled on a stool and struck his chest with two fists. "I loved him like an elder brother."

"Thank you."

The standard condolences issued from his mouth in a higher pitch than usual, which signaled different intentions for his visit. Through the porthole, funeral smoke from the pavilion striped the darkening sky. Birds flew toward the hills. He finished his speech with another fist to the chest.

"Isn't it too soon to start this?" I said.

"Start what?" He was such a bad liar; it was almost comical.

"You know very well," I said. "What everyone I'm sure is talking about behind my back."

"Dear bereaved wife of my beloved friend, you question my integrity! But since you bring it up, well… The question of the leadership, and of course your fate, have crossed my mind once or twice."

"My fate?"

"My dear friend, you're too young to remain a widow."

I laughed in spite of myself. How this fool misread me after all. "Wah! You waste no time! Aren't three wives enough?"

"Ha! Too late! I've a fourth now. And with my brothers' hens always fluttering around, I'm practically married to seven! Anyway, I could never handle you."

"And you never will."

"But somebody else inevitably will, and then—"

"Whoever that unfortunate man turns out to be might compete with you for the Confederation leadership."

Wu's high, raucous laughter echoed from the walls. He hunched forward and wagged a finger at me. "Oh, my dear, dear, dear. I always knew you were smarter than me."

"Oh? I've known it from the moment we met. Please have your say, then leave. I'm tired and have medicine to prepare."

I had obviously disrupted whatever speech he had composed in his head. He looked down nervously at his hands, then up again, his mask of humor pushed aside.

"Fine. Let's be direct about it," he said. "When you add up vessels and men, the three Luichow fleets have the edge over your eastern fleets.

And we have an older, well-established base."

"So, you're proposing Tunghoi Bat to lead the Confederation? How generous of you."

Again, he wagged a finger. "I've been the most loyal and devoted follower of the Chengs since—"

"Cut the storytelling, please. I can guess what you want. Or can I?"

Wu laughed again, but nervous now. I was glad to see him squirm, considering the presumptuous nature of his visit. Still, I also knew him as Cheng Yat's oldest and best friend.

"What could I possibly want from you?" he said. "Only your charm."

"Mister Man-with-four-wives, when have I ever been less than charming toward you?"

"Your enchantments make the moon itself shy away in shame. Perhaps you might be persuaded to apply them on certain other commanders."

I fought the urge to laugh in his face, just to see his expression. "What makes you think I can convince anyone to support you?" *Including me,* I thought.

"Ha! I've never met a woman so expert at making men dance without even realizing there was a tune!" Hands flat on his chest, he leaned forward with a conspiratorial whisper. "I pledge my loyalty to you, Cheng Yat Sou, wife of my benefactor and friend. I'll make sure you're cared for in the most luxurious of—"

"Crazy! Do I look like I need taking care of? Thank you for coming. I need to prepare my herbs."

"Ah-Yang, forgive me, forgive me. We're old friends, nothing changes that, right? I'm just a fatty with a big mouth."

I immediately regretted my outburst. The pot had been pierced; the leadership contest was out in the open. If I wanted to play these men, as he put it, to my own silent tune—once I figured out what that tune was—I had to overcome my exhaustion, transcend the pain, and keep calm in words and demeanor.

I offered a conciliatory hand. "I've had a difficult day. I'll be pleased to discuss the matter another time. You've always been a faithful friend."

"I'm as faithful to you as a dog, Cheng Yat Sou."

"So long as you don't turn into a dog in heat."

His laughter followed him out the doorway. "Aiya! Too bad I have a surplus of wives."

The medicine made me drowsy, robbing me of the chance to think, but it did me good in other ways. For the first time since the typhoon, I slept through the night without waves crashing in my head. In the morning, the pains had subsided. My arm was stiff but functional. I sent for breakfast and strong bo lei tea, and renewed my order for no visitors except the children.

A brisk knock at the door didn't sound like Ying-shek. An older boy, son of one of my helmsmen, stood rigidly at attention, trying to appear older than his twelve or thirteen years.

"A thousand pardons, Cheng Yat Sou. Commander Kwok asks if you're well enough to see him."

I must have looked like a savage, arm greased with salve and tangled hair in my face. Did I want to see Kwok Podai? After so many days of confinement and illness and ritual, the voice inside me screamed no— it was inappropriate, I needed to think things over first. Still another voice, from below, hungered for his charm and wit. I told the boy I'd receive him in the first watch after midday.

I latched the door and flung open my clothing chest. For one moment, I caressed my favorite red quilted robe. Absolutely unsuitable for a grieving widow, or a woman who, I presumed, was about to be put upon with questions about the leadership. I settled on sober black trousers and a businesslike knee-length black woolen tunic. I spent the rest of the morning in front of my copper mirror, pinching life into my cheeks and rubbing ointments into creases and shadows. Who was I fooling? The woman staring from the mirror could no longer pretend to be a pretty young girl; thirty-three years was nothing less than ancient. We were meeting to talk business, I reminded myself. After setting my hair with sandalwood combs, I added a garnet hairpin—a single spot of red for the Red Flag Fleet.

We met on deck in a light drizzle. Up close, he too had aged. His neck had thickened, the lines on his face reminded me of seasoned wood grains. But that look he gave me came from the same eyes engraved in my memory, the same subtle swell at the ends of his lips, his strong brow tilted as though poised to scoop me up. He arrived without a jacket, making a show of defying the weather. He had a parcel tucked under one arm.

I led him to a canopied shelter beside the deckhouse. "You've been avoiding me, and now you ask permission to see me. That isn't like you."

361

"I heard you weren't well. But you look—"

"Like an old bent-over widow with pains in my back."

"Cheng-tai, even in mourning dress, you're quite entrancing, such that fish—"

"Might drown themselves upon seeing my reflection. I know the tale."

"Indeed." He handed me the parcel. Its size and weight made me think of a human skull. My fingers trembled as I removed the wrapping. Cradled in padding sat a lacquered black drum with red stripes, crowned with taut, creamy pigskin.

"For you, the living reincarnation of Leung Hung-yuk, the great woman warrior." Two crewmen walked past, too obviously curious to overhear. "Might we go inside?" Kwok said. "I have a private matter to discuss."

I tapped the drum, my fingernails making a light, pleasant sound. "What sort of matter requires being alone in my cabin?"

"A private business matter."

The cabin was dark despite the time of day. I pointedly left the main door open, set the drum on the floor, and refilled the lamp. "I predict that your gift is accompanied by a poem."

I wanted a poem. Before we discussed anything else—memories, Cheng Yat, leadership—what I wanted was a poem.

"A legend, I'm afraid. But I think you'll appreciate the allegory. Leung Hung-yuk was a Song Dynasty...shall we say..." His pause filled in the rest.

"Let me guess—a whore?"

"Your crudeness is charming. I would have said entertainer, but, well...among her various talents, she was a songstress and drummer who caught the attention of a young soldier named Hon Sai-chung. He swore to marry her once he gained a respectable rank, and when he at last earned the title of General, he kept his vow. She accompanied him on military adventures and became known as a rather lion-hearted woman."

"Finally, the story gets interesting."

"She proved her worth at the battle of Wong Tin Lake. The Song Emperor sent Hon to defend the province from the rival state of Jin. Hon arrived at the lake with eight thousand weary soldiers who discovered themselves up against the enemy's one hundred thousand troops and an entire fleet of warships."

"And then his lion-hearted wife fought them single-handed and the empire was saved," I said.

Kwok laughed. "You're not far from the truth. Madam Leung suggested a cunning plan. She carried her drum to a vantage on top of nearby Gold Mountain from which she could see the entire surroundings. Her husband General Hon sent his men to hide in the reeds while he launched a small flotilla onto the lake. She pounded her drum once."

Kwok struck the drum. *Boom!*

"This was the signal they had arranged to indicate that his boats should advance. Then when enemy ships left the shore, she banged the drum again, this time in double beats."

Boom boom!

"Which was the signal to pull back. The Jin navy thought the Han boats were retreating and pursued them toward the southern shore. Once Madam Leung saw that the enemy had been lured into position, she signaled once more, with triple beats..."

He slid the drum to me. The game he was playing was so transparent; let him play it alone.

He took the hint.

Boom boom boom!

"Hon's men rose from the reeds and rained flaming arrows onto the Jin ships, raising an inferno as high as the sky. Up on the mountain, Leung Hung-yuk drummed up a frenzy, stirring heaven and earth and the hearts of their forces while striking terror in the bowels of the panicking Jin, who were slaughtered to the last man. Hon Sai-chung achieved a stunning victory thanks to the ingenious strategy of his wife."

"And then?" I said.

"That's the end of the story."

"I want to know what happened next."

He shrugged. "The Song Dynasty was saved."

"What was her reward? Did her husband die before her?"

Kwok laughed, "Ah-Yang, your ambition is showing."

His familiarity grated. The story had been amusing, its intention too obvious. I pushed the drum away. "You had a business proposal."

"Business, yes. And a proposal."

I sensed movement outside the door. A sailor padded past on the companionway, whistling softly. I waited until I heard his steps climb to the poop deck. "I suppose this proposal involves you as Confederation leader."

"What do you mean?"

"I'm simply finishing your story for you. I'm getting tired and feeling chilled." Reaching into the clothing chest for a shawl, I tried not to let him see my displeasure. Whatever irresponsible notions I'd entertained earlier had evaporated during his transparent little performance. I was no longer a girl easily enchanted by stories.

"That wasn't my meaning at all," he said.

"I'm sorry. You come in here with a story of a woman helping a man gain power. I've done that once already. Unless your tale has a new ending?"

"You haven't heard my proposal. I regard you quite differently, Yang."

"Do you? As what, your advocate? I won't bang a drum to rally the others to your support. Wait until Tunghoi Bat arrives, and we can—"

"Will you give me a chance to answer your questions?"

His angry outburst stunned me and at the same time, pleased me for having cracked through his smooth facade.

"I've never met a woman like you, Shek Yang. You fear nothing. You think nearly like a man. Yet you have the softness of a woman." His hand slid from his lap. I wanted to slap it away, slap his face, but my hands were smarter and stayed still. "As for my proposal—"

Only then did I slide out of his reach. "I'm in mourning, you may have noticed. And I'm not interested in being anyone's concubine."

"I would be offended at your accusation, but it's precisely your frank honesty that draws me to you."

In his face I recognized the madness of desire. The fool. The beautiful, arrogant fool.

"Thank you. Change the subject." I said. "You told me you have a private business matter. I hope it has something to do with your proposal."

He nodded. "My business proposal."

"Then get straight to the point. Why do men take so long to say what they mean?"

"The point is...the Red and the Black are big, powerful fleets. Imagine if we were one. We would be unconquerable! There would be none of this..." he swept his arm through the air "...jockeying for power. The triads, the navy, corrupt ministers, no one could lift a hand against us."

"With you as Confederation leader."

His back snapped straight. "What do you mean?"

"I'm simply helping you reach your point. It's getting late. Every man in Tung Chung thinks it's his turn to be leader of this or commander of that, and they all seem to consider me as having the power of influence. And, by the way, our fleets are already linked through the Confederation. So, I don't see the need—"

"May I make my own point, please? I mean a total merger," he said. "Of Red and Black. Yes, I know your next question. A joint command, of myself and you, as equals...and, yes, best cemented through marriage."

Finally, that word.

He continued: "Before you say anything, I know what you're thinking. Wong-yan becomes Second Wife, you will be First. I've always held feelings for you, Yang. Please consider that."

Though I'd anticipated his move, its brazenness stunned me. Nevertheless, there was logic to his proposition: marriage as a business arrangement. It was the easiest solution to my current situation—and more. I couldn't deny the attractiveness of his intellect, his stories, and of course the man. Kwok was unquestionably handsome, carrying himself like a leopard. A warrior who loved poetry. Was my chest pounding right now with desire for him or merely for the idea of partnership in power? If I were to even flirt with the thought of remarriage, Kwok was the man least likely to shunt me aside into a weak little wifely role— hadn't he just said so with his story? Something, though, some tiny feather tickling the back of my skull, asked questions and demanded answers. Was his proposal just a ploy to crawl into my bed? To steal my fleet? Or both?

His hand moved as though to embrace me, then changed its mind on its own, his face giving away everything. He was transparent in his affection as much as he was in his ambitions. I couldn't tell which was the stronger.

We both knew the whole notion was preposterous. A widow was the property of her husband's family and could never remarry without their approval. No Cheng cousin would condone a union between myself and Kwok Podai, essentially ceding half the control over the Red Flag Fleet. Without their consent, not a single member of the boat community would accept it.

"You're thinking about it," he said.

My face burned. If I gave an answer now, it might be the wrong one.

I tapped the drum twice: retreat.

He smiled at the reference.

"Thank you for the gift," I said.

The four-times-seventh day since Cheng Yat's passing. The ritual service was short, but the rumors went on and on.

Everyone, in every wine shop, around every gambling table, had a suggestion about who Cheng Yat would have appointed as successor. No one asked me, the pitiful widow with no say in the matter. Little did they realize that I alone knew the secret of Cheng Yat's thoughts on the matter: that he had been a fit forty-two and "invincible", safeguarded by the gods. He'd never given a moment's consideration to who might succeed him one day.

Just in case I wasn't filled to the eyes with scandals, Ah-Yi happily blessed me with more. She arrived with a basket of snacks and fresh hearsay: a naval squadron was sighted west of O Moon.

"How many junks?" I asked.

"They say twenty or more." She poured red melon seeds into a bowl.

"Who is *they*? Who saw them?"

"Somebody saw them," she cackled. "That's all we know. Hee! *Somebody.*"

"Probably just fishing junks. We'll have to send a patrol to check."

I cracked a melon seed between my teeth. It felt almost obscene to indulge even such minor pleasure at a time like this. Ah-Yi unfolded a half-finished vest and settled down to sew.

"What do you think, Ah-Yi? Convene a conference already, or keep waiting?" I was, of course, referring to Tunghoi Bat, whose failure to come to Tung Chung to honor Cheng Yat was raising suspicions even in me.

"Hee! First time you ever asked my advice. What do I think? I'll tell you. You should think less and sleep more. And you haven't been eating. Just look at your hair. So thin!" She tossed back her head and laughed. "See? You're still a woman. Husband gone, men plotting right and left, navy attacking, but when I mention your hair—" She mimicked my mouth dropping open. I laughed, despite everything else in the world.

Ah-Yi turned suddenly serious. "A lot of men have eyes on you, more than you know. Some for your unfairly pretty face, and some because they think power lies in your bed. Ha, of course I know! And a few would be happy to see your throat slit. I don't know which is the most dangerous, and I guess neither do you. That, my precious, is what I think. Now, pass me that ball of thread."

Cold winds and colder rain pellets heralded the five-times-seventh day ceremony. Even the monks seemed happy to hurry through ritual prayers.

Like Ah-Yi said, I was popular among the men. Wu-shek Yi invited me to a meal. Son of a Frog and General Bo each inquired more than once about my health. Only Kwok Podai kept his words to a minimum. What remained between us best remained unsaid.

More ships than I'd ever seen in one place filled Tung Chung harbor, including several from neighboring Fukien, all here to honor Cheng Yat. But still not a single ship of the Yellow Flag Fleet. What upset me more was Cheung Po Tsai's continued absence: Cheng Yat's adopted son, and my...I had trouble defining his relationship to me.

I had no time for such concerns. Only fourteen days until the end of official mourning. If no leader was decided by then, the Confederation might crumble. It was time to put things into motion, with or without its eleven-fingered second most powerful commander.

I invited the eldest surviving Cheng kinsmen for a private memorial in my cabin. Cheng Yat's nephew Cheng Bo-yeung and Cheng On-pong, son of Cheng Chat by a previous wife, were different heights and only distantly related to one another, yet they shared the characteristic Cheng jutting brows and generous lips. Both had distinguished themselves as captains more through family name than by crafty leadership.

Though between them in age, I welcomed each formally as an elder would. "Fraternal Nephew and Younger Cousin, your loyalty and respect were a constant source of strength to Cheng Yat. I assume that your allegiance remains undiminished even in death."

There was something almost deliberately false about their bows; to them, I was still the outsider. "Eternal loyalty," said cousin On-pong.

Bo-yeung made his attitude clear: "Younger Sister—"

"You may call me Paternal Aunt."

"Aunt, may I ask if this little gathering has to do with the Red Fleet command?"

"It might, yes."

Bo-yeung, the elder of the two, appeared to be their spokesman.

"We've discussed this between ourselves, and of course we welcome your comment."

"And I value your thoughts on the matter."

On-pong cleared his throat, glanced at his cousin, and continued, "The Red Flag has over three hundred ships. If we divide them between us—"

"Wait! What are you saying?" I asked.

"If we split the fleet—"

"I would rather die!" I could barely contain my outrage. No wonder Cheng Yat had given neither of these...boys...more than a few ships to command. "You think a fleet can simply break in half like a worm?"

"The Red Flag is already many times larger than other fleets—"

"Because your uncle and paternal cousin built it that way! You would dismantle his life's work? How dare you even speak such words!"

Bo-yeung puffed out his chest. "Aunt, permit us to finish. Of course, we prefer to keep the fleet together. When On-pong's father Cheng Chat left this life, the command passed to my paternal uncle Cheng Yat. No one doubted his right to the succession. But the question of who takes over now is not so straightforward. I am Cheng Yat's rightful heir, and On-pong is Cheng Chat's."

On-pong broke in: "That's why we've agreed that one of us assumes command of the Red Flag Fleet and the other leads the Confederation as Dai Lo Ban."

"You've been discussing such a thing without consulting me?" I said.

"Out of respect to Cheng Yat's widow, we're prepared to accept your decision as to which of us assumes which role." Bo-yeung bowed to me, the falseness of his respect rising like fumes from his back.

An unthinkable proposal! And a dangerous one. These hulking creatures with more muscles than brain imagined themselves to be leaders simply because the men who fucked their mothers were surnamed Cheng? I was so very tired from all the rituals, the rumors and scheming, the pain in my back and the night terrors. And now these foolish men presented me with this.

"What if I choose someone else?" I said.

Bo-yeung was indignant. "What was Cheng Yat but the son of Chat's father's brother? Am I not the same in relation to him? With due respect, you don't make decisions except those I put to you."

"Cheng Chat was the first to unite us. I am his sole surviving son," On-pong said. "For two hundred years, this has been the Cheng family fleet!"

"My name is Cheng, too!" My fist banged the floor. "I built this fleet! With my husband, a true man! He made us powerful, but I made us rich! As long as I'm alive, I represent the will of Cheng Yat. It is *my* responsibility to choose the next leader for the Red Flag Fleet! It's *your* responsibility to offer me absolute deference."

They sat like mirrored images beside each other, hands on thighs, elbows out like wings. "Honored *Daai Neung,*" Bo-yeung lingered on the formal address for a father's brother's wife. "You twist our words. We mean no disrespect. But the positions must remain in the family."

"Honored Fraternal Nephew, honored Younger Cousin," I said. "You know how to sail, and you know how to fight. But leadership, like wealth, needs to be earned. And I determine who earned it."

"And we decide whether to accept your determination or to split the fleet."

"If either of you ever farts another word about splitting the Red Flag Fleet, I will rip you apart."

My words bounced off their backs as they left the cabin, undismissed.

Once I would have considered it a superstitious waste of time to visit a funeral pavilion every day for a month. But the daily ritual made the end feel slower in coming, that day when the Widow Cheng would be ready for disposal, a withered stump to uproot and shunt aside. Praying also gave me time to calmly think. The storm had finally receded from my dreams, replaced by long stretches lying awake while my mind turned, debated, planned, composed speeches. Here, by day, chanting brought orderliness to my thoughts, freed from the turbulence of solitude.

The boys came with me this day. Hung-shek was content to sit on a mat, though where he got hold of a prayer candle I couldn't tell, and I had to pry it from his mouth. Ying-shek planted incense sticks with the solemnity of a little priest, until he became bored and wandered to the edge of the platform.

"Ma! Look!"

I counted more than twenty-five junks entering the bay, all flying yellow pennants. Tunghoi Bat's lead ship sailed at the point, every line of rigging decked with multiple banners of blue,

369

green, white, black, and red.

"I think we know who assumes they're already in command," I said.

"Where's *Suk-suk?*" Ying-shek said. *Uncle* meant Cheung Po Tsai.

"I wish I knew."

More and more Yellow Flag ships turned into the bay as if they were invading.

Ying-shek protested when I sent him and his brother off with the nanny, but I knew he was eager. I'd promised candies in the village, and Ah-Ping was always more lenient than me about extra portions. I told the priests to bring more candles and sacrificial wine.

I was praying and chanting, surrounded by monks, when a white-robed figure knelt beside me. He placed incense into urns, kowtowed three times, his sword sheath bumping the floor with each bow. I drew out my chant until even the priest lost patience and tapped his bell. I sat with eyes closed in feigned meditation while the man beside me breathed louder, cleared his throat, muttered a hasty prayer, then sat still. His impatience was audible.

I looked at him sideways without turning my head. Tunghoi Bat offered me the slightest, most stingy of bows. My eyelids dipped in reply, then I returned to my prayers.

When I sat up, he was gone.

Wu-shek Yi tried to lighten the mood at Tunghoi Bat's welcome banquet with a string of bawdy jokes. The guest of honor smiled and drank, saying little, his stony-faced wife beside him. Other than the usual florid condolences, neither offered me a word.

I was so tired I could scarcely sit up. All afternoon I hadn't let myself rest, entertaining well-wishers and, more importantly, informants relaying rumors of plots and meetings I wasn't supposed to know about.

Dishes were cleared, plum liquor poured. Tunghoi Bat rapped the table for attention. "Time to lay chariots and horses on the game board. We're all one family. Sometimes we argue. Sometimes we compete. But we're inseparable as brothers." He paused for the few grunts of affirmation. "When a family becomes leaderless, the number one brother must prepare to take charge."

"Thank you, Eleven Fingers," said General Bo. "As the eldest among us, I accept your endorsement!"

"Too late. As the number one fattest among us, *I* accept his endorsement," Wu-shek Yi said.

Tunghoi Bat didn't take the jokes. "I'm speaking about the one among us who has served longest."

General Bo tapped his chest. "I worked Annam since the first campaign, longer than any of you. That makes me senior on all counts!"

"We all served in both campaigns," said Kwok Podai, "except our 'brother' from Tunghoi."

"Exactly!" Bat's six-fingered hand dangled in the air like a spider. "I'm not talking about serving foreign kings, but about the business of this Confederation. While the rest of you were playing soldier, I kept business going here at home. That makes me the most senior in this line of work."

"Ha! Some argument!" General Bo said. "If he thinks we had it easy, he was never in Qui Nhon!"

"Or Thi Nai," said Wu-shek Yi. "Some fight!"

"A massacre!" said Son of a Frog.

And then, as always happened, they fell into the same old talk about the glory days in Vietnam. The ships were bigger, enemies taller, cannons louder. Crushing defeats were recast as victories.

I had nothing to add until Wu decided I was being ignored. "Let's not forget what brings us together, to honor this woman's great husband. May she be well taken care of by us all!"

Taken care of. An old chicken shrunken and beyond use. If only they could have seen what was in my head. My fury would have dwarfed their battle stories.

"Thank you. I'm strong enough to take care of myself," I said. I raised a bowl in toast to me.

XXXVI
Po

At last, on the six-times-seventh day, the fortune tellers declared
Cheng Yat released from the Courts of Hell.

There was no such release for me. In the past two days alone,
besides the never-ending influx of condolence leavers, gossip mongers,
and pursers bearing accounts, Kwok had called twice to remind me of
his proposal, Wu came to repeat that I would be "well taken care of",
and Son of a Frog and General Bo—and a host of other captains—had
paid their respects. I was almost grateful that Tunghoi Bat kept his
distance. They called me strong, all those men, then they expected me
to hand that strength to them. But today, I felt no power at all. I was
tired, my back pain had flared. With seven days left until the end of
mourning, when I would be officially classified as a widow, my mind
was a battleground of conflicting schemes and notions.

The head priest led me through a private ceremony, witnessed only
by a few clergy and professional mourners. A white-clad apparition
kindled incense at a side altar until the rituals finished. Then he
knocked back his white hood, and Cheung Po Tsai smiled at me
with hands raised in prayer. This was how he announced himself after
forty days' absence? I rushed through the final chant and left the platform.

Stones and shells in the sand poked my feet but didn't slow my
stride while he called me from behind. He caught up with me as I
crossed a stream dividing the beach. I spun around and backhanded Po
across the face.

"Where have you been, you bastard? You missed the funeral. His
adopted son! You know what people are saying?" My throat felt raw; it
hurt to breathe.

His cocky reply infuriated me more. "Tell them I was with San Po."

What did an obscure goddess have to do with anything?

"You should have been here, showing respect!"

"He would have wanted her blessing," Po said.

I remembered Cheng Yat once stopping at a temple to San Po, Tin Hau's youngest sister, on an island somewhere, but he had never mentioned her again.

"Aiya! I'm tired of hearing what he would have wanted!"

I limped up the rocky stream bank, then stopped to catch my breath. My back ached, head pounded, and feet hurt.

"Where did you really go?" I said.

"I told you. The San Po island temple."

He removed his mourning cloak and placed it around my shoulders. I must have been shivering.

"He and I went there once, said his father used to bring him," Po said. "I gave him the full rites for the dead."

"Forty days?"

"Nine, ten days, maybe longer, I think. Sometimes I worshiped all night and slept all day. Sometimes I forgot where I was."

"Why didn't you come back?" I said.

"Taking care of business. Someone had to."

Everything around me went into a spin, as if Cheng Yat's spirit had launched itself from the edge of the world, setting it turning—his soul released, like the priests promised. Po Tsai was speaking, but I caught only snippets of words.

"...you all sitting here jawing...O Moon, Crow Island, Ji-nai, I was everywhere...chewing out triad bosses, agents...no holiday from payments. I know you're tired of hearing it, but I think he would have wanted me to do it."

Clouds chased past my eyes while he talked, as if the storm had returned, not in my dreams, but in full waking horror.

I managed to choke out words: "Bring me to the—"

My foot slipped on slick stone. Pain ripped through my spine. The spinning ended.

I came awake bathed in an oil lamp's warm glow and the familiar fresh wood smell of my cabin. A pair of arms wrapped me from behind—one draped over my waist, the other supporting my neck on a cushion of muscle.

Po Tsai's breath tickled the base of my skull. He stirred a little, his tunic's smooth silk whispering across the stiffer fabric of my robe.

My first thought was to pull away.

My second thought was that I was too tired to.

I was so very tired. Tired of the rituals, tired of entertaining gods and spirits and priests. I was tired of the coming and going of visitors and pursers and ambitious men, of combing with all ten fingers and all ten toes through every new rumor and every plot. I was eager neither for the coming leadership contest, nor for putting it off any longer. I was ready. Or would be if I could only get some rest.

And so, I settled into Po's embrace. My body softened like it hadn't in half a lifetime while I willed my mind to follow and flush itself free of thoughts. His chest pressed into my back with every breath, air from his lungs spilled over my neck. I felt wistfully at ease lying in his arms, like—what? A brother? A friend? What did one call the only man among all of them who wanted nothing from me, with whom I shared a common bond through Cheng Yat, with whom I could speak my mind without measured words?

I eased back against him and held the hand that dangled over my belly. I felt myself drifting back into sleep.

"Do you miss him?"

I thought the words were enclosed in a dream until they sunk through my ear into my brain.

"I miss him," I said softly, in case it had been a dream.

"I also miss him," he whispered back. "In most of my heart."

"But not all?"

"What about you?"

"I asked about you," I said.

We lay quietly, not facing each other. I felt his breath quicken. I knew what Cheng Yat had done to his father, that Po had been as much a hostage as I had been, until we'd both given in for our own separate reasons.

"That other part of my heart is where I made my own freedom. That's the part you saw," Po said.

"When do I see the rest?"

"You've seen that too. Many times. Today. The dutiful son."

Now it was my breath that rushed. I slid out of his hold and lay on my back, watching the lamplight dance on the ceiling.

"How do you create your own freedom?"

Po raised himself on his elbow and supported his head in his hand. "What kind of question is that? Isn't that what you've been doing since the instant you were dragged aboard?"

"I did a poor job of it, don't you think? I'm still here while men argue over my fate."

"Ah-Yang, you don't know yourself. You're always fighting, that's why. Fighting the world, fighting people, fighting yourself. You listen only to your own voice, never pay attention to those other voices inside you—remember your 'woman's sense'? Remember when it might have saved us all?"

Whether intended or not, he left the thought dangling in the dark: *If I'd listened to that sense—that voice—if I'd insisted...oh, if only I'd insisted! I might have saved Cheng Yat, and everyone else aboard those poor, doomed ships.*

Still, I couldn't accept such intuitions as spirits or gods or ghosts talking. The voice that I was fighting was my own. It was speaking now, loud inside my head. What was it saying? What was I fighting?

It told me to stay right here and lie in Cheng Po Tsai's arms.

I turned on my side. This time. I faced him.

"Hold me," I whispered.

I would make my own freedom starting tomorrow.

XXXVII
Three Visits

W u-shek Yi accepted my invitation to a private midday meal, stuffing himself on steamed chicken and bamboo shoots. We talked of the weather and seasonal trade until I set down my chopsticks and said, "What do you think of Eleven Fingers's little performance? He seems rather convinced of his indisputable authority."

"Ha! He'll have to do a lot more convincing. Everyone knows Cheng Yat would never have wanted him as successor."

"Everyone should stop guessing who or what my husband might have wanted. May I get you tea?"

"He never mentioned names? You can tell me; I'm your loyal friend."

I rinsed both cups with a splash, then poured. Wu's vows of loyalty stemmed from something, and it wasn't simply honor. No man in the world I lived in pledged allegiance to another unless they had something to gain or had racked up debt.

"Cheng is the only name that counts, isn't it?" I said.

"I can only think of Cheng Bo-yeung and Cheng On-pong—Aiya! You're not saying..."

"They're the eldest male kin. One of them by rights—"

"Now I know you've gone mad. There's a reason Cheng Yat never gave either of those wooden heads a squadron. Wah! If only we could get rid of them. You would make a better commander than either of those nitwits!"

"Now you're being ridiculous."

He wagged his finger at me. "Ah, ah, ah, you cunning girl. I'll bet that's why you invited me here. Commander Shek Yang! For such scandalous talk, I require wine!"

I uncovered a jug hidden in the corner and filled his cup with golden liquid.

"Shame on you," I said. "I blame you for putting such ideas into my head."

"Ah-Yang, let's stop pretending. You're clever, but a flimsy liar. I promised you days ago that you would be well taken care of, but you bristled at the suggestion, like I was trying to rope a wild horse. You think I don't know? Tell me what you want from me."

"To begin with, I want to know your chances of becoming Dai Lo Ban. Do you really think Eleven Fingers would put aside his ambitions?"

"He and I are old friends, but maybe not good friends."

"And Kwok Podai? Would he support you?"

"You can answer that question better than me," he said. "Don't look at me that way. It's common knowledge that you and he are plotting something."

"My dear friend, how much more knowledge do you have about me that I don't know about myself? More to drink?"

I changed the subject to other fleet leaders, meanwhile refilling his cup until he'd had just enough wine to keep most but not all his senses. When his face turned persimmon red, I replaced the stopper and pushed the jug aside.

"How would you do it?" I said.

"What are we talking about?"

"Before. You mentioned getting rid of the Cheng cousins."

He stared into his empty cup. "Cheng Chat's own son? If I said such a thing, then please slit my throat."

"My fat friend, you and I can help one another." I raised his chin with my finger until we each looked straight in the other's eyes. "You described your loyalty to me, remember? Like a dog, you said."

"I—"

"And dogs kill rats to protect the master."

His face stretched as if he'd been splashed with cold water. "Ha, you know me. Always joking. Can't keep my blabbermouth shut."

"Some jokes are taken seriously. Oh, look, there's still wine left."

I spent the afternoon shuttered inside the cabin with a trusted scribe, flipping backward and forward through stacks of ledgers, trying to decipher the former purser's cryptic handwriting, while the young man transcribed my comments with his brush. I scolded myself for never having learned to write more than a few words, for who could trust anyone in this society, in these times? My important plans and ideas for the conference remained securely inside my head.

My thoughts were scattered by a loud rap at the door. Fortunately, it was Ah-Yi. I'd have bitten the head off anyone else.

"Don't look now, but here comes Mister Good Old Days," she said.

"Who?"

"General Bo is who."

"I told everyone: no visitors. Signal him to turn around."

"Too late. The old dog's already out there spitting on our nice clean deck."

I dismissed the scribe, stacked the ledgers in the corner, checked my hair, and changed my coat before descending to the deck with a sculpted-on smile.

"Fine looking ship you have here," General Bo announced. "Very fine. You wouldn't happen to have a drink to warm these old bones."

I ordered heated wine and tea brought to the canopied shelter beside the deckhouse. General Bo glanced up at the cabin, clearly expecting to be received there.

"Child's sleeping," I told him in a loud whisper.

We sipped our drinks while he doled out more compliments about my flagship. Then he cleared his throat and wiped the ever-present saliva from his lip. "Eleven Fingers and I were talking last night. About the leadership."

"I see. As has everyone, apparently."

"Yes, well..." He gulped wine and swished it in his mouth, then continued: "Just trying to clear up some speculation."

"There's a lot of that going around. What is it you came here to ask?"

"Everyone wants to know—about the Red Fleet—which of the Cheng boys—"

"You know, I would rather talk of something else. Anything else." Which was true. If Tunghoi Bat thought he could pry information through this wheezing old man, then he was a fool on two counts. Here was a chance to reverse places. "Tell me one of your stories. You tell them so well."

Who said I was a poor liar? The old sea captain took my bait. I peeled a pomelo while he resurrected an incident from the first Annam campaign, before my time, when he'd captured what he'd thought was a salt barge but turned out to be full of ammunition. I laughed along and poured him a generous cup of wine.

I asked him, "During your time in Annam, I wonder whether you encountered General Xuan Bui Thi?"

He nodded. "The woman with the elephants. Remarkable general, absolutely fearless. I could tell you some stories…"

"So, you think a woman can be as great a general as a man."

"Ha ha! Don't think I haven't suspected your ambition, Cheng Yat Sou."

"Then you're cleverer than I am, old uncle. I haven't any ambitions to speak of."

The junk bobbed through a swell. We both looked to the side by instinct, checking sea and sky. Cheng Yat once told me that a swell is a messenger from the past, the vestige of weather that had already happened somewhere else. General Bo himself was like a sea swell: a once-vigorous commander of navies whose time had passed, reduced now to fewer than thirty vessels; one could barely call that a fleet.

"I sometimes wonder if too much ambition can lead to loss of control," I continued. "Take for example the Red Flag Fleet. More than three hundred ships. Almost too unwieldy for one commander, don't you think?"

"It is a large number."

I plucked seeds from a juicy pomelo section. "I would think that whoever leads the Confederation might wish to balance the numbers. For example, the Red Flag Fleet could afford to divest a few ships. That is, if another fleet would accept the burden."

"Yes, I had a similar notion," he said. "Of course, it would depend on which fleet might benefit from such a transfer."

"I was thinking that the White Flag Fleet has the capacity for a few more."

He rocked back and forth, pretending to give it thought. I recognized the look of a whore negotiating with a customer. "Perhaps, perhaps. It would depend on how many."

"I was thinking that trimming, oh…maybe twelve junks and their crews would be a good start."

General Bo's face split into a wet, gap-toothed grin. "I could take on twice that many."

We rolled through another swell, gentler than the last. An egret dove into the bay, emerging moments later, clutching a fish in its beak. I said, "Fifteen three-masters with full crews, and another ten after the conference, when we…ah…see which direction everyone sails. There may even be a rather large eat-water junk in the repair yard which doesn't yet have a crew."

"I'm certain I could find men for that."

"Our little secret."

"Our little secret indeed." He drained his wine cup and set it down with a thump. "Madam Elephant."

I was back with my ledgers and my thoughts for the conference—quotas, shares, new names, new rationales, new titles—one idea stacked on top of another. The slightest interruption would send everything toppling, like a child's house of sticks. Which is exactly what happened when excited voices erupted outside the door.

"No visitors! Cheng Yat Sou's orders!"

"Stop! We told you: no one allowed inside!"

"She'll allow me."

That voice.

Po's voice.

I scrambled to the door. It was the night of the moonless tide. I could barely make him out, standing in the doorway dressed all in black—even a black turban—against the dark sky.

"Come in. I'll make tea," I said.

"I'm not staying."

"Where are you going?"

"With you. Come. Something to show you."

"I couldn't! Tomorrow is—I'm right in the middle of—ah, wait, is something wrong?"

"Nothing's wrong. Come, come. I want you to see." He extended a hand, his teeth glowed in the dark, his little boy's grin.

My mind had been turning all day like a spin toy, and I was spent. "Make it fast," I said.

He took me out in a *siu chat pan,* which reminded me, not unpleasantly, of a Kwangchow sing-song girl boat, its matted cowling long enough for two people to conduct themselves in private. The perfect vehicle for a serene night time excursion. Except that this time, the man did the singing.

The night was still and black, almost liquid. Stars burned holes in the moonless sky. The water was as smooth as a lake. Po Tsai sang his old, interminable song about the seasons in a voice as clear, if lower pitched, as the first time I'd heard it from that cheeky young boy on the mast top. I waited for him to sing it all through to the final verse:

> *Winter-stored wine is drunk happily,*
> *Everyone showing what he can do.*

Only then did I interrupt his show. "Where are you taking me?"

He set down the yuloh and anchored us with a stone at the end of a rope. "Here is as good as any. Quiet now. Watch."

Leaning over the gunwale, Po pounded the hull with a block of wood. Either side of us the surface exploded with tiny leaping fish, lines of them fanning out into the night. A few landed in the boat. Po dangled one in my face with a laugh before tossing it back home.

"This is what you brought me way out here to see?" I said.

"Ha! Yes."

"This was more important than the presentation I've been working on all day?"

"Yes!"

"Dancing fish?" As if I'd hadn't seen such a thing ten thousand times.

"So many tonight!"

I had to admit, I'd rarely seen such multitudes, though I'd never had the leisure to drift around Tung Chung Bay, by day or night.

"Is there...ah...some message you're trying to show me? I fail to see—"

"No message, Ah-Yang. Maybe *that's* the message. Nothing to think about: no ledgers or pursers, no one to pound the door demanding attention. Just fish and stars."

"And you."

"You can ignore me if you want."

His timing had been right. I'd needed the diversion. The air was refreshing, his humor contagious. "This has been nice. I think we should go back now."

"Haven't you worked hard enough? Yang, look at you, tense as a claw. You can't just plan and think and plan some more and believe that makes you prepared. Clear your mind and spirit first, then you can face the world."

We sat in silence, watching the lamps in the village extinguish one by one. I took his wood block and slapped the hull. New legions of fish burst from the water. There was no message in their movements, just their natural response to fear, a brief flash of beauty in the world. But not even this could stop my thoughts popping in every direction, just like those fish.

"All right, just help me lay this one to rest," I said. "How to approach Tunghoi Bat? Better to tease him into saying something he can't back down from, or to come on strong? What do you think?"

"Aiya! You're not listening to me! I don't know how words work. I only know that if you feed chickens too much grain, they blow up and die. That's you right now, gorging on thoughts."

The boat creaked. A chilly breeze swept over us. Po reached into the canopy and placed a cape or a blanket over my shoulders, then another on himself, leaving only his face visible, a crooked smile lit by reflections in the water.

"See? Maybe I don't think so much, but still I'm always right," he said.

"Oh, you!" I swatted him with a corner of my blanket.

I raised the blanket for another playful blow. He grabbed my hand and held it, pressing my fingers into the warm softness of his palm through three slow rocks of the boat. His pulse throbbed against mine.

He let go. Weariness swept over me like a current. I leaned my head into his chest.

"I'm cold," I said.

"Take you back?"

I planned an early start to the day, arranging the conference area, fortifying myself with strong tea. But the spirit he kept reminding me of, the voice—whatever it was inside me—told me to stay. For once, I listened.

He followed me into the cowled space. I lay on a pile of mats and pulled my blanket around me. Po Tsai offered a short prayer to the shrine in the back, and then lay facing me, though I could hardly see him in the deep shadow.

Was it merely kindness I felt radiating from him or something more, a spirit rising like heat and entwining with my own? I wanted him to touch me.

383

"You hated me," he said.

He caught me off guard. I forced myself to breathe.

"You hated me," he repeated. "I knew it. But I didn't believe it."

"No. I despised my father. I hated all Punti. Hated pirates. In the beginning, I hated Cheng Yat," I said. "What I felt for you wasn't hatred."

"Aiya! All those things I did to make you hate me...years of effort, wasted!"

"I swear that I never hated you."

"And I swear I never believe your lies," Po said. "Did you have a brother or sister?"

As if he'd dug a well into my heart, a flood of sickness and truth gushed out. All my hatred, all my anger, had begun that day my brother was stillborn. If he'd survived, my life would have ridden an entirely different current. My mother may have lived. Ah-Ba wouldn't have drunk himself into gambling away his junk, and I...I wouldn't have been taken away. I poised on the verge of ultimate wealth and power, but maybe I'd have had an easier life if only I'd had a brother.

"Be my brother," I said. Echoes of Cheng Chat's wife: Elder Sister, Younger Sister. But not the same.

"I've always been your brother." Po opened his arms.

I lay awake a long time, wrapped in his embrace and he in mine, until I drifted into light, easy sleep.

XXXVIII
Conference

He dropped me off just after sunrise, by which time a canopy had been raised on the forward deck; a round table was wheeled into place.

After freshening my face and hair, I slipped into a red silk gown and went down to supervise the preparations. Women arranged bowls of jerked meats and fruits; others polished tea cups. A stack of cushions, one in each fleet color, stood to the side. I picked up two, placing red on the forward stool, nearest the bow, yellow to the right—no. Give Bat face, but not too much face—yellow forward or stern? Flanked by blue and green, or did that divide the table between east and west factions? Black beside red—did that suggest the wrong message? Aiya!

Eyes closed, I circled the table with my arms full of cushions, dropping them at random. Let spirits guide me in seating these face-obsessed men.

Son of a Frog arrived first, then old General Bo accompanied by his adopted son. Wu-shek Yi showed up with a brother. Then a long wait for Kwok Podai and Tunghoi Bat.

Their sampans approached at the same time, each gesturing the other to tie alongside first. The standoff might have lasted all day had Kwok not given in and allowed Eleven Fingers the trivial distinction of being received last like a little emperor. Tunghoi Bat's wife stepped aboard before him, wearing a stunning Vietnamese knee-length blue tunic, an unsubtle reminder of her husband's senior role in the first Annam campaign. She hooked my arm like an old friend and presented a slim wooden box.

"Lovely candied limes from Luichow. A little treat for us ladies while the men jabber." Could she have been blunter?

"Thank you," I said, sliding my arm free. "We'll save them for after."

Tunghoi Bat nodded approval at yellow being nearest the bow; the other four sat on the god and spirit sides. General Bo's son, Wu's brother, and Tunghoi Bat's wife were offered observer places beside the gunwale.

Tunghoi Bat nodded to the red seat, which remained vacant at the stern. "It seems we parley with a ghost."

I settled onto the empty cushion. "Thankfully, I'm very much alive."

"Madam, you have our sympathy and tears," Bat said, "but this is a meeting of fleet commanders, not wives or widows."

"Thank you for your benevolence, Tunghoi Uncle," I said, pausing for chuckles at the pun on the name *Bat*. "I was married aboard your ship and bore my eldest son in your harbor. I would think of you as my real *suk-suk,* except that you're too handsome to be my father's brother. But, respected uncle, unless some other officer of my fleet dares to oust me from this stool, you are all to regard my word as that of the Red Flag Fleet."

"By rights, that word belongs to Cheng Chat's son," Bat said.

"That is for the Red Flag Fleet and none other to decide. Furthermore—good men, let me finish!—until a replacement is decided by this council, the Confederation command also resides in this seat."

Everyone spoke at once, all except Bat who fixed me with a glare, until Kwok Podai struck the table for silence.

"I believe Cheng Yat Sou initiated this conference," he said. "We all acknowledge that she was the brains behind many of Cheng Yat's—"

"Brains or tits, who cares?" Tunghoi Bat said. "Someone who's never captained a ship, never conducted a battle, never led a raid on sea or land, expects to lord over those who have? What has she commanded other than a captain's bed?"

I was saved from a rash response I might have regretted by a sudden commotion at the opposite rail. Bat might even have planned it. Cheng On-pong had one foot in his boat, the other over my gunwale, shouting at the men who blocked him, "Let me aboard! I represent the Red Flag Fleet!"

I stepped away and called over my chief helmsman.

"Tell him nothing has been decided about the Red leadership and that this show of temperament will weigh against him when the time comes. If he still doesn't leave, lock him below where I won't hear him."

Back at the conference table, I forged a smile.

Wu-shek Yi slapped his thigh. "If she wants to play commander for a day, why not? Better a pretty plum than an ugly old dog. Let's get this over with."

An uncomfortable silence was broken by Son of a Frog farting. I looked at each man and lightly cleared my throat.

"Thank you for coming," I said. "I wish there were no need for us to be here right now. I lost a husband, and all of us have lost a leader. I know for certain that he respected every one of you great men. Whatever you may have thought of him privately was no concern of his. What mattered to him was that, as men, as commanders, you treated this Confederation with respect, and I am grateful to each of you for demonstrating that allegiance by being here today. I place the health of the Confederation above my own. And with that, I want to offer each man here my devotion and begin this council by letting each speak his mind while the others listen. Uncle?" I bowed my head in Bat's direction. "You have a lot to say today."

Tunghoi Bat let a dignified silence pass. "It would be arrogant of me to deny that we're all richer and stronger because of the Confederation. But respect by itself doesn't hold us together or bring in wealth. Respect goes without saying. It's strength we need! If we're to continue after the sad demise of this woman's husband, we need a strong man to lead us."

A joke formed on Wu's lips. I flashed him a cautionary look.

Bat continued: "The kind of strength I'm referring to isn't about muscles or guns. It's about experience, it's about position, it's about strength in here." He tapped his forehead. Then he repeated his same old arguments: his seniority, a lifetime of piracy, this or that official in his pay. He launched into a long-winded justification for sitting out the second Annam campaign. Other men nibbled snacks. Son of a Frog twirled his teacup in his fingers. General Bo spat into a cask.

My mind wandered to last night under the stars. Something small had shifted inside me, a sense of calm strength that I seemed to have inhaled from the crisp air. We'd held each other all night in an innocent way, his chest warming mine, our breath in each other's faces. Shaken from sleep by birds hopping on the canopy—magpies or mynahs, I couldn't tell—the first look he gave me was bashful, even embarrassed. He'd returned me to the ship without a word.

Bat's voice broke my thoughts. "Isn't that right, Cheng Yat Sou?"

"If you say so," I replied.

"If I say so! Hear that? Of course I say so. Tunghoi makes better sense as Confederation base—far from Kwangchow and the Governor-General's palace with their sympathetic locals, not like this backward island."

"Ah yes, lovely Tunghoi," Kwok Podai said. "Where even the most bumbling admiral can trap us like turtles in a jug, as we've experienced twice."

"And ran them off twice," said Tunghoi Bat. "I've said enough. Who's with me?"

"With you for what?" Kwok said. "No one else has had a chance to speak. Anyway, what's the use of these little speeches? I can fart from my mouth as well as the rest of you about strength and respect. But who among us can read and write? Oh yes, I know you all think this is an affectation of mine, an entertainment. What good does it do a common thief to read history and verse? The fact is, we're no longer ordinary bandits. We're a business, a big business, for which we can thank our late Dai Lo Ban. And those who advised him."

The atmosphere chilled. His acknowledgment of me was not lost on the rest.

"Our big, and rather complicated enterprise does not and cannot survive on brute strength or stubborn heads alone. It requires management and knowledge as much or more than fighting skills. Shouldn't a literate man, well read in history and strategic thinking, be at the helm? Mm. I see your faces. I know your answers."

"Useful if the navy challenges us to a poetry contest," Wu-shek Yi said.

Kwok pushed his stool back and stood as if to leave. How fragile the unity of this group! I fixed Kwok with a glare that sent him back to his seat. *Later,* I tried to let him understand, *we'll talk in private later.*

"If we can all refrain from ridicule, please," I said. "Who else wants to be heard?"

Every man stared ahead at anything but each other. General Bo cleared his throat.

I nodded, "General Bo."

The old captain wiped his lip. "Seems to me every man here would claim to be the smartest among us. So, I'm going to do the smart thing and admit I never was interested in being leader. Doesn't mean I don't want something out of this. I'm the man with the smallest fleet. A little less small would bring me joy. I'll give joy in return to whoever offers the most ships. There, I said it."

He deliberately avoided looking at me. I could have strangled the treacherous bastard.

Son of a Frog laughed. "That's a true rascal thief speaking. First honest thing I've heard here all day. Me? No speeches. Not ready to rule this mob nor be a whore for ships. I'll keep the wind in my mouth about who should take the job. I just want to get this done with and go back to robbing and plunder, and that's all I have to say. Thank you."

"Aren't we forgetting something?" said Wu-shek Yi, without the usual smirk in his voice. "This Confederation was Cheng Yat's notion, and we all bought into it, and all profited by it, as has been said. But has anyone asked who he might have chosen as successor?"

"I believe we all have, numerous times," Kwok Podai said. "And I think we all agree—and Cheng Yat Sou might confirm this—he never let his preference be known."

"That isn't what I said," Wu replied. "I said, who he *might have* chosen. Who would have been his most likely choice?"

"I believe that has been the primary topic of conversation among every sailor, fisherman, and hawker for a hundred *li* in every direction for an entire cycle of the moon," Kwok said. "I expect you have some novel ideas on the topic? Shall I guess?"

"My guess is that his confidence would be in the man among us he knew the longest, the first man he groomed to be a fleet leader, a man who's been doggedly loyal to him from the beginning."

"And who, if rumors have any credence, has been plotting against Cheng Yat's nephew. An odd sort of loyalty."

The remark took me as much by surprise as everyone at the table, judging by their reactions. Wu stood up, shouted, "Turtle's egg!" and launched a bowl still filled with dried plums at Kwok Podai. Son of a Frog, seated beside Kwok, knocked it out of the air. Plums hit the floor like cannon shot.

I rose to my feet and was about to shout for order when Tunghoi Bat began applauding. "A most productive meeting." He slid his stool away from the table and slapped his knees. "At least we've all had our say."

"I have not," I said.

Slowly, gradually, Bat and Wu resumed their seats. In the icy silence, I heard a fish jump.

I stood and looked past the men's shoulders over the sparkling water of the bay.

Clear your mind and spirit, Po had said.

I was ready.

"Thank you for your attention," I began. "What a lucky woman I am! That's what some of you think, right? A common whore who was fortunate enough to be taken by one of your own. Don't look so surprised at my language. Yes, I was a whore, a lowly flower boat girl. I gave myself daily for a handful of coins. I gave!

"What about yourselves? Bandits your whole lives. What has any of you ever done but take, take, take? But that isn't the difference between me and each of you. What sets me apart is that I wanted something better. I would have died rather than remain a prostitute all my life. But I was a slave. What's your excuse?

"My good men, you all enjoy sharing your memories, many of which are quite entertaining. May I have your indulgence while I share too? I remember the time when I was—can we say *initiated?*—into the sea bandit life. We would sit poised in a cove somewhere for days until by chance some unsuspecting trader drifted by. If we came away with a hold full of sugar and a crate of lacquered bowls, we would sing to the moon! Sometimes we would band together and gang up on a salt convoy, remember? A few men might lose their lives, but what did it matter? We could pawn off our winnings and live like kings and queens for a few months and forget about the other months when we starved or were held back by the weather. That's how it was, was it not?"

A few shrugs and cleared throats. I waited a moment and went on.

"Maybe that's why, when you share drinks and reminisce about the good old days, the stories all revolve around fighting in Annam. Because the rest of the time was rather a poor source of tall tales. We were plain pirates, petty thieves, often getting in each other's way, feasting on stale rice and caterpillars. How did someone once put it? *A flock of ravens content to pick up scraps.*"

I hesitated. Suddenly the thought I wanted to convey seemed too complicated, too analytical, but their blank looks hurried me along.

"Of course, you wanted more. We all did. But wanting more isn't the same as wanting *better.* I know—who ever heard of bandits bettering themselves? Has any of you tried? You have the ships, the men, the guns—have you, you, you, you, or you ever had a dream of using that power to create something better? I did. That's why this Confederation exists at all!"

There, I'd finally come out with it. Every one of these thick-headed men thought all one needed was force of will—a wave of a sword, stubborn arms folded across a chest—to command a ship, a fleet, or an operation as vast as this one. Why had it taken so long to say out loud, even to myself, that the Confederation, from its conception, if it had been the result of anyone's force of will, it had always been mine alone?

"I know some of you—all of you—saw me as an outsider who didn't know her place. An overbearing wife to Cheng Yat, always trying to shove ideas into his head. Well, you were right! You were right all along. That was me, always whispering in that poor man's ear. He protested, he argued back, too often wanting to hit me. But in the end, he was man enough to listen. And what did those silly womanly ideas accomplish? Look at yourselves to find out! You're all fat and wear fine clothes without patches. Look at *us*. The roving bandit days are over. We are the masters of the coast for ten thousand *li*. Of course, the Mandarins don't call us that. They smear us as *scum floating on the sea* or *robber hornets*. But that's all they can fight us with: their words. We achieved the impossible, which their incapable navy never could. We brought stability to this coast. And we're rich from it. Everyone's happy! Merchants beg to pay our protection fees. Villagers no longer run to the hills. Even foreign barbarians are wary of us. We're the true power, and neither the emperor nor his shoe-shining governors can stop us. Isn't that right?"

Tunghoi Bat appealed to his fellow captains: "And she accuses us of exaggerating? True enough, her husband accomplished a great deal. But this former wind-and-dust girl needs reminding: it wasn't her, but Cheng Yat and you men and me who led every last raid, every last fight. Men, we don't need to drag out this meeting. Let's choose now."

My voice rose from deep in my gut: "Not until I'm finished. I've heard a lot of speeches about who's the strongest, who's the most senior or the most educated, who was who's favorite catamite-turned-commander. Or who might be willing to make a deal. But I haven't heard anyone talk about leadership. I've heard no one with a plan."

Kwok raised his head. General Bo shuffled in his seat. Bat stared into space.

I continued: "I've heard all about your connections, wits, and strength, but not your visions. What are your intentions for our business, other than the same old robbing and ransom?"

"Robbing and ransom—a tidy summary of what we do," Wu-shek Yi said. "Maybe we should expand into inns and teahouse theaters?"

"First new idea I've heard from any of you," I said. "Maybe we need a new round of speeches. Who wants to be first to share your vision for the Confederation of the Flags?"

I wet my throat with tea, waiting for a response and getting none. "I'll go first."

"Enough! Who wants to listen to a widow's nattering?" Tunghoi Bat said.

"Transshipment of goods," I said, each syllable beating a slow, deliberate cadence.

I let the words sink in, watched their confusion take hold. Only Kwok Podai looked faintly amused.

"That's what we do from now on," I said. "It's no longer piracy, and we are not pirates. We are in business. We are transshippers of goods."

General Bo spat on the floor. "Put a fancy name on it, it's still plunder and blackmail."

I ignored the remark. "We expand the pass system inland. We appoint agents in every port, spies in every town, a reliable schedule of fees for cooperative officials. We establish supply lines with our triad partners for those goods we're forced to confiscate."

"Forced to confiscate. That's hilarious!" Tunghoi Bat said. "You want to turn a simple, successful operation into some unnecessarily complex web of fees and agents and whatever you call your transshipped goods? How do you even keep track?"

"I told you. We're in business, the biggest in the region. So, we act like one. Hire every scribe on the coast. Every one of them. Offer salaries and shares of the spoils such that government offices will be bare of literate men."

The mention of literacy didn't move Kwok Podai. As my speech went on, his brow was more pinched, his eyes sunk deeper into his skull.

General Bo's face puckered into a lopsided smirk. "How many scholars wish to be ship's pursers—that is, *criminal sea wasp* pursers?"

"That's why we don't call them pursers," I said. "They will be taken on board as Ink and Writing Masters. The same with helmsmen. New titles for every specialized job. They'll all be working for us, all profiting with us. This is just the beginning of my vision for the Confederation of the Flags. Continue to be glorified *scum floating on the sea* or own the whole world as we know it? What is your choice?"

I took my seat. Whether the men thought my words mad or sensible, it didn't matter. They were ideas, plans; they formed a vision. I caught Kwok Podai hiding a scowl.

"Who goes next? Let's compare each leader's plan," I said.

The bamboo frame creaked. Water rippled around the ship clear as jewels. Kwok Podai avoided my eyes.

Tunghoi Bat grabbed the table's edge and helped himself up. "Is none among you intending to say a word? Well, then, let me be the one. It's all well and good to make up words like 'transshipment' and 'Ink and Writing Master' and to pretend that we'll be nothing but glorified merchants in floating accounting rooms. That doesn't disguise the truth of what we are. We're hunters. We hunt ships. We hunt treasures. We hunt men. We are wolves of the sea, six big packs of proud and hungry wolves. Give it another name, but that's all we are and ever have been. Clever ideas—'visions' she calls them—didn't make us what we are. Striking fear into the hearts of victims and enemies did. Whoever leads this operation has to be the toughest wolf of all, ready to rip the guts from whoever gets in our way, to kill and send even our own men to their deaths."

Bat leaned toward me, head hunched and shoulders raised, like the wolf he claimed to be. "I've heard that she once killed a man in the heat of battle, in defense of her own life no doubt. That doesn't make her a leader. Oh, but I know which weapon she uses best—the one no one else here has: the one inside her trousers! Not a sustainable way to run a fleet of twenty thousand men."

This went too far. I stood to face him.

"What? She denies it?" he said.

I was ready to strangle him where he stood. However, he didn't grasp that his dog fart insult revealed the threat he felt from me, an acknowledgment of my power. We both were wolves.

"I believe this meeting is concluded," I said.

XXXIX
Night

Kwok Podai stopped me at the companionway stairs. "We need to talk."

"I'm very tired." Of course, I knew what he wanted.

"We need to talk now," he said.

"Later." I hurried past him up the stairway.

While my body ached with fatigue, the rest of me was strung like a crossbow. My eyes and ears were sharper and clearer than ever before. I had to finish what I'd started.

The young scribe arrived quickly at my summons, carrying his writing kit and an oracle book. First, he confirmed what he'd reiterated twice before: the Dog Hour on the second day of the twelfth lunar cycle of Emperor Ka-hing's twelfth year of reign was the precise auspicious time to bestow an official position. Tomorrow morning.

Vowing deep secrecy, he set to work with his brush. I understood now what Cheng Yat had said about loyalty. I had no reason to trust this young man except a deep feeling in my gut. I knew he wouldn't reveal what he was writing until the appointed time. I could rely on him with my life. I offered my departed husband a silent apology. *I'm turning into you.*

Alone at last, I picked at my supper until the soup noodles turned to glue. Hot tea helped ward off the fatigue of waiting.

The noises settled throughout the bay—families dousing cook fires, shutting hatches against the cool evening. I changed into a fisherman's black tunic and trousers and did my hair into a single long braid. In the dark, I would be just another boat woman.

I strapped a short dagger to my calf.

A passing sampan responded to my whistle. Filling the surprised boat girl's hand with silver, I took the yuloh and put her ashore.

A delicious chill rose from the bay. Tiny fish leapt before the bow, breaking the young moon's white eyebrow into silvery shards. My shoulders ached from the long-out-of-practice exertion of sculling, and I worried I might have trouble identifying ships in the lightless water alleys until at last I pulled alongside Wu-shek Yi's junk, its dark wood blacker than its own fluttering shadow.

I had a leg over the gunwale when four female figures skittered down the companionway stairs. Wu-shek Yi stepped from his cabin, still in the jacket he'd worn at the day's conference, as though he'd been expecting me.

"Ah-Yang, what a nice surprise, though as you can see, I'm already well stocked with women."

"We need to talk. Away from other ears."

"Yes, well, I'm in need of a morsel. Join me in the galley?"

Wu dismissed the cook from his cleanup duties and helped me down into the cramped space reeking of vinegar and shrimp paste. In the weak glow of a nearly spent lamp, he pretended to examine a shelf full of dried roots and herbs.

"Strange that you want to speak 'away from other ears' when every ear under heaven has heard about my apparent assault on the precious Cheng morons."

"That's what I came to ask you about," I told him. "The first I heard of it was at today's meeting."

"Is that so? If I were a suspicious man, I'd say one very sly woman set me up. And I wouldn't understand why, after all I've—"

"All I asked of you was to speak to them."

Wu lifted a jar cover and picked out a plum dripping with syrup. "Oh, now you say it. Funny how my memory has you wanting me to 'get rid of them.' I must be getting old. Plum?"

I waved away the fruit. "In my memory those were your words. I hope you didn't—"

"All I did was talk to one." Wu sucked down another plum and sealed the jar. "Something to the effect that those of us who knew his uncle before he was born would not be entirely cooperative with a Red Flag Fleet commanded by someone who didn't have the endorsement of Cheng Yat Sou. Or who wasn't Cheng Yat Sou herself."

"You didn't say that!"

"I only told him the truth."

"My dear friend, you don't know the truth."

"Don't 'dear friend' me, lovely woman. You don't think I have you figured out? You aren't here to talk about those petty little Cheng boys. You've come to talk me into supporting Kwok Podai. What's this surprise on your face? You don't think everyone knows? I hope the wedding banquet is well portioned!"

I laughed a bit too loud and covered my mouth. "Even if you were right, he wouldn't stand a chance. You'd support a slug before you'd line up behind Kwok, am I right? Eleven Fingers thinks everyone naturally should back him. Even you."

"Ha! You amuse me, Yang! But you may be right. None of us can win, so I need to support someone else. Who, I'm guessing, might that be?"

"The one who has no long-seated rivalry with any man. Who helped establish the Confederation in the—"

"No speeches," he said. "Make your point."

I folded my arms. "The one who would owe you the most favors in return for your backing."

At my smile, Wu-shek Yi laughed so hard he nearly knocked the shelf from its supports. "Yes, one who wraps men in her coils like a snake. A slim, beautiful snake!" He gagged on his laughter. "Wah, too hot to think. Let's get out of here and share some wine."

"I'm glad we understand each other, old friend." I patted his bouncy cheek. "I have other visits."

While I climbed from the galley he called in a whisper, "Wait. What do I tell those nosy girls up there about why you came?"

"I don't know. Tell them I got lost."

"You, lost? Never!"

When I left General Bo's junk sometime later, the sliver of moon had dipped behind the hills, leaving a few scattered deck lamps straining through night mist. I could barely see the way forward.

I hadn't gone far when the sampan received a violent jolt.

Ribs struck wood. My neck crunched. A tight grip on the yuloh saved me from tumbling overboard.

A larger sampan turned until our beams touched. A man's silhouette;

I couldn't make out who. Then a flash, like a mirror, or steel. Another. Whoever he was held a sword or a cutlass.

I reached into my trouser leg for the dagger and stood. The sword swished through the dark. Ducking in time, I grabbed a paddle from under the thwart. In that instant light reflected on the attacker's face.

Tunghoi Bat's Taumuk faced me with mad, empty eyes.

I aimed my swing at his head. The paddle struck metal; tremors shot up my arm. The sword poised for another strike. I raised the heavy wood in one hand, the dagger in the other, but with the boat rocking under me and nothing to cling to, my legs faltered. His blade came down invisibly fast. As I fell, I flung my dagger wildly. Then black water swallowed me whole.

I broke the surface with my sampan between us. Unable to see a thing, I heard painful groans, then a yuloh creaking as his boat turned away.

Kwok Podai stood at the rail of my ship with his hand extended to help me aboard. I refused his offer and ran past, feet splashing in their own puddles.

"What happened?" he said. "Where have you been?"

"Not now."

He followed me bounding up the stairs. I nearly crushed his fingers shutting the door between us.

"We need to talk!" he said from the other side.

I yanked off my dripping clothes and rummaged in the dark for oil. The lamp had burned out.

"You and I had an arrangement!" he called.

"Oh, is that what it was. I thought it was a marriage proposal."

"A marriage of fleets, and of man and woman."

"Which comes first," I said, "the fleets or the fucking?"

"Don't be vulgar! I came to seal our deal. Don't you want that, Yang?"

At last I found oil and a flint, but it took force of will to subdue the trembling in my hands enough to kindle a flame. In the light the bruise on my ribs looked worse than it felt, just a mild throb. I heard my robe rip as I tore it off its hook to cover my nakedness.

"Yang? I know you hear me. Let me in."

"I'm not in the mood for poetry."

"Ah-Yang, listen to me." Then his voice penetrated the wood. "Ah-Yang, I've held...special affection for you."

I had to calm down. He knew full well by now what my intentions were, but I couldn't risk angering him further. What he didn't know was how much I'd been tempted by his proposal. What would union with such a man hold in store? Despite the gentility of his words, I knew him well enough. Kwok Podai wanted to consume me in body and spirit.

"I'm sorry. I'll see you at the meeting," I said.

He banged the door. "Let me in!"

"I'm not decent."

"Were you ever?" The door rattled against a furious kick. "We had an arrangement!"

"What arrangement?" Another man's voice. "I said, what arrangement? Whatever it is better have nothing to do with Cheng family business!"

I recognized Cheng On-pong's bullish lowing. Then Cheng Bo-yeung: "What deal have you made with that woman?"

Kwok muttered, "Fuck your old mother." Feet stomped away.

Two sets of knuckles rapped the door.

"Paternal aunt! Let us in."

"I'm not dressed."

"Then dress! We gave you a chance. We gave you respect. Said you'd give us a decision! Well?"

"We know your plot with Kwok Podai. You can forget it."

I threw open the latch. I didn't care how I presented myself.

"Fools!" I said. "Yes, let's decide this once and for all. No, don't you take one step into this chamber until you've gathered every one of the Red Flag Fleet squadron commanders. I'm calling a full meeting, this moment! Go!"

I'd once swum into a school of jellyfish as a child. That was how I felt now, in this room full of men: that if any of them so much as brushed me with a finger it would burn deep through to my bones.

The two Cheng cousins sat facing me. Completing the circle were Cheng Yat's former Taumuk, Leung Po-bo, and five other of Cheng Yat's most trusted squadron chiefs. I confiscated a wine jar; the only thing to drink, I informed everyone, would be tea. We exchanged respects until there was movement at the door. If envy had a flavor, it would be what

I tasted from these men's breaths when Cheung Po Tsai stepped inside, wearing flowing purple robes fit for a stage opera prince.

The entire bay must have been kept awake half the night. The cabin walls hummed, my ears rang from the roar of oaths, fists pounded timber so hard they might have triggered waves. By the time the noise died, my throat felt like it had been scoured with coral. But consent had been wrung from each of them. The question of who would command the Red Flag Fleet was settled.

Po Tsai lingered after the others left.

"What happened?" he said.

"What do you mean? We just finished appointing—"

"I mean with you. I heard rumors of a fight. I see you wince every time you turn."

I told him about the incident with Tunghoi Bat's Taumuk. He made me repeat certain details while his face sagged deeper and deeper. At the end he strode to the door.

"Don't do anything," I said. "It isn't your matter!"

"That rat attacked you—of course it's my matter!"

"Please don't make decisions for me. Stay," I said. "I need company."

"You have fifteen guards stationed outside, and I don't know how many on deck. You're safe."

"But I'm asking you to stay."

I was excruciatingly, deliriously tired. Tired of hurting, tired of mourning, tired of putting on a brave face. I was tired of being strong around tough-talking men, tired of worrying about being cast aside, tired of everything I'd built collapsing around me. Here in the lateness of the night, I simply needed him with me.

"Don't you dare walk out!" I said.

But he did, leaving the door open behind him.

I heard rather than saw the figure padding into the room. I regretted leaving the door unlatched—in the darkness, anyone might have entered. But, no, I had many guards. It could only be Po.

My breathing quickened, back went stiff, at the acute sense of an animal approaching—a feral musk-like smell mixed with blood and sweat, his breath hissing through tightened lips—an animal returned from the hunt. He'd brought a gift, he said, the only words he spoke.

I slid aside to make room on the mat. He lay facing me, not touching, one eye a sparkling ember, the other lost in shadow. His seething was now that of a man, one who was maybe frightened of what he'd just done, or maybe of what he held himself back from doing. A man who needed something, from me.

I opened my arms.

We held each other tight, rocking gently, and settled into a firm, warm embrace, heart against heart, in a way no one had ever held me, not since my mother, and never any other man. It felt like the fulfillment of something I couldn't recognize—ten times ten thousand *li* away from the way I'd held other men as a transaction or even the best times of gratitude and dependence with my late husband—I'd never held man or woman before out of raw joy.

His lips pressed my neck below my ear, crossed the precipice of my jaw, found my cheek and lingered, giving soft kisses. This couldn't be happening. This shouldn't be happening. I was...he was my... Struggling for breath, my lips parted to say something, to beg him to stop, but then his mouth was on mine with a feral abandon that swept all other thoughts into the void. I felt myself sinking, tasting his tongue, holding his head as I turned onto my back.

Buttons snapped. Fabric parted. Soft flesh touched flesh. My hunger for him took me completely by surprise. I had lived with one man for how many years, slept and eaten and fought with him, transformed his seed into children. Yet I had never truly, desperately wanted him the way I wanted this rapturous man gliding his belly on mine, long fingers shaping me like a potter forming a vase.

The voices in my head screamed. They shouted. They beat against my skull, telling me this had to stop. Had to stop now! It was wrong. I was a grieving widow. He was my adopted son!

He slid down and kissed where no man had ever kissed me before, and all the voices melted.

Then he was upon me, his eyes shining into mine. He entered me casually, without introduction.

We moved like a swelling sea: rolling, pitching, unhurried. I pulled him deeper, urged him faster. He circled, teased, explored. Of course, I know how to mimic pleasure—no different than striking a flint to make sparks, sometimes fooling even myself. I didn't want that this time; I summoned the strength to let go. I felt him release. The sun burst behind my eyes.

I held him until our sweat chilled and he raised himself to reach for a blanket. I wanted to freeze this moment, in the quiet and dark, the faint slap of water and creaking timber, Po's breathing beside me.

He was asleep when I crawled from the blanket. As quietly as I could, I threw on a robe and grabbed a sack of coins and the papers the scribe had written.

The first hint of dawn haloed the hills. My scribe had done well: a small fleet of sampans was waiting. I stepped from rail to rail, my hands soon emptied. The sampans scattered to deliver the announcement to every vessel, temple, and market throughout Tung Chung:

> *Cheng Yat Sou is hereby the indisputable Dai Lo Ban of the Confederation of the Flags.*

XL
Drum

My face looked smooth and still youthful in the mirror, though it may have been an effect of the subdued morning light. I smoothed the rouge on my lips and tucked back a stray strand from my neatly parted hair. I sat back to admire the woman in the mirror, resembling a young bride, with matching gold phoenixes linking tails across the red landscape of her jacket.

I'd kept the men waiting long enough. It was time.

As my last act before leaving the cabin, I placed one foot at a time on a stool by the door and pulled on my mother's red slippers.

Today, Ah-Ma, I avenge your powerlessness.

It didn't escape my hearing that they were talking about Cho, Tunghoi Bat's Taumuk, whose mutilated corpse had washed ashore early this morning. Their talk died as soon as I stepped outside the cabin.

The table had been removed from the conference place. All that remained were six stools and colored cushions, with one addition: in the center stood Kwok Podai's gift, the little black and red drum.

Tunghoi Bat threw shouts before I was halfway down the steps. "By what big audacious bladder do you go about spreading a false announcement?"

"I wasn't aware that we had made our choice," General Bo said.

I took my place on the red cushion, struggling to maintain the appearance of calm as Bat raised an accusative six-fingered hand. "She's confused about her place."

"On the contrary, I've never been more certain." I removed a balled fabric from my pocket and rolled it toward Bat. Along the way it unraveled from around a wrinkled slab that might have been mistaken for an oyster until it came to a stop near his feet. His mouth opened so wide I could see down his throat as he recognized what it was: a severed human ear.

"This one heard the wrong advice."

"You dare! What's the meaning of this?" Bat kicked away the hard scrap of flesh.

Did it really require explaining? I stood with such force that my stool toppled over.

"Which of you has murdered men less deserving than that lowly worm Cho who bought his own death? When do I get to hear your congratulations? Where's my welcome into your bloody-fingered brotherhood?"

"Anyone who kills another's loyal deputy and then declares their leadership without consensus has no right to speak of brotherhood," Tunghoi Bat said.

"I would have to agree," Kwok Podai said.

I righted my stool and sat. "Then let me make you understand. It's very simple. The Red Flag is the largest fleet. It's the Cheng fleet, and Cheng is the Confederation leader. I suppose you know my name: Cheng Yat Sou. Nothing more to discuss."

Tunghoi Bat pretended to be calm, but his hands clenched like claws. "I'm the last person to belittle the Cheng name, but you...you..."

"Face it, Eleven Fingers. It's settled," General Bo said.

"Some of us won't sell our loyalty for toy boats," Tunghoi Bat shot back. "What about Fatty Wu? Your lips are unusually still."

Wu-shek Yi looked to me and back to Bat. "Women are cleverer than men. Call me a dog, but I'll keep my allegiance with the Chengs."

"So, Madam Cheng," Bat said. "You have the support of a self-proclaimed dog, and of the smallest fleet."

"Size doesn't matter. Ask any woman," I said. "A dagger cuts as well as a sword. The only number which counts right now is six."

Bat tossed a look at Son of a Frog. "Who do you support? Out with it."

Kwok Podai's brow twitched as if possessed by a demon. He believed I had tricked him, and he was somewhat correct, a gamble I had taken; and now, I feared his next move. The Confederation was strong as iron but as fragile as jade—one crack, and the whole thing would shatter. I held my tongue until I was sure of my words, then kept my voice calm and deep.

"I remind you that this Confederation gives us all strength, and any who makes a move to abandon this union betrays the tens of thousands who serve under him. If any one of the commanders of the Confederation of the Flags thinks he's incapable of being led by a woman, then be sure to know that I will fight him. I will hunt him down and burn his ships because the Confederation is a dragon—and I am the dragon's head."

"Bold words, Cheng Yat Sou," said Tunghoi Bat. "You should bang your little war drum during such a performance."

His remark was well-timed. At the poop deck rail, my young scribe nodded once and withdrew from view. The Dog Hour had arrived.

"Thank you. We all will," I said, picking up the instrument and setting it in my lap. "This was given to me as a symbol of a great woman warrior who beat a drum to guide a great army to glory. And now..." I raised the wooden drumstick and held it out toward the center "... we play a similar game. Whichever man supports me to lead our great union, show it by striking this drum."

I offered General Bo the distinction of being first with the drum. An old man with a proud past, reduced to bartering for ships, but still tough inside, a worthy ally. His face went crimson, staring at the skin for what seemed an age. He tested the drumhead with his fingertips, finally raising the stick to his forehead, then brought it down with a high-pitched thump that lingered in the air. He slid the drum and stick to Wu-shek Yi.

Fatty Wu, the quick-tongued man with a whale's belly and maiden's voice, whose passions for food and women were as pronounced as his sense of loyalty, was probably the toughest among them all. My breathing stopped while he twirled the drumstick with a flourish. He struck once, then twice more, and raised the drum toward Tunghoi Bat, but changed his mind and passed it in the other direction.

Son of a Frog would be better named Bear. Big and soft outside, he was the man I knew the least. He hesitated before clamping the drum between his knees, studied the stick as if the wood held the answer to a question, then lowered his hand until it hovered a finger's width over the drumhead. He glanced at me, at the stretched pigskin, and back at my face. His wrist flicked twice, beating a lighthearted *pong pong*.

Son of a Frog glanced between Bat and Kwok, both of whose hands remained rigid at their sides. He leaned past Wu and dropped the drum onto Tunghoi Bat's lap.

I studied Tunghoi Bat's scarred face. He was an arrogant, loose-tongued, irritable figure on the verge of old age, but he was also a man who stuck to his principles. I was determined to earn the loyalty he was so reluctant to pledge. He held the stick in both hands as if to snap it in two.

"Cheng Yat Sou," he said with resignation, "you're a difficult, obstinate woman. I don't know whether it's your cleverness or your arrogance that makes me wary. But while my mind is screaming not to do this, my heart is pounding. Like this!" He raised the stick and brought it down with all his strength, nearly knocking the drum from his lap. "And this!" He hit it again, twice. "And finally, this." He pounded a triple beat so fierce I thought the skin might tear. I placed my palms together and bowed to him.

Bat held the drum to Kwok Podai. "Let's hear your music."

Kwok Podai, so refined, so intelligent, his education so under-appreciated among the pirates. He'd offered me a cunning plan, for which he must have held hope even until today. But of all the pirate chieftains, my instinct told me to beware of him the most.

"I see I've been ambushed, like the Jin defeated by the roll of Leung Hung-yuk's beat." He spun the stick in his fingers, pausing for thought. "I was first among us to recognize this woman's potential for authority, though I'd imagined a somewhat different arrangement. So..." He offered me a half-smile, oddly warm and infinitely sad. "Let me court you with your drum, Cheng Yat Sou, and play the song of the Pirate Queen." Five beats pealed through the air.

He leaned across and placed the drum at my feet. "Each colored flag has drummed in your favor, all except the Red."

Wu-shek Yi slapped his thigh. "True! You're Red Dai Lo Ban. Strike a beat for yourself."

I nudged the drum aside. "I never said I was Red Dai Lo Ban."

"But you—"

"I said I spoke for the Red Fleet, until now." I rose and stepped to the canopy entrance, where I cupped hands around my mouth. "Commander of the Red Flag!"

Cheung Po Tsai moved down the companionway steps, shimmering in his swaying purple robes and charcoal-black turban, a dagger tucked firmly in his belt. He stepped into the enclosure and accepted the drumstick from my hand.

"They want to hear you play," I said.

"Wait!" Tunghoi Bat's lips fluttered, trying to find words.

"Hilarious!" said Wu-shek Yi. "Is anyone surprised she appointed her adopted son?"

"He's not my son." My hand rested on Po Tsai's shoulder while he pounded three joyful beats.

"The Commander of the Red Flag Fleet is my husband."

XLI
The Pirate Queen

The seven-times-seventh and final day of mourning dawned bright and crisp. The drumming started with the rise of the sun. Red-frocked priests spread along the shore, their chants sounding like echoes. Old women scattered colored paper in the water.

The mourning platform was already being dismantled. The larger idols were wrapped, some to send aboard the flagship, others for local temples. The sailcloth panels were coming down.

I walked hand-in-hand with Ying-shek to the mountain of offerings on the beach. In the center, an enormous junk built of wood and paper in the image of Cheng Yat's ship. Stacked around and on top were buildings, animals and servants, clothing and weapons, all made from paper, and one hundred and eight chests of shaved wood, stuffed with golden paper ingots.

A monk offered Ying-shek a flaming stick, which my boy held over his head, and threw it as high as he could into the heart of the pyre. Flames shot up; a fountain of smoke billowed to the sky, carrying all those fine gifts to this earnest little boy's father in the other world.

The ceremony was finished. Cheng Yat was a liberated spirit. Life could go on for the living.

Cold gusts strafed the poop deck. Pinching my collar tight, I watched fifty ships of the Yellow Flag Fleet list almost to their rails as they tacked toward the headlands. A flock of white egrets crossed low in their wake, showing off their ease against nature's forces.

True to form, Tunghoi Bat had lingered until last. A private banquet in his honor had been friendly, even managing a few laughs at other men's expense. I had played his game and won, and though maybe offered with a little bit of visible grudge, he'd voiced his respect.

When asked for first orders, I repeated what I'd said publicly: conduct business as usual, as if nothing had changed but the name: transshipment of goods. Further developments could wait.

"Wait for what?" he'd challenged.

I had no answer prepared. Would he accept the truth? Wait until I was confident not to make a mistake? I could usher in my reign with some big, bold move. Instead, I chose caution. I told him I needed time to consider, the way a boat maker imagines the ship he'll build from a stack of freshly cut trees.

Ying-shek ran past, chased around the deck by Po Tsai in some silly game. My two beautiful men: one a man-child with a fierce hunter's heart; the other a frisky, proud cub. More questions crept forward: had I been hasty in declaring myself to Po?

Watching him: *No, of course not.*

There was no ambiguity in my life right now. I just had to get reaccustomed to that odd, funny, remotely familiar feeling, buried so deep in my past: the feeling I had when I ran around on the flats swinging a bucket full of shells while my mother waved, and my heart tingled, and the whole wide world was mine.

It was mine again. I'd made it so.

The harbor mouth burst into flashes and smoke. Po and Ying-shek joined me to watch as the noise of a thousand thousand firecrackers rumbled across the bay. The Yellow Flag ships were warding off evil spirits for their journey, but it made me think of Spring Festival—new year, new beginning.

Thousands of frightened black birds erupted from the trees and coalesced into a dark fluttering cloud, spiraling and whistling high into the air, then swarmed into the hills.

"Do you think they have a leader?" I said.

"They must. She's probably a stubborn old *baat po*, don't you think?"

"I'm serious. How do birds choose their leader? Do they divide into squadrons? When a leader dies, how do they decide who takes over? Is it passed to a son?"

He hugged my shoulder, pulling me close. "Dear Yang, too much to worry about. Just be the Pirate Queen." But my questions wouldn't stop. Did birds feel pride or shame? Did they love and honor each other?

A single black bird dashed overhead, chirping with full-throated joy.

"Is that one lost?" Ying-shek said.

I lifted him into my arms, surprised at how heavy he had become. "No," I told him. "She's going her own way without anyone telling her what to do."

There was so much my sons might learn from me.

There was much I might learn from the birds.

ACKNOWLEDGEMENTS

I first heard of Cheng Yat Sou in snippets of legends from an old sailor in Tai O. It was infatuation at first listen. She may have been one of history's most notorious criminals, but the more I learned about her, a picture formed of a courageous, brilliant woman forced to navigate against her will through the worst that life, history, and the weather could throw at her. Besides, her main base was on the same island where I live, while her second husband remains a local legend.

I submerged myself in research, excitedly sharing each newly discovered gem of information with my wife Cathy, often lamenting, "I wish I could find a book about her."

"Write it yourself," she said, again and again.

Not only was this book Cathy's idea, but she supported me every step of the way. Her psychologist's insights into the characters' personalities and motivations were invaluable. Her cultural insights, being native Cantonese, were essential. But it was her emotional and practical support and Buddha-like patience through the difficult years of researching and writing that I am most grateful for. Thank you, my love.

My search began at the source, in the seafaring community of Tai O, where Mr. Leung Kin Fung and his family regaled me with stories of the old days and invaluable information about traditional sailing terminology and folklore. While lost on a back trail during a cross-island hike, I met an old woman whose name I sadly didn't note, who shared her first-hand account of a pirate raid on her village back when she was a girl in the 1930s, of which some details made it into this book. Graeme Morris coached me on the fine points of traditional junk technology and handling on his Fukien vessel, Long Hai, lovingly renovated with local old-timer shipwrights. The account of a sail anchor in a storm is based on his harrowing first-hand experience, with my embellishments.

Ten thousand bows of gratitude to the world's leading experts on 19th century Chinese pirates: Dr. Dian Murray, who generously shared rare, otherwise inaccessible historical documents; and Dr. Robert Antony, who bravely endured barrage after barrage of detailed questions, and guided me in my attempts to fill in the gaps in the history. Dr. Libby Lai-Pik Chan and other staff of the Hong Kong Maritime Museum were of great help with minutiae of Chinese sailing paraphernalia, maps, terminology, and countless other questions.

A special thank you to Karen Ackland, who suffered through the first draft, one raw chapter at a time. I am indebted to numerous mentors and readers for their feedback, including Pete Fromm, Mary Helen Stefaniak, Mike Magnuson, Deborah Reed, Susan DeFreitas, Pat Dobie, Anastasia Edel, Brian Taylor, Stephanie Bane, Larry Krone, Annika Feign, and Cathy Tsang-Feign.

My gifted editors Caroline Leavitt, Jessie Campbell, and Rita Ray made me humble and the manuscript readable.

Finally, blessings to the MacDowell art colony and the Obras Foundation for providing heavenly environments in which to write, and to the Hong Kong Arts Development Council for its generous financial support which helped make this book a reality.

CHARACTERS & GLOSSARY

PEOPLE

*Names follow the Chinese format of surname
followed by given name(s). Thus, Shek Yang's family name
is Shek. Most pirates went by nicknames.*

*All characters listed are actual historical figures,
except those marked with an asterisk**

PRINCIPAL PIRATES

Cheng Chat 鄭七	Pirate commander; elder cousin of Cheng Yat
Cheng Yat 鄭一	Red Flag Fleet commander; a.k.a. Cheng I
Cheung Po Tsai 張保仔	Adopted son (and catamite) of Cheng Yat
Leung 'General' Bo 梁保	White Flag Fleet commander
Kwok Podai 郭婆帶	Black Flag Fleet commander
Shek Yang 石陽	Wife of Cheng Yat; a.k.a. **Cheng Yat Sou** (Cheng I Sao) 鄭一嫂
Son of a Frog 蝦蟆養	Green Flag Fleet commander; real name Lei Sheung-ching 李相清
Tunghoi Bat 東海八	Yellow Flag Fleet commander; real name Ng Chi-ching 吳知青
Wu-shek Yi 烏石二	Blue Flag Fleet commander; real name Mak Yau-kam 麥有金

OTHER PIRATES

Chen Tin-bou 陳添保	Chinese commander in Annamese mercenary navy
Cheng Bo-yeung 鄭保養	Nephew of Cheng Yat
Cheng On-pong 鄭安邦	Younger cousin of Cheng Yat

Cheng Sing-kung 鄭成功	a.k.a. Koxinga; 17th century pirate leader turned rebel
Cheng Hung-shek 鄭雄石	Second son of Yang and Cheng Yat
Cheng Lau-tong 鄭流唐	Seventh founding fleet commander of the pirate confederation
Cheng Ying-shek 鄭英石	First son of Yang and Cheng Yat
Leung Po-bo 梁婆保	Cheng Yat's principal Taumuk
Ng Sheung-tak 吳尚德	Cheng Yat's purser
Wu-shek Tai 烏石大	Wu-shek Yi's elder brother
Wu-shek Sam 烏石三	Wu-shek Yi's younger brother

OTHERS

Ah-Yi* 阿姨	Widow serving aboard Cheng Yat's ship
Cheng Chat's wife 鄭七嫂	(real name unknown)
Cheng Wong-yan 鄭往認	Kwok Podai's wife, and Cheng Yat's cousin
John Turner	English sailor captured by pirates
Leung Hung-yuk 梁紅玉	Liang Hongyu; Song Dynasty woman general
Madam Le*	Annamese tea house proprietor in Chiang Ping
Na Yin-sing 那彥成	Two-Kwang Governor-General 1804-1806
Quang Toan	Tay-son Emperor of Annam 1792-1802
Quang Trung	Tay-son Emperor of Annam 1788-1792
Suen Chuen-mau 孫全謀	Chinese admiral
Ng Hung-kwong 吳熊光	Two-Kwang Governor-General 1806-1809
Xuan Bui Thi	Annamese woman general

LOCATIONS

Annam	Former name for Vietnam
Chek Lap Kok 赤鱲角	Small island off the north coast of Tai Yue Shan (Lantau Island)
Chiang Ping 江平	Giang Binh; pirate haven on China-Annam border
Chicken's Neck 雞頸	Taipa 氹仔；island south of O Moon (Macau)
Fukien 福建	Fujian; province northeast

of Kwangtung (Guangdong)

Ha Moon 廈門   Xiamen; port in Fukien province

Hoinam 海南   Hainan; major island off the south China coast

Ji-nai 紫坭   Zini/Tzu-ni, market town south of Kwangchow

Kwangchow 廣州   Guangzhou, a.k.a. Canton; capital of Kwangtung

Kwangshi 廣西   Guangxi; southern province, jointly governed with Kwangtung

Kwangtung 廣東   Guangdong, a.k.a. Canton; southern Chinese province

Lei Yue Moon 鯉魚門   Village at east end of Hong Kong harbor; birthplace of Cheng Yat

Luichow 雷州   Leizhou; large peninsula in southern China

Ningpo 寧波   Major northern Chinese trading port

O Moon 澳門   Macao/Macau; Portuguese colony at the mouth of the Pearl River

Phú Xuân 富春   Former name for Hue; Annam imperial capital

Punyu 番禺   County in the Pearl River delta near Kwangchow

Spirit River   Sông Linh; river in Vietnam; now named Sông Gianh

Sun-wui 新會   Xinhui; coastal district in Kwangtung Province

Tai O 大澳   Fishing/smuggling village on Tai Yue Shan (Lantau Island)

Tai Yue Shan 大嶼山   Lantau Island; large island in east Pearl River delta

Thang Long 昇龍   Former name for Hanoi

Tin-pak 電白   Dianbai; small port in western Kwangtung

Tunghoi 東海   Island and village on east side of Luichow; home of Tunghoi Bat

Tung Chung 東涌   Bay on Tai Yue Shan; eastern base of the confederation

Two-Kwang 兩廣   Kwangtung and Kwangsi Provinces jointly administered

Wong Po 黃埔   Whampoa; foreign merchant district near Kwangchow

Wu-shek 烏石   Village on west side of Luichow; home of Wu-shek Yi

DEITIES

Hau Wong 侯王	Local deity of Tai Yue Shan and nearby Yuen Long; said to be the deification of the uncle of the last Song boy emperor
Hoi Hau 海口	Ship spirit; literally "mouth of the sea"
Hung Shing 洪聖	God of the Southern Sea, worshipped mainly in southern China
Kwan Tai 關帝	Kwan Ti, Guan Yu; God of War and, oddly enough, of Literature
Kwun Yam 觀音	Guanyin, Kuan Yin; Buddhist goddess of mercy
San Po 三婆	Goddess; Tin Hau's youngest of two sisters
Sheung O 嫦娥	Chang'e; Goddess of the Moon
Tin Hau 天后	a.k.a. Mazu/Matsu; goddess of sailors and fishing people

TERMS

Ah-je 阿姐	Miss; informal term of address for a young woman
Ah-sao 阿嫂	Madam; informal term of address for an older woman
áo dài	Traditional Vietnamese women's outfit
baat po 八婆	Meddlesome old hag (strong insult)
baat gwa 八卦	Nosy old gossip (moderate insult)
bai nin 拜年	Traditional New Year visits to family and friends
bak gei 白鱀	Chinese white dolphin, often seen with bright pink skin
bo lei 普洱	Pu'er; dark tea made from fermented tea leaves
braves	Civilian vigilantes recruited by local officials
catty 斤	16 taels; approx. 1.33 pounds/600 grams
chau mui 臭妹	Literally "stinky girl", equivalent to *little bitch*
chek 呎	Approximately 1.2 feet/0.37 meters
Ching Ming 清明	Mid-spring festival devoted to grave sweeping
comprador	Chinese warehouse manager for foreign traders in Kwangchow

congee 粥	Rice porridge, eaten plain or with salted fish, meat or vegetables
eat-water junk 吃水船	Large, fast-moving ship that could be propelled by sails or oars
Dai Lo Ban 大老闆	Supreme leader
Daai-dai 帶弟	Nickname for daughter; literally means "bring a younger brother"
Dong Jit 冬節	Winter solstice
erhu 二胡	Two-stringed bowed musical instrument
faat din 發癲	Crazy, hysterical
fan-tan 番攤	Game played by guessing multiples of coins
feng shui 風水	Fortune-telling based on geographical features and alignments
fook 福	Good luck; used in written blessings during Chinese New Year
foreign mud 紅毛泥	Opium
god side 大邊	Also called "big side"; left (port) side of a junk
gogo 哥哥	Elder brother (familiar term)
gwa ji 瓜子	Melon seeds
Hakka 客家	Later settlers in Kwangtung, culturally distinct from Cantonese
Hoklo 學佬	People and dialect of Fukien Province and other coastal regions
hong 行	Guild of Chinese merchants licensed to trade with foreign traders
horse-trough junk 烏艚船	Common black-hulled vessel resembling a horse watering trough
ji-ji-ja-ja 吱吱喳喳	Gibberish
Ka-hing 嘉慶	Jiaqing; era name of seventh Ching Emperor, reigned 1796-1820
Kin-lung 乾隆	Qianlong; era name of sixth Ching Emperor, reigned 1736-1795
kung hei 恭喜	Good luck blessing
lai see 利是	Lucky money given inside red envelopes at Chinese New Year
li 哩	Approximately 1/3 mile or 500 meters
lo ban 老闆	Boss or leader; also a general title for a shop or restaurant owner

lo yi 老二	Second-in-command
longan 龍眼	"Dragon eye" fruit native to southeast Asia
lotus feet	Women's bound feet
Ming Heung 明香	Descendants of Ming Dynasty loyalists who fled to Annam after the establishment of the Ching Dynasty
mudskipper	Amphibious fish; lives in mangroves and mud flats
Outer Ocean 外海	Any part of the ocean beyond the sight of land
pit 撇	Short vertical stroke in Chinese writing
Punti 本地	Land-dwelling people, considered native to Kwangtung
sampan 三板	Small boat, holds anywhere from 2 to 16 people
sao/Ah-sao 嫂/阿嫂	Wife (familiar term of respect)
Sit Tou 薛濤	Xue Tao; Tang Dynasty poetess
siu chat pan 小七板	"Seven plank boat"; small boat, larger than a sampan
spirit side 細邊	Also called "small side"; right (starboard) side of a junk
suk-suk 叔叔	Uncle
sycee 細絲	Gold or silver ingots used as currency
tael 兩	Approx. 1.3 ounces/38 grams; measure for precious metals
tai 太	(as suffixed title) wife or Mrs.
talk-three-talk-four 講三講四	Chit-chat or gossip
Tanka 蜑家	Boat dwellers (insulting term)
Taumuk 頭目	Ship second-in-command, though sometimes command own ships
Tay-son	Faction that ruled Annam for several decades
turtle egg 龜蛋	Insulting term, equivalent to "bastard"
wai 喂	Greeting, as in "hello" or "hey"
wu lung 烏龍	Oolong; fermented tea, often pressed into disks
yamen 衙門	Government office in imperial China
yau fui 油灰	Putty made of shells, oil and bamboo fiber, used for boat caulking
yuloh 搖櫓	Elongated sculling oar

ABOUT THE AUTHOR

LARRY FEIGN is a writer and artist who lives walking distance from notorious pirate haunts in a Lantau Island village. He is the author of several books about Hong Kong, as well as a children's book series under a pen name.

LARRYFEIGN.COM

OMENS

THE MISSING CHAPTER

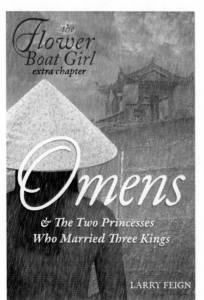

Made in United States
North Haven, CT
10 August 2023

40151924R00262